THE POWER

BUILDING THE CIRCLE - BOOK 2

MAGGIE M LILY

Cover design by Melony Paradise of Paradise Cover Design

Standard Print ISBN: 978-1-7353887-1-7

Large Print ISBN: 978-1-7353887-3-1

for my boys - always.

PROLOGUE

*A*t twelve years old, Adrian Trellis understood what it was to love. He had met the girl he was going to marry. In years to come, people would talk about the grand love affair that began at such a tender young age.

At least they would—once he talked to Whitney. The spring dance was coming. After admiring her from afar for most of the school year, this was his opportunity to strike. He was going to ask her to the dance.

Whitney would be delighted. Together, they'd dance the night away, recognizing their mutual young love for what it was. They'd remain hopelessly devoted to each other until the end of time.

Just as soon as Adrian talked to her.

Right after that happened.

The problem was that Whitney Langcaster was beautiful and popular. Her dark brown hair with chunky auburn and blond highlights topped sparkling hazel eyes. She was funny, kind, and smart. Perfect.

And popular.

She was always surrounded by a gaggle of giggling girls.

Adrian was…Adrian. At five-four, he was the shortest boy in his class, shy with bad acne. Adrian was nerdy, rather than smart. He was awkward, not popular. The second of nine Trellis siblings, he often compared himself to his brothers and found himself lacking.

His elder brother, William, was tall, strong, and sporty. He had already been invited to try out for the varsity football team when he started high school in the fall. Girls followed Will around, hoping he'd smile at them or talk to them. Even though he was a year ahead of Whitney in school, she often tried to get Will to sit with her before school started in the morning.

His next closest brother in age, Jake, was naturally popular. Always quick with a joke, knowing precisely what to say, everyone loved him. Girls liked to flirt and tease with him; they'd leave notes in his locker. The other guys wanted to surprise Jake, catch him off guard, try to pull pranks. It never worked. Jake was just too cool to be fooled.

"Just go up and tell her you want to take her to the dance. This doesn't need to be such a production, Adrian," Will said one morning as they waited for the school doors to open.

"Yeah. What's the worst that can happen? She might say no. Oh well. But she'll probably say yes. Have some confidence in yourself, Adrian. If she says no, then you know, and you don't have to keep agonizing about it," Jake coached.

"All the girls are *always* with her. Always. If she said no when it was just me there, I think that'd be fine. But with everyone watching? That'd be terrible," Adrian said for what felt like the thousandth time.

"You want me to ask her for you?" Will offered.

"No!" Adrian's voice cracked.

Will's eyes went to slits. "Why not? I would. I don't care."

"She likes you. If you ask her, she'll think you're asking her, not me," Adrian mumbled.

"Whatever, man. I'm not taking that girl to the dance," Will declared.

That surprised Adrian. "Why not?"

"Well, because you like her. That wouldn't be right. But she's also annoying. She whines a lot and wants everyone to do things for her," Will said.

"She's not annoying! You just—"

"Whatever, Adrian. I'm not taking her to the dance, but I'll ask her if you want me to," Will offered again.

"Does she take the bus or walk home from school?" Jake asked.

"Usually she walks," Adrian muttered.

"Somehow, I knew you'd know the answer to that. Just follow her home one day, and talk to her then, after the girls split up. If they don't split up before her house, ring the bell and ask her. Job's done," Jake said.

"I can't follow her home! That's creepy!" Adrian exclaimed.

"Dude, you already know where she lives. Give it up. Don't follow her then, just meet her at her house," Jake grumbled.

The first bell rang as the doors opened.

JAKE IS A GENIUS. *This is going to work! Only one other girl is walking with her now,* Adrian thought.

He followed more than a half-block behind the girls walking home from school so it would seem less creepy. Adrian watched, one by one, as the girls split off for their own houses or blocks. Audrey was the last girl left with Whitney. Adrian knew for a fact that Audrey lived down another block because he went to her house once to work on a science project.

This was it. This was his chance. Audrey was waving goodbye and laughing as she walked away from Whitney. Adrian picked up the pace, but he knew he had almost two blocks to catch up before her house—no need to run.

"Uh, Whitney?" Adrian called as he got closer.

"Yes?" she asked, turning to face him.

"H-hi. Um. I'm Adrian. I'm in your class," he mumbled.

"I know, you're Will's brother." She looked around him, like Will might be hiding somewhere.

"Uh, he's not here. It's just me." Adrian blushed.

"Oh. Well, what do you want?" Her tone was less polite.

"Wouldyougotothedance with me?" he blurted.

3

"Huh?"

"The spring dance. Would you like to go with me?" Adrian asked slowly, with better enunciation.

There. It's out. It's done, he thought.

He glanced up at her beautiful face. Hazel eyes glowing with happiness, her mouth was opening. She was going to say yes. He knew it! They'd be in love forever!

Laughter burst from her mouth in a loud giggle.

"OMG, what? Did you just ask me to the spring dance?"

"Um. Yeah."

"You. Asked me. That's so funny! I can't wait to tell Audrey. She'll be so upset." Whitney continued to laugh.

"Um. So, do you want to? Go to the dance?"

"Why in the world would I go to the dance with you? You're a geek. I'm going with Alex Brutus unless Will asks me."

Adrian blinked, trying to think of what to say next.

Whitney's voice turned scornful. "You're a nerd. I wouldn't go with you if you were the only boy who asked. I'd rather go alone than go with you. Why would you think to ask me? Why would I go with you?"

That hurt. Adrian had spent most of a year idolizing this girl, only for her to laugh in his face and call him names. The pain quickly morphed into something more.

For the first time in his life, Adrian was furious. Humiliated. His body was overwhelmed with energy, fueled by the anger that he poured into his words.

"You'd go with me because we'd have a great time! Alex Brutus is a jerk! I've seen him spit in your lunch and then brag to the guys that you've swapped spit. I would never do that because I'm not a jackass. You should go out with a nice guy like me!" Adrian yelled at her.

As he yelled, there was a sharp spike of pain in Adrian's forehead that made him double over. Blood was dripping from his nose.

"Ouch," he muttered, wondering if he was going to be sick.

"Adrian, are you okay?" Whitney asked in a soft, gentle voice.

He stood up straight again. Adrian's head was still excruciating, but he wouldn't let her see that. She'd probably laugh at him again. He scowled at her.

"I'm fine," he growled.

"You're bleeding," she said while reaching out to touch his face. "I think I have some Kleenex in my bag, one sec."

He took the tissue from her and wiped his face. The bleeding had already stopped. "Thanks. I'll see you around, I guess," he muttered.

"Wait! Adrian?"

He turned around. "What?"

"Are you picking me up for the dance? What time? Or should I meet you there? My mom might be able to take us if your mom can't."

"I thought you were going with Alex Brutus." Adrian's tone was flat.

Whitney shook her head. "No. No, Alex Brutus is a jerk and a jackass. I'm going to go with a nice guy like you because we'd have a great time."

Convinced she was making fun of him, Adrian started the long walk home, heart-sore and sorry that he hadn't listened to William.

By the time the Trellis boys got to school the following morning, Whitney had told everyone that she was going to the dance with Adrian.

She also outed Alex Brutus as a jerk and a jackass that spit in girls' food. Alex didn't live it down until he went away to college.

William ended up going to the dance with Audrey Stevens, the sweet, smart girl that had a crush on Adrian since fourth grade. On the day that Whitney announced her date to the dance, Will found Audrey crying alone, around the corner of the school. He asked her to the spring dance immediately, knowing that his little brother had gotten it wrong.

FOR THE REST of middle school and well into freshman year of high school, Whitney Langcaster followed Adrian around every chance she got. If Adrian walked by while Whitney was talking to someone else, she'd pause in the conversation to talk about what a nice guy he was. She'd bring up the dance they went to together, where they had a great time.

It didn't matter if she'd told the story before. Whitney said it every time she saw him. If they spoke directly, she'd repeat, over and over, what a nice guy he was and what a great time she had at the dance.

Adrian learned to avoid her. It saved Whitney from the humiliation of people laughing at her repetitive conversation.

By the time Whitney was free of the mental compulsion, Adrian had figured out how the angry energy worked, if not what it was. Terrified of the effects and ashamed of what happened with Whitney, he learned to control his temper and let the energy out in other ways.

1

"*A*unt Lucy, I found help," Ree muttered while pulling on her hand.

"Ree, I told you to wait on the bench. What are you doing, honey? You're going to get too tired if you stand here with me." She bent down to adjust a shoelace.

"I'm okay! Really! He's going to help!" Ree exclaimed.

"What, baby? No. We don't know him," Lucy muttered.

Ree's *help* was touching her papers.

Lucy slapped his hand. "Don't touch my stuff."

"Gah," he yelped.

Really, jackass? It was a hand slap. Lucy mentally rolled her eyes.

"Why would you tell him that? Leave my kid alone. You have nothing to do with this."

"No, really, Aunt Lucy. He said he'd talk to the money people." Ree was all in on this guy.

The guy nodded. "It's true. I did."

"Why would you say that to a little kid? What the hell's wrong with you, man? He's five. He doesn't know you're full of it and trying to hit on me. Get the—" Lucy paused to reconsider her wording choice. "Get the heck out of here."

"Ah, I'm not—I wasn't—I wouldn't. Well, okay, I would, probably would… Maybe. Maybe not. But not like this. I mean, maybe in other circumstances. I agree. Guys that would do that to a little kid—no good. Anyway, no. I really am going to help. If you want help. I can help."

What the fuck? Idiot. Piss off.

"I don't know who you are. Just go. Please," she said.

"You all need to go!" the billing bitch yelled.

"Nancy, we're not going to go—" the guy said.

"You are going to go. You don't have anything to do with this," Lucy told him.

"I'm not going to go," he said. "Wait—"

"You're all going to go, or I'm going to call security."

"I'M NOT GOING ANYWHERE!" Lucy yelled. They'd driven almost an hour to talk to this woman. "We're going to figure this out!"

"I'm calling security! Other people are waiting. You need to go. There's nothing more I can do for you, lady! You need money or a different type of insurance. Those are the two options. Medicaid won't pay for this," the bitch yelled.

Oh, okay. Money and Insurance. Thanks, I'd love that. Where can I get that? Lucy cursed to herself again.

"Holy hell. NANCY! Don't call security! I don't want you to get fired!" the guy yelled.

"You're a nutter!" Lucy had enough. "You have nothing to do with this! What the fuck, man!"

Henry gasped.

"Sorry, baby. Sorry, I didn't mean to use the bad word. Sorry," she apologized.

The asshole was laughing.

"I called security," the billing bitch sneered.

"Henry, my man, we've made a mess of this," the guy said to Ree.

Why did Ree give the guy his name?! He knows better than that.

Henry nodded at him.

"Don't you talk to him! You leave us be!" Lucy yelled.

"I run a foun—" he started to say.

"I don't care! GET OUT OF HERE!" she yelled.

The guy sighed. Ree was watching him. This asshole got Ree all worked up.

"We'll straighten it out," he said to Ree.

"Folks, it's time for you to go!" the security guard called as he entered the room.

"I'm not going—" Lucy yelled.

"This woman needs to—" the billing bitch yelled.

"Time to—" the security guard tried to yell over them.

The jerk yelled something that made the billing bitch pause. Everyone in the room stopped and stared at him, including Ree.

"My name is Adrian Trellis. I run my family's Beloved Foundation for Children. I'd like to help get this sorted out."

Foundation? What foundation?

Everyone in the room was still staring at him. Lucy was thoroughly confused.

"Well, it's for children. And other stuff. It's a big foundation. But part of it is for children. That's the part we care about here," he babbled. "Yay, kids!"

Ree laughed at him.

"Let's step out into the hallway and talk about what's needed," the guy said to Lucy.

As the door to the billing office was closing behind them, someone yelled, "Oh. There he is. AAADDDDRRRIAAAANNNN!"

"Oh, boy," the guy said.

Adrian? He must be Adrian. I think he said his name was Adrian, right? This ought to be good, Lucy thought.

The guy came to a full stop a few yards away. "Oh, there you are, Lucy. Hi."

Do I know him? Maybe from the bar?

"I don't think I know you," Lucy said.

"You don't. Hi, I'm Sam." They shook hands.

"I'm not going to be weird. Hey, this guy wants to kiss your ass." Sam gestured to a guy in a suit.

He's not going to be weird. We have that going for us. I gotta get Ree out of here.

Sam took a coffee cup from the other guy. Adrian. "It's cold and tastes like teenage angst. He won't drink this." Sam handed the offending coffee to the suit guy.

"Mr. Fuller, nice to see you again. I'll take that back," Adrian said as he took the coffee back.

"Have you seen the 'rents?" Sam asked.

"No, they're probably with Jake and Matty," Adrian replied.

Sam looked puzzled. "No, I don't think so."

"What do you need, Mr. Fuller?" Adrian asked.

"I was hoping to give you a tour of—"

"BOYS! WHERE IS SHE?" a woman yelled from down the hall.

The Adrian guy turned to Lucy and Ree. "I apologize in advance. We're having a bit of a family crisis."

"Where is she?" the woman growled.

He said something too fast to understand.

"How is she?" the woman asked.

"Better. Much better. We can go see her. Let's go see her now," he said.

The woman turned to the guy in the suit. "Who are you? I don't know you. Are you someone looking for money? Go away. We'll do the money thing later."

The suit guy didn't know what to do.

"Go away," she said again.

The woman turned to Lucy with a toothy smile. "Why, hello there. Who might you two be?"

Why is she hugging Henry? What the fuck, woman? Don't touch my kid!

"Someone looking for money," Lucy grated out.

"Well, you found it!" The woman grinned.

Adrian pulled a business card out of his wallet and a pen from his pocket. He scribbled a name and phone number on the back of the card.

"Lucy, here's my card. On the back, I wrote a phone number for Martha Washington—and yes, it's her real name. She's my assistant. Tell her I said Lurie Children's Hospital. They're probably the best at what he needs in the area. We'll figure it out. She'll be expecting your call and will get everything rolling," Adrian said.

"Put your phone number, too," the woman instructed.

He gave the woman a look. "My number is already on the card, Mom."

Oh, fucking-a. She's going to play matchmaker? What's with this shit show?

"Your cell number is not on that card. Put your cell number down," the woman coached.

Adrian rolled his eyes.

"Don't you roll your eyes at me!"

"I wasn't rolling them at you. I was rolling them at me. My cell number is on the card front. It's just easier than arguing with her," he said, handing Lucy the card.

"Uh, great. Thanks, I think. I'll call Martha on Monday," Lucy said as she put the card in her pocket.

"He's a doctor," the woman said. "Pediatrician. Great with kids. Saves lives."

"Um. Okay. Thanks," Lucy said with a nod.

"All right, Mom, let's go see Matty. Bye, Lucy. Bye, Henry." The guy waved a coffee cup at them as he walked toward the elevator.

"Do you have your graham crackers, Ree? You didn't leave them on the bench, did you?"

"No, I finished them. The baggie is in my pocket."

"Good boy. Let's go back to the car. We can go home."

"Aunt Lucy, do you think he'll help? He said he would talk to the money people. They got mad at him, though." Ree looked at her with hope in his eyes.

No, Ree, I don't think he'll help. I think he's scamming.

"I hope so, baby. We'll see, I guess. How did you meet him? What did you talk about before you came into the money room by me?"

"He sat down on the bench and asked if I was lost. I didn't talk to him because he was a stranger. He asked if we needed help, and then I nodded. He told me his name, and then I told him mine, and we shook hands. Then I told him about the money people, and then we went to the money room to find you. He's real nice. I like him."

"He didn't touch you or anything?"

"I made him hold my hand walking to see you. I don't like money offices. The people are all mean."

She pulled the card out of her pocket: *Adrian Trellis, Executive Director of the Beloved Foundation.* The name Trellis was vaguely familiar, but she couldn't place it.

Over the last year, Lucy had applied to every nonprofit she could find that had anything to do with rare childhood cancers or diseases. She was still getting rejection letters. She didn't recall applying to anything called Beloved.

"Henry, want to take a ride to the library? We can get new books, but I want to use the computer first."

"Okay!"

As they walked through the hallways, Henry was skipping over the crack pattern in the tile.

"Aunt Lucy?"

"Henry Leap Frog?" Lucy asked as she jumped with him.

"Do we have to go back to the apartment?"

"Not right now, but tonight Erika will come to stay with you. I have to work."

"Oh." Henry clearly was not a fan of this.

"What's wrong with hanging out with Erika? I thought you liked her?"

"I do. It's fine. I don't like it when she leaves, though."

"Leaves? What do you mean?" Lucy's brow furrowed.

"Sometimes she leaves after bedtime, and then there are people in the hallway, and if they bang on the door, I hide."

Lucy paid the downstairs neighbor twelve dollars an hour to watch Henry while she worked. *She better not be leaving him alone.*

Henry climbed into his booster seat and buckled his belt. Lucy said her mental prayer to the god of working cars as she got behind the wheel of her 1992 Ford Escort. It was a good day. The car started on the second try.

Twenty minutes later, Lucy and Henry were walking into their favorite public library branch. It didn't look crowded.

"Well, there's my Henry! How's my best reader? Hi, Lucy!" the librarian, Leti, greeted them.

"Hi, Ms. Leti!" Henry ran to give her a hug.

"Hey, Leti, is the computer working today?" Lucy asked.

"I think so. More letter writing, huh? Henry, want to look at the new books with me? We'll be over here, Lucy. Good luck."

"Thanks, Leti!"

THIRTY MINUTES LATER, Lucy was still staring at the screen, dumbfounded. The Adrian guy. That Sam guy. The woman. The older guy. The pictures all matched. He wasn't scamming. These people had serious money. The not-going-to-be-weird Sam dude was worth billions.

Ree might have actually found help. I shouldn't have slapped his fucking hand! Should I apologize? I didn't know. It'll be fine. It seemed like he would still help. He didn't seem mad, did he? I could call him? No, he said to call the lady on the back of the card. I'll talk to her about it. I really hope I didn't fuck this up.

"How's book hunting going, Ree?"

THERE WAS a knock on the apartment door at six thirty that evening.

"Hey, Erika! He's all fed and bathed. He's coloring," Lucy closed and bolted the door behind the babysitter.

Erika was wearing sweats and a t-shirt.

Those aren't going out clothes. She's not going to leave him. It's fine. Maybe she ran down to her apartment for something once, and he got scared.

"You working to two or four tonight?" Erika asked.

"I'm working till four," Lucy said. "You'll be staying here until I get home, right?"

Erika paused and looked at Lucy like she was nuts. "Yeah."

They'd never had a problem before. Erika wouldn't leave him alone. It was fine. She was worried about nothing. Erika had been babysitting for almost a year, and they had no problems.

"All right, see ya in the wee hours then!"

2

$\mathcal{A}$ drian got home from the hospital a little after seven p.m. on Saturday evening. Matty was in good hands. Jake was calming down. They'd be fine. He wasn't helping anything by being there, just serving as the resident Trellis for ass-kissing.

"Ugh," Adrian said out loud at the thought.

No one responded because the house was empty. Adrian's house was always empty. He set the two large pizzas he brought home down on the dining room table then walked through the house to make sure everything was as it should be.

It was. Clean. Tidy. Empty.

After grabbing a beer, he sat down and ate the entire large sausage, mushroom, onion, and green pepper pizza. The other pizza was for later.

Letting his food settle, he wrote a quick email to Martha with what he knew about Lucy and Henry. He was pretty sure of the type of cancer from looking at what had been ordered on the paperwork Lucy had. Or at least what he saw before she slapped at his hand.

Adrian laughed out loud at the memory. He'd been startled by her reaction, not the slap. So few people were snappish with him. It was funny. Especially because the Foundation would help them with whatever Ree needed. Maybe Lucy, too. There were parts of the Foundation that dealt with adult education and career training.

Thinking it over, he understood Lucy's reaction. She was absolutely gorgeous. Blond hair, royal blue eyes, oval face, athletic build with understated curves in all the right places.

Random assholes using the sick nephew to hit on her was probably a common thing. Ree was someone she cared about, a problem wanting a solution. She radiated fatigue and stress, too—great fodder for assholes and abusers everywhere. She was right to be skeptical.

"We'll set that to rights. It'll work out. I'll call Gretta on Monday. She'll see him quickly," Adrian said, again out loud.

"There's no one here," he continued. "I'm talking to myself. As usual. I should get a dog."

Adrian sighed. "Then the dog would be lonely because it's just me, and I'm only here and awake for a couple hours each day. Maybe two dogs? Two dogs might be the way to go. They could keep each other company."

Then, of its own accord, his mind drifted back to the curve of Lucy's neck as it joined her shoulder and the small amount of skin that showed in her v-neck t-shirt.

"Oh, absolutely not. It's time to go beat the shit outta myself," he said with determination to the empty house.

Adrian stuck the extra pizza in the fridge and headed to the basement for a workout. He'd be back upstairs to eat it in a few hours.

BARTENDING the late shift on Saturday nights was hard work. The bar was packed, and no one was bussing tables. While Lucy was grabbing empty glasses off tables, some asshole tried to put his hand up her shirt while grabbing her ass.

"Hot fucking damn, woman. You wanna ride my dick like a pogo stick?" he leered.

Fuck this shit, Lucy thought as she kicked the guy in the shin.

"Hands off, man. Next time, the kick will be higher," she warned.

The guy bellowed something at her as he reached for her ponytail.

Always with the damn hair, she internally sighed. *I guess I didn't really need the job after all.*

Lucy dropped the tray of glasses on the table and slugged the guy in the face. He fell backward into the guy behind him, who took offense. Loudly and with violence.

Lucy scooted back behind the bar, hoping no one noticed her role in the ongoing bar fight. Maybe she wouldn't get fired. Tonight. Maybe she wouldn't get fired tonight.

HENRY WOKE up in his bed to the neighbors fighting and screaming bad words. He went out to the living room to find it empty. The people were in the hall again. Something thudded against the door. Someone was groaning.

Scared and shaking, he ran for the phone. *Aunt Lucy!*

The call to Lucy's cell went to voicemail. Henry thought the phone number for the bar was on the fridge with Aunt Lucy's schedule, but the paper was gone. He called her cell number again.

LUCY WAS dead on her feet. She'd been up since six a.m. She had made good tips, but it was hectic and busy. There were two more bar fights before the bar closed at four. Cleaning up and balancing the register took time. It was now four thirty in the morning. She'd been awake for more than twenty-two hours.

Sleep. Sleep. Sleep. Almost home. Sleep. Sleep. Sleep, she kept chanting to herself. She counted the minutes from the bar to the apartment to stay awake. She cranked the music up and sang along with songs she didn't know. She was almost home. *Sleep. Sleep. Sleep.*

In total, she'd made two hundred thirty dollars in tips. Half were credit, so she'd have taxes withheld. After paying Erika and taxes, she ended up clearing about a hundred bucks for nine hours of hard work.

I should open a daycare.

The apartment building door was busted again. *Fuck this place, this building, this neighborhood.* There was a used condom hanging off the door handle. *At least it's not needles.* She opened the door without touching it.

Lucy headed up the stairs, climbing over someone who'd passed out on a landing. *And there's that needle in the stairwell. We gotta get out of here.* Their lease was up in four months. She'd start applying for other places that accepted rent assistance soon.

Someone else passed out in her hall. He'd managed to piss himself.

She put her key in the lock and opened her apartment door to find Adrian Trellis sitting on her couch.

She yelped, completely startled. *WHAT THE FUCK?!*

He was putting his finger over his lips to signal for her to be quiet.

While she tried to catch her breath, he picked Henry up from the couch and walked toward the bedroom with him. He closed over the door on his way back to the living room.

What the fuck is he doing here?! Is this some kind of trap, after all? Is he following us? Henry was breathing, right? I didn't see him move. But he had to be breathing. If I start screaming, what kind of "help" will come? It's four thirty in the fucking morning.

"You put my card on the fridge," Adrian said quietly. "He called me a few hours ago, crying after the babysitter split. He couldn't find the number for where you work, and your cell went directly to voicemail. I've tried calling your cell several times."

"Holy fuck! Holy fuck! Jesus! I don't have any missed calls. None. I check my phone," she stammered. She was shaking with fear. "You need to leave right now. Right now. Get the fuck out. You don't belong in my apartment. I don't know you. Please. Leave. Please. Please get out. GO—"

She was backing away as he pulled a phone out of a pocket. "Is this the right number?"

She didn't want to take her eyes off him. If she looked away, he was going to take a swing at her, and then she'd be down with no chance at fighting. She was starting to hyperventilate.

Adrian sighed at her. "Lucy, I'm not going to hurt you. I'm just trying to figure out why a terrified five-year-old called me at eleven thirty on Saturday night, saying he was alone and scared in a dangerous part of town." He recited the number from his phone.

Lucy blinked. "No, my number ends in 01. Is he okay? Oh my God, he was here alone?!"

A different sort of terror was settling in on top of the existing terror. *Henry was here alone?!*

"He's fine, zonked out on the couch around one thirty. He woke up for a minute when the babysitter showed up around three. Pretty sure I scared the crap out of her. I'm not really sorry about that."

"Oh my God. He was here alone!"

Aunt Lucy's on her way to a panic attack. This is not normal for them, I guess, Adrian thought.

Henry had seemed well-mannered, clean, well-cared for, and loved when they met earlier. He was alone on the bench at the hospital, though. Adrian understood that having Henry in the billing office would have been overwhelming for him. And it was a hospital. In a good area. Not terribly dangerous. The bench was less than fifteen feet from the office. Someone would have heard if he started yelling for help. Adrian was willing to overlook it at the time.

When Ree called his cell phone earlier, crying and terrified, Adrian intended to get over here and then call the police. He'd get an emergency court injunction. He'd get Henry the hell out of here.

Ree knew his own address and could tell Adrian the numbers for the building and apartment. He knew the street name but couldn't spell it correctly. Still, Henry got it close enough for Adrian to find him. Pretty good for a five-year-old.

While driving into the neighborhood, Adrian wondered if he should have called his brother, Will, to go with him. It was one of the worst areas in Chicago; police would be slow to respond.

The main apartment building door was kicked in, so he didn't have

to worry about getting buzzed into the building itself. The hall stunk
of piss. There was a hypodermic on the stairs. This wasn't safe for
anyone, let alone a woman raising a sick kid. Henry was about to go to
a new home. Aunt Lucy might get some visitation, but this couldn't
continue.

The door opened before Adrian could knock. Henry had been
standing on a kitchen chair, looking out the door peephole to watch
for him. Adrian was surprised to find him in superhero pajamas in a
spotlessly clean, rundown apartment. Given the rest of the building,
he was expecting the place to be a pit.

The apartment was small. Adrian walked through it to make sure
everything was as it should be with nothing dangerous lying around.
There wasn't much. A living area that barely fit a sagging old couch
and a TV that wasn't a flat panel. A tiny table for two along one wall.
Around the corner, there was a kitchen so small it didn't look like the
oven door could be opened all the way. One bedroom with two twin-
sized beds and a bathroom. Everything was clean and orderly, the beds
were made, and the bathroom smelled of cleaner.

"What happened, Ree? Where's your aunt?" Adrian asked as he
returned to the living room. Ree was checking all the locks on the
door. The door was the only thing in the place that looked new. It
appeared to be reinforced, too.

"Erika left! She was supposed to stay. Aunt Lucy even asked to
make sure. Erika was supposed to stay, but then she left! Adrian, she
left. She's not supposed to leave!" Ree babbled, starting to break down
in tears. "She's supposed to stay!"

"Okay. It's fine, buddy. When did Erika leave? Where's your aunt?"
Adrian said quietly, calmly. Henry hadn't been crying when Adrian
arrived; he'd been brave by himself. Now that he wasn't alone, he was
done being brave.

"I don't know when she left. I was asleep. But then there was a big
bang, and I woke up, and it was loud, and then I came out here, and
she wasn't here. The door wasn't even locked. The door is *always*
supposed to be locked. It's the rule. The door stays locked. Erika
knows the rule," Ree continued to cry.

"Henry, where's your aunt?" Adrian asked again.

"Work! She's at work! I don't like it here, Adrian. I want Aunt Lucy. Can we go to Aunt Lucy? Will you take me to Aunt Lucy?"

"Where does she work, Ree?" Adrian asked.

"The bar," Ree sobbed.

"Which bar? What's the bar's name?"

"I don't know. I'm not allowed to go there. I don't know what it is. There was a paper on the fridge with the phone number, but I don't know where it went. It was there earlier."

"Does Aunt Lucy have a cell phone? Is that number somewhere?" Adrian picked him up off the chair he was standing on and put him on his feet.

Ree recited Lucy's cell number with confidence while Adrian put the chair back at the little table for two.

"I've been calling her, Adrian. I've been calling. She always answers. What if something's wrong? What if Aunt Lucy got hurt? I want Aunt Lucy!"

"Okay, buddy. It's okay. Everything is going to be fine." Adrian sat cross-legged on the floor next to Henry.

Without hesitation, Henry climbed into Adrian's lap, wrapped his arms around Adrian's neck, and sobbed.

"Henry, it's okay, buddy. Everything is fine. Aunt Lucy is fine. I'm here. It's fine. We'll be fine," Adrian repeated while rocking and soothing the little boy.

Not the police. I won't call the police. I'll wait for Lucy to get home, get the story, and then help her work with Family Services. This is a childcare thing, not a neglect thing, Adrian thought, relieved.

Lucy seemed like a caregiver willing to go to bat for the kid. Adrian hated the idea of that not being accurate. Poor with terrible options was one thing. Intentionally leaving the kid alone and terrified was another thing altogether.

AROUND THREE FIFTEEN A.M., someone started jiggling and pushing on the locked door. When the pushing didn't work, a voice started calling from the hallway.

"Ree? Did you wake up? I'm right here, Ree. Open the door, Henry."

That was not Aunt Lucy's voice. The missing babysitter?

"Henry! Open the door right now, you bad boy!" the voice snapped.

"Hello," Adrian said as he threw the door open.

"Holy fuck, man. Who are you?" a short Latina lady said.

"I'm a friend of the family," Adrian said with deliberate calm. The woman smelled like beer and pot. "Who are you?"

"Pst, shut it, man. Lucy ain't got no friends. Get out the way," the woman said as she tried to push around him. "You waitin' to bang her? I'd bang you. Lemme in. I gotta check on the kid."

"Are you Erika?" Adrian asked tersely.

"Yeah, man, get the fuck out the way," she said, still trying to push him.

"You're not coming in. Go away before you wake Henry up. You're fired," Adrian said slowly, calmly.

"Fuck you, man. I don't take no orders from you. Fired, my ass. I'm due money."

"For what? You left." Adrian could feel the anger rising in him.

"I was here. I just ran down to my apartment," she lied.

"I've been here since eleven thirty."

"Yeah, so that bitch owes me five hours. You ain't got nothing to do with this. Get out the way, dick!"

"Adrian?" Henry mumbled from the couch.

"Everything's fine, Ree," Adrian soothed quietly.

As Erika started yelling at Ree, Adrian let the anger slip out a bit. "Erika."

Her eyes snapped to his.

"Go away."

Then she was gone.

LUCY WAS STARTING TO HYPERVENTILATE. "When? How?" she gasped out.

Her face was drawn with big dark circles under her eyes. She was visibly shaking.

"Lucy, he's fine," Adrian said, back to his soothing voice. "I've been here since about eleven thirty. He did a good job of knowing the address and everything. He just transposed your phone number."

Lucy squatted down, rested her elbows on her knees, and covered her face.

Adrian couldn't tell if she was crying. He turned around to give her a minute, grabbing his car keys and going to the window that looked over the parking lot. He was pretty sure his car was still there.

Well, that's a pleasant surprise, he thought.

When he turned back, Lucy was still folded in on herself with her arms over her face.

"Lucy, are you okay?"

"Why did you come here?" she mumbled, face still covered. "Thank you for staying with him, but what is it you want from me? It certainly isn't money."

Adrian sighed. "I don't want anything from you, Lucy. I came because he called me for help. I thought he was in trouble, and I came to help."

When she picked her head up, her blue eyes were spilling tears and makeup down her face. "I'm so sorry. I'm so sorry I slapped your hand earlier and gave you grief, and I'm sorry he had to call you and that you had to sit here tonight. I'm so sorry. I'm so tired. I don't know what to do right now. I'm so sorry. He was here alone. He was here alone. I'm so sorry. I'm so sorry, Ree. Oh God, what am I going to do?"

Sigh.

Adrian sat on the floor in front of Lucy and pulled her into a hug. She flinched when he touched her like she thought he was going to hurt her. After a second, she realized it was just a hug and relaxed. Before long, she was curled up in his lap, being rocked and soothed.

"You know, I sat with Henry like this for a while earlier, too," Adrian chuckled.

Lucy didn't respond.

"Oh, come on. The circumstances are a little funny."

She still didn't respond.

He tipped her head to the side to find her fast asleep.

"Well, now I have to figure out how to get us off the floor..."

Thirty minutes later, Lucy was in her bed, shoes off, sound asleep. The man passed out in the hallway was roused and helped to his door. Paramedics were treating a guy that was drunk and stoned when he fell down the stairs. The hypodermic was cleaned up. And Adrian was on his way home.

When Lucy woke up six hours later, Adrian was long gone, and her keys had been slid under the locked apartment door.

3

---

*I*t was almost six a.m. by the time Adrian was home again.

"He's probably awake," he said out loud. To himself. Again. "He never sleeps. If he's sleeping now, he'll sleep through the call. I can call. It'll be fine. But I'll feel like shit if I wake him up."

Adrian's cell phone rang in his hand.

"What?" his younger brother, Sam, asked.

"I feel like you're getting weirder since Jake moved out," Adrian said.

Sam sighed. "I'm not getting weirder since Jake moved out. My weirdness is just more apparent. Jake did a good job muffling shit in and out. What do you want? I could hear your babbling five miles away. You live alone, Adrian. Stop talking to yourself."

"You know that woman we met yesterday at—"

"Lucy and Henry. Yes. Have you fixed that yet?"

"Uh, no. That's why I'm calling—"

"I called you. It's why we're talking, though. I'll give you that," Sam pointed out.

"Do we have to do this, Sam? Really? So pedantic?"

"You're the one that wanted to talk before eight a.m. on a Sunday," Sam bitched.

"Were you sleeping?"

"Of course not, but that's not the point. If I come over, will you make me eggs?"

"Yeah, sure. Come on over."

"Ugh, never mind. I don't want anger eggs. What's with Lucy?"

"She lives in a truly awful, dangerous part of town—"

"Why do you know where she lives?"

Adrian sighed. "The babysitter split on Ree last night. He found my card on the fridge and called for help."

"The card that you gave Mom stink-eye over? The card she made you put your cell phone number on? That card?" Sam asked gleefully.

"Is there a point?"

"Just pointing out that *Mom* did that little nudge. Not me. I'm pretty sure Mom is why I'm weird."

"Well, I mean, psychology says—"

"Back to the kid," Sam snapped.

Adrian sighed. Every conversation he and Sam had went like this. Sam did it intentionally.

"Terrible part of town. Like, old hypodermics in the stairwell part of town. I would like them to not live there. Acquiring a property is outside the bounds of the Foundation. Would you acquire property and give it to the Foundation?"

"Well, is the building for sale? I hadn't really thought of that before, but—" Sam started.

"No, I didn't mean to buy the building they are in. I meant buy somewhere else for them to be while he's going through chemo," Adrian clarified.

"Oh. Well, we can do that, too. But what about everyone else that lives in that building? In that neighborhood?" Sam asked. "How do we make the neighborhood safer?"

"You want to build a new neighborhood? What do we do with the people that live there right now?"

"I want to build it for them. They stay. But we help make it better. Drug rehabs and schools and career training initiatives. Stuff like that. Why can't we do that?" Sam asked.

"There are all kinds of social works programs out there, striving to do that now. We give them lots and lots of money. It takes time, though," Adrian explained.

"Well, why aren't the social works programs working? Are the programs flawed? Could we do it better? Can we help make the programs better? Do they just need more money or people?"

Adrian lifted his eyebrows, smiling into the phone. "Do you want the information on the social works programs for the greater Chicago area, Sam?"

The was a pause of hesitation.

"Will you be mad at me if I look at it? This is your thing, not mine."

Adrian laughed. "Not at all, Midas. I'd love for you to pick a winner and make it a reality. There's no downside to you looking at it."

"Send it over when you can. Thanks, Adrian," Sam said, sounding like he was about to hang up.

"Wait. Don't hang up. Lucy and Ree don't have time for the neighborhood to be rebuilt. He's going for chemo sooner rather than later, and it'd be good if he didn't live there," Adrian reminded him.

"Oh. Oh yeah! That means I get to go buy property, right? Without getting in trouble?" Sam sounded tentatively hopeful.

"Yes, that's what I'm asking you to do," Adrian confirmed.

"And you'll tell Dad that you asked me to do this, so he doesn't freak about my OCD property-buying behaviors?" Sam asked.

"It's true. I will tell him I asked you to do it. Somewhere close to Lurie Children's Hospital. They'll be spending a lot of time there."

"What kind of house does she want?" Sam's voice vibrated with excitement and happiness. Buying property was Sam's favorite hobby.

"The kind that doesn't have heroin addicts next door."

"Woo, that humor's a little dark for you. That was William-level cynicism, Adrian. Not a good look on you. Go punch the bag some more."

"I'll do that later. Once we're done with this conversation, I'm going to call Lucy and see if I can get her out of there today."

"No." Samuel's voice came through the line in a way that made the cell phone lose signal.

"What? No, what?" Adrian asked.

"Not today. Don't call her today. Tuesday. Talk to her in person on Tuesday." Sam was breathing a little hard.

"You okay?" Adrian asked. "Should I come over?"

"I'm okay. Just caught off guard. Tuesday, though. Not today. Not tomorrow. Wait it out."

"Why?"

"Because I said so," Sam said, the annoyance clear.

"Of course, that'd be the reason. Fine. Let me know on the house front."

WHEN ADRIAN WALKED into the big room of his parents' house on Sunday afternoon, he was greeted with his father's scowl.

"Did you tell him to go buy property?" Hank demanded.

"I asked him to buy a house and give it to the Foundation, yes," Adrian admitted.

"See!" Sam said, defensively.

"He asked you to buy *a house*. Not three houses, Sam. We don't need three more houses in Chicago. You own eight houses in a ten-mile radius. What are we going to do with these new houses?" Hank sounded defeated.

"I figured Lucy could pick one and we'd do something else with the others. Maybe give them to the hospital or something. I don't know." Sam shrugged.

"You have to stop doing this, Sam!" Hank yelled.

Sam sighed. "Why? It's not like I don't have the money. It's not like I'm going to run out of money. I keep trying to give it away, and it's not working. I like buying property. Why can't I buy it when I feel like it?"

"Because you can only live in one at a time, Sam! You own, like, eighty-three houses around the world and won't let anyone outside of the family use them because you don't want someone else sleeping in your bed. The bed that *you don't even sleep in.* That's weird, son," Hank said, resigned.

"Well, I never claimed to be not-weird," Sam said, defensive again.

The room was quiet for a moment while everyone acknowledged the reality of that statement.

Sam smiled a full-fledged, adoring smile of joy. A smile that would make any sane woman's heart melt into a puddle at his feet.

That smile isn't for a woman. He's smiling like that about the houses. I just know it, Adrian thought.

"They're good houses, Adrian. The frisky one is empty, and we'll close on it fast. Its upstairs bathroom is sad; it needs a new one. The impulsive one still has a large family in it. They just listed it on Friday. The rebellious one is my favorite, though. There's a tree in the back that needs a swing. The old couple that lives there now doesn't have grandkids, though. So, the tree's lonely," Sam explained.

Hank scrubbed his hands over his face.

"Sam—?" Noah started.

"NO, NOAH. NO. ABSOLUTELY NOT," Hank yelled.

"What makes a house rebellious?" Noah finished with a grin.

"I walked in the front door and said hello to it—" Sam started.

"Wait," Hank interrupted. "Who was shopping with you? Andrea or the other person?"

"Andrea," Sam said.

"We're fine. Go ahead," Hank nodded.

"So, I said hi, and I thought the dining room would be to the right, but it was to the left, *behind* the living room. I didn't see that coming. And then I thought the kitchen would be a certain way, but it wasn't. The cabinets opened in the other direction, being contrary. I thought the house and I wouldn't be friends. But the closets upstairs were just how I thought they'd be. The tree in the backyard said it wished it had a little boy. It was lonely. Then it occurred to me that the house was just rebellious. Going through a phase. It'll get over it."

By the time Sam was done talking, everyone in the room, except Hank, was grinning. This was typical Sam behavior when evaluating properties and land.

"At regular intervals throughout every day, I wonder what your mother and I did to make you like this, Sam. I can't even really complain about it, either. It's not like you're a failure-to-launch guy living in our basement, playing video games," Hank said through laughter.

"Please get a girlfriend. You've gotten weirder since Jake moved out," Hank begged.

Sam glared at Hank. "I can't find—!"

"Get a real girlfriend. Like, one that exists. Not this dream woman. Give a real person a try. You might like it," Hank interrupted.

"Ahem, Mandy Baker!" Ethan fake cleared his throat, making everyone in the room, including Hank, smile.

Sam dated Mandy Baker before he started his company. They were college friends. By the end of the third date, they agreed to just be friends. Sam began to visibly glow while they were making out on her couch. When he touched the bare skin of her shoulder, her skin burned, leaving a mark.

Mandy was the third non-related person Sam hired into Trellis Industries. She ran the legal department and had long since been wealthy in her own right. She kept working because the company did good things for the world. As far as anyone could tell, she had never once said a word against Sam, but they weren't really friends anymore.

Sam had not tried dating anyone in almost ten years. Before Mandy, attempts at dating were awkward and strange. Being physically intimate with a woman made him ill. After Mandy, he wasn't even willing to try. Sam had been genuinely fond of her; he had a rough time when she started avoiding him.

At Ethan's mention of her, Sam smiled, but it was a sad smile. Bittersweet.

"Back on track," Adrian said after a pause. "I'm going to have Martha talk to her about the house tomorrow—"

"I said no, Adrian. Tuesday. Why are you ignoring me?" All traces of humor were gone from Sam's face.

Will and Hennessy walked into the room together. "Woo, what'd we miss? Why's he pissed off?" Will asked.

"Adrian is helping a woman and kid through the Foundation. He asked Sam to buy property because they live in a bad part of town. Adrian just said he was going to have Martha talk to the woman tomorrow even though Sam told him to talk to the woman on Tuesday," Ethan summarized.

"What? I'm not ignoring you. You told me not to call—" Adrian started.

"I TOLD YOU TO TALK TO HER ON TUESDAY. Do as I say. First, the appointment, help her be calm, let the kid swing his feet, tell her about the house, and then do the car," Sam instructed. The air crackled with a little bit of energy, though his voice didn't echo.

Adrian blinked. "I have no idea at all what you're talking about. I will do whatever it is you want me to do, but I'm going to need a little more information. I'm not trying to be contrary. Tell me what you want me to do."

Sam seemed to calm down. "I want you to meet her at the hospital on Tuesday and talk to her. It has to be you, not Martha. And it has to be in person."

"It has to be Tuesday? I can't take Will and go down there right now?" Adrian clarified.

"Tuesday," Sam confirmed.

"Why would I go with you?" Will asked.

"She lives in Englewood."

"Oh, you got that wrong, little brother. You aren't going down there at all. Hennessy and I will go. You get to stay home," Will said without humor.

"I was down there on Saturday night. It was fine. Just not a place for a kid on chemo," Adrian muttered.

Hennessy cleared his throat. "Why would you go there, Adrian?"

"Because a small child called me alone and afraid," Adrian said, forcing himself to be calm. "The building was not good. The apartment had a war-proof door, though. And let's be honest. If the young blond lady and her little nephew can *live* there, I should be able to visit for an evening, don't you think?"

"This is Lucy? You're talking about the woman from the hospital?" Darla asked, coming into the room.

"Yeah, Mom."

Darla started to look happy. "She called you? That didn't take long."

"No, Mother. She didn't call me. Henry called me at eleven thirty at night. The babysitter split, leaving him alone and terrified in the apartment while Lucy was at work. So I went down and stayed with him," Adrian explained.

"Well, now I'm delighted I made you write your number on that card. Poor baby. He can come to stay with me when she works. We'll have fun. Tell her," Darla instructed.

Will's face was a mask of irritation. "Let's go back to the part where you went to Englewood in the middle of the fucking night."

"Let's not," Adrian snapped. "It's fine. I'm fine. I'll talk to her on Tuesday. Moving on. How's Matty doing?"

AFTER THREE RINGS, an older woman's voice answered, "This is Martha."

"Uh, hi. Hi, Martha, my name is Lucy Wallace and on—"

"Oh, hi, Lucy! One minute, one minute. How's Henry feeling? We need to go to Lurie Children's Hospital. It's AML, right? Acute myeloid leukemia? That's what Adrian thought it was, but he wasn't sure. Wait. Wait. What's that say? Tom! What's this here?" The woman moved the phone.

Well, he said Martha would be expecting my call, I guess. Lucy almost laughed.

"Lucy, I'm back. Sorry about that. Can you bring him to Lurie tomorrow morning? Like nine thirty or ten, somewhere in there?" Martha asked.

"Yes, yes, of course. What kind of paperwork do you need me to fill out? I'll fill out anything you need," Lucy said, startled. "It's tomorrow? Not next week?"

It typically took weeks and weeks to get an appointment.

"No, no. The doctor Henry wants doesn't have office hours on Monday. So it's tomorrow, not today. Now, when you go in the main doors of the hospital, you go to the information desk and give them your name. They're going to have all the paperwork you need, okay? Bring any records or previous tests or anything like that with you. Now, do you work tomorrow? It might be a long day," Martha said.

"No, I don't work tomorrow," Lucy replied flatly.

She got fired yesterday after telling the bar owner she couldn't work nights until she found a babysitter.

"Oh, good," Martha said. "Now, is your legal name Lucy? One of my granddaughters is Lucille. Such a sweet girl. She's in college now. I can't believe how fast that happened. How do you spell your last name? What's Henry's full name? Does he have a social security number? We'll get these forms filled out, and things will be better, you'll see. It's going to be fine."

"Uh, Martha, is Mr. Trellis in?" Lucy asked. "I was hoping I could talk to him for just a minute."

"Oh, um. I don't know if Hank's in. They had a bit of an emergency with Jake's girlfriend. In the hospital with some kind of seizure, I think. She's a cute little redhead, impish little woman, so funny with Jake. So good to see one of the boys in love. I can find out if Hank's around," Martha replied. "What did you need?"

"He goes by Hank? I thought his name was Adrian?" *Holy shit, I've been calling him the wrong name.*

"Oh, no. No. You're looking for Adrian? Or his dad? Adrian is Adrian or Doctor Trellis, I guess. But no one calls him that, even his patients. Sometimes he's Dr. Adrian. Mr. Trellis is his dad, Hank. But no one really calls Hank by the formal name, either. None of the boys go by Mr. Trellis. There's just too many of them for that. Everything would get all confused.

"Anyway, Adrian's not here. He had to go to some silly lunch thing. I don't know. Something with the mayor. He'll be back later this afternoon. What do you need, honey?" Martha asked.

"Nothing. Nothing at all. I just wanted to say thanks and apologize. I was very rude when we met," Lucy tried to explain.

"Oh, honey. Don't you worry about that. Adrian doesn't offend easily. Everything's fine. It'll all be fine. You'll see. Don't worry. Are you worried?" Martha asked, concerned.

"I just, I didn't think he would actually help. I thought he was making a pass at me, and I yelled—" Lucy stopped talking at Martha's laughter.

"That's funny, honey. You don't know how funny that is. I can't wait to tell Tom. No, don't you worry about the hanky-panky business. He's much too shy for that nonsense. He's a good boy. Momma Trellis raised all those boys right, except for maybe Noah. That one's trouble, but some girls like that kind of thing. But no, Adrian's a good boy," Martha prattled on.

Did she really have to laugh that hard at the idea of the wealthy do-good doctor hitting on me? Lucy wondered.

"Um, maybe I'll call him later and apologize anyway. I'd feel better," Lucy said.

"Well, you do that if you feel like you should, but I'm sure he won't know what you're apologizing for. He probably didn't even notice."

"I yelled at him and called him a nutter," Lucy admitted.

"Eh, well, these things happen. Don't you worry about it, honey. Do you need anything else? Nine thirty or so tomorrow. At Lurie. Main entrance. Do you have a way to get there?" Martha asked.

"Yeah, yes. I can get there. But what else do you need from me? For the paperwork?" Lucy hadn't given the Medicaid numbers or anything.

"Nothing, we're all set, honey. Now you have a good day tomorrow and tell Henry to be brave, and you give us a call and let us know how it went, okay? We'll be thinking about you," Martha said.

Lucy was tearing up a smidge. "O-Okay. Thank you for your help."

Maybe Ree actually found help. Lucy was trying not to get her hopes up, but that nice chatty old lady wished them well and said she'd be thinking about them. That was nice, a nice thought.

4

$\mathcal{H}$enry skipped in the main entrance of Lurie Children's Hospital with his aunt at nine twenty on Tuesday morning. The person at the information desk said they were "starting with the doctor" and would go from there. Lucy wasn't sure what to make of that. An elevator ride later, they were hopping over cracks in a different hospital's tile pattern.

They had seen a doctor here before. The doctor was willing to work with Medicaid for the visits. But they required a bunch of testing that Medicaid wouldn't cover. Since Lucy didn't have an extra thirty thousand dollars lying around, they were shit out of luck. Lucy had moved to the next doctor on the list.

"Hello," the chipper receptionist said with a wave for Henry. "Which doctor are you here to see?"

"Uh, I don't know," Lucy admitted.

"What time is the appointment for?" the receptionist asked.

At Lucy's blank look, the receptionist's face fell. "You have to have an appointment. We can get you scheduled, but it won't be today. We're already overbooked."

"I think there's an appointment. The information desk was

supposed to have papers, but the guy sent us here," Lucy explained. "I can call and—"

"Oh. Is this Henry?" the receptionist asked.

Henry smiled and nodded.

"Hi, Ree! We have some background stuff for you to fill out, Ms. Wallace. You're a little earlier than we thought you'd be. That's great. Makes it easier to fit you in somewhere. Dr. Garaff is going to see you. She's the best with his type of cancer. We're kinda folding you into the schedule, so today might be a little rough," the receptionist explained as she handed Lucy a pile of paperwork.

Lucy nodded. "We'll do whatever you need."

An hour later, they were still sitting in the waiting room, rereading Henry's library books. It didn't bother either of them; this was par for the course.

"Henry Wright!" the nurse called from the door to the exam rooms.

Lucy jumped up. "We're coming!"

A quick stop at the scale and height ruler later, they were in an exam room with a table, guest chair, and doctor stool. The room was so small, Lucy had to fold her legs under the guest's chair.

There was a knock on the door almost immediately. A middle-aged woman in a white coat with silver-streaked brown hair and overly large hazel eyes came into the room.

"Well, hi, Ree! I'm Dr. Garaff. I'm sorry you waited so long, but you were perfect out there. I saw you reading when I walked by. Are you reading Elephant and Piggy books? Those are some of my favorites! Ms. Wallace? Lucinda? What do you prefer?"

"Lucy, please. Thank you for seeing us so quickly. I can't believe—" She was talking so fast she was difficult to understand. This doctor might actually help Ree. They might be on the road to improvement.

"Oh, psh. Anything for Beloved folks. Dr. Adrian is one of my favorite former students. Such a kind heart. I was disappointed when he restricted his practice for the Foundation.

"Let's take a look, okay? Can I look at you, Henry? My hands aren't cold. Your glands are a little swollen, sweetheart. Does your throat hurt?" Dr. Garaff asked.

"Only a little. I'm good!" Henry said.

Lucy's eyes went wide. "Ree, you have to tell me. Even when it's a little hurt, honey. Little hurts become—"

"It's fine, Lucy. Take a breath and let it out," Dr. Garaff said in a calming tone of voice. "We're going to do just fine."

Lucy nodded. There were tears in her eyes again. She hated crying, hated crying in public, and hated crying in front of people she didn't know. This doctor must think she's a basket case. But a cold could kill Henry. A scratchy throat could turn into something much worse. This was probably their last chance for help. Lucy had almost given up hope before Saturday.

The doctor sat on the stool. "Tell me about what medication he's on, what tests have been done, what treatments we've tried..."

Lucy shook her head. "We've done three rounds of chemotherapy. The cancer hasn't changed.

"He's had eight courses of different antibiotics over the last year. He did a course of steroids last month. After that, the pediatrician told us there wasn't much else to be done. Insurance won't pay for more treatment. One of the doctors had suggested a different type of chemo, but the insurance said it wasn't approved for his type of cancer."

"Do you know what types of chemotherapy they've done?"

"Yes," Lucy said. "I keep records." She handed the doctor the pile of old paperwork.

Dr. Garaff flipped through the folder. "They did three rounds of the exact same type of chemo. Of course. We're going to—"

There was a knock at the door.

"What?" the doctor called. "You know I hate— Ah! There he is."

Adrian Trellis walked into the room and had to scoot to the side to close the door. "Gretta, I think you need smaller exam rooms. This is just too extravagant. Are you tucking your students into your pockets?"

Lucy's already racing heart skipped up another notch.

Oh God. He's here. I can apologize. And maybe find out what his foundation will cover. Was it just part of the treatment? All of it? I could try another Go Fund Me, Lucy thought.

She took a moment to really look at him. She hadn't paid attention when they first met, too busy arguing with the hospital. She thought he was working a scam. Saturday night was fuzzy; Lucy had freaked out.

He was tall, six-two or three with medium brown hair streaked with natural dark golden blond. Clean-shaven with blue-grey eyes. Handsome. The blue shirt and tie suited his coloring.

"Adrian!" Ree cheered.

"Hey, buddy! Hi, Lucy!" He high-fived Henry without looking at Lucy.

"Hey, you know, I wouldn't need to make the rooms so small if people didn't *overbook* my calendar," the doctor said with a smile. "I wondered if we'd see you before the day was done."

"Can I stay?" Adrian asked, looking in Lucy's direction, but not really at her. "Do you mind if I listen?"

"No, I don't mind," Lucy said, somehow embarrassed. She didn't know what to say to him. He hadn't looked at her. She must have offended him. Or maybe he'd written her off as a terrible parent because Ree was alone.

Her stomach flipped again at the thought of Ree alone in the apartment.

"Am I allowed to look at the paperwork? I don't want to get my hand slapped again," he said with a smile aimed at the folder of paperwork.

"I'm so sorry about—" Lucy started.

"No, no. I was teasing, Lucy. Martha told me you were upset. Don't be. It's fine," he said with a laugh as he flipped through the file of old paperwork.

"Back to the point," Dr. Garaff said. "We're going to do some bloodwork today. We're going to start a course of a different type of drug and see how it is tolerated. I want a specific supplement, too. I'll prescribe it. Get this all filled here at the hospital. They have what I want.

"I would like you to come back on Friday for another set of blood-work. Next Tuesday, then again on Friday, more bloodwork. I'll see you again two weeks from today. Depending on how he tolerates the meds and how the blood work goes, we'll start chemo after that. I need him as strong and healthy as he can be.

"He looks terrific, Lucy. You're doing great. We're going to take this one step at a time and see how he does. Lots and lots of fluids, Henry. As much as you can drink. As much food as you can get him to eat, too, Lucy. It doesn't matter what the calories are. We just need the calories right now.

"He's had a lot of antibiotics and steroids in the last year. I'm not going to prescribe anything for the throat. Manage the discomfort with Tylenol or Advil. Call the office immediately if he starts running a fever. Even if it's the middle of the night. There is always someone on call, so you can call with questions or concerns or anything you need.

"How does this sound? I know it's a lot of time at the hospital."

"We'll make it work," Lucy said.

"Good. Now, you! My favorite rich boy. How are you? What's new? You'll take my referral? Are you building that new wing or what? That building is still next door. I thought it'd be torn down by now," Dr. Garaff said to Adrian.

"Of course I'll take your referral. I told you I would," Adrian replied with a smile for the other doctor. "I don't know what's happening with the building. Sam's working on it. We'll get it done. But this room is seriously ridiculous, Gretta. Poor Lucy is folded in half over there!"

"Small rooms let me see more patients, help more people. Get over it," Dr. Garaff smirked as she stood up. Adrian gave her a quick hug.

"Thank you for seeing them so fast," Adrian murmured.

"Psh. For you, sure. Too much stress on Aunt Lucy, Adrian. She's going to crack before our boy does," the doctor said as she was leaving the room. "The nurse will be right in with the orders. I'll see you in two weeks, Lucy and Ree!"

As soon as the door closed behind the doctor, Lucy started talking. "I didn't get a chance to—"

The nurse came in with a pile of papers. The prescriptions had been sent to the pharmacy. The bloodwork orders had been sent to the lab.

LUCY LOOKED ROUGH. The dark circles were still under her eyes. Her cheeks looked pinched. Her posture was stiff with tension and stress. She was still beautiful—platinum blond hair, vibrant blue eyes, tall and leggy.

I just won't look at her. It'll be fine. I'll walk with them to get the bloodwork, we'll get some lunch, and I'll talk to her about the house. I just won't focus on her, Adrian thought.

"Come on, I'll walk with you to get bloodwork, and then how about some lunch?" he asked Ree.

"Okay!" Ree said, excited.

In his peripheral vision, Adrian saw Lucy open and close her mouth like she was going to say something but decided not to. After putting Henry on his feet, he handed the file of old paperwork to Lucy and let them lead the way out of the room.

On the way to the lab, Henry held both Lucy's and Adrian's hands, walking between them. Adrian felt Henry's arm stiffen and waited for him to swing his feet up off the ground.

A few good swings later, the kid was giggling. "I've always wanted to do that," he squealed.

Oh man, these two have really been on their own, Adrian thought.

The lab was packed, standing room only. "Wow, hang on a sec. Let me see what's going on. Sign in," Adrian said as he opened the door to the back rooms.

"HEY, HEY, DR. ADRIAN!" Lucy heard someone call from the back.

A minute later, Adrian called someone into the back. After that, a technician came out to the front desk and started shuffling papers.

Over the next fifteen minutes, the waiting room cleared quickly. The tech called people in order and got them checked out.

Lucy could occasionally hear Adrian talking to the kids. Once, she heard him pretend to yell in fright.

"Gah! It's a needle. Oh my gosh, oh my gosh, don't look. Don't look! Ahhh!" he called. Lucy could hear the little girl laughing. A minute later, the desk tech was giving the giggling girl a sticker and checking her out.

Two kids later, she heard Adrian yell, "Hey, Rob, new orders are coming through for this one now. I just hung up with them. These orders are wrong. I'm gonna pull it but reprint the stickers."

The guy at the desk shook his head, muttering, "Top notch."

Things slowed for a few minutes as they waited on the new orders.

When Ree got called, they were ushered into a room where Adrian was spinning around on a doctor's stool. Ree giggled.

"Ah-ha! There's Henry. Come here, Ree," Adrian said in a teasing voice. "I vant to take your bloud!"

Henry climbed up into the chair with a grin. "I'm real good at this. I don't get scared."

"I bet you are good at this," Adrian said with a little smile. "You've had lots of practice."

As he drew Henry's blood, he asked Lucy, "How's the waiting room? They're missing two techs right now. One's at lunch, and one called in. Are they close to caught up?"

"Seemed like. There were only a couple of people left out there. You're good at this. I've never seen a doctor do this," she said as he put the cotton ball Band-Aid over the needle prick.

"Oh, don't be fooled. We can all do it and have done it. Some of us are just not as comfortable with it. Cut open a body and move some parts? Sure! Pull bloodwork? Ewww. The nurses and techs do that," Adrian said as he smiled at Ree. "All done, buddy. Let's see what things look like out there."

As they entered the hallway that led to the waiting room door, another tech walked through it. "Hey! Dr. Adrian! Thanks, man. We'd be hosed all day."

"Sure, Jose. You back now? Has Rob gone to lunch?"

"Rob's got another hour before lunch, and Jackie will be in by then," Jose said. "I think we're good to go."

"Sweet, we'll see you guys later, then." Adrian did a backward wave to the guy at the desk.

"Are you hungry yet?" Adrian asked Ree. "Starving? Wasting away? You were in there for hours and hours and hours."

Ree giggled. "No, we weren't."

They were quiet for a couple of heartbeats as they walked toward the cafeteria.

"That was really nice of you," Lucy said. She must have startled him because he turned to look at her.

"Huh?"

"That was really nice of you. Helping in the lab like that."

"Oh," he said, still looking at her. "It was backed up. It, I, we would have, I mean..."

He turned his head forward and took a deep breath. "We would have been in for a long wait. I couldn't just take Henry back and then leave. That wouldn't be fair to the people that had been waiting. The cafeteria is around that corner."

As they loaded lunch trays, hospital workers greeted him as Dr. Adrian with big smiles. He was popular with just about everyone. He got in line to check out with Lucy behind him.

The cashier greeted him by name. "What are you doing here on a Tuesday, man? Tuesday ain't your day. Today's Tuesday, right?" The cashier scanned something on the register.

Adrian smiled. Again. He smiled easily. "Just looking after my man Henry here."

"Hey, Henry." The cashier bumped knuckles with Henry and then asked Adrian, "How many?"

"Whatever. Surprise me. Henry and Lucy don't count," Adrian replied as he picked up his tray to walk away. "See you tomorrow."

"See you, man," the cashier called as he scanned Lucy's food. "Bye, Lucy. Bye, Henry," the cashier said.

"We didn't pay," Lucy said to the cashier.

The cashier laughed. "Dr. Adrian's buyin."

Lucy didn't see Adrian pay, either.

ADRIAN HEADED toward an empty table being cleared in the corner. The room was crowded but not yet full. When the lab was backed up, he worried they'd be hitting the cafeteria at noon, and it'd be crazy. But it was just now eleven thirty. They made good time.

After Lucy and Ree were seated, Adrian sat down across from Ree.

"What happened there?" Lucy asked.

"What do you mean?" Adrian asked back, taking things off his tray.

"With the cashier. How many?"

"Oh, it's not important. So, Dr. Gar—" he started.

"What happened there? I didn't pay. I didn't see you pay. What happened?" Lucy asked again, annoyed.

Adrian sighed. He disliked talking about these types of things. He chanced a glance at Lucy. She was opening Ree's chocolate milk and getting him situated. Adrian watched the care she took when selecting his food and now getting him set up to chow down. He saw the kiddo settle into his chair, calm and comfortable. This was routine for them.

Lucy looked up at him with raised eyebrows. Adrian looked at Ree.

Damn it, Sam. I'm so bad at this, Adrian thought.

"The cashiers have a barcode that scans to my account. He scanned it after each of us went through. Usually, when I come through the line, I buy lunch for everyone in line behind me. If the cashier notices someone coming through the line that looks like they can't easily swing the lunch they need to eat, I buy that lunch, too. It's not a big deal."

"You really are a do-gooder, aren't you?"

He nodded. "It's actually my job."

She smiled a little but still looked tense as she picked at her tacos.

"I didn't say thank you on Saturday. I thought you were scamming, offering 'help.'" She made air quotes. "I'm sorry I yelled at you."

"Lucy, it's fine. Really. I wasn't upset with *you* on Saturday. I was rather offended by the hospital, though. Telling someone to go find more money isn't helpful."

She nodded. "When I walked in the door Saturday after work, and you were in the apartment, I thought you were stalking me. I really thought I was about to die. I mean, who does that? Comes running when some random kid calls in the middle of the night. People don't do that."

"To be completely honest, I intended to get him out of there. When he called and said he was alone and scared in the middle of the night, I had every intention of calling the cops and getting him removed from the home."

She nodded again as she studied the side of his face. "Thank you for not calling family services. Thank you for staying with him."

"Lucy," Adrian began in a more pensive tone of voice. "You can't continue on like this. You can't stay in that apartment. It's not safe for *anyone,* let alone a kid like Henry.

"Assuming he tolerates the meds and starts chemo again, he's going to need a lot of care. You can't keep caring for Ree all day and then working all night. You're lucky you didn't fall asleep driving home from work on Saturday. You zonked out with someone you don't know well in your apartment."

"I know," she admitted. "I was surprised to wake up okay, still in my clothes with the apartment door locked. I got fired on Sunday when I told them I couldn't work nights until I found a reliable babysitter. So I need to find a new job again. I'll find one that's daytime work."

Henry sighed. His voice wavered a bit. "I'm sorry, Aunt Lucy. I don't mean to get you in trouble."

"No! Henry, no. It's not your fault, baby. It's going to be fine. I'll find a new job," she assured him.

"Actually, I was hoping you wouldn't find a new job right now," Adrian said.

"Huh?" Lucy asked, her eyes on his face again. He was still looking at Ree and looking around the room. At anything but her, really.

"The Foundation can provide you with a stipend to cover living expenses. Sam bought a couple houses reasonably close to here yesterday. Two are not yet vacant. One is vacant, and he'll close on it today or tomorrow. He said something about remodeling one of the bathrooms. Otherwise, he thought you could move into it shortly after that. We can go look at it after we pick up the meds if you want."

Lucy's mouth was hanging open in shock.

"Um. I. Um—" she stammered.

"In the interim, we've reserved space for you at a hotel near here. You can stay there until the house is ready. You won't have a full kitchen, but there's room service in the hotel and a fridge in the room," he continued.

Adrian chanced a glance at her. *Well, she doesn't look mad. Maybe I won't trip over her pride.*

"Or, if you don't want to live in the hotel, I don't live far from here. I can go live at the hotel for a little bit. Or with my parents. Or Sam. You can use my place. The main goal is that you no longer live in that apartment building in that neighborhood. Ideally, you'd make a list of what you want from the apartment, and then someone goes and gets it for you while the rest of the stuff is recycled."

"I don't understand," Lucy said. "Um. What do you...? How? Why would you do this for us?"

Adrian met her eyes and spoke calmly. "Because you need help, Lucy. It's not safe where you are now."

"I don't understand," she said again. "What do you want from us? Why are you helping us?"

Adrian was confused. "Want from you?"

"Yes. What do we have to do to get this help? We desperately need it. I'm not saying otherwise. I just don't understand what it is that I have to do to get it," she clarified.

"You mean like paperwork? There's a non-disclosure agreement to sign. You can talk about the foundation and the help, but you can't disclose dollar amounts."

"No, Adrian. I mean, what is it you or your brother or whoever wants from us? Do I have to sleep with someone? Am I going to be a slave or something creepy like that? Do one of you intend to hurt him? I won't allow that. You can't hurt him."

Adrian turned bright red and looked back at Henry. Henry was looking at his aunt with a confused expression. *Holy fuck. Me too, kiddo.*

"Uh, no. No Lucy. Nothing like that at all. I don't...we don't...I mean... That's not how we do things. Not at all. Never. We would never."

The table was silent for a full minute. Lucy studied Adrian while Adrian studied his plate.

"The foundation is a non-profit, Lucy. We help people. Other charitable organizations, mostly. They can distribute the money to the people that really need it the fastest. But there are some people, like you, that we've happened upon through the years. When we find someone that needs help, we try to help directly. With a legitimate need like this, we can throw money at it faster to get it resolved rather than going through another organization. That's all," Adrian explained.

"I don't know what to say to that. I don't know much about the foundation. There wasn't much information about it online," she said.

"I know. We mostly give money to other organizations," he said again. "Not directly to people in need. We don't really take direct requests for assistance unless they come from an employee or a contractor. We will always look after our people. But, otherwise, we don't look for people to help directly. It's harder to determine what's a legitimate need versus someone working the system. So we try to leave that up to other organizations that already have mechanisms in place for it. No need to reinvent the wheel."

LUCY WAS BAFFLED. No one does this kind of stuff. She'd contacted a hundred organizations over the last year. She couldn't find one to cover the cost of bloodwork, let alone living expenses. Something was fishy with this.

"I don't understand. Something seems off with this. One of those, 'if it seems to be too good to be true' type things."

Adrian looked startled. "Um. Okay. How do we resolve that?"

Lucy shook her head. "I don't know. I don't know what to do right now."

"I don't mean to sound like a jerk when I say this, so please cut me some slack. But what exactly do you have to lose by trusting an accredited, documented, well-respected global non-profit? Even if you don't trust me, why question the organization that's actually funding the help?" Adrian asked.

Lucy sighed. "I just don't know why you'd do this for us. Do you know how many organizations I've applied to for help in the last year? I'm not claiming that we don't need the help. We do need it. My other option is to do nothing, and that's not an option. I'd just really like to know what I'm getting into here."

"Have I done something to offend you?" Adrian was starting to sound annoyed. "Seriously. Have I done something that makes you think, 'Yeesh, this jerk is out to get us?' Because from where I'm sitting, it seems like I saw a kid that needed help on Saturday, offered support, and got yelled at. Then I sat with that kid all night, comforted his distraught aunt, put everyone to bed, locked the war-proof apartment door behind myself, helped the drunk and stoned neighbors, and cleaned up dangerous medical waste. Then I got you in to see one of the best doctors on the planet for Henry's type of situation in very short order and have now purchased lunch. What have I done to warrant the distrust?"

Lucy was quiet for a minute as she stared at her plate. "Absolutely nothing. You've been incredibly kind to us. It's just my experience that people don't do stuff like this. I feel like we're being set up for a giant letdown."

They sat quietly for a few minutes.

"That was your family? At the hospital on Saturday?" Lucy asked to break up the silence.

"Yes, my brother's girlfriend is in the hospital. She was in the ER on Saturday. When I met Henry, I was wandering around, trying not to be found by the hospital administrator looking for donations."

Lucy nodded. "And that was Sam? The guy that looked tired? He started the business and made you all rich? I snarked at your mom?"

"Yes, Sam always looks tired. It's his company. When I called him on Sunday, he was brainstorming about how to buy and rebuild your neighborhood." Adrian rambled a bit, clearly uncomfortable. "Darla likes sass. Don't let that faze you."

"I'm sorry Sam's girlfriend is sick," Lucy said, just to say something.

Adrian shook his head. "No, it's Jake's girlfriend. Jake's future wife, really. It's just a matter of time. I have seven brothers and a sister."

Adrian was blushing again, looking around the room.

"I'm sorry. I must seem like a lunatic," she said.

His eyes snapped back to her. "No, that's not... No, Lucy. Please stop apologizing. You haven't done anything wrong. I just. I'm not good—I'm not good at talking about this stuff."

It was his turn to take a few deep breaths. "I'm not good at stuff like this. Talking with little kids, talking with parents, talking with people at fundraisers. That's fine. Talking about the money, one-on-one with someone like this...it is very awkward for me. I would much rather hand you a pile of cash than have to explain why we're giving you the pile of cash. Martha is much better at this part."

That made Lucy laugh. "Martha, your assistant, Martha?"

"Yeah, she's much chattier. Usually, she does this part. By the time people get to me, they are already expecting the pile of cash," Adrian explained. "Sam was very insistent that she not handle this. And I figured you already knew who we were and had a good sense of what was to come. I wasn't prepared for you to question the motives of giving you help. I thought I'd just be tripping over your pride a bit today, and we'd muddle through."

That made Lucy laugh. "I have no pride left. None at all. I've spent close to two years begging every last state and federal agency that I could find for more money to help him. Every last foundation. Charitable hospital. Local churches... I'm not too proud to beg or accept a handout. Honestly. I just want to understand what I'm getting into."

Adrian sighed as he watched Henry play with the remnants of his mac 'n cheese. His voice was flat. "There's an NDA to sign.

"I'd like it very much if you didn't stay another night in your apartment.

"You'll need to decide which house you want to live in while Ree is going through treatment. We can look at the vacant one today, but the other two won't be empty for a bit.

"Decide if you want room service or a kitchen for the next couple weeks. And then, catch up on sleep. Lots of fluids and food for Henry. The upside to hotel living is that there are a maid service and a pool. You can both do with some pampering, I think.

"The only thing we want is for Henry to get better, Lucy. There are no strings attached." He met her eyes briefly and nodded. "Are we done eating? Do you want to go look at the house? Do you need some time?"

THEY WALKED out of the hospital, holding hands with Henry again. "I'll walk to your car with you, and then if you drop me off at my car, you can follow me to the house. Does that work?" Adrian asked.

"Uh, yeah," Lucy said.

Lucy pulled out her keys and then stopped at a battered old Ford. There was duct tape holding the exhaust pipe in place. The front passenger door handle was missing. There was plastic over one of the back windows. The front windshield had a crack that ran the length of it.

"Are you super attached to this car?" Adrian asked.

They were quiet leaving the cafeteria. Henry was more subdued and less playful. Adrian wondered if he'd be leaving friends behind at the old apartment.

Lucy started a bit at the sound of Adrian's voice. "Not at all. It just barely runs most of the time. But I need a car, even if we are going to stay close. I'll eventually get a job again."

"It's fine, Lucy. We'll replace the car," Adrian muttered.

"You're just going to give me a car?" Lucy asked, sounding skeptical again.

"We can walk to my car. We need Henry's seat, though. Is there anything of value that you need out of the car?" Adrian yanked the booster out of the tiny back seat.

Lucy collected a few library books and checked the trunk. Before they walked away, Adrian took a picture of the license plate and the lot letter.

"What are you doing?" Lucy asked.

"Someone will come to get the car and scrap it for you. It can't possibly be safe."

"It runs. I can take it where it needs to go," she said.

"You have other things to get done. Let's delegate where we can. If you keep on this path, you're going to have a heart attack. And I'm not really exaggerating," he said, tone still flat.

Adrian stopped walking when they reached a black Audi compact SUV.

Lucy ran her hand across the light grey leather interior as she got in. "It still smells like a new car."

Once Ree was buckled in, Adrian fired up the car, and they were off.

They were all quiet. Adrian didn't know what to say. The disparity between the way they lived bothered him. The foundation needed to do more. He needed to find a way to do more.

Maybe Sam's brainstorming about how to revive a neighborhood should be more than hypothetical talk.

"WHAT TYPE of doctor are you, Adrian? General pediatrics?" Lucy asked quietly.

"Ah, no. I mean, I can do general pediatrics. But I specialize in

Pediatric Infectious Diseases. I treat kids with HIV and AIDs, mostly," he said. "I don't spend a lot of time in the practice anymore."

HIV babies. He treats HIV kids. That has to be worse than treating cancer kids. There's no cure. Every one of his patients is on a clock, Lucy thought. It made her chest tight.

He had been withdrawn after her rampant skepticism. She kept saying and doing the wrong thing and didn't know how to set it right. The life changes discussed over lunch were not yet real to her. It felt strange to empty out her car.

"Adrian, I'm sorry I—"

"Lucy, please. Stop apologizing. Please stop doing that," he snapped.

He didn't seem like one to snap at people. Lucy was at a loss for how to continue.

Adrian turned the car into a driveway and put it into park.

"Now it's my turn to apologize. I'm sorry. I didn't mean to snap at you. I'm not upset with you. At all. I know you're doing the best you can with what you have. I'm upset that you don't have better. I'm upset that not everyone has better. We should be doing more. I should be doing more." The car door slammed behind him as he went to let Henry out.

"This house is particularly nice because it has a driveway and a garage. You don't have to find street parking. The other two are bigger houses, but they don't have driveways. The other yards are a little smaller, too," Adrian said.

AFTER DRIVING by the other two houses, Adrian took Lucy and Henry to his own home. It looked like a little house on a large city lot from the outside, but it was a deep brick bungalow. As they approached the front door, Lucy could hear a woman's voice talking inside.

He has a wife. Or a girlfriend. There's no wedding ring. I didn't put that together. It's not my business. I'm sure she's as wonderful as he is if she's willing to give up her house for a few weeks, Lucy thought. *But damn. I hate this bitch.*

Lucy paused at the front door, unsure of what to do.

"Just open the door," Adrian said. "I can hear Beth laughing inside. It's unlocked."

Henry gasped.

"I know, right?!" Adrian's voice was back to teasing. "Beth doesn't follow the rules. But there are giant guys in there with her. She's safe. Don't be scared."

Henry nodded as Lucy opened the door. To the right of the little entryway were a kitchen and dining area. To the left was a living room. There were, in fact, giant men in the living room.

Lucy paused again as the people stared at her. "Uh, hi."

"Hi, Lucy! Come on in!" a tall, slender woman in her early twenties said as she tugged the door all the way open. She had light brown hair and pale eyes, a beautiful face that smiled as quickly as Adrian's. She wasn't wearing a bit of makeup. Her skin glowed naturally with health and good humor. Lucy sighed.

One of the guys followed behind the woman. He was huge. Maybe six-four or five with blond hair and blue eyes and an exceptionally built body. He also had two guns holstered on his sides.

The other guy was smaller by comparison. Maybe six feet even, but just as built, if not as wide-shouldered. He also had two holstered guns and something that looked like a tactical knife on his belt.

What the fuck? They're wearing guns. I don't want Ree here.

Lucy turned around to go back out the door, but Adrian and Ree had followed her into the house.

"Why are you wearing guns in my house? I'm telling Mom," Adrian said with a completely straight face.

"Am I going to Englewood? Because if I'm going to Englewood, the guns go, too. Relax, Nancy. Safety's on. I'll Barney Fife it and put the bullets in another pocket," the blond guy said. "Kid, don't touch the guns, K? We clear on that?"

Henry nodded from behind Lucy.

"Jerk." The woman smacked him. "You're scaring him. It's okay, Henry. They're not going to hurt you."

"Hey, kid, are you Henry?" the blond guy asked as he knelt down. "I'm William. Will. Did you know Henry is my dad's name?"

"It's Adrian's dad's name, too!" Henry said excitedly.

"What a coincidence! Crazy, right? Wanna shake hands and be friends?"

As Henry finished shaking Will's hand, Will grabbed Henry's ankle and yanked him off his feet, dangling him by one leg and swinging him. Henry squealed with surprise and delight.

Lucy squeaked in terror. *What the fuck!* "Don't, don't, he can't do that!"

"Hennessy! Go long, man!" William yelled while swinging Henry toward the other guy.

"STOP!" Adrian bellowed. Everyone in the room froze.

Will flipped Henry around and set him down, seated, on the couch. "You know, you're no fun at all. I feel like you used to be more fun. The kid loved it. Right, kid?"

Henry giggled and nodded.

"See, he's fine. Oh. Aunt Lucy's gonna lose her shit, though. I didn't really consider that angle. Come here, Lucy. I'll dangle you by your leg, too—zero risk. I swear," William said.

Adrian turned to Lucy. Her eyes were huge, and she was terrified. "He's not my smartest brother. But there's no chance at all that he'd let Henry get hurt. Are you breathing, Lucy? You have to breathe. Henry, are you okay?"

Henry nodded, still laughing.

"Please don't do that again," Lucy gasped. "He gets hurt very easily."

"No more rough-housing. At least until the cancer's done. Once that's over, we'll throw down. Yeah?" he asked Henry. At an enthusiastic nod from Henry, William said, "We're in agreement. I'm sorry I scared you, Lucy. Stop glaring at me, Adrian."

Adrian sighed. "Lucy and Henry, this is my elder brother William.

That guy is an adopted brother named Hennessy. This is my little sister, Beth."

Somewhere, the names registered in her brain, but for the most part, Lucy was still trying to keep her shit together.

"Lucy, Will and Hennessy will go down to your apartment and get your stuff."

IN THE END, Lucy decided to go with them. It was hard to think through everything she wanted. She didn't plan to move out when she left the apartment that morning.

"It would be better if you didn't go, Lucy. The strong preference was for you *not* to go with us. We'll just take pictures and text them to you," Will offered.

"Henry and I will go. It's fine. I've lived there for most of a year. It's really not *that* bad," Lucy said.

"The kid can't go." Will's tone meant business.

"He's fine. He lives there," Lucy disagreed.

"Not anymore. Sam specifically said Henry stays here. The kid is staying here. Beth will stay here with him."

Beth nodded. "Milkshakes are coming soon. And maybe french fries. And whatever else looks good. Drink your juice, Ree. We'll watch movies. All good."

"I really appreciate what you people are doing for us, and I don't want to downplay that, but I don't know you at all. I'm not leaving my kid here alone."

"Then stay here with him," Will said. "Henry stays here, or we don't go at all. He was very clear about this. Sam said it like six times."

"I can just go get my stuff. We don't need to make a big production out of this," Lucy argued.

"Lucy, Sam says either Will and I go, and you stay here. Or you come with us, and the kid stays here. You don't go alone. The kid doesn't go at all. Those are the rules of engagement," Hennessy explained. "We're not trying to be difficult. It's just what needs to happen. It might even make sense later."

Lucy opened her mouth to argue.

"I'll stay here," Adrian cut her off. "Will that ease the worry?"

Lucy looked surprised.

"I sat with him all night on Saturday, Lucy. I understand the distrust, I really do. Logically, I get it. But I'm having a hard time not being offended when you'll leave him with someone like Erika but not my sister," Adrian said, annoyed again. "Let's just get this done. I'll stay here. Will and Hennessy will take you. It seems to be important that they're there with you, so I'll stay here."

"We don't bet against Sam. Ever. Please believe me," Will said.

Adrian didn't look happy. "There's not much to do. You're just taking what you want. No furniture or dishes or anything. Clothes. Toys that Ree really likes. Anything of value—sentimental or otherwise. Leave everything else. A service will come through and get rid of everything that's left."

"Thanks," she said quietly, knowing that she'd offended the people trying to help her.

"Do we need one truck or two?" Hennessy asked, unfazed.

$\mathcal{W}$illiam drove an oversized Suburban. "Is there enough space in here for the three of us and your crap? Do we need another truck?"

"No," Lucy replied. "We wouldn't need a second truck even if we were moving furniture."

"Okay. Let's do this," Hennessy hopped into the front passenger seat.

"I can give you the address—" she started to say.

"I have it," Hennessy interrupted.

"Oh," *Well, okay then,* Lucy thought.

"In the interest of full disclosure, I will tell you that I am a security consultant and investigator. I do a lot of work for Adrian, specifically around verifying if a need is legitimate. Monday morning, after you talked to Martha, she called and gave me your name and phone number. From that, I did a background check. The only information shared with Adrian and the Foundation was that your need is legitimate," Hennessy said matter-of-factly.

"Between those of us in this car, is your sister going to be a problem?" he asked. "This family doesn't go halfway. You're about to fall into a shitload of fucking money, probably for the rest of your life. Do I need a contingency for her?"

"I—I don't know. I don't know where she is. I haven't heard from her in a little over three years. She dropped Henry off for me to babysit for a few days and never came back. What was in this background check? Why would you do that without my permission? And this isn't for the rest of my life. The Foundation is helping Henry and then we'll—" She stopped talking when Will chuckled.

"Yeah, sorry if this wasn't clear, Lucy. When Darla starts huggin', you're family. It might take some time, but you're gonna be expected at Sunday dinner. They collect strays like us," Hennessy said through a laugh. "It ain't a bad thing. You'll see."

"What about the background check?" Lucy asked.

"What about it? You really wanna talk 'bout it? It was all publicly available data. We didn't interview anyone or pull credit reports or any of that. It's not that kind of check. You wanna see it, I'll show you later. But you don't want to talk about it now, Lou," Hennessy said.

"Jessup?" Will asked.

"Na, Reap. Not like that. It's fine," Hennessy replied.

"I'll plan for Linda," Hennessy muttered with a sigh a few minutes later.

"Jesus Christ," Will said as he wrangled the building door open. "Fucking used rubbers and needles. No wonder he had a shit fit. How long you been here, Lou?"

"Last October," Lucy mumbled. She was starting to be embarrassed by what was to come. These guys were going to judge her apartment. Her life. Somehow, she wished she'd kept her mouth shut so that Adrian was here.

"He came down here alone at night. Remind me to beat the shit outta him later," Hennessy said. "How fucking hard is it to call? And how did you make it here for eight fucking months without shit going sideways?"

"Third floor, far end of the hallway," she muttered.

There was a note from Erika on the door, demanding her money from Saturday. There had been a note on the door on Sunday and Monday, too. Lucy would file this note with those notes—in the garbage.

"On the upside, I don't have to pay that bitch now. She left my kid alone," Lucy said as she pushed the stuck door open.

Will walked through the apartment. "Clear. Lucy, start with clothes? Where do you want us to start?"

Thirty minutes later, Lucy was dragging the last of the bags of clothes to the truck. As she climbed the stairs, Erika came out of her apartment.

"You owe me something, honey," Erika said.

"Yeah, I owe you a call to the cops. You left him alone. I'm not paying you. Give it up," Lucy called over her shoulder.

"Bitch, you're going to pay one way or another. I need that money," Erika yelled up the stairs.

"Ain't happenin'," Lucy called back.

Back in the apartment, Hennessy was in the bedroom, moving the furniture to make sure nothing was left behind. Will was in the kitchen, moving the fridge to check for anything that might have been missed.

Lucy heard Will start laughing. "Here's your fucking schedule, Lou. With the bar number. You should fucking frame—"

Someone shot at and then kicked into the wood around the door. They did it well; the door opened.

Before she could react, Lucy got hit in the face with the gun. It went off as the gun hit her, shooting the couch as Lucy fell to the floor. "You're gonna pay my—"

And then Will was there. Before the guy with the pistol realized what was happening, Will ripped the gun out of his hand, ejected the clip, dismantled it, and tossed it over his shoulder for Hennessy. With a sickening crunch, the guy's knee joint cracked the wrong way as Will backhanded him to the ground.

"Will. He's down," Hennessy said.

William didn't move, standing over the guy.

"Reap! He's out. Down. Job's done," Hennessy said. "I'm callin'."

"Oh my God," Lucy cried. Nose broken and bleeding, she looked around the apartment. The gun went off. Did it go through the floor? Was anyone screaming?

When Lucy saw the couch, her blood went cold.

As William handed her a kitchen towel, he followed her gaze. "That Ree's spot?" he asked.

At her nod, Hennessy said, "See? Sometimes it even makes sense."

"Police will be here soon. Then we'll go, okay?" William murmured, trying to soothe her panic.

She didn't make it to the bathroom before she vomited.

AFTER LUCY LEFT with Will and Hennessy, Adrian paced.

"Are you going to pace the entire time they're gone?" Beth asked.

"Probably," Adrian said with a little smile. "Don't judge. Did you come here with them to babysit while we went down to the apartment? Sam got that wrong?"

"Pfft. Is Sam ever wrong? No. I just came to hang out. Nothing going on right now."

"Henry, do you want a snack? Want to go raid the pantry with me?" Beth asked. "We can have more ice cream!"

"No, thank you," he mumbled from the couch.

"Tired, buddy? It's okay to nap. It's not even two. Your aunt will be back when you wake up," Adrian said.

"K," Henry said.

About two hours later, Sam showed up.

"She went with them?" Sam asked, upset. He walked the circle of the living room to the kitchen without finding Lucy.

"Yeah," Adrian agreed. "Why?"

"I told them not to take her! Why did she go?"

"She wanted to. What's wrong?" Beth asked.

"Just go call them," Sam snapped. "I told them to avoid taking her."

ONE OF THE cops that showed up was former military. That helped things along. Erika came upstairs, crying and screaming from the stairway entrance. He never had a gun. They attacked him (in Lucy's apartment). Lucy broke her own damn face. And the bitch still owed her a hundred bucks.

"Enough with this fucking place," Will muttered as he shoved a hundred-dollar bill into Erika's yapping mouth. "Can we go? You have our contact info. She's gotta get to a hospital."

EMTs were loading the guy onto a stretcher, still unconscious. "What'd you hit him with?"

"My hand," Will said with a completely straight face. "Wasn't even a fist."

The cop calling in the IDs and gun permits yelled over his shoulder, "Hey, He-man. Trellis? You one of those Trellises?"

Will nodded.

"Here's your shit, man. Get gone. What are you doing down here to begin with?"

"Getting Lou moved," he said with a smirk.

When Hennessy opened the door to lead the way out, Erika was by the stairway, still yelling. "I will dump your ass over this railing. Shut it. Move. Now."

AS THEY WERE TURNING out of the rougher part of town, Hennessy's phone rang to the tune of "Black Magic Woman."

"That's new," he muttered. "Yeah, boss."

Lucy could hear a female voice on the other end that might have been Beth.

"We're out. Her face is broken," Hennessy said. "Nah, no fatalities. Okay."

He hung up. "Northwestern."

"Yes, Miss Daisy," Will muttered. "Anything we need to talk about?"

"Nah, that's all she said," Hennessy shook his head.

Stitches and a pain pill prescription later, they were back at Adrian's house just in time for Ree to wake up.

"I TOLD YOU NOT TO TAKE HER!" Sam yelled for the sixth time.

"No. You said it'd be better if she didn't go. You told me not to take the kid. And I didn't take the kid. See? He's fine," Will argued.

"YOU KNEW WHAT I MEANT!" Sam continued to bitch.

THERE WAS deep dish pizza for dinner, a rare treat for Henry. Lucy ate as much as she could, but the pain was settling in. The adrenaline was fading. Fatigue was hitting hard.

"Where are we sleeping tonight?" she mumbled to the room at large.

"Here. Take this." Adrian squatted down next to her and handed her a pain pill. As she swallowed it, he whispered, "Everything's okay, Lucy. Rest now."

As she faded out to oblivion, she heard Will clear his throat.

JUST A LITTLE PUSH. A tiny one, so she could sleep, Adrian thought. *No harm done.*

Lucy's head wobbled as she nodded off. Adrian caught her as she tipped sideways out of her chair.

"Want me to take her?" Will asked.

"She's not heavy," Adrian replied as he stood with her cradled in his arms.

"Aunt Lucy?" Ree asked, eyes huge.

"She's just sleeping, buddy. She needs to rest. You'll stay here with me tonight, okay?" Adrian said as he walked out of the room with Lucy.

"I'll get their clothes and stuff out of the truck. There's not much," Hennessy muttered.

When Adrian came back into the kitchen, Will was staring at him. "What?"

"I can take them with me or bring them to Hank and Darla," Will offered.

"We'll figure it out in the morning. She's sleeping now," Adrian replied.

"Amazing how quick that medication kicked in, huh?" Will said, still staring at his little brother.

LUCY WOKE up the next day in an unfamiliar bedroom. It took her a minute to remember where she was and what happened. As soon as she moved her head, her face reminded her.

She wanted a shower. And a toothbrush. And Ree. Where was Ree? The last thing she remembered was eating pizza.

She got out of the bed and walked into the hallway. She could hear people talking in the living room. She walked in that direction to find the short, middle-aged woman from the hospital on Saturday coloring with Ree.

"Aunt Lucy!" he called as he ran for her.

"Holy cow," the woman exclaimed, looking at Lucy. "There was a mishap."

"Hi, baby," Lucy muttered. "You okay? Did you take your meds?"

"Yes, Adrian gave them to me earlier," he said.

"Good boy, thank you," she mumbled.

"Hi, Mrs. Trellis, I'm so sorry for snarki—" Lucy started to say.

"Sweetheart, I'm Darla. And I have *nine* children. You have no idea what my definition of snark is. Go get cleaned up, then I'll make us some lunch. With an ice pack to go with it. And maybe some drugs. There's a bigger, fancier walk-in shower upstairs if you want that. A tub, too. Probably not a bad idea to have a soak."

"What time is it?" Lucy asked.

"Twelve thirty. Adrian thought he'd be home by two or so. So, probably three thirty."

"Thank you for—"

"Lucy, go get cleaned up," Darla said in a flat tone of voice.

A warm shower and a good tooth brushing later, Lucy was exhausted. Darla fed her hot ham and cheese sandwiches with tomato soup. She fell asleep in the living room chair before she was finished eating.

When she woke up, Adrian and Henry were cooking in the kitchen.

"Hey, guys," she said as she wandered in.

Adrian glanced up and flinched.

LUCY'S NOSE WAS BROKEN. Both eyes were severely bruised. One of the blood vessels in her right eye broke, so her eye was bloody. Her upper lip was torn and swollen. Adrian could almost see the shape of the gun in the bruising.

"How do you feel?" Adrian asked.

"Like I got hit in the face with a gun over a hundred bucks," she admitted.

"Well, that seems wholly accurate," he said with a smile.

"Smiling makes my face hurt. Don't make me smile." She tried to relax her mouth.

"Aunt Lucy, you look bad," Henry exclaimed.

Lucy started laughing. "Thanks, Ree, thanks a lot."

"Henry, up until this point, your life has lacked a strong male influence. I can tell. I will now guide you in the ways of smart men everywhere. Rule number one: women always, and I mean *always,* look beautiful. They never ever look bad, understand?"

Henry was giggling along with Adrian and Lucy.

"But Adrian, she looks bad. Not as bad as the bar fight, but bad. I'm not supposed to lie," Henry objected.

Adrian's smile turned brittle at the mention of a bar fight, but he didn't want to scare Henry. "No, no. Henry, this is not a lie. It is a partial truth. Because, as we all know, under all the bruising, Aunt Lucy is very beautiful. So we ignore the short-term bad in favor of the long-term beauty. That's how we justify it. Understand?"

"Aunt Lucy is always beautiful?" Henry asked.

"Yes, that is correct. Aunt Lucy is always beautiful," Adrian said while stirring a pot of something saucy. "Except if there's something stuck in her teeth. You gotta tell her about that. She'd want to know."

"Thanks, Adrian, thanks for the coaching." Lucy chuckled. "What's the second rule of smart men everywhere?"

"Ensure proper coverage before zipping," he said without missing a beat. "We'll talk about that later, Ree."

"Ow, ow, ow," Lucy said through laughter.

"Sorry! Sorry," he exclaimed.

"What's for dinner?" Lucy asked. "Smells Italian."

"Spaghetti and meata-balls!" Adrian said in a bad fake Italian accent.

"You sound like Super Mario Brothers," she teased.

"Eh, nobody's perfect."

After dinner, Adrian put on a kid's movie for Ree. Lucy was asleep in the chair again before the opening credits were done. She wasn't even sure what the movie was.

THE FOLLOWING DAY, she woke up to Adrian and Ree eating apples and peanut butter.

"Hi," she said, walking into the kitchen. "What time is it?"

"Eleven thirty," Adrian replied. "Hungry?"

"We have to go for bloodwork. We were supposed to be there an hour ago! I'll get dressed, give me—"

"Lucy, today is Thursday. Not Friday. I brought consent forms home yesterday for you to sign. Ree will go to work with me tomorrow. I'll take him down to the lab. My calendar is already blocked. We'll be home in the early afternoon."

"Oh. I lost track of the days with all the sleeping," she said lamely.

"I know. It's okay. I didn't." He smiled. "How do you feel?"

"Uh, better, I think. Hungry. I want a shower."

"Go upstairs to shower. It's nicer," Adrian said. "By the time you're done, lunch will be ready."

"What's for lunch?"

"Chicken strips and tater tots."

"Your mom made hot ham and cheese sandwiches and soup yesterday. It was like an idealized childhood lunch." She chuckled.

"Why is that idealized? I ate that all the time as a kid."

"Of course, you did." She laughed.

"No grilled cheese and tomato soup for you?" Adrian asked.

"Not really."

LUCY GRABBED stretch pants and a t-shirt for the day. She didn't even try to pretend the previous day. She had showered and put on fresh pajamas. Today, she'd do real clothes. But not too real in case she ended up sleeping in them again.

She chuckled at Adrian's weird house. It looked like a grandma's house outside, right down to the rose vines in the side yard. But it was completely remodeled inside. The kitchen was not big but wasn't lacking in anything. The downstairs bathroom was a good size with a walk-in shower and excellent water pressure.

The upstairs dormer was one large bedroom area with a master bath attached. The master bath included a giant shower with five shower heads that each had different programmable temperature and pressure settings. There was also a bathtub meant for two people, complete with skylights.

For a hot minute, Lucy wondered what kind of woman shared

Adrian's showers and baths. Then she backed away from the thought. It was none of her business.

But I hate that bitch, Lucy thought then laughed at herself.

She stood in the fancy shower for at least thirty minutes without running out of hot water. Then she felt bad about wasting water. As she reached to turn the water off, there was an unexpected romantic encounter with one of the water jets. She felt less bad about wasting water.

She stepped out of the shower feeling better. Relaxed. She smelled like Adrian's sandalwood products because she didn't have any shampoo or soap of her own.

Whatever. His stuff is much nicer than my White Rain Shampoo and off-brand Dove.

As she toweled off with the fluffy soft bath sheet and combed out her hair, she reflected on the last week.

What a weird couple of days. Saturday, I thought Adrian was a stalker. Now, I'm staying in his house, using his shampoo. Ree is seeing a new doctor. I'm unemployed and homeless but, somehow, better off.

Lucy glanced in the mirror and regretted it. Her entire face was covered with a mottled blotch of purple and blue bruising.

Mostly. Mostly, I'm better off.

ADRIAN LOOKED up as Lucy entered the kitchen. "Hey, you look better!"

"You're lying. I looked in the mirror," Lucy said with a small smile.

"I'm not lying. That has to make you wonder what you looked like yesterday," he replied, completely serious.

"How are you feeling, Henry? Is your tummy okay?" she asked.

"Just tired, really tired. I'm not hungry."

"Ah, nope. What's the deal, Ree?" Adrian said.

"One book per meal," Ree answered with a happy little wiggle.

"Do you want another book?"

"We already ordered it!"

"We did, but I might not give it to you," Adrian said. "I might keep it for myself," he followed up with a teasing smile.

"What's this?" Lucy asked.

"Adrian said he'd get me a book every time I ate with him," Ree said, excited. "We ordered like thirty books yesterday!"

Lucy looked like she didn't know what expression to put on her face. After a few heartbeats, she turned around and walked out of the room.

Adrian didn't expect the negotiation to bother her. Now he wasn't sure what to do. Maybe she was mad that he was bribing Henry?

"Five minutes to lunch, Ree. Go wash your hands, okay?" Adrian said as he followed Lucy's path out of the room. The door to the room she had been using was closed.

He knocked. "You okay?"

"Ah, yeah. Just needed a minute." Lucy's voice was muffled.

"Can I open the door?" *Is she crying?*

She didn't respond, so he opened the door a smidge and peeked in. She was standing in the far corner, looking out the window with her back to the door.

She took a deep breath. "Thank you for taking care of him. Taking care of both of us. I know there are a million other things that you need to be doing. We...we will get out of your way as soon as we can, okay?"

Definitely crying. Sobbing. Over kid's books?

"Okay," he said. "You're not in my way. Can I ask why you're upset, or are we pretending like you're not upset?"

"I don't know why, so maybe we're pretending like I'm not upset," she replied with a sob-laugh.

Another deep breath. "He loves reading. It's a good bribe." She nodded her head. "Thank you for buying him books."

"You're welcome. I'm going to go pull the food out of the oven. Come eat when you're ready."

When she made it back into the kitchen, the guys were eating quietly. She made a plate and sat down.

"Everything okay?" she asked them.

"Yeah." Ree nodded, looking tired.

Adrian nodded but didn't look at her.

He must think I'm nuts. Sobbing over books. What the fuck's wrong with me?

After lunch, Ree laid down for a nap. Adrian went upstairs.

Lucy didn't know what to do with herself, so she cleaned the kitchen and washed the floors. Then she cleaned the bathroom and dusted the living room.

"There's a service that comes in and cleans," Adrian said from the living room doorway, startling her.

"I figured. There's no dust or dirt anywhere."

"Then, what are you doing?" he asked, sounding annoyed.

"I don't have anything else to do right now," she mumbled, feeling completely useless.

He nodded as he ran his hand through his hair. "I was coming down to suggest that you start researching cars and order whatever you need online. Maybe start making a list of the stuff you're missing if you don't want to shop or research right now. We can go shopping if that's eas—"

She was shaking her head. "I'd rather not go out like this if that's okay?"

"It's fine. My laptop is on the kitchen table whenever you're ready," he said before heading downstairs to the basement.

When he came upstairs a few hours later, Lucy and Ree were coloring at the kitchen table. He went upstairs without saying a word.

Around five thirty, Adrian came into the kitchen and started making hamburger patties, still quiet. Withdrawn. Like the car ride from the hospital to the first house, Lucy wasn't sure where she'd gone wrong. Again. Didn't know how to make it better.

ADRIAN WAS ANNOYED. Between Tuesday night and Thursday afternoon, Lucy had slept for a day and a half. What would Ree have done during that time if they were on their own? She was battered beyond recognition right now. How would she have taken care of herself over the last couple of days if they were on their own? Why the sudden rush to get out?

"Do you want to leave?" Adrian asked over dinner. "Or do you want me to leave?"

Lucy looked confused.

"You said earlier that you'd leave as soon as possible. I've been thinking about that. This was not what I offered on Tuesday. It's probably not terribly comfortable here for you."

"Leave? Why would we leave? Where would we go? It's safe here. No bad people. We have to stay here. Aunt Lucy, we're not leaving, right? Adrian is helping. We need help! We have to stay." Henry was fighting back tears.

Surprised by the reaction, Lucy gave him a hug. "Ree, it's okay. We're okay. We are kinda taking over Adrian's house and life—"

"Adrian, you don't want us to go, do you? I'll be good. I promise. I'll eat and eat and eat. I'm sorry. I don't need the books. Please don't make us go," Henry said, tears welling in his eyes.

Yeah, I deserve this. I shouldn't have put Lucy on the spot in front of Ree, Adrian thought. *One hundred percent my fault.*

"I want you to be comfortable and happy, buddy. Both of you. Plus, I told you on Tuesday that you could stay in a hotel with a pool," Adrian said.

"Honey, we can't stay here forever. This is Adrian's house. He let us stay because we needed help—"

"We still need help! We can't go yet. Not yet."

Lucy met Adrian's eyes as she hugged Ree. "I'm sorry," she mouthed.

He shook his head. "My fault," he mouthed back.

THAT NIGHT, Ree woke up screaming shortly after two a.m. Lucy crashed into Adrian while running out of her bedroom at the same time he came running around the corner from the stairway. He caught her before she could slam back into the wall.

"Jesus, I'm sorry, Adrian!"

"Are you okay?"

"Fine," she confirmed as they entered the room Henry was using. "Ree, everything is okay. It's okay, honey. You're okay."

Adrian turned on the bedside lamp while Lucy scooped Ree into a hug. Sweating and crying, he was twisted in the bedding.

"The bad people are coming, Aunt Lucy. The bad people. We have to hide. They're gonna hurt you again. The bad people! We have to hide," Ree sobbed, eyes still closed.

"Shhh. I'm okay, Henry. I'm okay. Everything's okay. No one's going to hurt us," she soothed.

Stop talking, Ree. Please stop talking. Stop talking. Please stop talking, Lucy thought.

"Henry, wake up, buddy," Adrian said. "It was a dream, Henry. Just a bad dream."

"Adrian! The bad people. They're gonna hurt Aunt Lucy," Henry yelled as he tackled Adrian in a hug.

Wrapping his arms around Ree, Adrian began rocking back and forth, soothing him. "No one's going to hurt her, Henry, no one. It's okay."

As she watched him soothe Henry, Lucy realized Adrian was shirtless.

Holy hell. He's not as bulky as Will, but definitely more built than I'd imagined, she thought. *Pecs and a six pack, holy shit. So buff…*

She gave herself a mental head shake. *This is so not the time.* She avoided staring. Mostly.

Twenty minutes later, Ree was back asleep. Lucy and Adrian were headed back to their respective beds.

"Lucy?" he whispered as she was walking into her room.

She turned toward him.

"Do you want to go?" he asked.

She sighed. "It seems unfair to take over your home like this."

"That wasn't an answer." He ran his hand through his hair. "Please don't go. At least until you're healed. Please stay. I don't want you to go."

She walked back to him and hugged him. "Thank you, Adrian."

Then, to both their surprise, she kissed him.

She meant to kiss his cheek. The next thing she knew, she was kissing him. Really kissing him, ripped lip and all.

His right hand came up to gently touch her cheek and nudge her away.

"I'm sorry. I didn't mean to do that," she said with a hand covering her mouth.

Adrian seemed to be looking at her feet. "Did it hurt your lip?"

"Not really," she said, putting her hand down.

"Oh." Then he was kissing her.

A minute later, he pulled away.

"I meant to do that. Keeps things from getting awkward. G'night, Lucy," Adrian said as she laughed.

"Good night."

6

*a*drian woke at five thirty a.m. on Friday. Up with the sun, as usual. Ree was resting comfortably. There wasn't another peep out of him all night. He cracked Lucy's door open to check on her. She was sleeping on her back, covers pushed down and tangled with her legs, shorts and tank twisted around her. Either it wasn't a restful night or she moved a lot in her sleep.

He debated untangling her and covering her up properly, but that seemed like an invasion of her privacy. If she woke up, he wasn't sure how he'd explain it. Then shit would be *really* awkward. He quietly closed the door and continued on to the basement.

He had worked out for a few hours yesterday, after Lucy's talk of leaving took him by surprise. The angry energy was still sitting there. Ree's nightmare made it worse. He considered options and possibilities as he stretched and then wrapped his hands.

Ree mentioned the bad people on Saturday. Adrian assumed he was talking about the loud people in the apartment hall. Or the neighbors dealing drugs. Maybe that was a wrong assumption.

That apartment door was new. It was the only new thing in that building. And it was steel reinforced. Inconsistent with the other doors.

Had someone hurt them? Hurt Lucy? Beyond collateral damage in the bar fight that Ree mentioned on Wednesday?

Adrian groaned as the energy surged forward, and the anger rose to the surface. He thought of Lucy's broken face and the feel of her ripped lip, Henry crying, sobbing, begging to stay. The energy grew, stoked toward rage.

Lucy, bleeding and broken. Cancer. Cancer taking over Ree's tiny body. Lucy begging for help. Lucy hopeless and cynical in the cafeteria on Tuesday.

Adrian saw red as he pulled the boxing gloves on. The heavy bag swung hard on his first strike.

Oh yeah, this one's gonna be good.

After bag time, six-minute miles on the treadmill. Then push-ups, chin-ups, sit-ups. All the -ups. Then weights.

LUCY HEARD a door creak around seven thirty and then heard the stairway door. She climbed out of bed and pulled some clothes on over her pajamas. She wanted to apologize before Ree was up.

She made her way out of the room quietly and headed toward the kitchen. She expected to find Adrian there, but it was empty. The sound of the water turning on upstairs was evident in the quiet house.

Okay. I'll just wait for him. I can make breakfast. He's done all the cooking. I can make some eggs. If there are eggs. I really hope there are eggs. Otherwise, I'm just going to be useless again.

There were eggs. Three dozen eggs.

What the fuck? He must eat a ton of eggs.

She cracked six eggs in a bowl and began whisking them with some milk.

Does he like scrambled eggs? Who doesn't like scrambled eggs? People that like eggs eat scrambled eggs, right? Now I just need a pan, she thought, rifling through the cabinets.

"Frying pans are in the cabinet on the bottom right," Adrian said as Lucy yelped. "Sorry, I thought you heard me coming down the stairs."

"I was too distracted with an internal dialogue around whether or not you liked scrambled eggs," she admitted.

"I do," he confirmed. "Eggs in all forms are good. They're an easy meal for one."

"Ah, that makes sense, I guess," Lucy mumbled as she turned to look at him. Pale yellow dress shirt, blue tie, dark slacks. He was Dr. Adrian again. Yesterday's jeans and plain t-shirt were gone. She thought of his washboard stomach and was suddenly glad her face was bruised. It hid the blush.

"How'd you sleep? How are you feeling?" he asked. "The bruising is magnificently colorful."

"I slept okay. Weird dreams after Ree's nightmare. The stitches are starting to itch. So, I'm healing, I guess. Adrian, before he's up, I just wanted to apologize for last night. I shouldn't have gone there. You've been so incredibly kind to us, and it was wholly inappropriate. And I'm sorry. I won't do it again. And we'll leave when you're ready for us to leave. Or I'm healed. Whichever comes first. Or whichever you want. And yeah. That's it. I think," Lucy babbled, not entirely sure what words were coming out of her mouth.

"OKAY. Did you start looking at cars yesterday? Want to test drive this weekend?" Adrian asked, looking at his phone.

I'm not going to get annoyed. I'm not. It's fine, Adrian thought. *But it's fucking annoying that she keeps apologizing.*

"Uh, I started to. There's a car lot not far from here that has a couple of cars that are probably worth looking at," she said, distracted by his blatant dismissal of her apology.

"What's the dealership? What make of cars?" he asked, still not looking at her.

She's looking at used cars. I just know it. Why the fuck is she looking at used

*cars? I'm not going to get annoyed. I'm not. It's fine. The thought of having
money hasn't sunk in yet.*

"There was a Ford Explorer that looked in good condition and a
Chevy—"

"Lucy. Are you looking at used cars?" he asked, eyebrows raised at
his phone, sounding annoyed.

"Well, yeah. They're more afford—"

"Come here." His tone was sharp as the angry energy surged again
without warning. "Please."

She was moving before he finished speaking, eggs still cooking on
the stove.

"There's an app for everything," he murmured. "Including one to
estimate your net worth across all your accounts and liquid invest-
ments. This is my personal net worth."

"Oh, Adrian, I don't—"

"Look at it, Lucy," he said, tone still sharp, voice heavy with the
energy.

Her eyes snapped to the phone and the number on the screen.
"Uh, okay."

"Would you please look at new cars? You're right that used cars are
a smarter investment and more affordable, but we're way past that
point," Adrian said as he got up to rescue the eggs.

FUCK. I need food, and then I need to get out of here, Adrian thought. *I'm
losing control of it. It's been years and years since I lost control like this. Time
to go.*

She was still standing by his chair, looking at his phone. *FUCK.*

"Lucy?" he asked.

"Yeah," she turned around to face him. "Sorry, zoned out. I'll look
at the cars. Sorry. I didn't really think about it."

"Nothing to worry about," Adrian said, tone gentle as he plated up
the eggs. "Unless you really want to go, I suggest staying here today.
There would be an alarming number of stares. It wouldn't bother me,
but I suspect it'd wear on you."

"Agreed. I'll stay here if that's okay. Is there anything you need me
to do?" Lucy asked, hopefully. "I can make dinner."

"Would you order some groceries? The link is bookmarked. If you order by noon, they'll deliver by four. Whatever you want, whatever you guys normally eat. The account's hooked up. Just use the saved card. Ree and I will be back before you know it. Otherwise, order what you want or need. Did you do that yesterday?"

"Ah, no. I put some stuff in the cart—"

"There's a saved card on there, too. Whatever you want, all right? Don't worry about it. Your cards should be here today. We have to go soon, so I'll go wake Ree."

"No! I'll get him. You eat. We'll be just a second," she said on her way out of the room.

"HENRY, YOU OKAY BACK THERE?" Adrian called from the driver's seat, on the way to the hospital.

"Just tired," he said, perking up.

"You had a rough night. Do you remember your nightmare?" Adrian asked as he stopped at a light.

When Adrian turned to look at him, Ree's eyes were welling with tears. "Buddy! It's okay. I'm sorry. We don't have to talk about it. I won't ask again."

"Adrian, I don't want to go. Not yet. Please, not yet? Don't make us go yet? I'll be good," Ree promised.

"Henry, I'm not going to make you go anywhere. Your aunt and I talked last night. You're going to stay with me. At least until she's all better. Okay?" Adrian said soothingly. "I'm sorry that upset you last night."

"Aunt Lucy's going to stay, too?"

"Of course, Ree. I wouldn't take you away from your aunt. Everything's okay, buddy."

"When we were eating lunch, you said you were going to have the people take me away," Henry said in a tone bordering on betrayal.

It took a minute for Adrian to realize what he was talking about. "Yes, I did say that. When you called me over the weekend, I thought you were in trouble, that your aunt wasn't taking care of you—"

"Aunt Lucy takes care of me! She takes good care of me!"

"I know that now, Ree. I didn't know that when you called me on Saturday. But when I got to you and saw you—"

"Erika lied! She was supposed to stay. Aunt Lucy even told her!"

"Ree, I know that now. I didn't know that when I got to you. Once I understood, we just waited for your aunt to get home. I didn't call anyone. And I won't let anyone take you away. I'm not going to make you leave. We're okay just the way we are," Adrian soothed.

"And you won't let the bad people hurt Aunt Lucy?" Ree asked.

I shouldn't ask. The energy is already at an unsafe level. I won't ask. He's had enough upset for today. I'm not going to ask. I'm not going to ask. I'm not going to—

"Who are the bad people, Ree? What's that about? Is someone trying to hurt you?"

"I KNOW," Hennessy said as he looked out Adrian's office window.

"You know?" Adrian asked, clearly startled.

Hennessy's tough. I can beat the shit out of him and not feel bad about it. Why would he fucking know this and do nothing?

"Yup. She's filed several police reports over the last eighteen months or so. It came back in the background check," he said, calm as could be.

"Were you going to mention it?" Adrian asked. His tone sounded merely curious instead of enraged.

"Nope."

"Why not?" Adrian asked.

"I didn't want to worry you. And you shouldn't worry. We're hunting them. And the kid's parents, too. Speaking of, where is Ree? I thought he came to the hospital with you this morning," Hennessy replied, all casual.

"How do you know he came to work with me?"

"Because we're keeping tabs on the house. Who goes in and comes out."

"You're spying on me?" Adrian asked, eyebrows raised.

"No."

"It sounds like you're spying on me."

"I'm not."

"What would you call it then?"

"I'd call it security. It's a security detail. You should all have security details. Except for Reap. He's his own security." Hennessy sighed.

"I want to put a security system on your house and give her a panic button," he continued. "I thought they were going to a hotel and staying with you was only for a night or two. I would have talked to her about this at the hotel because it's none of your fucking business." Hennessy shot Adrian a look. "But if they're with you for a bit yet or, you know, forever—whatever—I want to button up your house."

"Someone is watching the house right now?" Adrian asked, ignoring the comments about Lucy and Ree staying at his house.

"Four people are watching the house," Hennessy clarified. "Two pairs. One for each door. The security system helps monitor windows."

"Do it," Adrian said. "And I want to read the file."

"I want Beth to be gloriously happy, dating some guy that's not a pig. And I want Will to laugh like he used to. We don't always get what we want."

"I'm not kidding, Hennessy. I want the file," Adrian said again.

"I'm not kidding, either, Adrian. No."

"You'll never work for the Foundation again," Adrian threatened, just to see how Hennessy responded.

Hennessy shrugged. "Life is hard."

"Why are you so obstinate about this?"

"She deserves her privacy, Adrian. She's earned it."

"I'm not asking to be nosey, Hennessy. I keep blundering into shit that's painful and hard—like this 'bad people' thing. Then I don't handle it well because I didn't see it coming. I just want to avoid making her uncomfortable."

"Okay. You want to avoid painful shit? Talking about anything from Tuesday forward should be reasonably okay. The broken face thing doesn't register on her scale of bad," Hennessy offered.

"Smartass comments aren't helpful, man." Adrian was beyond annoyed and seriously wondering if the mind mojo would work on Hennessy.

"I'm not being funny, Adrian. Let's do it this way. Scale from one to ten where one is your childhood and ten is the worst childhood imaginable. You know my background pretty well. I'd rate it a seven. With me so far?"

Adrian nodded, already sorry he pushed this hard. Hennessy didn't voluntarily talk about his childhood. This was too close to home for him.

"Lou's childhood ranks a nine."

Adrian rocked back in his chair as if Hennessy punched him. There were a couple seconds of silence before Adrian nodded.

"You want to know? Ask her. Tell her you want to understand. I don't think she has any idea at all how friendship works. She is very alone in this world. Be a friend. I won't give you the file without her permission. Hard no, Adrian. She gets to share what she wants, not what you want. She gets to choose. She hasn't had a lot of choices. I ain't taking this one from her. Understand?"

"I apologize, Hennessy. I didn't realize it hit so close to home. I thought you were just being a pain in the ass."

Hennessy nodded in acceptance. "Call and tell her I'm bringing lunch. I owe Lou a chat. And don't try to bully me again. You're bad at it. It ain't a good look on you. You're a better person than that, and we both know it."

SOMEONE KNOCKED on the front door. *Shave and a haircut. Two bits.* "It's me. Open the door, Lou," Hennessy called.

"Holy fuck, your face is epic. I gotta take a picture. The guys from our old team post pics of the most interesting injuries we encounter.

This is gonna win the month of June." He laughed as she pulled the door open.

"Shut up, Hennessy. What's for lunch?" Lucy asked.

Hennessy snorted. "Italian beef, chocolate shakes, and chocolate cake."

"You're a god among men."

"I know, right? Hungry?" he asked.

"Adrian eats a lot more eggs than you'd anticipate."

"Adrian eats almost nothing but eggs. Guy needs a life. And a wife. Care to apply?" he asked with a cheeky grin.

"Haha. So funny." Lucy rolled her eyes.

"Not really kidding, Lou. Time to talk. Just you and me," he said.

"What is it you need to know, Hennessy? I'm not lying to him."

"Let's eat. Here. Little bit of lunchtime reading for you." Hennessy threw a folder on the kitchen table.

"Background check?" she asked.

A gasp escaped as she opened the file. It was definitely a background file, but it wasn't hers. There was a picture of a young boy on top of the pile of papers. His face was battered, his right eye swollen closed. Hennessy couldn't have been much older than Henry in the picture.

"I figure I seen yours, you can see mine. You and me, we're a matched set of fucked up," Hennessy said.

She flipped quickly as she ate. Dad died in jail. Removed from Mom's care. Long series of foster homes, then the military. SEAL team.

"How'd you end up here?" she asked.

"Will and I went through training together. Didn't get along too well at first. He struck me as a pampered, spoiled momma's boy. And he is.

"Our team's first mission out went bad. I fucked up. Got separated. Far out of position. Then I got shot. I was due for a bullet in the brain in short order. Not a fucking thing I could do, either. Just watched them come for me. Then Will jumps outta nowhere.

"You saw him move. No hesitation. Faster than seems possible. He rained death down like the Grim fucking Reaper. Scooped my ass over his shoulder and hiked halfway down a mountain to rendezvous with the rest of the team."

Hennessy took a big bite and chewed before he continued.

"We've had each other's back since. I owe him my life. Figure he can make use of what I got left. So, I left the team when he did. Showed up for Sunday dinner.

"All of a sudden, I joined the fucking Waltons. But God damn, they are the best fucking people on this planet. They make it real easy to walk away from the shit in that folder."

"I thought SEALs were Navy? Water-based stuff. Were you swimming in a lake on the mountain?" Lucy asked.

"That's adorable, Lou." Hennessy laughed. "My turn?" he asked after chewing another bite of his sandwich.

Lucy nodded. "Okay," she said, dread pooling in her stomach. She stopped eating.

Hennessy was right, though. They were a matched pair of fucked up. He'd understand.

"Lucinda Lee Wallace. Twenty-three years old. Born and raised in Chicago. Only child, removed from Dad's care at eleven due to an unspecified type of abuse. Cycled through foster care, removed from one home after your foster brother—David, right?—raped and tried to kill you. The last foster home had multiple kids, including Linda Jane Wright. At sixteen, you ran away with Linda and stayed off the grid until your eighteenth birthday. Why'd you run? Where'd you go?"

Lucy shook her head. "Ah. Wow. That's sealed files, not public record."

"I've known Adrian for years. He's a do-good kinda guy. Sees someone in trouble, wants to help. Always. Seen him dressing homeless people on the street and helping a random woman in a parking lot to leave a bad situation all at the same time.

"He's like, 'Here, man, it's freezing. You need a coat. Gotta stay warm.' Sees a guy dragging his wife and kid around by the fucking hair, screaming about how she's gonna learn her lesson. Adrian walks over, says something to the guy. The guy runs away. Literally, hauls ass, running away. Lady's crying. Doesn't know what to do. Adrian gives her all the cash in his pocket, the keys to his car, and tells her about a center in Ohio that'll help them start over.

"I shit you not. The guy's always got a new car because he keeps giving them to people. He just signs the title now and leaves it in the glovebox for whoever ends up with the car.

"Anyway, Adrian gives her the car, and he walks back over to the guy that needs a coat. He starts digging through the pile to find one that's the right size while talking to the guy about a men's rehab that could help him put a life back together, that living on the street never ends well."

Hennessy took a drink of his shake before continuing.

"You know how many of the people he's helped have visited his house?" Hennessy held up his hand in a circle. "Zero. So, I dug deep on Wednesday. You can be offended. But you're still gonna answer me. Why'd you run? Where'd you go?"

Lucy took a deep breath and blew it out. Closing her eyes for a minute, she slouched back in the chair.

"This is you and me talking. No one else gets to know through me," Hennessy said.

She looked at him with raised eyebrows.

He nodded at her.

"One of the boys didn't respect boundaries. Linda had an aunt she thought would help us. It didn't work out. She…Linda started collecting boyfriends that would take care of her. That wasn't a solution for me, just more of why I ran in the first place.

"I was homeless for a while, panhandling and doing small jobs that I could find, avoiding people as much as possible. No shelters. No homeless camps. I didn't want to be found. Linda would help when she could.

"The weather turned cold. A little old Polish lady found me trying to huddle in her alley to keep warm. Said she could hear my teeth chattering in the wind three blocks away. She let me stay with her. I cleaned. Shopped. Took care of her. She was dying of cancer. Her kids didn't spend much time with her. She died two months before I turned eighteen. By that time, no one was looking for me."

"No prostitution? Drugs? I ain't judging, and neither would Adrian. If there's history, proof, I need to dig for it now, before it's in circulation."

"No. No drugs. No selling. That would have been more of what I ran from."

"You resurfaced. Got a job. A place to live. GED. Community college. Linda lived with you off and on. She got pregnant. You had a falling out. She calls one day, and what? What was the story when she dropped the kid off?"

"She thought I was trying to steal her boyfriend. His family was well off, her ticket home, she said. He made a pass at me. I declined; she took it badly. Didn't want to talk to me for a while. When she called, she said she was in trouble and needed to leave Henry somewhere safe for a day or two. I told her to come to stay, too. She said no.

"I called the cops four days later. Took what money I had and hired a lawyer. Got guardianship of Ree."

"Where did John come in?"

"Wow. You were thorough," Lucy said as she took a drink of shake. Hennessy nodded.

"I was tending bar. Two years ago, a little more. He was a regular. Not much of a drinker but liked being out and about. He was nice. Interested in me. Interested in Ree. A kind ear when Ree was diagnosed when all this started.

"I'd known him for most of a year before he asked me out. Dinner seemed innocent enough, and it was. The next day, he buzzed my apartment. I was surprised he knew where I lived but wasn't really alarmed. When I opened the apartment door, David was standing with him. I couldn't close the door fast enough. The guy that lived next door was a cop. He heard me fighting, yelling for help. Came running in his fucking underwear. He was dead asleep.

"They weren't armed when they came into the apartment. They got off on a plea. John had never been in trouble before; David had no record as an adult. The cop next door helped me file for restraining orders.

"Over the next few months, I would see David or John following me. Following Ree. I made reports. No one seemed to care.

"About that time, Medicaid wrote Henry off as a lost cause. Everything I had and more went into treatments that didn't work. The state gave us rent assistance. We moved to that horrible apartment. On the upside, they couldn't stalk me there. They stood out worse than I did."

"Have you seen either of them in the last couple of months?" Hennessy asked.

"I thought I saw John last month in a hospital parking lot, but then he was gone. Do you know how they're related? I'm not sure what the connection is between them," Lucy said.

"They were foster brothers when they were younger. Does Ree know you're not his biological aunt? Does Adrian?"

"No. And it doesn't matter."

"Pfft. You're telling me that? Fuck you too, Lou. All right. You sure there's no dirt to dig?" Hennessy asked.

"I'd tell if there was."

"Has he seen the scars?" Hennessy asked.

"Adrian? No."

"Don't let the scars take him by surprise. Have this talk with him."

"This whole thing confuses the fuck out of me, Hennessy. What do you think he wants from me? Someone to play house with?"

Hennessy snorted. "I think he wants you and Henry to be safe and well. That's all. You're not the type of woman he gets involved with. He ain't looking for anything."

"People aren't this nice," Lucy disagreed.

"These people are." Hennessy shrugged. "Always have been to me, at least. Took me a while to get used to it, too. Your cynicism irritates the fuck out of Adrian, and it's hard to irritate him. Might want to tone that down a bit. When I saw him this morning, he was as close to truly angry as I've ever seen. I don't want to see any closer."

Hennessy's cell phone started ringing to Pat Benatar's "Hit Me with Your Best Shot."

"The fuck," he muttered before answering. "Yeah, boss. Wrapping up. Maybe an hour." And then he hung up. "We're putting a security system on the house. You're getting a panic button—"

"Hennessy, you can't do that. This isn't my house. I don't want to bother—"

"Lou, he told me to do it. Ree told him about the bad people this morning. He called me before they were even in the door of the hospital," Hennessy said gently.

"Oh."

"It was a five-year-old's perspective, which he interpreted to mean that there were a pair of guys stalking you. Not wrong, but not really a complete picture. He's super pissed off at me, by the way. It'd be good if you had this talk with him."

"Why's he mad at you? It's my bullshit."

"Because I knew and didn't tell him. It ain't his business until you make it his business. But you should make it his business. He wants to help."

"I'm not sleeping with him, Hennessy. I'm not dating him. He doesn't need to deal with my bullshit," Lucy said, looking at her sandwich.

"I know this is a novel concept—completely foreign to you. But I'm going to throw it out there for consideration. I think he's trying to be a friend. Now, a friend is a person that cares about your wellbeing and is involved in your bullshit. Typically, they aren't paid or—"

"For fuck's sake, shut it, Hennessy," Lucy said with a small smile.

"That's better. Now say cheese for the picture!"

"AUNT LUCY! LOOKIT WHAT I GOT!" Ree yelled as he charged into the house.

"Hi, baby! I missed you. Were you good today? What you'd get?" Lucy asked.

"I was good. Uncle Sam came, and we played Go Fish, and then I had bloodwork. And then Grandma Darla came to say hi, and then Uncle Ethan brought me this!" He was waving a tablet around.

"Wow, Henry. You seem to have acquired a lot of family today," Lucy said, giving Adrian side-eye.

"That was not my doing. That was Sam's doing," Adrian clarified. "Also, watching Sam play Go Fish was one of the funniest things I've ever seen."

"Smart man rule number three: Never bet against Uncle Sam," Henry said, entirely serious.

"Really?" Lucy asked Adrian.

"Words to live by," Adrian replied with a grin. "I see Hennessy was here."

"Uh, yeah. About that—" Lucy started.

"Nope. It's done. Did he tell you there are also people watching the house?" Adrian asked.

"Like spying?" Lucy's eyebrows hiked up.

"Ha! That's what I said, too. No, a security detail. Apparently, they've been watching since Tuesday. He told you he's looking for them?" Adrian asked.

"Looking for who?"

"What exactly did Hennessey tell you? Because it doesn't seem like he told you anything. They're looking for the guys. You have the panic button?"

Another nod. "I'm sorry—"

"Lucy, the only part that makes me mad is that you didn't say anything. The rest of it is inconsequential."

"What's the matter? Adrian, you're not mad at us, are you?" Henry asked.

"No, I'm not mad at you! Everything's fine." Adrian smiled at Ree. "Can I show you some things, Henry?"

After a tour of security panels and teaching Ree the code, Adrian showed him the sensors on the windows and the cameras outside. Then Adrian asked Lucy to hit the panic button.

At her doubtful look, he said, "Hennessy suggested it so he wouldn't be scared if they came in the house at some point."

She flipped the clasp on the bracelet and hit the button. In less than a minute, there was a loud banging on both doors as the two teams let themselves in.

"Wow," Lucy said.

"Aunt Lucy, they have guns. Maybe they'll shoot the bad people!" Henry yelled, excited.

After a round of introductions, the teams went back to work.

"No more worrying about the bad people, okay?" Adrian said.

"That was so cool!"

"WHAT ARE YOU MAKING? It smells lemony," Adrian asked while setting the table.

"Is lemony okay? Do you not like citrus?"

"Lucy, I will literally eat any type of food you put in front of me besides live bugs and Brussel sprouts," he said, looking at his phone with a smile.

"You'll eat dead bugs?"

"I have eaten dead bugs, yes. They're crunchy." Adrian looked up to find her staring at him with a perplexed expression. "What?"

"Why in the world did you eat bugs? Was it a dare?"

"Ah. *Where* is a better question. Where in the world did I eat bugs? I spent six months in Uganda before I took over leadership of the Foundation. Bugs, grasshoppers, in particular, are a common dietary element. Definitely not something I crave, don't get me wrong. But that tells you exactly how nasty Brussel sprouts are to me." Adrian grinned at her. "Why are you smirking at me?"

She laughed. "I didn't mean to be smirking at you. But there have been times that I have been starving. I've eaten food out of dumpsters. I don't think I could knowingly swallow a bug, dead or alive, if my life depended on it."

Adrian's expression changed to something unrecognizable for a few seconds then shifted back to curiosity. "You didn't answer me. What are you cooking?"

"Chicken Vesuvio. Impractical for Chicago in June, but it sounded good."

"Are there potatoes involved in this?" Adrian asked.

"There are," she confirmed.

"Did you make a lot of it?"

"I did. I learned after the eggs. It's a giant roaster full of chicken and potatoes. We'll be eating leftovers for a week."

Adrian smiled. He wasn't smiling at her. Wasn't looking at her. But the smile was definitely for her.

"The bruising really bothers you, doesn't it?" she asked before she thought better of it.

"What do you mean? You're healing well. It's deep bruising and a broken nose. It's going to take a while to get better," he said, looking at his phone again.

She chewed on her lip and then remembered her lip was torn.

Should I ask? Do I want to go there? I want to know why, but it'll be awkward, Lucy thought.

Adrian lifted his eyebrows, still focused on his phone. "I can almost hear your mind spinning."

"Ha, the hamster is off the wheel right now. I'm on my own." She laughed. "You don't look at me. Make eye contact. Unless you're startled into it, or you're upset, you look at anything else but me. I assumed the bruising makes you uncomfortable—"

"The bruising makes me angry," he interrupted. "Not uncomfortable. Angry. I should have pushed harder for you to stay here. You brought back like five bags of clothes and two pictures. Will and Hennessy could have gotten that stuff.

"In retrospect, I should have given that woman the money on Saturday night before I sent her scurrying away. She would have had no reason to bother you."

An alarm went off on his phone. "Hey, Ree. Did you finish your juice box? Thirsty?" he called into the living room.

"You have an alarm on your phone for his fluid intake?" Lucy asked.

"Don't judge. I get distracted."

"I'm not judging," she said. "I'm wondering why I didn't think of that."

Adrian was laughing as he walked toward the living room.

REE WAS ASLEEP, sitting up on the couch, tablet in his lap.

Poor kid. No nap today, Adrian thought.

The juice box was empty. Adrian took the tablet out of his lap and shifted him to laying down so he wouldn't hurt his neck. It was just about six o'clock.

"He's zonked out in there," Adrian said quietly as he walked back into the kitchen. "He didn't nap today. Do you want to wake him up for dinner? He had mac and cheese for lunch. My mom fed him cake and ice cream. Ethan brought him chicken nuggets and french fries. He ate all of it."

"Dinner will be done in about ten minutes. He might wake up on his own," Lucy said, subdued.

"What?"

Lucy shrugged. "It's like with the books. I couldn't do this for him. Stuff him full of food and keep him busy and happy and stress-free. The only thing I could do for him was watch him die. Hennessy told me earlier that you and your family were the best people on the planet, and I'm starting to agree."

"You know that's a load of shit, right? Not the Hennessy thing, but the other stuff. Well, probably the Hennessy thing too, but that's not the point. You've kept him alive and in fighting shape. He's smart, relatively healthy, amazingly well behaved. And if you hadn't been at the hospital arguing with that woman in the billing department, fighting for him, we wouldn't be here now," he said.

Adrian chanced a quick glance at her; there were tears on her cheeks. He pulled her close for a hug. She fit against him well, the top of her head just a little bit higher than his chin. As her arms wrapped around him, she started crying in earnest. Heaving sobs shook her body against him.

"Lucy, it's okay. Everything's going to work out. You'll see," he muttered to her. "Don't do this to yourself."

"I'm getting your doctor clothes weepy," she said to his shoulder.

He chuckled. Her arms stayed around him as she turned her head to rest in the crook of his neck.

"It's been a bizarre week," she muttered.

They both chuckled at that. As their bodies shifted together with the laugh, a different type of energy rose in Adrian.

Turn your head. Take her mouth. Take her body. She is ours, the energy said, clear as day. The command was clear in Adrian's brain. Unmistakable.

His face turned to meet hers, both sets of lips parted, a scant inch between them, anticipating the contact.

If Adrian hadn't had a lifetime of controlling the angry energy, it would have won.

Holy fuck. What the fuck was that? What the fuck is wrong with me now?

In an effort of raw willpower over the impulse, Adrian's arms dropped from Lucy as he stepped back. "Speaking of doctor clothes, I'm going to go change. I'll be back in a minute. You're okay, right?" He didn't wait for an answer before he briskly walked away.

THEY TALKED about cars over dinner. As Lucy was loading the dishwasher, Adrian moved Ree to his bed.

Once the living room was free of sleeping children, Adrian said he was going downstairs for a while. He didn't come back upstairs before she went to bed at eleven.

We're really screwing up his routine. We'll get out of the way soon enough. I wonder what's in the basement, Lucy thought. Then, *It's really not my business.*

AFTER ONE A.M., Adrian's muscles gave out. He fell backward off the treadmill, into the cement basement wall, knocking himself unconscious for a minute. When he came to, he had trouble making his body stand.

He had fed that new energy all the rage he could find in himself. He cycled it all in and then beat it out of his body. It didn't help. That other energy was still welled in the pit of his stomach, waiting, completely unchanged.

The rage had never spoken to him before. Never in words. Impulse. Reaction. *Never* words. He had no idea what this new thing was.

He wouldn't think about it now. Too tired. And hungry. So hungry. He'd eaten an entire box of energy bars. He needed more. There were leftovers in the fridge. Just as soon as he could climb the stairs.

LUCY WOKE to the sound of rustling in the kitchen shortly before two a.m.

What the hell?

The alarm hadn't gone off. There were no alerts on her phone. She'd have an alert if a security alarm had been triggered.

Did Ree finally wake up, looking for a snack?

She headed toward the kitchen to help him, only to find a sweaty, shirtless Adrian standing in the kitchen eating cold chicken and potatoes out of the storage bowl.

"Oh my God! Are you okay? Adrian, sit down! You're swaying in place. Sit! Here, I'll bring a chair," Lucy said. "Is your head bleeding? Oh my God!"

"I'm fine, Lucy. Shouldn't you go back to bed?" he asked. Tone flat, lifeless.

"You're bleeding! Or you were bleeding. You're not fine! Did you fall? Sit down, Adrian, before you fall again! Should I call an ambulance?"

He laughed. Actually laughed. "No, Lucy, I don't need an ambulance. It's just a bump. I'm fine. Hungry. I'm going to eat this, take a shower, and go to bed. It's fine. I'm fine."

"Did you fall asleep downstairs or something? Why are you all sweaty?"

"I was working out," he said.

She shook her head. "What? You went up to bed earlier, couldn't sleep, and then went to work out? You look terrible, Adrian. Your eyes are all dark underneath, and your cheeks are sunken like you haven't eaten in a week. We should go to the hospital. Something's wrong."

ADRIAN'S whole body tingled anew with *other* energy. Little lightning sparks of energy that crawled down his skin, reviving his body, if not his mind.

She's ours. Take her. Take her. She's right there. Standing there. Take her. Take her. Take her. Look at her. Take her. She's ours. Ours. Take her.

She touched his shoulder. "Adrian, we have to go to the hospital."

Mmm. The sound of her. Smooth skin. Long arms, long legs. Take her. Ours. She's ours. They're both ours. You know they're ours.

"Lucy, I worked out too long. That's all. Lost track of time. I'm going to eat this, drink a bunch of water, take a shower, and go to sleep. I'll be fine in the morning."

"Have you...? Have you been downstairs working out since after dinner?" she asked.

"Yup."

"Adrian! That was hours and hours ago! Look at me!" She pulled his face toward her so she could look at him. When their eyes met, the energy screamed at him. "You're barely—"

OURS! OURS! OURS! Take her!

"Lucy," he said as he kissed the palm of her hand.

"This is a dream," he whispered.

"Sleep till morning," he mouthed with no sound.

Adrian caught her just before she hit the floor, dead asleep.

By the time Adrian ate all the leftovers and rehydrated, he was almost back to normal. Exhausted, but lucid. He'd need to think of a reason for all the leftovers to be gone. "I worked out too long and then ate seven chicken breasts and three pounds of potatoes," would probably sound strange.

The rage energy and whatever this new energy was sucked up a lot of calories. Along with the working out, he had to be careful to eat enough. That was hard to do with Lucy and Henry in the house.

Happily, when there were enough calories in his system, the energy seemed to repair his body quickly. He could completely shred his muscles in a workout, eat a dozen eggs, go to sleep for a couple hours, and wake up refreshed and ready to go.

He turned to see Lucy lying on the kitchen floor as he washed the empty bowl from the leftovers and put it in the dish drainer.

I can't believe I fucking did that. It wasn't necessary. I should have just agreed when she assumed I had gotten up to work out. Three times, today. I fucked with her mind three times today.

He needed to be careful. More careful. He swore to himself that he'd never do this, that he'd never allow this to happen. Now, look at him.

His mind wandered back to middle school and Whitney Langcaster. Thoughts of her were a regular reminder that anger and rage were dangerous. The wrong combination of words spoken in the wrong tone of voice while meeting someone's eyes could have horrible consequences.

So, he generally didn't meet a person's eyes. He was so careful with words, they often came out as a garbled mess. He tried to ask questions instead of making statements. He didn't speak to anyone in anger. And, on the rare occasion he dated, the woman had to be simple-minded. The echo of a command seemed to fade much faster in the dim-witted.

Over time, he'd found that pulling the rage forward before a workout made it easier to manage throughout the day. Or it used to be easier to manage. The pool of other energy still swirling in him after six hours of hard exercise hinted that things were changing.

Lucy was many things; dim-witted wasn't one of them. She surfaced strong, uncontrolled emotions in him very easily. When he had quietly suggested that she rest on Tuesday night, she ended up sleeping for a day and a half.

This was so dangerous. A slip of words, a few seconds of anger, a focused thought. She'd be lost. He had to be careful or he really would be the monster he feared.

He picked her up from the floor easily now; his body had fuel again. Muscles were weary but working.

I should send them away. Work more for the next week or two and then send them to the house Sam bought. It'd keep them safe, Adrian thought.

As he set her on her bed and covered her, Adrian looked at Lucy's battered face. She was still beautiful. Bruised with a broken nose, her blond hair still shone in the pale light, the shape of her jaw defined against the column of her neck and the relief of flesh around her collar bone.

The thought of sending Lucy and Henry away made his stomach lurch and his chest tighten. The rage and the new energy roared through him in revulsion.

Adrian heard his phone vibrate with a text upstairs.

SAM: House will be ready next Thursday.
ADRIAN: Thanks, Sam.

I'll be more careful. I'll focus on control. I'll keep them safe.

7

---

*L*ucy shook her head when she woke up in bed on Saturday. *What a weird fucking dream. Shirtless Adrian was lovely, but how bizarre.* The memory was fading before she was even out of bed.

As she started making breakfast, she paused at the clean, empty bowl that held the leftovers from dinner last night, sitting in the dish drainer. It seemed odd, but she couldn't figure out why.

AFTER BREAKFAST ON SATURDAY, dealerships brought her cars to test drive. Adrian argued for an Audi. In the end, she ordered a Mazda.

"Do you really give your cars away? Hennessy told me that yesterday, but he has to be exaggerating," she said as they walked back into the house. Ree was ready for a nap and headed to his bed.

Adrian's cheeks turned pink. "Why were you and Hennessy talking about my cars?"

"He was making a point about the kind of person you are."

"That's actually kinda interesting. Hennessy and I aren't really close. What kind of person does he think I am?" Adrian asked.

"The kind of person that gives cars away to women in abusive relationships while also dressing homeless people for cold weather." She was watching him closely as he poured iced tea for both of them and then sat at the kitchen table, looking out the windows.

"Well, that's accurate. I did, in fact, do that. And I have been known to give my car to someone whose life would be better if they had a reliable way to make a break for it. Sometimes, all someone needs to make a better life for themselves is a way to physically get away. Did Hennessy tell you the rest of that story?" Adrian asked.

"There's more to that story?"

"Yup. The woman I gave the car to is Martha's granddaughter."

"Martha, your assistant? That Martha? Is that why you gave her the car?"

Adrian laughed. "No, I didn't know Martha at that point. Her granddaughter had been in a bad situation for years and couldn't exit it. Her then-husband told her he'd kill her if she left, and she had no money of her own. She was forbidden from talking to her family. The husband monitored every aspect of her life. She couldn't leave the apartment unless he was with her. It was bad. I didn't know it was that bad when I got involved. I saw him dragging them through the parking lot, screaming at her that she'd learn her lesson eventually.

"I walked over, told him that if he didn't get away from her and the child immediately, we'd have problems—and I included Will and Hennessy in that 'we.' Coward that he was, he turned and ran for it. Dana was wigging out, talking about him killing her. I handed her the car keys and the cash. I wrote the name of a shelter in Ohio on the back of one of my cards. The shelter would help her without question. If she had issues, she could call me. She took it and ran. I wished her well and thought that was the end of it.

"Two months later, I got this rambling voicemail on my Foundation phone number from a grandma, thanking me for her granddaughter's life and that she'd like to talk to me. I thought the granddaughter was a patient—I was still active in the practice at that point. It took me a good ten minutes of Martha rambling to figure out who the granddaughter was.

"Martha wanted to repay me. I decidedly did *not* want that. She was living off a pension, forced into early retirement from being a schoolteacher. After a lot of back and forth, she told me that she was coming to work for me, and I gave up arguing with it. She's better with people than I am.

"That's how Martha came to the Foundation. She bosses us all around and has tried fixing me up with every granddaughter, grand-niece, and random attractive woman that she has met or talked with. Last month, I just had to meet some woman she talked to from the QVC channel. Martha is personally affronted that I am both single and unwilling to live in a mansion. She's a trip."

Lucy was chuckling. "I'm sorta with Martha on this. I don't understand why you're single. But I'm also a bit mad. When I talked to her on Monday and tried to explain that I was rude and wanted to apologize for thinking that you were hitting on me, she got a great big laugh out of it. What the hell, Martha? I'm cute when I'm not bruised and stitched!"

Adrian grinned, looking at his glass of tea. "She was still laughing when I got back from that awful lunch. I'm a great big oaf when it comes to dating, and she knows it. Her entire family laughs at me. Anyway, people that we work with through the Foundation are off-limits. It's a conflict of interest that I won't tolerate. I've had that conversation with her in the past."

Lucy's chest suddenly felt tight, making it hard to take a deep breath. Adrian was frowning at the condensation on his glass as they were quiet for a minute.

"What else did Hennessy say?" Adrian asked finally. "He obviously didn't talk much about the security. What did you talk about?"

"Oh. Uh, he shared his background with me, I think because he felt bad about digging into my background without asking," Lucy started.

ADRIAN WAS STARTLED into looking at her. "Hennessy talked about his time in the military?"

"Well, that too a little bit. Explained how he ended up here. But mostly we compared notes on our childhoods. He had some questions about my background, which I answered. He's very protective of you and your family," Lucy said, still subdued.

At that moment, Hennessy's ranking of her childhood as a nine sunk in. *What the fuck? What kind of notes were they comparing?* Adrian was quietly freaking out inside.

Realizing he'd been quiet for too long, Adrian tried to pick up the thread of their conversation. "He is a part of our family. Long since adopted. My mom refers to him as her ninth son. He doesn't have any family worth mentioning."

Lucy has a sister, right? There has to be a sister for Ree to be her nephew.

"He said my cynicism bothers you immensely, that I need to learn what trust and friendship are. He's a smartass," she finished.

"All of those things are true. Very true. Logically, I understand the lack of trust and the cynical outlook. But they make me batshit crazy. Extremely batshit crazy," Adrian admitted.

Crazier than they should make me, Adrian amended to himself.

Lucy was looking at her hands. "I'm sorry. I don't mean to upset you. I really don't. I've just never had someone genuinely want to help me to this degree. I'm extremely grateful for everything you've done for us. I'm just not sure what to do with myself. I'm used to being on the move for twenty hours per day."

"It's going to work out okay. You'll see." Adrian kissed her forehead as he walked by to start making lunch.

Fuck. I need to not do that, he thought as both energies went crazy, zooming through his body.

When he turned around, she was touching the spot he kissed on her forehead.

"Sorry, it seemed like the thing to do. I wasn't really thinking about it."

Lucy's lips twitched into a little smile. "S'okay."

"You look...confused?" he asked.

"I am." She nodded.

"Sam said the house will be ready next Thursday," Adrian blurted.

"Okay. Ready for us to go, huh?" Her expression was unreadable.

YES! This is not safe, Adrian thought.

"Not especially," his mouth said, without consulting his brain.

THEY HAD Italian sub sandwiches for lunch. They seemed to spend a lot of time eating. This was the best fed Lucy could ever remember being.

Henry and Adrian kicked a ball around in the backyard that afternoon.

"He needs a dog," Adrian said as he sat next to Lucy.

"He does NOT need a dog." Lucy laughed as Henry worked on dribbling the ball.

"Yes, he does. He's a little boy. All little boys need a dog. It's a partner in crime."

"I take it you had a dog growing up?" Lucy asked.

"Always. At one point, we had five dogs. Nine kids, five dogs, and a snake. Darla is a saint. My parents still have a dog. Hank loves dogs," Adrian said with a smile.

They were sitting under the patio table umbrella. It was June in Chicago, hot and steamy with lots of sunshine. Lucy sipped iced tea while rocking in her chair, relaxed and calmer than she'd been at any point so far.

"Did you have pets?" he asked.

Her relaxed smile faded. "No."

"Are you coming to Sunday dinner tomorrow?" he asked to change the subject.

"I don't think going like this would be good," she said, gesturing to her face. "Your family is celebrating your brother's engagement. I'd detract from that."

"No, you wouldn't. If anything, Darla's going to be pissed you didn't show."

Lucy didn't respond.

"Did you order stuff yesterday?" Adrian asked, trying to think of a safe topic.

"I don't really need anything, Adrian. I'm better fed and rested than I think I have ever been."

"I'm glad for that. But you and Henry don't have much in the way of clothes, and what you do have is...well-loved, let's say. Other than the tablet that Ethan brought him, the books I ordered, and the ball from Roscoe's last visit, there are no toys.

"You can get anything you want. Anything at all. Don't you want to go nuts spoiling yourself? Spoiling him?"

Adrian watched Lucy staring at her hands in her lap. The bruising was slowly fading into the yellow and green stages. Her body posture was less tense, so long as they didn't talk about money or childhood pets, apparently.

He kept touching her without meaning to. Walking into the kitchen while she made breakfast, he rested his head on her shoulder to watch what she was doing. Stepping around her to get to the utensil drawer, he'd put a hand on her waist. The kiss on the forehead. He needed to be more careful.

She didn't react much. He was probably making a bigger deal out of it than he should. But random touching was *not* being careful. He needed to be careful.

"Adrian, you've been so kind to us. So generous. There's nothing I can give you in return that you don't already have. No stellar way to say thank you. I can't bring myself to abuse your kindness more than I already have," she said in a wavering voice. "There really isn't anything I need."

The words were out of his mouth before they went past his conscious brain. He was surprised to hear his own voice. "It bothers me that Hennessy knows more about you than I do. If you wanted to give me something in return, I would ask for that trust."

She nodded. They sat in pensive silence for a few minutes.

"My mom died of a drug overdose when I was nine. I came home from school to find her dead on the living room floor.

"My dad was a drunk and a drug addict. I was removed from his care when he was caught trying to trade me to settle a debt shortly after my eleventh birthday. There was no home. I've never really had a home. Just places to live. So, no. No dogs for me.

"I don't think Hennessy knows. When we discussed it on Friday, he summarized as 'removed from the home for unspecified abuse.' So now you have that over him."

A deep breath later, she cleared her throat. "If all goes well, I'll owe you Henry's life by the time this is done. And probably mine, too. That's not a debt I can repay. It's not that I don't trust you. I just can't imagine why anyone would want to know something like that."

The power surged through him without warning, like it was lying in wait, battering at his brain and chest. The impulse was strong but the direction unfocused. Adrian swatted it down.

"Thank you for telling me," he whispered, staring at her.

When she finally met his gaze, he smiled and dropped his eyes. "Wouldn't you enjoy shopping? I mean, really. *Anything* you want."

8

---

*a*drian made baby back ribs on the grill Saturday night to go with potato salad, corn on the cob, and marinated tomatoes. Lucy was openly laughing at him by the time they sat down to eat.

"What?" he asked.

"You made six slabs of ribs for two adults and a five-year-old. I made five pounds of potato salad at your request," she said, still laughing.

"I eat a lot." He smiled at her laughter.

"I noticed. What happened to last night's leftovers? Did you get up for a snack and then drop the bowl or something?"

He gave her a rueful smile. "Accidents happen." It was not a lie. It was a truth about life.

"Henry, don't fall asleep in your food, buddy. You okay?" Adrian asked to change the subject.

"Huh?" Henry asked, eyes drooping.

Lucy's brow furrowed. She reached over to feel his forehead. "Does he feel warm to you?"

Adrian touched Ree's head and then held Lucy's hand for a second. "No, he's not warm. You're cold. We were outside for a long time earlier; he's been busy today. He's okay," Adrian said, trying to ease the look of panic on Lucy's face.

"I'm okay, Aunt Lucy. Just tired. Really tired," Ree muttered.

"Ree, are you sure? Your throat doesn't hurt? Your tummy's not upset? You don't feel sick?" Lucy asked, talking almost too fast to understand.

"No, I'm okay," he said again.

"Lucy," Adrian soothed, looking at her. "Breathe. He's okay. He was busy today. Lots of playing. The drugs will make him tired. He ate plenty of food today. He did a good job snacking. It's okay."

Lucy's eyes were welling with tears when she looked at Adrian. The look of panic and despair on her face made his chest ache. Going around the table and squatting next to her chair, Adrian pulled her close for a hug. Her body shook with her sobs. "Shh. He's okay, Lucy. It's okay. Shh."

When her tears eased a bit, Adrian whispered, "I'm going to put him to bed. He doesn't need to see you upset like this. I'll be back, okay?"

She nodded.

"Come on, Ree. Let's get your face washed and your teeth brushed for bed."

Without another word, Adrian picked up Henry and walked out of the room, carrying him off to bed.

I need to get it together. Adrian's absolutely right. Ree doesn't need to see this. I need to calm down. Adrian's a doctor. He knows when it's time to worry. This is not the time to worry. I need to calm down. I need to get it together. Weepy and splotchy with bruising is not a good look, Lucy thought.

Then she shook her head at the thoughts about her appearance. *What the fuck, self. Not appropriate.*

By the time Adrian was back in the kitchen, Lucy was calm and picking at her food, staring at her plate. "Thank you," she muttered.

Adrian pulled out the chair next to her and took her hand. As usual, her system went on hyper-alert at his touch, heart speeding up.

Good grief. This is just pathetic. He could not have made it any clearer this afternoon. Not happening, she told herself.

"Calmer?" he asked.

She nodded. "Embarrassed. Sorry."

"S'okay. You two have been on your own for a long time. I'd be terrified of losing my family, too. There's nothing to be embarrassed about. I just didn't want Henry to get worried. When I met him last week, his primary motivation for asking for help was so you didn't have to cry anymore. Yesterday, in the car, he told me he thought I was going to send you away and make him stay with me. That's how the 'bad people' thing came up."

"Oh," she muttered.

Please don't ask. I don't want to talk about it right now, she thought.

"I'm not going to ask. I suspect you don't want to talk about it right now."

Lucy burst out laughing. "I was just thinking that."

Adrian smiled as he got up to walk around the table, back to his plate.

OTHER THAN LUCY laughing at the sheer volume of food Adrian ate, they were quiet through dinner and cleaning up the kitchen.

As Adrian turned around from hanging up the dish towel, Lucy hugged him. Surprised, he wrapped his arms around her. "What's this for?" he murmured.

"It's a 'you're great' hug. Full disclosure: other than forcing hugs on Ree, I don't do this often, so I might be doing it wrong." She laughed, slightly weepy.

Lucy could feel the rumble of his laughter in his chest.

"Nope, you got it right. This is exactly what a hug is." Adrian's hand ran up her back to stroke the back of Lucy's head, holding her to his chest.

Reflecting back on it, Adrian wasn't sure who started the kiss. But it began as a simple meeting of lips. Just a peck. A comforting bit of contact between two friends. Then it became a merging of mouths, something deeper, breath commingling, air dancing between them.

This is not safe. This is not good for her. I need to not do this, Adrian thought.

He stepped back, away from her. It was physically painful to break contact with Lucy. Adrian struggled to breathe for a second.

"I'm not sure how that happened. I'm sor—" Lucy began.

OH, FUCK IT! SHE'S NOT GOING TO APOLOGIZE AGAIN, Adrian thought just before he seized her mouth, tongue exploring and teasing hers.

"Okay," he said, pulling away and stepping back again. "This is a terrible idea. For a lot of reasons. Terrible idea. I don't want to take advantage of you and the situation you're in with Ree, and this is not—"

Lucy kissed him again, her body pressed to him.

"Ethical. This is not ethical, and I need to stop this. Now. In just a minute." Adrian kissed her again.

"Wait. Wait, just a second. Let me—" Adrian said, reaching for his phone. There was a text message from Sam from an hour ago.

SAM: Forgot to tell you. Dad and I closed Lucy's Foundation case. We'll handle it privately with Dad as executor.
ADRIAN: You're my favorite brother.
SAM: Pfft. I get that a lot.

"What? What does that mean? The foundation isn't going to help us?" Lucy was starting to panic again.

"No, everything's fine. They just removed me from the equation of determining need and assistance. They funded an independent trust for you and Ree, outside of the foundation," he explained.

"Why? Why would they do that?" she asked, confused.

"So that I can stand around in my kitchen making out with you and not worry about you feeling like you have to participate in this so Ree gets the help he needs. You can do as you please, without concern of being 'punished' or whatever if something goes sideways between you and me," Adrian explained.

Lucy blinked. "They're making it easier for us to stand around in your kitchen making out?"

Adrian nodded, noticing her arms were still around him.

"How would they know that we want to stand around in your kitchen and make out?" Lucy's cheeks turned pink. "Okay, how do they know *I* keep wanting to stand around in your kitchen making out?"

"Oh, no. No, Lucy. That's definitely a 'we.' Not just a 'you,'" Adrian said, still screwing with his phone, not looking at her.

"Okay, we. But how?" she asked again.

"Uh, Hank actually suggested it last Saturday when my mom got all giddy at the sight of you. I rolled my eyes at him, thought he was overreacting. My mother has long lamented my unattached status. Sam's just…different. Like him knowing your name. He had never met you before. That's just how he is. I can be sitting here, thinking about calling him, and then he'll call me and ask why I'm thinking so loudly at him."

"So, what does this mean?" Lucy asked, still slightly concerned.

"For Ree's health stuff?"

Lucy nodded.

"Absolutely nothing. You'll still get all the care and support needed. Probably forever. I have to operate within the bounds of the non-profit charter. They don't. Hank will ensure that everything is handled properly."

"Like your dad wouldn't cut us off cold if he felt I wronged you," Lucy muttered.

"He wouldn't, Lucy. Never. Hank has more integrity than any other person I've ever met. The thought would never cross his mind. You could murder me in my sleep. He'd still help Ree. You haven't really met him. That's just how he is. But that's the point of this. It's done. You don't need to see any of us ever again if you don't want to."

"Adrian, I couldn't see you denying Ree help if we had a falling out. I refuse to believe that's who you are."

"I can't imagine it, either. But now none of us have to worry about it. It's out of my hands."

"So, what does this mean?"

Adrian's lips turned up a bit at the corners as he finally glanced at her face. "What do you want it to mean?"

Lucy smiled a small, secret smile without answering. As her lips tilted up to meet his, the energy exploded through Adrian, doing something like a little happy dance.

As he pulled away from the kiss again, Lucy grabbed Adrian's head. "Stop hedging. Please? I don't want to stop again. Can we make out and get all hot and bothered like functional, consenting adults? Because that sounds like fun."

"I wasn't going to stop," Adrian murmured in her ear, giving her goosebumps. "I was going to do this," he continued as he nibbled her earlobe and kissed a line down her long neck to her collarbone.

"Oh. Contributing to the hot and bothered state of affairs," she gasped as he kissed around her jawline and sucked her other earlobe gently.

Completely unaware of how she got there, Lucy found herself being pulled on top of Adrian on the couch in the living room.

"Change of venue?" she asked.

"Seemed like it would be more comfortable," he muttered.

"Mmm," she said, running her hand up the sculpted flesh of his abdomen and chest under his t-shirt. "I don't understand how you're this fucking ripped."

Adrian chuckled. "I work out a lot."

"Yeah, I guess so." Lucy laughed, kissing his jawline and neck, down to the collar of his t-shirt.

Adrian's hand slipped under her t-shirt, thumb gently stroking the skin at her waist. Lucy froze immediately. The happy, feel-good energy she was buzzing on froze in place as she struggled to breathe.

Adrian sat up, taking her with him. "Lucy?"

"Ah, sorry," she said, turning bright red. "Momentary lapse in the hot and bothered status. Picking back up." She tried to laugh, reaching for him.

He waited, neither pulling away or moving closer. She couldn't budge him if he didn't let her.

"Can I opt-out of talking about this right now if I promise to talk about it later?" she asked.

Adrian watched as she wrung her hands, refusing to make eye contact. Refusing to make eye contact was his thing, not hers. Something was really wrong. "You can, but I'm not sure it would be wise. For either of us."

Lucy nodded. "That's probably right."

She sat quietly for a minute.

Adrian counted the seconds, trying to calm the rage that was anticipating some new excitement. He wasn't angry with Lucy, but he suspected that whatever was going through her mind would enrage him. He thought of Hennessy's nine rating, trying to mentally prepare himself.

"I'm worried this will change things between us, and I don't want to change things between us," she finally said.

"Okay," Adrian said. "What is it you're afraid is going to change?"

Lucy blinked at him, looking terrified.

"How about I say a bunch of things that are all true, and you stop me when I get to the ones we need to talk about?" he asked, trying to make this easier for her.

Lucy blinked again then nodded.

"I'm pretty into you. More into you than I have been in anyone. Ever. The love and care you share with Ree make me feel better about life. I love that you're both feisty enough to not let some strange dude paw through your medical paperwork but also vulnerable enough to cry when that dude buys a bunch of kid's books.

"I know that you and Ree have had a rough road. Based on what you told me about pets, I've assumed your road has never been easy.

"I asked Hennessy for your detailed file yesterday after Ree talked about the bad people. Hennessy refused, and he would not typically refuse me anything. He's protective of you. He does not share his background easily. So he trusts you and wants you to understand that he's familiar with uneasy roads.

"I know you wouldn't be in this house right now if he thought you were a danger to me or mine, if you were an active drug user, or if you had a recent history of prostitution.

"Knowing all that, there's not much that you can tell me that would make me not interested in you. That includes telling me you don't want to stand around in the kitchen and make out or that you don't want to lay on the couch and make out. And also includes telling me you're not ready to go to bed with me yet. All of those things are fine. You can tell me you're just not interested at all and walk away. That would make me sad, but not uninterested in your wellbeing."

When Adrian stopped talking, Lucy made a little snort through her nose. Without looking at him, she started talking.

"I am so ready to go to bed with you, it's amazing. That's actually not the problem. The problem is that I've never actually *wanted* to go to bed with anyone. The problem was a sensory memory that passed quickly and has now left us in this weird place."

"You've never had sex?" Adrian asked, dumbfounded.

Lucy shook her head. "No, I've had sex. Sort of. Are we counting involuntary sex?"

"No." The rage clawed at Adrian's brain.

"Well then, not much sex. I dated a guy when I was in community college. He talked about it like it was the greatest thing ever. I laid there, thought the whole experience was overhyped. I didn't see him again afterward. I've been busy since Ree came along," she said, somehow humiliated and defiant at the same time.

They were quiet for a couple heartbeats. "You know, this is really ruining the hot and bothered thing we had going.

Adrian tried to smile. "It's just on a break, not ruined. The sensory memory?"

"Ah," Lucy muttered. "That's a little harder to explain, but I will."

She sighed. "I was in foster care after my dad did…what he did. Cycled through a lot of them."

"Hennessy, too," Adrian noted, more to remind her that she wasn't alone than anything else.

Lucy nodded.

"One of the homes was a large family. The couple had four biological kids. They had just finished adopting another. The caseworker told me it was a lovely family, good kids. If I fit in, I could probably stay there.

"My second night in the house, the eldest biological son came into the room I slept in, stuffed a sock in my mouth, zip-tied my hands, and raped me. He said if I told, he'd kill me. No one would believe me, and he'd kill me.

"I didn't know what to do. I was terrified. My entire body hurt. There was blood everywhere. Marks from the zip ties on my wrists. When the wife came to wake me the next morning, she asked if I got my period in the night. I said no and tried to explain. She didn't believe me or didn't want to believe me. David was just teasing, he did it with all the kids, it was like a rite of passage.

"I was terrified. Hurt and terrified," she repeated, shuddering at the memory.

Adrian squeezed her hand, reminding her that she was safe. Lucy started, roused from whatever thoughts were running through her brain.

"At dinner the next night, I hid a steak knife. I wasn't going to be a victim again if I could help it. When he came for me that night, I caught him off guard and sliced him good a couple of times. He liked it, liked the pain.

"He eventually overpowered me. When interviewed later, the parents told police they heard me screaming but thought we were 'just playing.' He had raped me again and stabbed me six times with the knife I had taken from the dinner table. There are scars on my abdomen."

Adrian could actually taste the rage. His vision was red. He didn't move. Didn't try to talk. Wasn't sure he could, even if he wanted to. The new energy, the rage, and his nature were in accordance. Aligned. For the first time in his life, Adrian intended real harm to another human being. If he found this person, Adrian would kill him without hesitation.

"David is the bad person Ree talks about. He teamed up with another foster kid that had lived with them when David was younger to stalk me. They showed up at our apartment one day, tried to hurt us. The off-duty cop that lived next door heard us screaming.

"In retrospect, I'm confident this is why I was so…harsh when you and I met. It was similar to meeting John, David's former foster brother. He was all about listening, interested in Ree, wanted to be a friend, wanted to help. When I came into the apartment and found you on the couch, I really thought two crazy fuckers were going to jump out and kill me. I wondered if Ree was already dead. There was no off-duty cop next door. It was four thirty in the morning. I was certain I was about to die."

Adrian sat quietly for more than a minute, processing and trying to decide how to move forward. He had to put the rage down. The rage couldn't get near her. He would not hurt her. The rage had to stay away. At that conscious thought, the energy that was the rage, clawing at his brain, disappeared.

Well, that's new, Adrian thought. *Since when is it obedient?*

Voice calm and neutral, eyes forward, speaking carefully, Adrian asked, "May I see them? The scars? I won't touch."

Lucy stood, pulling up her tank top to show her flat tummy. The scars were staggered in a horizontal line, a little higher than her navel. "You can touch. Not sure why the touch triggered me earlier."

"Do they go through to your back?" Adrian asked, tone still neutral.

She turned so he could see her back. "Two did, the rest, no."

LUCY COUNTED to thirty in her head. Then to sixty. He still hadn't spoken. Reacted. Touched her.

Does this make me damaged goods? Why did that fucking happen? Why did I freeze like that? This hasn't bothered me in years!

"Adrian?" she asked quietly.

With one smooth movement, he had pulled her back to the couch and directly into his lap. "Thank you for telling me. Thank you for showing me."

"What are you thinking?" Lucy asked in a small voice.

Adrian sighed. "I think he was trying to kill you, inflicting as much pain as possible. I think he should be in a mental institution. I think you're amazing. And I think if the opportunity arises, I will kill him. Doing so violates my oath as a doctor. Still, I have that whole horrifically wealthy family thing to fall back on when they take away my license to practice medicine, so there's that."

That actually made Lucy laugh, which made Adrian almost smile.

9

"I'm sorry I ruined hot and bothered time," Lucy said as she kissed the corner of his mouth. "Mostly, I'm sorry for myself. There is a serious lack of the hot and bothered type of enjoyment in my life. Except for the water jets in your shower. That frisky one caught me by surprise."

And then Adrian was laughing for real. "I wondered how that bottom one got angled to hit my thigh."

They were both laughing as Lucy rearranged herself to be facing him, straddling him on the couch.

"Lucy, there's no rush—" Adrian started before her mouth took his for a dance.

A few minutes of kissing and necking later, Lucy was tugging at Adrian's t-shirt. "Off," she grunted. "I showed you mine."

"I can't decide if you're trying to escalate things or if you just want to pet my muscles." Adrian laughed.

Lucy grinned. "Little bit of both."

"That's fair," he muttered, pulling the shirt off.

As her hands wandered and their mouths did the do-si-do, Adrian slowly inched his hands up Lucy's torso, over her shirt to her breasts.

She jumped and gasped a little when he squeezed her nipples through her clothes.

"So much better than the showerhead," she teased, mid-kiss. "There's none of this zingy zappy happy feeling running amok without you."

That gave Adrian a mental pause. *Can she feel it? Can she feel that other energy running rampant?*

Rather than lift her shirt up, he pulled the straps of her tank down, so the tank still covered her torso but freed her bra. Hands running up her body then down her back, kneading tension as he went, Adrian checked for any sign of hesitation.

When nothing but happy sounds followed his hands, he bent his head to kiss down her chest to her breast. With no sign to stop, he pulled the left cup of her bra down to kiss one nipple while his right thumb stroked the other.

Lucy let out a pleased little moan. She seemed to grind her hips against him on pure instinct. Adrian forgot to breathe for a second. Lucy gasped at the feel of him through his cargo shorts.

Alternating breasts, his ministrations continued as her breathing increased.

"Uh, Adrian?" she whispered. "Maybe upstairs?"

He nibbled a little harder than before, making her jump against him just enough for him to get a hand under her ass. That hand pushed her up to her knees, bringing her chest closer to his face. With Adrian still kissing, sucking, and nibbling, Lucy was unprepared for his fingers to rub that perfect spot between her legs, just so. Through the hard seam of her jean shorts, the motion was just enough to send her spiraling over the edge, gasping in surprise.

"I blame the pecs," Lucy sighed, coming back to herself, body relaxed and head resting on Adrian's shoulder. "I was turned on by the pecs, which made me easy pickings for that. The six-pack, too. Pretty muscles. I feel like it shouldn't be that easy for you to make that happen. So I'm blaming the pecs. And maybe the medical degree. It's a little humiliating how quickly that happened, but I'm pretty okay with it. Hot and bothered time for the win," she rambled before falling silent again.

"Adrian?"

"Hmm?"

"You should do that again."

She could hear the smile in his voice. "Okay. We should go upstairs, though."

"REALLY?" Lucy looked at him skeptically.

"Bath time," Adrian declared.

"Why is it bath time rather than bedtime?"

"Several reasons, really. I'm assuming there are no traumatic experiences tied to a bath."

"That's true," Lucy confirmed.

"It's fun, it feels good, it allows playtime. You can explore—we can explore—without being embarrassed because the bubbles hide things. It'll be highly enjoyable, even if we don't have sex," Adrian explained.

"We're not having sex?" Lucy asked, sounding disappointed.

"What's your middle name?"

"Lee," Lucy said, baffled by the non sequitur.

"Lucy Lee? Really?"

"Lucinda Lee, actually."

"Lucinda! Fuck Hennessy and his privacy shit. That's amazing." Adrian laughed. "He could have told me that."

"What is happening right now?"

"Oh. Yeah. Distracted. Get in the tub, Lucinda."

"You're serious about this?"

Rather than answer, Adrian dropped his shorts and stepped out of his boxer briefs.

Lucy blushed. *Well, okay then. I guess we're taking a bath.*

Lucy pulled off her clothes, stress radiating from her. Hot and bothered time was great, but the bathroom lights didn't hide much. Adrian was about to get a good look at her scars.

"Into the tub, Lucinda," Adrian said, with a playful swat on her ass. It startled a giggle out of her.

"I ADMIT IT. This is really, really nice," Lucy hummed, reclined next to Adrian in the tub.

"Mmm. Sit forward for a second," he said, sliding behind her and pulling her back against his body.

"Bath time cuddling? Really?" she asked with a tense giggle.

Slowly and gently, to avoid startling her, Adrian began kneading out the knots of tension in her neck and shoulders, hands sliding smoothly in the foamy bathwater. Down the back of her head to the trapezius muscles in her neck, then across the shoulders, and back to her neck.

Lucy groaned. "You are an incredibly handy guy to have around. This might be the most luxurious experience of my life."

It's a bath and a neck rub. Family dogs are generally treated better than this. At the thought, the rage swirled within Adrian just a second before quieting back down.

Kissing her neck, nibbling at her ear, he inched his hands around to cup her breasts, thumbs circling her nipples again. This elicited a different type of sound as she shifted against him.

As her breathing picked up, he slid a hand down her belly and paused. "Can I touch? Is that okay?"

Rather than respond, Lucy shifted her legs, giving easier access.

"So beautiful, so brave," he muttered against her ear as his fingers gently circled and touched, following the same pattern circling her nipple.

"Adrian?" she breathed as her body tensed, close to climax, hips moving in rhythm with his hands.

"Almost, love," he muttered, moving the hand from her breast down between her legs and slowly inserting a finger.

"Oh!" Lucy cried.

Adrian paused, unsure if that was a good or bad sound.

"Don't stop!" Lucy scolded, making him laugh just a bit as he aligned the circling of the finger outside with the motion inside.

Breathing hard, body tense with need, "Please," she whispered. As quick as a tiny increase in pressure, Lucy was soaring again, rolling through another orgasm quickly.

Before long, she flipped herself over to kiss him, hands roaming free around his torso.

"You were right about the bath," she said.

He smiled. "Yeah?"

"Yep. It's fun. It definitely feels good. And there's exploration," she said, closing her hand around his dick without warning, slowly, firmly, stroking.

"Oh my God," he breathed. "I almost embarrassed myself there. Lucy, ugh, wait—" He groaned again as she cupped his balls and rubbed her teeth on one of his nipples.

The energy exploded through him without warning, mixing with lust and longing. And rage. Rage, battering at the inside of his mind, screaming to be free as the lust and other energy combined to raw power. "Lucy," he said, voice echoing through the room.

We need to stop. This needs to stop. I don't have control. Say the words. Say the words. Stop. Pause. STOP! Adrian's conscious mind screamed.

Lucy moaned. Unsure how it happened, he was inside her, shifting with her as she moved, power slamming through both of them.

"Oh, God. Adrian. Adrian, I don't, I can't—" she breathed as she orgasmed.

Adrian tried to slow down. Tried to pause. Tried to give her a minute. The energy continued to pound at his control, demanding an out. Completely baffled by where it came from so suddenly, Adrian fought the rage back and let the other power flow.

Shifting her with him through her orgasm, picking up speed, sloshing water over the edge of the tub, Adrian came with her when Lucy exploded again.

HOURS LATER, Adrian lay awake in bed with a peacefully sleeping Lucy tucked alongside him. He was unable to account for the rage. He'd been thinking about it for hours.

The angry energy, the rage, was *never* a part of sex. Never. He would never take a woman that elicited anger from him to bed. That energy was not allowed to be loose during intercourse. Ever. Adrian locked it down and had literally walked away once, mid-action, when it broke free.

The *other* energy that had surfaced on Friday night seemed to be something else. It wasn't hurtful. As Lucy said, it made things tingly and enjoyable. There was a power to it, but it didn't seem to be like the rage.

The problem with the other energy came from it interfering with Adrian's control of the rage. The other energy seemed to be trying to pull the rage forward, and rage did *NOT* belong in sex. Between the physical pleasure, the mental battle with the rage, and trying to understand that other energy, Adrian wasn't sure what happened. Or, at least, he wasn't sure of the order of events.

He thought Lucy initiated the sex. She had been touching; the non-rage energy went haywire. He let it free because he couldn't control it and the rage at the same time. Then, they were joined. She didn't seem upset or surprised afterward, didn't make any comments about it escalating quickly.

What if I hurt her? What if the power did it, and I hurt her? I will not hurt her, Adrian swore to himself. *What did I say? Did I say anything? Did the power slip into words? What did I say?*

Adrian continued to rehash things, over and over, throughout what would be one of the longest nights of his life.

LUCY WOKE up alone early Sunday morning, the sun coming in through Adrian's front windows. The clock said it was six thirteen. After a quick trip to the bathroom, Lucy threw on yesterday's clothes and headed downstairs to find Adrian.

He wasn't in the kitchen, living room, or bathroom. Ree was still fast asleep and probably would be for hours. Did Adrian go somewhere? His car was still in the driveway. His keys and wallet were on the shelf. He wasn't in the backyard.

Oh, wait. The basement. There's a basement, she thought.

As she opened the door, she could hear the sound of a punching bag being hit. She headed down the stairs to find him shirtless, drenched in sweat, hair stuck to his head, beating against a heavy bag hanging from the ceiling with practiced ease and power. There was a well-worn treadmill and elliptical, along with some weight-lifting equipment as well.

Wow. This is why he's so ripped. How long has he been down here?

"Hi," Lucy said, over the sound of the bag.

Adrian started, grabbing the bag before it could swing back at him. "Hi, everything okay?" he asked, coming toward her.

"Yeah, good," Lucy said with a blush. She had aches in unusual places, but she felt good.

"Why are you up?" he asked.

"The sun coming in the windows woke me. I'm glad to be up, though. Saves awkward Ree questions."

Adrian looked confused. "What time is it?"

"About six thirty now. How long have you been up?" Lucy asked.

"I'm an early riser," he said as he pulled off his gloves and began unwrapping his hands. "Come on, I'll take a quick shower and make some breakfast. I'm starving."

"Are you okay?" Lucy asked. "You have dark circles under your eyes like some bitch hogged your bed last night."

"I'm great, Lucy. Sweaty. Hungry. Thirsty. Ready for a good morning smooch, but way too sweaty and nasty for it," he said with a half-smile.

"I'll risk it." Lucy grinned, stretching to touch her lips to his.

"Brave woman. Upstairs!" he demanded, swatting her ass.

FIFTEEN MINUTES LATER, they were both clean and dressed.

"How are you, really?" Adrian asked while cracking eggs.

She lifted her eyebrows. "Tender in interesting places, *extremely* relaxed, and thinking that I should go to school to be a massage therapist."

That surprised a laugh out of him. "Why a massage therapist?"

"So I know how to do lovely things to your neck and back, too. I had no idea you boxed. That has to be hard on the joints."

"It hasn't bothered me yet. Orange juice or just coffee?" he asked.

"How long have you worked out like that? There was a full-on gym down there."

"High school. Maybe a little earlier with lifting weights, but boxing started in high school. Long time."

"Did it help to keep all the brothers in line?" She smiled.

"Bah. I'd never swing at them. That's Will's job. And he only does it when things are serious."

Lucy chuckled. "I appreciate that you used the present tense as if Will still beats the crap out of you guys."

Adrian grinned. "He does. This only surprises you because you haven't met Noah yet."

They fell silent while starting to eat. Lucy watched him as he worked on his eggs.

"How are you, really?" she asked, a bit on edge. "You look tired. Regrets?"

His eyes snapped to her. "No, Lucy. Absolutely no regrets, unless you felt rushed. I'm not entirely sure how things escalated so quickly, but I don't regret it unless you do."

Lucy gave a rueful little smile. "I may have gotten a little carried away. I think. I'm not sure, either. I'm just worried about you. You don't look good, Adrian."

"It's a fuel thing, Lucy. I worked out too long, that's all. I'll eat my pile of breakfast, drink some fluids, maybe raid the fridge some more. I don't know. I'm okay."

Lucy shook her head.

"What?" he asked.

"Weird feeling of deja vu." She laughed.

HENRY WANDERED into the kitchen a few minutes later, still yawning. He climbed up into Adrian's lap without invitation, settling in for his morning wake-up cuddle session.

Adrian readjusted in the chair, leaning back to give Ree more room. "Well, good morning, sleepy. How are you?"

Henry made a sleepy little grunt.

"Not yet awake?" Adrian asked.

No response.

Adrian took a moment to assess things. The rage was utterly silent. He could still feel it, sitting in the center of himself. But it was not pushing at anything. That was unprecedented. Even when happy and at peace, the rage still lurked just under the surface.

The other energy did a little happy dance through his body when Ree crawled into his lap, just like it did a short race around him at Lucy's good morning kiss. It didn't lurk. It wasn't centered, like the rage. It just existed. It was just there.

Adrian pulled the other energy forward, without the rage. "Lucy?"

She looked up immediately, smiling at him.

"Do you want more coffee?" he asked.

"No, thanks. Here, I'll get yours. You have a snuggly Ree in your lap." She went to pick up his coffee. "Your cup is already full. Why'd you want more coffee?"

"I didn't want more coffee. I wanted to know if you wanted more coffee," Adrian said, kicking himself for not thinking of something else to ask her.

Her name didn't feel or sound different when he said it with the other energy. Maybe it wasn't the same sort of thing. But it acted like the same thing. The energy behaved just like the rage, with the way he could push and pull at it. And it definitely tried to influence his actions—using actual words and commands.

As he had a thousand times before, he wished he could talk to someone about this crap. But this was not something anyone else would understand.

"Are you hungry?" Adrian asked Ree.

Head shake.

Adrian pulled the other energy forward. "Are you hungry if I make waffles?"

"I love waffles!" Henry exclaimed.

10

"You're really not going to dinner with me? Really?" Adrian whined.

"Adrian, look at my face. I can't go like this. Your brother just got engaged, and you'll be celebrating and all that. I don't want to be a downer," Lucy said. Again.

"Henry, are you going with me?" Adrian called, looking into the living room. Ree was asleep on the couch.

Adrian sighed.

"Lucy! Please come to dinner. Please! Darla's gonna be pissed if you're not there," Adrian continued.

"Why is this such a thing? We'll go next week," Lucy said, puzzled by his insistence.

He shrugged. "It occurred to me earlier that I've never actually brought anyone to Sunday dinner before. Friends, yeah. Buddies and whatnot in college. But never a girlfriend."

"Oh." Lucy's cheeks went a little pink. "I can go find something to wear and wake Ree up—"

"No, it's fine." Adrian laughed, realizing he was being ridiculous. "Next week. He's out like a light. Stay here and order things. Clothes, Lucinda. Girl stuff. Little kid stuff. Random crap you've always wanted to buy. Make that a reality. You should not have that panicked look when considering what to wear to a family dinner."

"I'm guessing Darla would not approve of a stained t-shirt and ripped shorts." Lucy smiled.

"She has nine kids. At least one of us is a mess each week. Usually Jake. Clothing wouldn't bother her. Plus, you come with a little kid. You'll immediately be her second favorite person, with Ree being her favorite person. But still, you looked decidedly uncomfortable for a minute there."

After a pause, Adrian continued. "Probably better to wait for next week. Hank will be agitated by the stitches."

"See, they look terrible!" Lucy agreed.

"They do not look terrible. Hank gets very…concerned about his people. You'll see. Battered Matty is probably enough for one week," Adrian admitted.

ADRIAN WAS the last to arrive for Sunday dinner. The dog didn't even greet him. "Well, fine, Roscoe. Be like that. I don't mind at all," he muttered with a frown. But it made sense when the big room was empty. Everyone was getting settled around the table.

Jake was the first to notice him and came over for a hug, Matilda close behind. Just because he could, Adrian picked Jake up off the ground mid-hug and swung him a bit. "Congratulations, little brother! It's about time! More than a year in the making. Horseshit, man. Horseshit."

Matilda was next; she was tiny. Barely five feet tall. A foot-swinging hug was mandatory. Always. "Awww, it's my soon to be teeny, tiny sister. Congratulations, Matty. You look *much* better than the last time I saw you. The meds are working okay?"

"Yes, Adrian. But I need the ability to breathe, you know," she muttered into his chest. "Honestly, you're worse than Will, just quieter about it."

As they made their way to the table, Adrian watched Matty move.

She was just about back to normal. The bruising was better; the stitches were out; the vertigo was gone. She was doing fine.

Adrian shook his dad's hand, kissed his mom's head, and smacked the brothers he could reach. Beth was in the far back corner, between Hennessy and Matthew, so he blew her a kiss rather than trying to get to her. He found himself seated in Sam's usual chair between Matty and William. Looking down the length of the table, he saw Sam sitting with Luke.

"I'm mixing shit up," Sam said. "Just for fun."

"Samuel," Darla said in a chiding tone.

"It's part of the fun, Mom. I'm trying on Jake's fucking foul mouth, too," Sam replied with a straight face.

Darla glared at him as she tried, and failed, not to laugh.

"Where are Lucy and Henry?" Darla asked when the table chatter died down.

"Yeah!" Matthew said. "What's this I hear about you living with someone?"

Adrian turned his head to glare at William.

"What day is today?" Will asked.

Adrian continued to glare.

"Today is Sunday, big brother!" Beth called down the table.

"Beth, what day was it that we watched him carry the lovely battered blonde into the back bedroom?" Will asked.

"Tuesday!" Beth called gleefully.

Adrian shared his glare with her.

"Tuesday night, Wednesday night, Thursday night, Friday night, Saturday night," Will counted off on his fingers. "I count *five* nights they've been at your house. Wait. They're still at your house, right? You haven't fucked that up?"

"William," Hank said.

"Dad, I really feel like we should get a swearing pass this week. Jake's getting married, and Adrian's living with someone," Will said.

There were unidentified snorts of laughter from around the table.

"Hey, wait a second," Adrian said. "You're the oldest. Jake's getting married. I'm living with someone. Where's your significant other, William?"

"We've talked about this. I'm ruined till the end of time," Will said, not missing a beat. "We're talking about *you*. The doctor. The one Mom wants to play matchmaker for *so very* badly."

"What? He's a wonderful person and painfully shy!" Darla said, indignant, as the table exploded in laughter.

"Is Lou still at your place?" Will asked.

"You know the answer to that question," Adrian replied.

"I do, but we need to establish it for the table at large. Is Lou still at your place?"

"Why do you know that?" Hank asked, confused.

"There's a security detail assigned to Lou," Will said without pause. "Answer the question, little brother."

"What was the question?" Adrian said, laughing.

William smacked him upside the head. Not gently.

"Yes, they're still staying with me. Henry is terrified of leaving."

"And?" William asked.

"And what?" Adrian asked back, all innocence.

"Don't make me fucking beat you," William threatened.

"Mom, William swore at the table," Adrian snitched.

"Oh well," Darla said to rampant laughter.

"Jake and Matty had sex on the pool table in Jake's office," Adrian yelled as he ducked away from Matilda.

"ADRIAN! WHY WOULD YOU BRING THAT UP?" Matty yelled back, horrified.

"Matty, it's times like this that it is painfully clear you grew up as an only child." Noah laughed.

Without warning, Will twisted Adrian's arm up behind his back, holding it in a way that would dislocate the shoulder if Adrian tried to pull away.

"Really?" Adrian asked, unfazed.

"Answer the question," Will coached.

"What was the question?" Adrian asked as Will twisted more.

"Are you hooking up with Lou or what? He's completely indifferent to this. Noah cries like a sissy when I do this to him."

"Hey! You twist that shit hard on me. It fucking hurts!" Noah bitched.

"Whatever, man. If I twist his arm any more, I'll rip the shoulder socket apart," Will said, letting Adrian go. "Answer the question! There are bets to be settled."

"Oh, well, in that case, I'm not answering. Let the pool roll forward." Adrian laughed.

Matty turned in her chair to look at him. "Really? Not going to play along?"

"Nope." Adrian gave her a grin.

Matilda smirked at him, reached over, and poked the only ticklish spot on his body.

Adrian jumped out of his chair. "Whoa, not fair! Don't do that."

"What the fuck did you just do?" Jake laughed.

"He's ticklish in the same spot you are," Matty said as the table exploded in laughter again.

"That's just evil, Carrots. I love it." Will cheered.

"Lucy is healing, I think both mentally and physically," Adrian answered without answering, once the table settled down.

Will snorted.

"What the fuck happened? She got pistol-whipped or something?" Jake asked. "Mom told us you met this woman at the hospital. Somehow, you ended up at her apartment on Saturday because the kid was scared. They were going to stay in a hotel or something on Tuesday, but she got injured."

"She didn't get pistol-whipped," Will corrected. "Her face got broken when some jackass tried to use a .38 special as brass knuckles."

"I got a picture! Wait!" Hennessy called, pulling out his phone. "It's from Friday, and this happened on Tuesday. Look at that shit."

Will smirked. "You definitely got June with that."

"I know, right?!!" Hennessy laughed.

"Holy fuck!" Jake yelled.

"Yeah. It was sorta like Fate looking at Matty, beat up and seizing in the hospital, and thinking, 'I can top that!' Lou's nose goes splat, her lip is ripped, and she's worried about the gun going off, through the floor, hurting someone. She puked when she saw the kid's favorite spot with a bullet hole through it, but otherwise, she couldn't give fewer fucks about the broken face," Hennessy said.

"I told you not to take her," Sam bitched.

"YEAH. I KNOW." Will growled.

"Heh, Lou's tough. She'll heal," Hennessy said.

"Did they get the guy who did it?" Matty asked.

Hennessy snorted. "Yeah, the Reaper sittin' over there got him, no problem."

Will looked around innocently. "What? I didn't kill him. I thought about it, but I didn't. It was fine. He just won't walk unaided again. They probably saved the leg. And he had a glass jaw. That's not my fault. You reap what you sow."

Beth looked at Hennessy. "Do you call him 'Reap' as in 'Grim Reaper' or more as in 'you reap what you sow?' I've always wondered about that. I can't imagine Will being the Grim Reaper when you're the tough guy of the dynamic duo."

Hennessy's face went blank as he glanced at Will. Will shrugged. "She isn't a little girl anymore."

Hennessy snorted. "Beth, I have nothing, and I mean absolutely nothing, on him. He is known across every branch of special forces as the Grim Reaper."

All heads at the table turned to William, who shrugged again. "Some things are worth fighting for. Killing for. Surviving for. I will burn in hell for all eternity, but those I love will be safe."

At the far end of the table, Sam gave an audible gasp, eyes wide. "Love? Will, love?"

"Yes, Sam," Will snapped. "Contrary to popular belief, I still feel, for fuck's sake. Don't be an asshole."

After an uncomfortable silence, the conversation picked back up.

"Have you two love birds started thinking wedding thoughts, yet?" Hank asked.

"Oh, no," Will interrupted. "Not so fast. There was no answer to the question. There was a well-crafted sidestep."

The entire table turned to stare at Adrian.

"What?"

"Adrian, I will beat you bloody. You'll have to eat like forty-five eggs to heal up. Answer the question," Will demanded.

"What was the question?" Adrian asked again, lips quirked into a half-smile. He helped himself to another piece of chicken from the platter in front of him.

"Pay up," William told Noah. "Why do you keep taking the bets? Sam has *never* lost a fucking bet. We do this like three times a week, man. Pay up."

"THERE WAS NO ANSWER! HE DIDN'T ANSWER. I'M NOT PAYING UNTIL HE ANSWERS!" Noah bitched.

"Booo!" everyone yelled at once.

Sam threw out a smug little smile. "Just so everyone knows, I'm Adrian's favorite brother."

Will snorted again. "Fuck off."

"Okay, I was Adrian's favorite brother last night. It might be back to Will by now," Sam acknowledged.

"Actually, I hate you all right now," Adrian admitted with red cheeks. "I'm wondering why I came to dinner tonight. Do we *really* have to discuss everything? Swearing at the table is the end of the world, but my sex life is perfectly acceptable."

"Ha," Hank said. "Jake and Matty are getting married. Time to move on to someone else. William won't play along. You're next."

"Dubious honor," Adrian muttered.

"To be clear: there will be no swearing or sex talk when there are little ears at this table. If you jackasses teach that child new vocabulary words, they better be G rated. DO YOU ALL HEAR ME?" Darla demanded. "I'm looking at you two idiots, Jacob and Noah. YOU WILL BEHAVE."

"Adrian, does Henry do the earmuffs thing?" Jacob asked, demonstrating covering his ears to block foul language.

Adrian shook his head, chewing a big bite of food.

"Could you teach him before Sunday?" Jake asked.

"I could," Adrian said with a grin. "What's in it for me?"

"I won't tell Lucy that you told everyone you two hooked up," Jake offered.

"I didn't tell anyone anything," Adrian corrected.

"See! The bet is not settled!" Noah declared.

William groaned. "You lost, man. Let it go."

"I'm kinda pissed Henry didn't come to hang with me. I get Lucy not showing while rocking the battered look, but why no Ree?" Ethan asked.

"He was sleeping," Adrian said.

Jake's brow furrowed. "Is that an okay thing? Not a bad sign, right?"

"It's fine. He's doing well so far. No fever, no trouble eating, happy and calm, aside from Thursday night," Adrian said before thinking.

Matthew's eyebrows shot up. "Thursday night?"

Adrian sighed. After a moment of consideration, he decided he really did want to discuss this. He needed to vent. "So, Tuesday, she got injured. Wednesday she was completely wrecked—couldn't keep her eyes open—"

"That was for the best, Adrian. She needed sleep," Darla interjected.

"I agree, Mom. That's not my problem. Thursday, she gets up at lunchtime, feeling better, takes a shower, comes into the kitchen, and gets all worked up that I ordered Ree some books. The kid loves books, so we made a deal about him eating in exchange for books. Lucy catches on to it and gets upset—like tears-level of upset. I ask if she's okay, and she says something about leaving as soon as fucking possible.

"I was floored. Seriously had no idea what to say, but I was pissed. She's beat to hell. Why the rush to leave, you know?"

Adrian paused. Everyone was staring at him with looks of shock. "What?"

"Don't worry about it," Will said. "Finish the story."

"So, I'm pissed. I go upstairs to do some work. I go back downstairs later to find her on her hands and knees, scrubbing the fucking *already clean* floors. I wanted to bash my head into a wall. Why can't she just watch TV and rest or something?

"I ask what she's doing. She says she doesn't have anything else to do. I give her the laptop and tell her to start ordering shit because they have next to nothing. She refused. I got pissed off again, went downstairs, and worked out.

"By the time dinner rolls around, I'm more annoyed than mad. I ask her if she really wants to go because fuck. If she doesn't want to be there, I'm not going to make her stay.

"Henry freaks out. And I mean *freaks*. Loses his shit, nearing panic attack levels. Tears and begging. 'Please don't make us go, I'll be good.' It fucking killed me. I felt like a giant dick.

"Then Thursday night he wakes up screaming in a night terror, babbling that the 'bad people' are going to get Aunt Lucy. Turns out, she's had a pair of guys stalking her for almost two years. She didn't say anything. Henry told me in the car the next day.

"She doesn't volunteer anything, doesn't want to 'be in the way,' won't spend any money at all, and will not ask for help. Logically, I get it. She's never had anyone willing to help. But it makes me batshit crazy."

After a pause, he continued. "And, by the by, Hennessy, fuck you. I know you know the background on this. I respect your point on it, but it's just making it harder for her to find her way when I'm blundering around like a fucking moron. She's answered every question I've ever asked. She's not trying to hide anything from me. I just don't know what questions to ask. So, fuck you for not helping."

The entire family was still and silent, effectively frozen in place.

"That was, without question, the longest rant I've ever heard from you," Luke said with a laugh. "I mean, that was like an entire year's worth of Adrian dialogue."

"And ten years of Adrian cussing." Noah laughed.

"Feel better?" Hank asked.

"I guess," Adrian replied. "I just don't know how to help. I'm a little out of my element here."

"You're gonna have to be patient, Adrian. She's never had anyone care for her before. The closest she got was a little old Polish lady that gave her room and board in exchange for cooking, cleaning, and medical care. That's it," Hennessy said.

"There has been no one else. At all. Ree's mom, maybe. But on paper, that looks more like Linda used her for support without giving much in return. If it's really bothering you, ask her if you can read it. I'll give it to you if she says it's okay."

William sighed. "Jessup—"

"Na, Will. No. Not with this. Her childhood makes mine look like a fucking walk in the park. He doesn't get to flip through it like a novel. If they end up in ugly places because he didn't ask something or she didn't volunteer something, well tough. That's part of building trust and understanding," Hennessy said, determined to stand his ground. "It's been five days. Give her some fucking time."

After an extended pause, Matthew cleared his throat. "Well, this is another one for the record books. Adrian used more than ten words in a row, and Hennessy is refusing to give Will something. Never thought I'd see that day."

Will looked at Adrian. "He's probably right, Adrian. Time and patience. Probably no shortcut to this."

"The time and patience don't bother me at all. Getting pissed off because I don't know what's going on bothers me. Seeing her hurt bothers me. Causing her to be uncomfortable bothers me." Adrian shook his head. "It is what it is."

The table was quiet until Noah handed Sam ten bucks.

"Fuck you," Noah muttered.

Sam smiled. "I'm framing this one."

There were a couple laughs, but the table was still tense.

"So, wedding plans?" Ethan asked Matty. "Are we setting a date any time soon?"

"I want to do something small," Matty admitted, feeling awkward. Trying to talk about happy things after the heavy conversation was strange.

"Yeah, small. Who do you want to sing at our wedding, Matty? I heard this idea yesterday during best-friend-not-shopping," Jake teased, trying to break up the heavy feeling.

"Oh. I was mostly kidding about that, but it would be amazing," she said with a blush.

"We might be able to make it happen," Jake offered. "Sometimes throwing enough money at something like that, or at the right charity, knowing her priorities, might get it done."

"Who?" Ethan asked, excited.

"Emma Gracen," Matty muttered.

"I just love her," Ethan said.

"Me, too," Matty sighed.

"That's why she's the most beautiful woman in the world." Luke laughed. "Mass appeal."

"We should totally make that happen," Noah said. "I could take her to bed, fall madly in love, and forever cure my man-whore ways."

Will snorted. "Now we're just being ridiculous."

"William?" Sam called from the other end of the table.

"Yes, Samuel?" Will called back, slightly entertained by the formality.

"What do you love?" Samuel asked, words heavy with power, making the air vibrate. "I need to know."

"Huh?"

"What do you love?"

Driving home from Sunday dinner, William continued to think about Adrian and his complete non-reaction to what was, in fact, an excruciating hold. The rage could absorb pain. Was there no reaction because Adrian has a high pain tolerance? Or was there no reaction because the rage was fucked up?

Will thought about Lucy and Ree, in Adrian's house for almost a week now, disrupting his little brother's rigid, vitally important routine. Shaking up his emotions.

Adrian's smart. He's figured it out by now. It's fine. They'll be fine, Will thought.

William's mind flashed back to Whitney Langcaster in middle school. And then to the dinner rant. Then the dark tension that settled over the table when Adrian was angry and frustrated with Hennessy.

Maybe I'll just stop by for lunch with Lou tomorrow. Say hi. See how things are going.

The Bluetooth system dinged with a call. The display read "Pip."

"Hello, love," Will said as the call picked up.

"How was dinner?" Pip asked.

Will smiled. "Adrian's got a girlfriend."

"Ha! Why does Noah keep taking the bets?" she asked.

"It's one of life's great mysteries." Will laughed.

"What did Sam's dinner taste like?"

Sam stories made Pip happy. Hennessy was Pip's favorite brother by default. He was the only brother that knew Pip. Knew of Pip. But if Pip had met his other brothers, Sam would be her favorite, no doubt about it.

Will talked through dinner, sharing his day with the woman who knew his family but had never met them.

Pulling into his driveway, Will sighed. They'd hang up soon. Maybe he could drive around for a while yet.

"I heard the car shift into park. You are home safe," she said.

"I'm home," he confirmed.

"I miss you so much it hurts," Pip said quietly.

Will closed his eyes. "I'll see you on Friday and talk to you in the morning."

"I know," she said.

"I love you."

"Know that, too. Please think about it, Will?" Pip whispered.

The line was silent for a solid fifteen seconds.

"Love you." She hung up without another word.

11

*S*topped at a red light, Adrian shot Lucy a quick text on his way home from Sunday dinner.

ADRIAN: I'm about a mile away. I'll be pulling up and coming inside soon.
LUCY: You're announcing your arrival? It's your house.
ADRIAN: It's dark. I didn't want to scare you.
LUCY: You've been to my apartment. You expect me to get scared by you coming home?

"Did you eat?" Adrian asked. "Darla sent you leftovers."

"I had chicken nuggets with Ree around six. He's been out since a little after seven. Is that concerning?" Lucy asked.

"That he's sleeping? No. It's actually a good sign. He's not throwing up or running a fever, right?"

"No, just sleeping a lot more than usual, and that's saying something." She met him in the kitchen with a smile.

"How was dinner?" she asked. "We missed you."

Adrian arched an eyebrow. "Did you?"

Lucy blushed. "Uh, yeah. Ree was looking for you at book time. It's lonely here by myself when he's sleeping."

"We missed you at dinner, too." Adrian kissed her as he walked by to put the food in the fridge.

"Hennessy showed everyone a picture of your Friday face, so if you were hoping to avoid that...sorry." He chuckled.

When he turned around, she was standing in the same place, touching the spot he kissed.

"Okay?" he asked, wondering if he shouldn't have kissed her.

Lucy's lips twitched into a little smile. "Yes, just not used to a kissy greeting."

"Me, either," Adrian admitted, walking back toward her. "It's fun, though. See?"

He kissed her again, more serious about it.

Lucy chuckled as she wrapped her arms around his neck.

"How are you?" he asked a moment later. "Lots of changes in less than a week."

She smiled. "I'm not sure it's caught up with me yet, honestly. Doesn't feel real."

"How can I help?" Adrian asked. "I keep trying to bully Hennessy into giving me your background check. I want to stop blundering into painful things. He won't budge on it."

That caught Lucy by surprise. She stiffened in his arms immediately. "Why in the world would you want to read that?"

"Because I keep doing and saying shit that makes you scared or uneasy or angry. I would really rather not do that, but I have no idea what to avoid," Adrian explained. "Anyway, he will not budge on it. Even when Will pressed him, and I've never seen Hennessy push back at William. He will let me read it if you say it's okay." Adrian raised his eyebrows.

Lucy stepped back away from him. "Uh, I don't know. I mean, I'll adjust quickly. You don't need to worry about it for long. You shouldn't worry about it now. It's my bullshit. You don't have to deal with it."

"I would like to make things easier if I can. Your dad, the stabbing, the bad people…I blundered into that stuff. I know it made things harder for you. I would rather not make things harder."

"But knowing the shit doesn't make it go away, Adrian. I appreciate what you're saying and understand your point. I just haven't seen the actual file. I don't know what's in it, how detailed it is. Can I talk to Hennessy? Are you going to be mad if you don't get to read it? It's not that I'm trying to hide things. It's just a lot to process."

"Okay. Whatever you want, Lucy. I'm not mad. And I won't be mad," Adrian promised. "Are you mad?"

"What? No. Of course not," she said, shaking her head like she was trying to clear her thoughts.

"Can I come over there to stand with you again?" he asked.

Lucy looked startled, noticing the space between them for the first time. "I didn't realize I backed away." She walked back into his arms.

The happy energy zinged through him again at her touch, feeling like static electricity where their skin touched. Lucy tucked her head against his shoulder, facing his neck. He could feel the wisps of her hair float against him as he hugged her tight.

This feels so right, he thought. *I need to not push. Hennessy is right. Time. Time will help.*

"I'm sorry, Adrian," Lucy whispered.

Without warning, Rage exploded, ripping through his body. His ears started to ring; his vision went red. The other, happier energy fizzled out in Rage's wake.

Before the conscious part of Adrian could even start to react, Rage tipped Lucy's head back to meet her eyes.

"You will never apologize for something that is not your fault again," Rage said, unrestrained, with full intent and focus, directly into her eyes. It watched as the command sunk into her mind.

And then it was gone. As suddenly as it surfaced, Rage disappeared again.

"Lucy! Lucy! Are you okay?" Adrian broke out in a cold sweat, panting for air through his terror.

HOLY FUCK! HOLY FUCK! What just happened?

Lucy stood in his arms, glassy-eyed and staring. At the sound of her name, she shook her head. "Huh? I'm fine. What's wrong, Adrian? You look like you're going to be sick."

OH MY GOD. WHAT DID I JUST DO?

ADRIAN WAS DRESSED and ready to leave when Lucy woke up on Monday morning.

"Wow, early start today?" she asked.

"Good morning," Adrian said with a quick kiss. "Yep, early meetings. I was just about to head out. Disregard the note I just left you," he said with a small smile. "Have a great day. Please take the security people with you if you go out," he said as he walked out the door without waiting for a response.

She had slept upstairs with him last night, but there was no hot and bothered time. He seemed like he wasn't feeling well, but now she realized he was upset.

He's mad about the background file. Why do I keep fucking things up? Lucy thought.

AROUND ELEVEN, her cell phone buzzed with a text message.

WILLIAM: How bored are you right now? Want some lunch company?

LUCY: Sure!

WILLIAM: Noah and I will be there in about a half hour. Any special lunch requests?

LUCY: Surprise me.

WILL and Noah found Lucy and Ree hanging out in the backyard.

"That kid needs a dog!" Noah yelled.

"Yay! Uncle Noah!" Ree yelled as he ran for him. When Ree made contact, Noah fell over in the grass, like he'd just been tackled by the raw might of a five-year-old.

Lucy laughed as Noah fake wrestled with Henry, eventually getting pinned and defeated.

She looked at Will. "See this? This roughhousing is fine, He-man."

"You're no fun either, Lou. He was perfectly fine," Will said defensively.

"Why? What did you do?" Noah asked.

"I swung him around by an ankle and made like I was going to toss him to Hennessy, roughly thirty seconds after I met them. It was not well received," Will admitted.

Noah blinked. "Sometimes, you're not so smart, you know?"

Will lifted his eyebrows.

"Ha! Just kidding, man. Yeah! Dangling the sick kid by a leg is a great idea. Please don't hurt me," Noah said with a completely straight face.

"Hey, Adrian told you it wasn't so smart, too. You didn't threaten him." Lucy laughed.

"Adrian has a much higher pain tolerance. I'd have to *really* hurt him to hurt him. This one, not so much," Will said.

"I'm a lover, not a fighter." Noah winked.

"It's nice to meet you, Noah," Lucy said, still chuckling.

"Likewise, tall, blond, and beautiful," he said with another wink.

Will smacked him upside the head. "Stop it."

"I feel like this is my role in our family. I'm the flirt. It's my job," Noah said defensively, rubbing the back of his head.

Will ignored him. "You look better, Lou. More rested. At least a little more relaxed. Stitches come out soon?"

"Adrian said probably tomorrow. Tuesday night is a little fuzzy. I don't know if I said thanks, but thanks. I'd probably be dead right now if you weren't there."

Will nodded in agreement without trying to soften the blow. "Probably. This is why we don't bet against Sam. Ever. The only one that bets against him is Noah, but he's an idiot. And he never bets about anything important. When Spooky Sam says something, we listen. Lesson learned?"

"Definitely, but it's weird."

Noah's eyebrows climbed his forehead. "You've met Sam, right? Did he scream 'normal' to you?"

Will smacked Noah upside the head again.

"Would you please stop doing that?" Noah bitched.

"I'll stop doing that as soon as you stop being a dumbass," Will promised. "Let's eat. Brought sandwiches."

"You people eat a *lot* of food. Like, *a lot*. I made five pounds of roasted chicken on Friday. I have no idea what happened to it. Adrian dropped it while midnight snacking, I think. The bowl was in the dish drainer on Saturday morning," she said with another laugh as they sat down at the patio table.

Will was watching her closely. "Hmm. Yeah, we do. Adrian and I burn through a lot of calories. How are things going with you here? Do you want to go to a hotel or come to stay with me? You don't have to stay here."

"We can't leave!" Ree said, alarmed.

"We're fine—" Lucy started.

William cut her off, crouching down to meet Ree's eyes. "Henry, I will not let anyone hurt you or Aunt Lucy. You are safe now. Understand? No more worrying about the bad people. No more being scared in the night. No more. You're safe, and you'll stay safe." Even pitching his voice low, Will couldn't stop it from ringing with truth and power.

Henry wrapped his little body around Will in a hug and burst into tears. "I didn't like it. I didn't like it at all. It was scary all the time, and Aunt Lucy cried about the money people, and the people were in the hall. It was loud next door, and the bad people came, and Aunt Lucy was scared, and the people in the bar hurt her, and then I was sick and—" he rambled into Will's shoulder.

"Ree!" Lucy exclaimed as she tried to take Henry from Will.

"He's fine, Lucy," Will grumbled. "We're just gonna sit here for a bit together. Leave us be."

"I don't understand what just happened! He was fine!" she said, shocked.

Well, Lucy, I intentionally asked a question I knew would scare him then followed that fear to all the other fear I could find in him. Now I'm taking the fear from him because he's got enough on his plate right now, William thought.

He wondered how she'd react if he said it, wondered if she knew about Adrian.

Fuck, I wonder how Noah would react if I explained it. Will laughed to himself, confident Noah had no clue.

"He's a kid. Sometimes just the reassurance of being safe helps clear the mind," Will said calmly. "He's good. We're good. How are you?"

Lucy frowned. "I was better before that little meltdown. Ree, are you really okay? Feel okay? Tummy okay?"

And now I'm going to siphon off your fear because you also have enough on your plate. You're welcome, Will thought, enjoying his little internal dialogue.

Henry nodded, wiping his eyes.

Lucy sighed in relief, breathing deeply. "Lots of stress and change and scary stuff. I'm so—" Lucy paused. "I was going to say I'm sorry, but there's really nothing I could have done differently. I'm glad we're out of there. Will is right, Ree. We're okay."

"You know what helps with relieving stress and fear?" Noah asked.

"Wha—?" Lucy started.

"Noah!" Will growled

"Orgasms," Noah said with a cheeky little grin. "I can help!"

And now Noah gets a little bit of fear. It'll be good for him.

"What's an orgasm?" Ree asked through his tears.

Lucy and Will both glared at Noah as he looked around in concern.

"Did anyone else just see a bee? I hate bees. I'm allergic," Noah said.

William laughed. "You're not allergic. You're just a sissy."

AFTER LUNCH, as they were saying goodbye, Will gave Lucy a hug. Quietly, he said, "I meant it. You don't have to stay here. Just say the word, okay?"

Startled by the severe tone of his voice, she said, "Uh. Okay. I think the house will be ready next Thursday. But we're okay. Or I thought so. Are we in Adrian's way? Did he say something about wanting us to go? Should we go elsewhere?"

"He hasn't said anything. I'm talking about you and what you want. Dad and Sam pulled Ree's foundation case. If you don't want to be here, you don't need to be here. Understand?"

"Okay," she said, concerned. "Will, Hennessy has that background file—"

"I know, and I know Adrian wants to read it. He means well. I haven't seen the file. I don't know what's in it. But the fact that Hennessy isn't sharing makes me think you should give Adrian the synopsis and not the detail. I think graphic details of you being hurt would be extremely bad for him."

William watched Lucy closely for some spark of recognition or fear at the thought of Adrian being angry and upset. There was none. She had no idea.

I need to talk to Adrian, Will thought. *It's time for a heart to heart.*

ADRIAN CAME into the house talking. "Hello, pretend dog, how was your day? My day was stupid. Ignorant people kissed my ass and told me childhood hunger wasn't a thing in the US. I didn't take it well."

Lucy met him at the side door as Adrian talked to his feet.

"If there were an actual dog here, I'd be scratching his ears right now," Adrian continued.

"Really? The dog thing again?" she asked.

He scrunched up his face. "Too much?"

Lucy made the "little bit" gesture with her thumb and finger.

"Huh, maybe next week," Adrian said as they walked into the kitchen. "How was your day? Where's Ree?"

"Sleeping in the living room."

"Ah, crap. I didn't wake him, did I?" Adrian peeked around the corner. Henry was still out.

"How was your day?" he asked again, quieter.

"Good. Will and Noah came by for lunch."

Adrian pretended to wince. "There's no excuse for Noah. How often did William threaten to beat the shit out of him if he didn't behave?"

Lucy smiled. "Less than ten times. Highly entertaining. Also, Noah is super scared of bees."

"He's not allergic. Just a sissy," Adrian said as Lucy laughed.

"How was your day?"

"My day really was stupid. I got in an argument with entitled rich people. Not worth talking about. I was glad to be out of the office. You should know, Martha is commenting on my propensity to leave work early or on time. She likes this trend and says you should call her.

"Please don't," Adrian continued with a headshake. "She'll irritate the crap out of me until the end of time about moving."

"Moving?" Lucy asked, surprised.

"I told you. Martha strongly believes I should live in a mansion. For years, I've maintained I do not need a mansion for just me. There is now more than just me in this house. For the last week, she's been leaving real estate listings on my desk," Adrian said.

"Poor you." Lucy laughed. "You're being bullied by your senior citizen assistant."

"Poor me," Adrian agreed, pulling her close and kissing her cheek and then collarbone as Lucy put her arms around his neck.

"Adrian?" Lucy asked.

"Hmm?" he responded, kissing her neck and not noticing the tenseness in her shoulders.

"Are we okay? I mean, is this okay? Us being here? Things got a little more complex, and I know this is your space, and I just want to make sure..." She stopped talking at the sight of Adrian's expression.

Adrian took a step back from her. "Do you want to go? If you want to go—"

"No, I just worry that you wish we would—"

"I don't want you to go, Lucy," Adrian said sharply. "Why are you worried about this?"

"I know you're upset about the file thing and when—" she started.

"I'm not, Lucy. I told you I wasn't upset, and I'm not. I would tell you if I was," Adrian said, annoyed.

"Adrian, you were clearly upset this morning and—"

"Lucy, I wasn't upset about the fucking file," he snapped.

There was a pause as they each stared at the other's feet.

"When Will was here earlier, he said he'd move us out of here if we wanted to go. I thought maybe you told him you wanted us to go," she said quietly, still not looking at him.

Adrian closed his eyes, sighing as he tipped his head back. The rage was chewing at his brain again.

"I'm sorry I snapped at you. I don't want you to go, and I'm not upset about the file. I had a really rough night last night. I didn't sleep well," he explained.

"I don't know why he said what he did, but I suspect William was just being William. He likes you and tends to be slightly protective of people he likes.

"Remember what I said about Hank's integrity? We were all raised with strong morals. The money didn't change that."

Adrian made a gesture between them. "This relationship, mixed with Henry's needs, makes us all a smidge uncomfortable. No one's suggesting we change things, but we all, collectively—the entire family—need you to understand that Ree's help is independent of you and me."

"Okay," Lucy choked out over the lump in her throat.

"Are you crying?" Adrian asked quietly.

"I don't know. Yeah. I think so," she said, trying to laugh at her stupid emotions.

"Are you crying because I'm an asshole?"

Lucy let out a snotty snort, head still hanging. "Your definition of an asshole is much different than mine."

"Am I allowed to hug you now, or are we still fighting?"

She chuckled through her tears. "Again, very different definitions of fighting. And I don't know why you're asking permission from *me*. You're the one that backed away this time."

Lucy's head tucked back into its spot on Adrian's shoulder, facing his neck, as Adrian's arms wrapped around her.

"I'm sorry," he breathed. "I'm sorry, Lucy. I did *not* make that easy. I didn't even let you finish your sentence. I'm sorry. The thought of you going away makes me feel ill."

"There are ribeye steaks and baked potatoes and broccoli salad with craisins for dinner," she offered. "You get to grill meat again."

"Well, that makes me feel better. I like grilled meats. Is there a lot of this feast?" he asked.

"Enough for six people, so I expect leftovers to be gone tomorrow."

"You're catching on quick!" Adrian chuckled, resting his forehead on her shoulder. "I'm so tired."

"I'll sleep downstairs tonight, so you get some..." Lucy stopped talking as Adrian's arms tightened around her.

"You know what helps with bad sleep?" he asked.

Lucy could hear the smile in his voice. "Hmm?"

"Hot and bothered time," Adrian said, starting to kiss her neck.

"Shocking," she said with a laugh, sucking on an earlobe.

"I'm a doctor. I know these things," he muttered as their kiss started and the happy energy picked up.

"Are you kissing?!" Henry asked from the doorway.

"Gah! We've been caught by a stealthy Ree." Adrian laughed.

"Is it okay if we kiss sometimes?" Adrian squatted down to catch Henry's running leap of a hug.

Henry clapped his hands excitedly. "Yes!"

"What would you have done if he said no?" Lucy grinned.

"I would have negotiated for toys and books," Adrian said without pause.

"Oh, man!" Ree sighed, realizing he missed an opportunity.

"Don't sweat it, Buddy. I gotcha covered." Adrian laughed.

12

"There. Done," Adrian said, pulling the last stitch out of Lucy's face on Tuesday morning. "Give it a few months, and there won't even be a scar. That ENT did a nice job. I approve."

"I'll say it again. You're a handy guy to have around, Adrian." Lucy grinned.

"I am very confident the lab will reschedule him to later today if I ask, and then I can go with you," Adrian said.

"We'll be fine. You're sending security guards with us," Lucy grumbled.

"Let's be clear. *Hennessy* is sending security guards with you. *I* just agree with it. Look at it this way. You have a chauffeured car."

"There are going to be people with guns following us around," Lucy said, looking decidedly uncomfortable.

"The guns aren't going into the hospital. We've agreed on that. So there will be people with tactical knives and tasers there with you. And ask, but I don't think they're going to follow and lurk over you. I think the goal is to be inconspicuous. I don't think they're trying to hide, but I don't think they're trying to be obvious, either. Hennessy's hunting. You're baiting the trap."

"You really think he's actively looking for them? What's he going to do if he finds them?"

"I know he's actively looking for them. I think his actions will depend on what they're doing when he finds them." Adrian met her gaze then looked at Ree.

Okay, Lucy thought. *We'll talk about this later.*

"Ree, be a good boy. I'll see you this afternoon," Adrian said, giving Ree a kiss on the forehead.

"I will. Bye, Adrian," Ree said, dancing in place.

"Lucy, be a good girl. I'll see you this afternoon," Adrian said, giving Lucy a grin and a kiss on the forehead.

She swatted at him, laughing.

"You're leaving the house for the first time in a week. Don't talk to strangers. Don't get lost. It's okay to ask for directions," he rambled off, still laughing. "Do you have your cards? Everything you need? I'm weirdly nervous about this."

"Yes, I'm all set. We're even going to Walmart after the hospital."

"GOD FORBID!" Adrian yelled. "You know, Lucy, people spend money there. Are you going to be okay?"

"I'll manage." She laughed at Ree's giggles.

"Okay, buy me something pretty," Adrian said with a laugh as he headed out the door.

"Eat up, Sir Henry! We have to get going soon, too," Lucy directed.

"Okay," Henry said around a bite of pancake. "Aunt Lucy?"

"Henry?"

"I'm happy. Are you happy?"

Lucy's heart warmed at that. "Yes, I am," she said, giving him a hug.

"Okay. One more time, just for fun," Joann, the security consultant, said.

"The car will be in the fourth row from the left outside the main entrance. If I have to exit in a hurry, head that way. You'll intercept us.

If I see one of the bad people, I hit the panic button and walk in the opposite direction of him. You'll be within five hundred feet of us at all times," Lucy recited.

"Henry?" Joann asked.

"I hold Aunt Lucy's hand and look both ways when crossing. If I see the bad men, I point and scream 'FIRE' as loud as I can so that everyone looks at me."

Joann nodded.

"Why do I scream 'fire' and not 'help?'" Henry asked.

"People are more prone to react to 'fire.' They don't want to get involved in anyone's personal situation that might be tied up in 'help.' But 'fire' affects everyone, so people look," Joann explained. "That's the theory, anyways."

"Wow," Lucy muttered. That made her sad.

"I know," Joann responded. "It doesn't matter if people look, though. It will startle the bad people, Henry. And we'll be looking."

"Henry, my man! How's life?" A hospital orderly on his way out the door bumped fists with Henry as they walked through the main entrance.

"Life's rockin', Gerald. Rockin'!" Henry exclaimed.

Lucy looked at Henry in surprise. He grinned up at her. "Adrian has lots of friends." He giggled gleefully, which made Lucy smile as he directed her toward the lab.

"I know where it is!" he said. "I know my way around. Adrian showed me."

Walking through the halls, random people greeted Henry and looked at Lucy appraisingly. She wasn't sure why, but Lucy wanted to blush every last time.

After signing him into the lab, the desk clerk told Lucy it'd be a short wait, and they sat down.

"I didn't grab a book to bring with us, buddy. I'm sorry," she said.

"We have to take our books back to Ms. Leti," Henry reminded her.

"I forgot about that," Lucy admitted, wondering if they'd be taking the books back or if someone else would. The library branch wasn't in the worst part of town, but it wasn't great, either. They could return the books at a different location, but Leti had been kind to them—one of the few people to contribute to Henry's Go Fund Me. Lucy would like to say goodbye.

At that moment, it clicked in Lucy's brain. She wasn't going back to their old life. Regardless of what happened with Adrian, she was confident they'd never be in another apartment where the people next door sold drugs. They were going to exhaust all possible treatment options for Henry. She wasn't going to watch his beautiful spirit wither because of money. They were going to find a way forward and have a real life. Maybe even a home.

Wrapped up in her thoughts, she started when Henry stood up. "Come on, Aunt Lucy, they're calling us."

Lucy hopped to her feet, following Henry to the door and back into the room.

As the technician sat Henry down, another technician stuck his head in the room. "Hi, Henry!" he called.

"Hi, Jose!" Henry answered.

"You know who this is, right, Jackie?" Jose said to the middle-aged woman setting up Henry's blood draw. "Dr. Adrian's boy," he said with a laugh, heading on his way.

Jackie's eyebrows climbed her forehead.

"Oh, no. No. Adrian's not his—" Lucy started.

"Psh. Girl, shut it. I know that's not what he meant. No. The gossip mill is all a buzz about our Beloved—pun intended—Dr. Adrian shacking up with some woman and her sick kiddo." She was clearly biting back laughter at the stunned expression on Lucy's face.

"Apparently, he was here on Friday, doing Dr. Adrian things, kiddo in tow, introducing him around like a proud papa. Every last person that knows this kid is eyeballing you with either wonder or envy." Jackie was openly laughing now.

"That one's been at the very tippy-top of the most eligible list for *years*. Even before the money hit with the super-freak brother. He has a secret fan club—and, yes, the only one it's a secret from is *him*."

Lucy's mouth was hanging open. *Holy fuck. What do I say?!*

Henry was giggling like a maniac. "Uncle Sam's not freaky!"

"Don't you tell him I said that." She laughed. "Don't want to get on Uncle Sam's bad side. *Uncle* Sam, even. This is just too sweet!"

Lucy blushed red as Jackie continued to laugh at her discomfort. "Henry and I were just staying in the extra bedrooms."

Jackie snorted. "Yeah, okay. We'll pretend like *Uncle Sam* doesn't own like eighty-five hotels and half the greater Chicago area. 'You just needed a place to stay.' If you aren't snuggling with him, you should be."

"They were kissing yesterday," Henry reported. "Aunt Lucy, why are you all red?"

Lucy started laughing and couldn't stop. "Whatever," she said eventually. "I don't work here."

"Yeah, that's the right outlook! Now give me the goods on the bruising, so I have truly juicy gossip. No way Dr. Adrian had a hand in that."

"No, nope, he did not. Squash that shit if it comes up," Lucy instructed.

"Psh," Jackie said again. "No one would dare to think it. So, what happened?"

"So, not this just past Saturday, but the Saturday before, I was at Northwestern Memorial in the billing department..." Lucy began.

"...then Will broke his kneecap and knocked him out. The cops came. I was a mess."

"Wait now, which one is Will? There are a lot of those boys."

"Blond, shoulders as wide as he is tall, looks like He-man," Lucy clarified.

"Mmm. That one's my favorite. Strong, silent type!"

Lucy laughed. "We ended up back at Northwestern to get my nose set and stitched and then back to Adrian's house to get Ree. I think I literally fell asleep at the kitchen table."

"She did!" Henry confirmed. "Adrian caught her before she fell out of her chair."

Jackie laughed and clapped. "It's *perfect.*"

Lucy shrugged. "I've done a lot of sleeping in the last week. Henry's been hanging out with Adrian. He took the stitches out of my face this morning."

"I love this story," Jackie said, putting a Band-Aid on Henry's little arm. "It's just so Dr. Adrian."

As Lucy and Henry headed for the door, Jackie followed behind Lucy. "Girl, you need to crawl in that man's bed and not get back out. Looking all ashamed and embarrassed. What's wrong with you!" she muttered. "Wrap them long-ass legs around him and go for a ride. Move your ass into that man's house and stay there. He's *way* too good of a person to not be married with like fifteen kids. Get on that. Better gossip by Friday, *Aunt Lucy.*"

AFTER A STOP FOR LUNCH, Ree and Lucy spent a long time in Walmart, replacing things left behind at the apartment. Lucy bought some makeup, and Ree got bath fizzes. An alarming number of toys were acquired, along with new pajamas for Henry and new stretchy pants for Lucy. Henry selected a Gonzo t-shirt for Adrian. Lucy opted for a tray of cupcakes.

As they got back into the car, the two security consultants were laughing.

"What?"

"I don't know how to break this to you, Lucy," Joann said. "But rich people don't shop at Walmart or buy Suave."

Lucy blushed as she shrugged. "I'm not rich."

"You clearly have *no idea* how much money I'm paid per hour, and there are four of us following you around." Joann continued to laugh.

"That wasn't my doing," Lucy said, slightly defensive.

"No, it was—" Joann paused to correct her language in front of Ree, "freaking HENNESSY, which just makes it *that much* better. The only way that gets better is if it's the Reaper. Who, by the way, rolled our asses yesterday because you were in the backyard unaccompanied. The Reap is batshit crazy about protecting his ladies. I love this gig."

ADRIAN CAME into the house talking to the dog again. "Hello, pretend dog, how was your day? My day was stupid again. Ignorant people kissed my ass and told me dental care was not important for a person's long-term health and wellbeing. Rich people suck."

Lucy met him at the side door again, laughing.

"If there were an actual dog here, I'd be scratching her ears right now," Adrian continued.

"Is this going to be a daily thing?" she asked.

He grinned. "I figure if I keep it up, you'll let me get a dog by the weekend."

"It's your house," she reminded him. "If you want a dog so bad, why don't you have a dog?"

"Historically, I've not been home enough throughout the day to take care of a dog. I'd be getting a dog for it to be alone all day and then sit in the basement and watch me workout every night. Not fair to the dog. But there's a little kid, now. Little kids need a dog!"

"Noah said the same thing when he walked into the backyard on Monday," Lucy admitted.

"Speaking of little kids, is he sleeping again?" Adrian asked as they walked into the kitchen.

Lucy nodded.

"How did bloodwork go? No problems, right?"

"Oh no, you tell me about your day first, and then I'll tell you about bloodwork. Everything went fine, but every last woman in the hospital gave me the stink eye."

"Really?" he asked, laughing. "My day really was stupid. I got in an argument with entitled rich people again. Same story daily."

"Poor you." Lucy laughed at the repetition from the day before.

"Poor me." Adrian grinned as he kissed her. "What happened at the hospital?"

"I totally spilled the dirt on us, and you have a secret fan club." She laughed.

"It's not a secret. They leave various bits of undergarments in my office, which makes me *extremely* uncomfortable," he said, chuckling as Lucy shook with laughter.

"Poor you," she said again.

"Poor me," he agreed again.

The next kiss got more serious. The happy energy was mixing with Adrian's hormones in new and exciting ways. It zinged around his body in response to Lucy. It craved her, zapping to wherever skin met.

Adrian had no intention at all of taking this little make-out session further. Henry was sleeping in the next room. It was four thirty in the afternoon. This was not going any farther; he was not getting a hard-on. He shut his baser instincts down.

Not happening, he told his body.

The energy surged anew, in previously unvisited areas.

Not happening, he told the energy.

Then Lucy nibbled his ear. Adrian was not prepared for the wave of raw lust. The energy, the power, tried to take over. As Adrian warred with his inner self, his body got confused. He started to lose control.

Adrian stepped back, pulling Lucy's arms from around him. "Okay, need a time-out," he gasped.

"Uh, yeah," Lucy mumbled.

Okay, Jackie. I am aligned. I will crawl into his bed and stay there. Sounds good. Let's do that. Right now, she thought.

It must have shown on her face.

Adrian gave her a sheepish smile. "There's a small, impressionable child asleep in the other room. It's not even dinner time."

"Yeah," Lucy said, nodding, not looking at him. Her cheeks burned with embarrassment.

"I didn't mean for that—" he started.

"Later?" she asked.

"Later," he agreed, eyes flashing with heat. "Remind me to never again make fun of Jake and Matty."

"Huh?" she asked.

"Okay, I will absolutely still make fun of them, but not as much." He laughed as he started telling her the story.

Ree woke up to the sound of Aunt Lucy laughing hysterically.

"NOTHING is sacred to you people. NOTHING!" She cackled.

"They were in an office with intentionally thin walls with no sound-blocking insulation! They spend all day, every day throwing tennis balls at the walls to irritate each other. Sometimes Sam attends meetings in Jake's office without leaving his desk!" Adrian laughed.

Ree wandered into the kitchen, still waking up. "Uncle Jake has a pool table in his office."

"OH MY GOD!" Lucy yelled, laughing again.

13

*W*illiam was making hamburger patties when his doorbell rang on Wednesday night.

"I need to know what you love, Will," Sam said as the door opened.

Will sighed. Sam had been asking this question every hour on the hour since Sunday night. Including in the middle of the night.

"Sam, I swear to God. I would tell you if I understood what you were after. I need a better question to help," Will said. Again.

"I need to know. I need it, Will. I can't think straight until I know. I don't know why. It's imperative, and I need to know. It's just you and me here. Can you tell me now? I won't tell anyone. I just need to know," Sam begged.

"When did you last eat, Sam?" Will asked, looking at his little brother. His eyes were sunken. "When did you last sleep?"

Distracted, Sam had to think for a minute. "I had macaroni and cheese for lunch when we had lunch."

"That was Monday, Sam. Come on. I'm making hamburgers," Will said gently. "We'll eat and try to figure out what you need to know."

"I don't think I can eat them anymore," Sam replied, eyes glassy.

That startled William. Sam usually ate with him, ate his food. "Why?"

"It tastes like fear, even when you put Fear away. I can still taste it now. It didn't use to be like this." Confusion and frustration were apparent in Sam's voice.

"Since Jake moved out?" Will asked.

"Before that. It started getting worse before that but got much worse after he moved out and even worse after I answered Matty's call. I can't find the girl now. Even in dreams, I can't find her. She has to pull me to her. I can't go to her. Something's wrong with it."

"Wrong with what, Sam? What is there something wrong with? Come on, let's sit down. We'll talk through it together, okay?"

Will and Sam didn't talk about weird shit. He was surprised that Sam knew about the fear. This was the first one-on-one conversation they'd ever had about the girl.

Hank and Darla thought the girl wasn't real, that she was a figment of Sam's weird brain, like it made up a dream friend for Sam to talk to in the nightmares.

But, Will had no doubt whatsoever that the girl was real. He had looked for violet-eyed girls and Wile E. Coyote in every bar he'd ever been in, across the globe.

The terror radiating off Sam was tangible to William. He tried to pull it away from Sam and into himself but couldn't. He'd never been able to help Sam, even as kids.

"You'll talk with me about this? It doesn't give you the creeps?" Sam asked.

Will's eyebrows shot up. "Does it give you the creeps?"

"Holy God, yes. Daily," Sam admitted.

Will shrugged. "Me, too. We'll be fine. What is something wrong with Sam? Go back to that."

"With me. With whatever this is with me. I can't stay in one time anymore. I don't always know when it is or where I am. I used to be able to stay. I could force it to stay in one time. But now there's more, and I can't make it stop. Like I'm in a lot of times at once, and none of it makes sense," Sam whispered.

"Can you eat in the other times?" Will asked.

Sam shook his head. "My body's not there. I'm just visiting."

"Are you hungry?" Will asked.

"I'm so hungry. So tired. But I can't find the girl, and everyone suffocates, Will. I can't rest because everyone dies."

Holy fuck. I thought my lot in life was hard. I spent all this time worrying about Adrian. Fuck. Poor Sam, William thought.

"Can you eat food that you make, Sam?"

"Not anymore. It tastes like terror, pain, and hunger. Jake's food tastes like Matty's campfire. Ethan's food isn't happy anymore. Adrian's food is angry—"

"Still angry? Even with Lucy there?" Will interrupted.

Sam paused. "I don't know."

Holy God in Heaven, how do I help him? Terror and Pain and Hunger and suffocating dreams. How is he still sane?

"Okay. Mom? Dad? Beth? Luke? Matthew?" Will asked.

"Luke won't help. He won't answer my questions, either," Sam said, eyes sad again.

"Sam, I know Luke would cook for you. Have you asked him?"

Sam sighed. "I make him wary. He's worried people are going to hurt me. I don't know why. He avoids me. It's why I moved seats at dinner. I wanted to talk to him.

"Matthew—no. He is afraid of me. Afraid of himself. Afraid of everything. Can you do that thing?" Sam asked.

Will was puzzled. "I don't feel fear from him, Sam. I'll see if I can find it, okay?"

Sam nodded. "Beth's heart hurts. Dad is terrified for Mom. Mom's love tastes like medicine. Do you know what's wrong with Mom?"

Will sighed. "I was going to ask you that. Okay. If I wore gloves while making your food, and thought of nothing but what I love in life, do you think you could eat? Can we try it?"

"Okay. Thank you, William." Sam sounded defeated.

Usually so self-assured, confident of what should and should not happen, seeing Sam vulnerable and lost made Will more than a little afraid for the future.

Twenty minutes later, Will watched as Sam literally gagged on his burger.

"The cow was sick. The cow was sick and suffering. They didn't treat it. Is this our meat?"

William nodded.

"Do you still have the packaging? We have to find this farm. It was horrible. Horrible pain. Oh God." Sam ran to the bathroom.

SAM COULDN'T EAT after that.

"Stay here tonight. Stay with me. Maybe it'll be easier with me here," Will said.

Sam nodded. "William, what do you love? It might help."

William sighed. "I love Mom. I love Dad—"

"*No.* It's a *what*, not a *who*. *What* do you love?" Sam insisted.

"I love my family. I love my friends. I love dogs. Warm sun on my face. Italian Beef sandwiches. My country. My home..."

Will stopped listing things after Sam nodded off. Twenty minutes later, when his cell phone vibrated, Will headed into the back bedroom, as far as he could get from Sam. He didn't want to disturb the rest that was so badly needed.

"Hello, love," he said quietly.

"Woo, why are we whispering?" Pip whispered back.

Will sighed. "Sam is sleeping on the couch. I don't want to wake him."

"Did he eat with you?" she asked, still quiet because he was whispering.

"No, I made burgers tonight. I wasn't expecting him. The cow was in too much pain. It fucked him over."

"What about fruits and vegetables? Organic fruits and veggies? No pesticides or anything. No animal life involved. He could even eat them raw," she suggested.

"I tried that last week. Made vegan pasta. He could taste the decay in the soil. Over the years, he's actually had an easier time with meat and grains than fruits and veggies."

"Did he figure out what you love?"

"No, I don't know what to do with that," he admitted. "I keep thinking it's you, but he keeps telling me it's a what, not a who."

SAM FELL asleep on William's couch, listening to the sound of Will's calm voice.

He dreamed of the house with ever-changing views.

Thinking about Will's question of eating in other times, Sam went to see if there was food in the kitchen. It never occurred to him to look before. He had never tried eating in other times, either, but didn't think he could.

There was no food in the kitchen.

It's a dream. Can I put food in the kitchen? Sam wondered, thinking about peanut butter and jelly.

No such luck.

There was a sound from the living room. There had never been a sound in this dream before. Sam went to go look.

The girl was standing in the middle of the room, looking confused. When she saw him, she ran for him, hugging him tightly.

She couldn't talk. Had never been able to speak. But, when she touched him, her thoughts were clear.

"Where are we?" she asked, amazed.

"The house with the changing views. How are you here?" Sam asked.

"I don't know. I was in the clearing, trying to find you. Then I heard love call, and I was here," she said. *"You are sick?"*

"Hungry. Tired. I think I'm broken now. I think I went to Matilda when she called, and now I'm broken."

She shook her head. *"No. You woke more. More of you is awake. Not all of you, not yet. Not even half. But more of you. You need a tether. An anchor. Like the clearing for me. You need that."*

"How do I make that?" he asked.

She thought about it, brow furrowed. *"I don't know. I will ask Mama. But she and I are of Life. We tether to Earth. You are of Time, constantly moving. I don't know how to tether time. I don't know if you can."*

"Why can't I eat? Even raw vegetables? It makes me sick," Sam asked, talking quickly. Sometimes dreams with the girl ended abruptly.

She sighed and nodded. *"For me, too. There is too much power. You have to release it."*

"How?" he asked.

Her pale violet eyes shone with tears.

"I will find you," he promised. "Can you tell me where you are? Outside the clearing, can you tell me?"

"I don't have the knowledge, Sam. It doesn't come with me when Walking. The wards take it from me."

"Why?" he asked.

"We are not the only ones to Walk, Sam. I am vulnerable without you," she explained, not for the first time.

He nodded, bending to touch his forehead to hers. "I will find you."

Shifting herself up just a little more, she kissed his lips.

Typically, at this point, Sam woke up abruptly, like the contact couldn't be sustained in the dream. This time, thunder cracked and lightning flashed outside the window of the house with ever-changing views.

They both sighed in relief as some of the power eating at each of them was released.

The girl gasped. *"How did that happen?! The power doesn't work like that when Walking! Where are we?! Quick, Sam,"* she said, grabbing his head again, slamming her lips against his in a deep kiss as the whole house shook around them, and the storm outside exploded.

Sam woke up, panting for breath, before the kiss ended. The morning sun was streaming in William's living room windows. His head was clear for the first time in over a week. He headed for the fridge immediately.

ON THURSDAY AFTERNOON, Darla had lunch at Claire Dermot's home. While they'd always been friendly, they were not close friends. So Darla was surprised when Claire called and asked for a lunch date. Darla agreed, suggesting a restaurant between their respective homes. Claire said she'd prefer to play host if Darla wouldn't mind coming for a visit.

Pulling up into the mansion driveway, Darla mentally rolled her eyes, wondering if they were going to eat cucumber sandwiches served by a butler. Thomas Dermot came from old money and was used to the trappings of it. He was also a dear friend of Hank's and one of Sam's earliest investors. Tom and Claire were good people, but Darla still mentally rolled her eyes at the manicured grounds as she got out of the Buick she drove herself around in.

As Darla walked to the front door, Claire came out to meet her with a hug.

"Thank you so much for coming all this way, Darla. I know this must seem odd, but I wanted us to be able to talk," Claire said as they walked into the house. "I've made some vegetable soup and paninis. Is that okay? We could also order in."

"Claire, I didn't realize you cooked! It sounds wonderful," Darla said, surprised as they walked into a blended kitchen and dining space.

"I love to cook. I have a garden in the summer and a greenhouse throughout the year. If I had my way, we'd live on a farm. But here we are, just Tom and me in this stupid house." Claire laughed.

Darla smiled. "You're full of surprises today. I always thought you enjoyed this lifestyle."

"I love my husband, and this comes with him. There are worse burdens in life," Claire grinned. "But Tom and I have always been a bit envious of you and Hank. All those kids running around, loud and chaotic. So much happy energy, always. You've always brought us joy. How is everyone? Is Jake engaged yet? I met his little sprite of a girl-friend at that fundraiser. So much fire and love."

"They got engaged a little over a week ago," Darla said with a smile. "Adrian is seeing someone. The rest of the herd is unchanged—loud, chaotic, and mostly happy. Sam is struggling a bit, as he does every now and then. How are you? To what do I owe the pleasure of this lunch date?"

After serving soup, Claire sat next to Darla rather than on the other side of the table. Taking Darla's hand, Claire asked, "May I be direct, Darla? I know we're not close, but I've always loved you and yours."

"Claire, of course. You and Tom have always been family to us as well. What's wrong?" Darla gave up on trying to set her expectations for lunch. This was not at all what she had anticipated. She'd roll with it.

Claire took a deep breath. "Where is the cancer, Darla? Are they treating it?"

Darla blinked.

"I know you're sick. I can see it in your energy. I want to offer help if I can," Claire explained.

"Ah, I'm not sure how you know that. I'd like to understand that better, as Hank and I haven't told a soul. Not even the kids know," Darla said, tone sharper than she intended.

Claire sighed. "I suspect most of your children know you're sick, Darla. But I'll explain. You'll think I'm nuts, but I'm being serious.

"There is energy in living things. Surely, we agree on that. Living things power their energy sources with food and water and rest. It's what makes us alive. We talk about burning calories when working out, burning fuel for energy. With me so far?"

Darla nodded. "That doesn't seem controversial."

Claire grinned. "Good. Now we get to the part that will make you think I'm a lunatic."

Darla laughed, preparing for something genuinely bizarre.

"There are some people that can see life energy. It's typically genetic. When I try, I can see your life energy. I can see the energy you share with Hank and the love that binds you.

"Your energy has always shown bright and clear. The night of the fundraiser where I met Jake's fiancé, your energy was duller than normal. It's more diminished now. You're sick. I don't think you're dying, but you're seriously ill. That distinction usually means cancer."

Darla sat in stunned silence for a moment. She had no idea what to say or do.

"I would not share this information with anyone, especially your children, Darla. As I said, I'd like to offer help if I can," Claire said, trying to alleviate concern.

After processing things for a moment, Darla decided that she'd like to talk about this with someone other than Hank. The timing hadn't been right to tell the kids. She'd just gotten the confirmed diagnosis a week ago. Matty was just getting out of the hospital. "I have stage three breast cancer."

Claire's eyes flashed with sadness but not pity. Darla was grateful for that.

"They're treating it?" Claire asked.

"Yes, of course. It has not spread. They're doing some treatment now, trying to shrink the tumor before doing surgery."

Claire nodded. "Good. Very good. Excellent news. Better than I had hoped. I'm so glad they're treating it." She sighed in relief.

"Me, too," Darla said. "But Claire, I'm not sure how you think you can help with this, even if you *can* see whatever life energy you're talking about."

"Oh. Yes. First, I'm sorry. I'm sorry, Darla. I'm sorry you're going through this. I've never known you to exude anything but love, light, and happiness."

Claire paused to take a deep breath, eyes misty. "Your children are beautiful; each one makes this world a better place, as you and Hank do. I wish you didn't have to go through this."

"Thank you, Claire," Darla choked out, giving her hand a squeeze. "I don't know how I'm going to tell the kids."

Claire nodded as they each took a moment to gather themselves.

"Okay, on to the help," Claire said briskly. "I can see the energy. Everyone in my circle can. Some of us can redistribute existing energy within the same person. Like, if you broke a bone, some of us might be able to help the break heal faster by focusing your energy at that spot. Some of us can move energy between people.

"I have a cousin in Dallas that can move energy between people. I've talked with her. She's willing to talk to you if you're willing to try it. Ava is powerful; she actually has too much energy. Sharing it with others helps her."

"You have a cousin that gives away her life energy? She wants to die young?" Darla almost laughed. Almost.

"Oh. Ha! No, the energy comes back. Just like you wake up refreshed from a good nap or feel better after eating when you're truly starving. Think of it as a rechargeable battery. I'm like an AA battery. Ava's like a car battery," Claire explained.

"How does this happen? How does she move it around?" Darla asked.

"That's a better question for her. But, conceptually, she'd help you maintain healthy energy levels so your body can withstand the cancer treatment. With some cancers, the treatment is worse than the disease. It weakens the body, weakens your immune system. Makes it harder for your body to keep doing its thing. The energy boost from standing a circle with Ava can help even that out. Rejuvenate you.

"You can go down and have lunch with her, like this. She and her husband run a restaurant," Claire said. "Regardless of where you decide to go with this, you and Hank would like Ava and Clyde. She can demonstrate. Explain better than me. I can't do it, and it's awkward to explain with words."

"Can I think about it? Get Hank's opinion? Would you mind if I shared this with him?" Darla asked.

Claire waved a hand. "Not at all. Please do. Tom and I would love to have dinner with you and Hank if you want to talk about it again. I know it must seem strange. But I need to tell you a couple more things about this, okay?"

Darla nodded.

"It would be best if you didn't discuss this with anyone outside your immediate family, and not just because they'll look at you like you're goofy. We're talking about energy and power and life. Think what you will of this, but some people would like access to that kind of thing. A person can feed off others.

"I would strongly caution you to *not* pursue this with anyone other than Ava. There are people here in Chicago that can do what Ava does. I would not trust them to help, even if you were paying them serious money. Okay?"

"Claire, I wouldn't even know who to ask about this," Darla said, again almost laughing.

"That's what I'm saying. Don't ask anyone about this outside your immediate family unless you trust them with your life. Because that's what we're talking about. Done wrong, this can weaken you, make treatment harder. Done right, well. Ah. Let's talk about that. But do you understand? Don't ask anyone you don't trust. Okay?"

Darla nodded again.

"Ah, okay. So. I'm an AA battery. I can't do much else but see the energy and maybe help my garden grow a bit more. Ava holds life. She can see it, move it within, move it outside, create new energy, and so on. She is very powerful in our crowd. Her abilities are highly coveted. Her power is some of the strongest around.

"Darla, uh, just hear me out on this. It's a little awkward on both sides because I don't know what you know, but I'm guessing it's not much.

"If Ava's like a car battery, most of your kids are like Niagara Falls. Forces of nature on a different scale. They don't seem to know it, for the most part. One of them understands a little bit, but even then, I don't think much. If you were to bring a kid or two with you, and their power is as I think it is, she may be able to just kill the cancer, like it was never there."

Darla opened her mouth to speak.

"Wait. Not yet. Let me finish," Claire said. "Niagara Falls. Most of them. Uh. Jake's Matilda. She is like the sun. Fire. Light. She absolutely radiates energy. Her life energy is the brightest I've ever seen or heard about. Even knowing your kids. And I don't think any of your kids fall on the usual scale of power. If you're going to take her to Ava, I need to warn Ava first."

Claire paused, taking a deep breath.

Darla stared at her. "And Sam?"

Claire nodded. "Yes, that's where I'm going with this. Don't take Sam. I don't know how to classify him. I can't even see his life energy."

"You think Sam is not alive?"

"No, I think Sam doesn't allow me to see his energy. He wields energy, tosses it around, speaks with it. The night of the fundraiser, he pulsed giant waves of it for hours. I don't think he knows what he's doing when he does it. But you know how his voice booms and echoes sometimes, even when he's talking softly? I'm talking about that. If Ava is a car battery, your other kids are Niagara Falls, and Matilda is the fire of the sun. Sam is gravity, the rotation of all the planets, and the power of time, combined."

They were quiet for a moment.

"I could have it wrong," Claire admitted. "Absolutely wrong. I don't see any of the kids clearly. Wherever they fall on the power scale, they're all stronger than me, without question. They also have more juice than Ava because I can see her clearly. They might not have a capability, but they have the raw power. Matilda is a different scale than the others. I think she's elemental, not life energy.

"Sam is something else entirely. He's dangerous when he chooses to be. Ava won't be able to hold that much power, even if he pushes it at a trickle. Don't get in a circle with him for healing. Ava can't hold that circle. It'll blow. And it isn't always clear that he has that kind of power. She might not notice throughout a conversation. He hides it very well when he chooses to."

14

The week passed quickly for Adrian and Lucy. By Friday morning, things were almost starting to feel routine. After bending to give Lucy a quick kiss, Adrian sat down next to Henry in the hospital lab as they waited for bloodwork.

"Woo, how far down the waiting list are we?" he asked. "I'm starving."

"You're always hungry!" Henry laughed.

"It's true. I am. You will be too when you're older. What do you want to eat?" Adrian asked Henry.

"When do you have to be back?" Lucy asked.

"One. It's eleven fifteen. Depending on how long this takes, we can go out."

"I like the cafeteria." Henry frowned.

Adrian shrugged. "We can stay here. It doesn't matter to me. Not exactly fine dining, though. Pizza Friday!"

When they were called back for the draw, Adrian followed.

"Gah! Be gentle, Jackie. Gentle. No more gossip, for the love of God." Adrian laughed. "If one more person collapses in my arms yelling, 'Dr. Adrian, you're my hero,' I'm going to cry."

"Bahahaha! Really?" Lucy chuckled.

"It's extremely awkward. Especially when I don't expect it. I failed to catch Jose earlier. He got dumped on his ass."

"He deserved it. He makes a terrible damsel." Jackie grinned.

"I thought you were off on Fridays?" Adrian asked.

"I usually am," she said with a snarky smile. "I traded days just so I could see your pretty-boy face. Figured you'd be down here with Miss Sweetie Pie."

"Jackie, please get them to stop leaving things in my office. Please? I'll fund your retirement," Adrian offered. "I changed the lock and everything."

"No, that's not going to help," Jackie said, shaking her head. "There are women that work in building services."

"How do I make it stop?" Adrian whined.

"Get married," she said without missing a beat.

"Woo, let's go out to eat." Lucy laughed.

"Now, when we walk into the house, what do you say to the dog, Ree?" Adrian coached on Sunday evening.

"ROSCOOOOE!" Ree yelled.

"Just like that. Perfect," Adrian complimented him.

"How come the security consultants get the night off when we come here? They've been carting my butt around all week," Lucy complained. "You don't need security consultants? Just me?"

"William and Hennessy are in that house, Lucinda. They count," Adrian said with faux terseness.

"Lucinda, even?" Lucy smirked.

"I love it." Adrian laughed. "I like to pull it out randomly."

"This is a giant driveway. It takes up half the yard," Lucy observed.

"I have eight siblings and a Hennessy. Those cars have to go somewhere," Adrian replied.

"True," she acknowledged.

"Why are we still sitting in the car?" Adrian asked.

"I'm nervous," Lucy admitted.

"Really? Why? You've met most of these people before," Adrian reminded her.

She shrugged. "What if they don't like me?"

"Oh. Okay. Get out of the car, Lucinda," Adrian said, laughing again as he opened the door for Ree. "You come with a ready-made grandchild. Darla will disembowel anyone that gives you a hard time."

Lucy could hear the dog's claws scrambling on the tile as the front door opened. A giant, fat rottweiler ran around the hallway corner.

"Roscoooe!" crowed Ree. The dog immediately flopped on his back and slid the rest of the way to them.

Lucy grinned at the dog antics as Darla came bustling around the corner from another room. "Ah! There's my favorite boy!" she called.

"Aww, thanks, Mom!" Adrian said. "I've always been the favorite," he explained to Lucy. The effect was somewhat diminished when Darla reached up and smacked his head.

"Shut it. Beth is my favorite, and you all know it," Darla said unrepentantly.

"Yes, but your favorite son is me," Adrian said as he kissed the top of her head.

Darla narrowed her eyes. "I have to think about that. It might depend on the day with the boys."

"I'm a doctor. I showed up to Sunday dinner with a woman and a small child," Adrian continued lobbying.

"It's true," Darla said, hugging Lucy. "You probably win today. Let's see how dinner goes."

"We're just missing Ethan and Sam. They're on their way. Come on, Lucy." Darla took her hand, pulling her toward the hallway.

Lucy followed along as Darla led her into a giant room. "This is, aptly named, the Big Room," Adrian explained. "It seats all of us with lots of room to spare."

"Too much room!" Darla groused.

The older gentleman Lucy vaguely recalled from the day she met Adrian was walking toward her. He walked right by her offered handshake to pull her into a hug. "How are you feeling, sweetheart? You've

healed well. Let me see you in the light. No, that scar won't stay. I'm
so glad."

"Yeah, okay. Right to 'sweetheart.' Lucy, this is my dad, Hank."
Adrian rolled his eyes.

"Oh." Hank looked sheepish. "I forgot that part. Hi, Lucy."

"Hi." She laughed. "It's so nice to meet you."

Henry was running around the room, jumping into laps to get hugs
and kisses.

"You know, kid, you're way too shy." Noah laughed.

"Okay! Speed introductions," Beth yelled. "Let's do this! Oldest to
youngest, you got this, Lucy. Ree already knows everyone because we
smother little kids with affection. It's fine."

"You know that one," Beth said, gesturing at William.

"You really, really, ahem, know that one," she continued, gesturing
at Adrian.

"Jake! Matilda! You've heard the stories." Beth laughed as Lucy's
cheeks turned pink.

"Adrian, you're my least favorite Trellis right now," Matty said with
no heat. "Why would you share that story?"

"OH, COME ON! I randomly tell that story to people I meet on the
street," Noah yelled.

"Yes, but I'm not going to meet those people and sit down to
Sunday dinner with them, Noah."

"What story?" Ree asked, all innocence.

"NOTHING," the entire room yelled.

"Moving on. Ethan's not here. Sam's not here, and you already
know him. He's still struggling, by the by," Beth said to Adrian. "You
may need to drug him."

"Still? Sleep? Food?" Adrian asked, alarmed.

Jake shook his head. "It's the worst I've ever seen. Ethan's staying
with him."

"He slept by me on Wednesday night and ate like mad on Thursday
morning," Will said. "I'm not sure he's eaten or slept since then. I'll
take him with me if he doesn't eat tonight."

"You're ruining my introductions thing," Beth bitched at Will, stamping her foot.

"Sorry, princess," Will said, patting Beth's head.

"I hate it when you do that," she muttered.

"I know, it's why I do it." Will laughed.

"Okay, you met Noah, that's Matthew, that's Luke, and, of course, me," Beth said with a curtsey. "The best Trellis, and that Hennessy person over there. We are not on speaking terms."

"Why?" Adrian asked.

"Because he's a dumbass and will not do as he's told," Beth grumbled.

Hennessy groaned. "Hi, Lou."

"What's for dinner?" Adrian asked.

"Lasagna!" the room yelled.

"Really? This is going to be a thing?" he asked Darla. "It's nine hundred degrees outside, and you made lasagna?"

"I did," Darla said, pleased with herself. "It's hysteri—"

The front door banged open as someone yelled, "Roscoe!"

"Let's eat!" Darla yelled.

Jake looked hopefully at Adrian as they made their way to the table. "Did you teach him earmuffs?"

"Nope, be a functional adult," Adrian answered.

Jake flipped him off.

"Jacob," Darla scolded.

"There was no new vocabulary involved in that. It was a gesture," Jake pointed out sanctimoniously. "Also, Beth swore!"

Darla raised her eyebrows.

"Sorry, Mom," Jake said immediately.

"Hi, Lucy!" a tall, slim-built Trellis called, walking toward her. This had to be Ethan.

"UNCLE ETHAN!" Henry yelled, running to hug Ethan and then Sam.

"Let it be known, here and now, I am clearly the favorite uncle!" Ethan declared smugly.

Much like Hank, Ethan walked right into a hug that made Lucy feel better about life.

"It's nice to meet you, Ethan," Lucy said, blushing again. "Hi, Sam."

Sam nodded to her. "Lucy, I'm glad the stitches are out. I told them not to take you."

"I'M GOING TO BEAT YOU BLOODY IF YOU DON'T STOP THAT," Will yelled.

"It's true!" Sam yelled back. "I absolutely told them it would be better if you didn't go."

"Boys, we're not doing this again," Hank said in a stern voice.

There was some confusion as people went to sit at the table.

"Jake, go over there. Matty, stay here with me," Sam directed.

"Really, Sam? I can't sit by Matty?" Jake asked, heavy on the sarcasm. "You're single. You sit on the other side of the table."

"I don't sit on that side," Sam said.

"For fuck's sake," Will muttered under his breath. "I'm going over there next to Ethan. Everyone just move down a chair."

Sam frowned. "I don't like this."

"Why?" Will asked.

"Because Ethan, Beth, Hennessy, and Noah belong over there. Luke can change sides as he wants, so long as he stays at that end. You belong here with Adrian. Matthew belongs to the left of Luke. You being over there makes us more lopsided. Come back over here with Adrian. Jake, go. You can be anywhere. Go over there," Sam insisted.

"This is fascinating," Ethan said. "We've never had assigned seats before. Whatcha doin', Sam?"

"Huh?" Sam looked up to find everyone staring at him.

"Whatcha doing?" Ethan asked again. "We move seats all the time. This is a new OCD thing. Last week, you sat with Luke."

"I'm not supposed to be on the outside like this. I always make it lopsided. But there's more of us now. We're really lopsided. We have to straighten it out," Sam said like it made sense. "It can't be like this. Jake, go!"

"Sam—" Jake started.

"I SAID, GO!" Samuel yelled, voice echoing, rattling the glasses on the table.

Beth yelped, grabbing her head as her nose spurted blood.

"What the hell?" she yelled at Samuel as she left the room.

"Oh, good. Good. That's done," Samuel said, voice still heavy with power.

Noah turned to Lucy. "Welcome to family dinner! Sorry. We're nuts."

"Uncle Sam?" Henry asked, concerned.

"It's okay, Ree. I'm not mad at you. It's fine. See, Uncle Jake is going," Sam said, himself again.

"BETH!" Will called, banging on the bathroom door.

"I'm okay," she said, opening the door.

Will could feel her fear. He took it from her.

Her head tilted. "Did you...did you just do something? I feel different."

"What? What do you feel? Energy?" Will asked, panicked.

He'd never actually been there when one of his siblings blew what he tended to think of as "the power hymen." Beth was his princess. He'd called her that teasingly since she was a little girl, but he'd left home and joined the military to keep her safe. He wasn't sure what he'd do if this power was something that was going to hurt her.

"Energy?" she asked. "I don't know. I just feel weird."

"Beth, look at me. That weird feeling, think about pushing it toward me and tell me to sit down," Will coached.

"What the fuck are you talking about, Will?"

"Please? Please just try it for me?" he asked.

"Sit down," she said, sounding confused.

Will didn't have the impulse to sit.

Everything is going to be okay. Beth is fine. Beth would love Pip. Maybe I could bring Pip home. Maybe it would work out, he thought.

"Oh! Oh! Thank God! Okay! Beth! That's great. Great. Okay. Let's go eat lasagna!" Will was yelling.

"Will, are you okay? Seriously. You're acting weird. I expect it from Sam, but…"

"Beth, I'm great. Absolutely great. I'm sorry I was weird. It's nothing. Nothing at all. Don't worry about it," Will said in his normal voice, turning to go back to the table. "Let's go eat."

"So, what was with the assigned seat thing?" Lucy asked. Adrian was driving back to his house with Ree asleep in the back seat.

Rage was clawing at the inside of Adrian's brain again. After Sam lost his temper and rattled the room, Rage slammed at his consciousness so hard he had trouble focusing his eyes. He'd been dizzy. Things were better now. But his head still felt like it was going to split open. He reached for Lucy's hand, hoping the happy energy would quiet things down. No such luck.

"I have no idea," Adrian said. "That was new. I swear he's not normally this nuts. He's having a tough time right now. Obsessed with knowing something that Will loves. Won't eat. Won't sleep. I'm really starting to worry that his mind is going."

"The glasses on the table shook," she observed. "I don't want to contradict your doctorly opinion, but typically mental breakdowns don't make the room shake."

Adrian nodded. "That's not new. Neither is the echo. He's done that since puberty."

"Beth's nose?" she asked.

"Absolutely new. Maybe something like with the glasses. I checked her out. There was nothing wrong. Her nose was fine, no sinus infection or anything. Just weird."

They were quiet for a few minutes.

"Thinking that it's time to run screaming?" Adrian asked.

Lucy shook her head. "Sam makes me uneasy, though. Not like he's going to hurt us or whatever, but…uneasy."

Adrian nodded. "Fair. For what it's worth, dinner is not usually like that."

"Okay."

"Really?"

"The food was good," Lucy said with a smile.

They were quiet until Ree was safely in bed, zonked out. When Adrian walked into the living room, Lucy charged him, starting an intense make-out session. Her hair blew toward him as the air conditioning turned on, strands tickling his neck as she tugged at his shirt.

"Lucy, wai—"

"*Now,*" she demanded.

"Now," Rage agreed.

"WILLIAM, WHAT DO YOU LOVE?" Sam asked again.

William, Ethan, Samuel, Jake, and Matty were in the big room with Hank and Darla.

Will sighed. "Sam, I would tell you if I knew what you were after. I really would. Are you coming home with me or going with Ethan?"

Sam hesitated.

"What?" Will asked.

"Can you come home with us?" Sam asked.

Will paused. "Yes. Of course. I'll go get some clothes and then come over, okay?"

"Maybe we should come by you?" Sam asked.

"You can do that, too. You can stay in the bedrooms. I can sleep on the couch. I can sleep anywhere."

"No! If I go with you, I sleep on the couch. Like last time. Exactly like last time, okay?"

"Whatever you want to do is fine with me, Sam. Just tell me what you want."

There was a long pause while Sam considered what to do.

"I'll go with Ethan," Sam said, sighing in frustration. "He can try to call to me again. That might not work if we're not in my space."

"Matty—?" Will asked.

"I've tried and tried. I don't know how I did it," Matilda answered before Will could ask the question.

"You could come home with us, Sam," Jake offered.

"No, I can't do that," Sam said tersely.

Matty rolled her eyes. "We'll behave, Sam. No hanky-panky."

Jake looked at Matty like she'd lost her mind.

"No, I really can't do that, Matty. It's lopsided. You and Jake are balanced. I can't unbalance it."

"What's the lopsided thing, Sam?" Hank asked. "You got really upset about that earlier. That's new. What's that about?"

Sam sighed. "When it was just us, it didn't matter so much. Things flowed, no matter where we were. Noah's girlfriends aren't part of the table. Stephanie-Bella wasn't part of the table. It didn't matter where they were. But when Matty joined, it mattered. She's a corner. She anchors things. I have to stay with her. I just have to, Jake. We can't be opposite each other. It's not right, then. Last week when I sat by Luke, it was wrong. It made my skin crawl. But it was tolerable because we were on the same side.

"But now Lucy has joined the table, and she's a corner. She anchors it, too. But her counterpoint is missing. Like, there's a person that should be in that corner, that can be in that corner, and isn't. There should be four corners, but we only have three. And when I have to be outside, it doesn't flow right," Sam tried to explain.

Everyone was staring at Sam.

"I don't know!" Sam said. "It just matters. Until someone can hold the last corner, it matters. We're missing a corner. The corner is there. We have someone that can fill it; they're just not here. We don't have the fourth corner yet."

"Sam, have you seen the girl?" Will asked. "Can you find her now?"

"No, I've tried, but I can't do it again. I don't know how I did it on Wednesday. Maybe I didn't do it at all. I don't know," Sam said, looking frustrated again.

"What? What happened Wednesday?" Hank asked.

"I went to see Will. He made hamburgers, but the cow suffered horribly. Did you find—?"

"Inspectors visited Friday," Ethan answered.

Sam nodded. "Then I couldn't eat. We sat down in the living room, and William listed off things he loves. I fell asleep and dreamt about the house with changing views.

"When Will and I were talking, he asked about eating in other times. I can't do that, but I wondered if I could eat in the dream house. I went into the kitchen, but there was no food. When I went back to the living room, the girl was there."

Jake's eyebrows shot up. "She was in the house? She's never been there before, right?"

Sam nodded. "She said she was in the clearing, looking for me, and then love called and she was in the house. We talked. We could stay there longer than we can usually stay in the field. Then she kissed me. A storm started outside, rattling the house. The dream still didn't end. My head felt better. Less pressure. My mind was clearer. She said something about the power not working like that normally, then we *really* kissed. Then the dream ended. I woke up. The sun was up, and I could eat everything. I felt so much better. So I ate a lot. But, by the afternoon, my head was feeling bad again. I ate some food, but it made me sick."

"Thursday night, I tried to get to the house again, but I could only be where people are suffocating. I couldn't find her. Friday, I felt worse. Now I'm lost again." Sam sounded utterly defeated.

"You ate some tonight," Darla said. "Is lasagna easier? Maybe the processed grains?"

"No, I felt better after yelling at Jake. But it didn't last."

"Do you want to yell at me some more? It's scary as fuck, but whatever," Jake offered.

"If you do that, go outside so you don't break anything," Hank said. "I think the roof may have cracked with that one."

15

*W*hen Sam finally nodded off, it was the suffocating dream. Beth was dying next to him in the dream.

"I don't want to see this!" he yelled into the silence. "I want to go to the clearing!"

Just like that, he was in the clearing. The girl was startled by his appearance. She reached for his hand.

"You got here! You got here on your own!" Her smile calmed him. Her touch soothed his head. He was in the clearing.

"I was in the place with no air, and I got pissed off. I yelled that I wanted to be here, and now I'm here. I had no idea I could do that," he admitted.

"Can you take us to the house?" she asked hopefully.

He wrapped his arms around her. In a clear, resonant voice, he said, "We want to go to the house with changing views."

Sam was in the house, but the girl wasn't with him.

"I want to go to the clearing," he said again.

Back in the clearing, the girl was lying on the ground, blood on her face and dripping from her nose.

"What happened?!" Sam yelled, wiping at the blood as he scooped her into his lap.

She blinked. Holding his hand, she said, *"I hit the ward. I can't go like that."*

"Well, take the ward down! Take it down, tell me where you are, and I will be here quickly. I will be here today. Within hours. Take it down!" he yelled, not for the first time.

"I am unbound, Sam. We cannot bind while Walking. Maybe at the house, I don't know. If we can get there again, we will try." She paused to think about it.

"If I am trapped like this, they'll drain me for a thousand years. Some do not need hours to get here. Just minutes. The wards will come down, they will feel me, and they will take me. I cannot stop them; I will not knowingly harm that which is alive. The wards cannot come down. They must stay. Death is better than the wards falling," she said with absolute certainty.

Sam took deep breaths, trying to calm down. "How do I pass through the ward? How does it work?"

She smiled a sad smile. *"It will let you Walk through because you love me and mean me no harm. I structured it so that you could come through."*

"Can you structure it so you can leave through it the same way? How did you pass through to the house?"

She sighed. *"Love called. I heard through the ward and could go."*

"Maybe if I go there and then call to you?" he asked.

She shook her head. *"Maybe. We will try it. But not now. I hurt."*

Sam could feel her pain; it was everywhere. The clearing was sad because of her pain. The air was still with it.

Mistress Life was injured by his doing.

The knowledge made it hard for Sam to breathe.

"I wish Adrian was here to help," he muttered as he ran his fingers through her hair, comforting her.

AFTER RAGE WAS quiet and Lucy was asleep, Adrian expected to be awake for hours. He was not in control during that sex. He tried to stop it and couldn't. Lucy could have been hurt. Really hurt. He'd always promised himself that he wouldn't do this. He'd rather die horribly alone than risk hurting someone with the anger.

He loved Lucy too much to risk this. It was time for things to change. He'd been selfish. She'd be the one to pay the price for it. He couldn't allow that. He was meant to be alone; he would be alone. The house would be ready soon. He'd make himself scarce until then and end things.

The thought made him physically ill. He barely made it to the bathroom before puking. After brushing his teeth and taking a quick shower, he climbed back in bed with Lucy. He intended to lie awake for the night, soaking up the feel of her next to him, knowing he wouldn't have this again.

But Adrian was asleep before his head hit the pillow. He was out before realizing it.

The dream started with Lucy. The look on her face when she slapped his hand that first day. The panic attack at finding him in her apartment. The look of hopelessness in Dr. Garaff's office. The laughter that came with teaching Ree the rules of smart men everywhere. Sitting in the sun, watching Ree dribble the ball—

And then he was walking through a dense forest. Not really an outdoorsy kind of guy, Adrian was startled by the new surroundings. He walked on, trying to figure out where he was. About fifty yards in, he reached a clearing.

Sam sat in the clearing, back to Adrian, holding a girl with blue-black hair in his lap. The girl started when Adrian walked into the clearing, jumping away from Sam and climbing to her feet.

"What?" Sam asked her.

She looked at Sam and then met Adrian's eyes. After a minute, she nodded toward Adrian.

Sam turned around.

"Adrian?" Sam asked. "What the fuck?"

"How am I here?" Adrian asked.

"I don't know. I thought about you. She's hurt. Maybe I said it out loud. I don't know. But you're here! How did you get here? How did you get through the ward? Can you talk to her?"

"Can you hear me?" Adrian asked the girl.

She nodded.

"Where are you? How does he find you?" Adrian asked. "He's been looking for you all his life."

Her eyes welled with tears. She nodded again.

"Can you write it down? Where you are? Even just a state," Adrian suggested.

She shook her head and reached for Adrian's hand.

At her touch, he could hear her, even though her lips weren't moving.

"Brothers?" she asked. *"You love him? Would not harm him? Would not harm me?"*

"Yes. Yes, he's my little brother. I'd never harm him. Or you," Adrian said, trying to understand what was happening.

"You need the Wind. Why do you fight it?" she asked.

Adrian shook his head. "I don't understand."

"Will you bring me Wind?"

He shook his head again. "What is the wind?" Somehow, he knew they weren't talking about air. This was very much like a classic Sam conversation.

She shook her head, sighing in frustration that Adrian could feel.

"What is your name?" Adrian asked.

Her lips tilted up. Not quite a smile, just like Sam. "Adaline."

ADRIAN STARTED AWAKE IN BED. He could hear his phone ringing in the kitchen.

"SAM?"

"Adrian. Adrian, what did she say? You believe me now, right? Adrian, you were there!" Sam panted, trying to catch his breath.

"I saw her, Sam. I saw. I've always believed you," Adrian said, feeling like he was being electrocuted by the raw energy running through him.

"What? What did she say? Did she talk to you when she touched you?"

"She asked me to bring her the Wind. Do you know what that is?"

There was a pause. "No, not yet. I don't see it yet. What else?"

"She couldn't tell me where she was. But her name is Adaline."

Sam gasped. "She could tell you her name? She's never been able to tell me before. I don't remember when I last asked. I wonder what changed."

"That's it, Sam. She didn't say anything else," Adrian said, vibrating with energy. "Too much energy, Sam. Too much. My brain is short-circuiting."

"Adrian! No. Don't hang up! Adrian!" Sam was screaming as Adrian hung up.

Adrian walked toward the stairs, intending to climb back into bed and wake Lucy up. The energy—the rage and the happy energy—were screaming for her.

Instead, he turned the corner and walked into the back yard. He wanted the breeze in his face.

He woke up lying in the grass a few hours later, covered in morning dew, in nothing but his boxer briefs.

When he got back to the house, he had sixteen missed calls and thirty-seven text messages from Sam.

The phone rang again as Adrian looked at it.

"Sam—" Adrian started.

"I'm out front. Open the door," Sam cut him off.

"CAN YOU PUSH IT OUT?" Sam asked as Adrian opened the door.

"Push what out?"

"The emotion. Whatever emotion you have. I know there is one, but I don't know which. Sometimes your food tastes angry, sometimes just red," Sam admitted. "Lucas can give peace. Maybe I'm not supposed to share that. I'm not sure. He told me not to talk about mine. That doesn't mean I can't talk about his."

"Peace?" Adrian was startled. "That would be...amazing."

"Yours is not peace?"

"No." Adrian tasted envy and rage, spitting out the word. *How fucking wonderful would it be to hand out peace rather than wrestle with fucking rage?*

"I hate Luke a little bit right now," Adrian admitted.

Sam smiled a real smile. "I had a hard time with it, too. I spend three-quarters of my life not knowing what the fuck is happening and the other quarter knowing things that scare the shit out of people. Giving peace sounds so much better."

"Right there with you, Sam."

"Can I come in?"

"Yeah, I'm sorry. What time is it?" Adrian asked, stepping out of the doorway.

"A little after five, I think."

Lucy was walking into the kitchen from the other doorway when Sam and Adrian entered the kitchen from the front hallway. "Hi. Hi, sorry. I thought I heard people talking. Is everything okay?"

Sam's eyes closed as his head tilted to the side. "Lucy, what is your name?" The words were heavy, and they echoed in the room.

"Huh?" Lucy blinked hard, trying to clear a wave of vertigo.

Samuel straightened his head and looked at her. "What is your name?" Samuel asked, quiet voice booming with power.

"Uh. Lucinda Lee Wallace," she said, confused and nauseous.

"No, Lucinda, what is your Name?"

"I don't know what you mean," she said as fear began to rise in her.

"Not yet, then. Not yet. Okay." Sam was Sam again.

"What did you just do?" Adrian asked.

"I have no idea. Other-Sam was driving. Do you have an Other-Adrian?"

"No, man. I don't think so. Not like that. It felt like the house was vibrating, like at dinner tonight."

Sam shrugged. "Oops. It's fine, though. Tell me again. Tell me what she said. Do you remember the exact words?"

"What's going on?" Lucy asked.

Sam looked at her. "I have dreams of a girl. Adrian was in the dream tonight. He talked to her."

"Wow, that was some epic shorthand, Sam." Adrian tried not to laugh. "So much for this being like a major family secret, huh? You told Matty."

"Matty can call me. I had to tell her. Lucy is highly skeptical. Of everything. Including me. And you. But it's fine. She won't tell. She won't tell because I wouldn't let them take Ree last week. When she was moving. She'll remember that." Sam was staring in her eyes.

Lucy nodded. "I won't say anything to anyone."

"So tell me again. What did you ask her? What did she say?"

Adrian rubbed his face. "She said I need the wind. I don't know what that means, but I don't think she was talking about gusty air."

Sam was quiet for a few heartbeats. "What else?"

"She told me her name. That's it," Adrian said.

"No, it's not. Tell me again."

"Sam, that's all she said—"

"No, it's not. Start at the beginning again. She walked over and touched you. What was the first thing she said when you realized you could hear her?"

Adrian tried to focus. He shook his head, wondering if he was going to be sick again. "She asked if we were brothers. If I would hurt you. If I would hurt her."

They sat down at the kitchen table as Lucy started making coffee.

"What did you say?" Sam asked.

"I said that you were my little brother and I wouldn't hurt either of you. I think she nodded. She said I need the wind, asked why I fight it. I asked where she was, told her you'd been looking for her all your life. She nodded, looked like she was going to cry. I asked if she could tell me the state she was in, even. She didn't say anything. I asked her name. She told me, and then I woke up."

"How many Adalines could there be in their early twenties on the planet?" Sam wondered.

"I suspect we're going to find out. I suspect there are fewer

Adalines then there are bars in the US. So, hey, that helps." Adrian smiled.

Sam shook his head and looked at Lucy as she put the coffee down in front of them. "Lucinda. Lu-cin-da. That's why Will calls you Lou. Lucinda.

"How did Ree come to be with you? He is not of your blood. Will you tell me? Hennessy won't. I've asked. Repeatedly. He will not tell me how Ree came to you, and he will not tell me what William loves, but he knows both."

Adrian snorted. "Hennessy is refusing to tell you things? You're losing your touch. He used to be fucking terrified of you."

"He still is. He won't tell me, though," Sam said, still watching Lucy.

Lucy's eyes flicked to Adrian.

"No, Lucy," Sam said. "No. I don't think there's anything you can say at this point that would make him stop caring. We're not built like that."

Lucy's cheeks flushed red.

Adrian's stomach dropped, knowing what was coming. Then he acknowledged the truth of that statement to himself. He'd love her until the day he died.

Face scrunched up, Adrian said, "It's true. You had me at the hand slap. BFFs."

Lucy burst out laughing, relieving some of the tension that Sam introduced.

"You're much better at this than Jake. It'd take him a year to admit that." Sam's lips turned up.

"Jake's an idiot."

Sam nodded. "Jake is an idiot."

"Will you tell me? How Ree came to be with you?" Sam asked. "It's important, but I don't know why."

"I was in foster care," Lucy said. She paused to take a deep breath as both men watched her. "Linda was also in the system. We were placed in the same home. We were foster sisters."

"Oh. Linda? Henry's mom is Linda?" Sam asked.

"Linda Jane Wright."

"Hmm." Sam tilted his head back and closed his eyes. "How old were you? When you knew Linda? How old?"

"Fifteen. I was fifteen when we were placed together. Sixteen when we ran away," Lucy said.

"You ran away?" There was a crease in Sam's forehead.

"Yes."

"You didn't stay together. For a little while, yes. But then you split up," Sam said. It wasn't a question.

Lucy nodded in confirmation, anyway.

"She's not dead. I know you think she is, but she's not. She knows about the violet-eyed girl. Did she tell you? Do you know?" Sam asked, focused.

Lucy gasped. "Wow! Wow. Holy fuck." The hairs on Lucy's arms stood on end, her mouth hanging open.

"Lucy, please. I...please tell me. Please. I need to know." There was a glassy-eyed look bordering on madness in Sam's eyes.

"Sam, relax," Adrian soothed. "Want something to eat?"

"Lucy, please tell me about the girl," Sam asked again.

"Holy fuck!" she yelled.

"Lucy, please. I'm sorry. I need to know. I need to know now." Sam was biting off the words.

"Ah, okay. Okay. Sorry, but this is seriously freaky," Lucy said, suddenly out of breath.

"Um, we ran away. Linda had an aunt that she thought would help us. She said her aunt was weird, new age, witches and Wicca and all that, but that she would understand. Understand and help.

"She lived on a farm about sixty miles outside the city. We walked and hitched most of it. When we got there, the aunt wouldn't let us in. She said we belonged to the violet-eyed girl, to the violet-eyed miss or something like that. No, mistress. The violet-eyed mistress, and that she would not risk the wrath of the mistress. She babbled about someone finding me if I stayed and that I couldn't be found.

"We left. The aunt died not long after that, of some kind of undiagnosed heart thing. But Linda brought up the violet-eyed girl often. She thought it was funny. Said she had dreams about her sometimes."

Sam frowned. "Do you dream of her?"

"Of Linda? No."

"The girl with the violet eyes. Is she in your dreams? Have you seen her?"

"Uh, no."

"Do you dream of fire? Or people suffocating?"

"Sam," Adrian said with a warning tone.

"You're really freaking me out." Lucy was starting to shake with adrenaline and fear.

"I'm sorry, Lucy. I'm sorry. I don't mean to scare you. I'm sorry," Sam apologized. "I dream of her often. I have for a very long time. Most of my life. I can't find her. Do you know where she is?"

"No," Lucy said, still shaking.

"I'm sorry. I'm so sorry, Lucy. Do you know where Linda is? Or the farm?" Sam asked.

"Sam, enough," Adrian said. "Leave it be for a while, okay?"

"I don't know where Linda is or where the farm is. I would tell you if I did," Lucy choked out through her fear.

"I don't mean any harm to you or yours, Lucy. I will do everything I can to help you. I don't think it was me you were supposed to hide from," Sam said. "I knew you at the hospital. That first day. When I saw you. I knew you. Remember, I knew your name? I knew you. You belong here. It's going to be fine. We'll find the girl."

"I MEAN THIS REALLY SWEETLY," Lucy started after Adrian walked Sam out. "Your brother freaks me the fuck out. My heart is still racing."

Adrian nodded. "Me, too, sometimes. He freaks himself out, too. I've never seen him this bad. The last two weeks or so have gotten exponentially worse. He's been dreaming of the girl since he was about twelve. Looking for her for his entire adult life. To the best of my knowledge, no one else has ever seen her. I don't know how I got there tonight, but I definitely saw her."

They sat quietly for a few minutes.

"Tonight was different," Lucy acknowledged. "It felt different."

Adrian nodded.

"What happened? What changed?"

He was silent and still for a minute. Lucy thought he wasn't going to answer.

Adrian rested his elbows on the table as he scrubbed his hands over his face.

"I'm going to make myself scarce for the next couple days," Adrian said, looking at his hands.

Lucy's shock quickly morphed to raw pain. "Adrian?"

"This can't be, Lucy. It just can't. I don't want to hurt you, and there's no way to avoid it if we're together. I know that's fucked up, but it's the truth."

"I don't understand," she whispered. "I don't understand what happened. We were fine earlier. Why? What happened?"

"I'm sorry. I know this seems nuts. But it can't be. I can't be with you. I can't do this to you."

Lucy was silent for a while, trying to figure out what happened. What to do. How to fix it.

Lucy cleared her throat. "If it's not what you want, it's fine, Adrian. I don't want to chase you out of your own house. We'll leave. But why? Why all of a sudden, don't you want to be with me?"

Adrian snorted. "Are you fucking kidding me? I want it so bad I can taste it. But it's not gonna happen."

"Why?"

He shook his head. "I just can't."

"We'll leave today. Stay elsewhere. The house will be done soon, anyway."

"You don't need to leave. Stay until the house is ready. It'll be easier for Ree. I'll stay away."

16

The following week was lonely for Lucy. Having spent most of her life on her own, loneliness was a new sensation for her. Other than Henry, she wasn't used to having anyone else around. While she never took his presence for granted, Lucy was still surprised by how much she missed Adrian. Romance aside, he was the first friend she'd had in a very long time. She felt somewhat lost without him. Every aspect of her life had changed in the last two weeks. There was no one to discuss it with.

Hank had given her the paperwork for the trust fund on Sunday as they were headed out the door to go back to Adrian's house. Before everything went off the rails. When she finally opened it on Monday morning, she had an anxiety attack. Glad that Ree was still asleep, she called Hank and asked him to take it back.

"Lucy, I wouldn't take it back, even if I could. Why are you upset?"

She was trying to sound calm. "We don't need that. Once Henry's through treatment, I'll get a job and go back to being a real adult."

There was a long pause as Hank thought about how to respond. "It's a trust fund, sweetheart. I can't and wouldn't touch it. It's for you and for Ree. It is my sincerest wish that you never want for anything that money can buy, including time for you to enjoy life with your nephew.

"I'm not sure what getting a job and being a 'real adult' means to you, but the way you say it concerns me. Please consider what happiness is for you and seek it out, Lucy. You have the means to do as you please. Now you just need to figure out what that is."

Lucy suspected she knew what happiness was for her and that it was already gone.

TUESDAY MORNING, Lucy drove her new car to Ree's doctor's appointment. There were security guards following her to a hospital that was treating her sick kid.

Two weeks. So much has changed so quickly, Lucy thought.

Ree would start chemotherapy next week, assuming his bloodwork and immune system held up.

Tuesday night, Ree picked at his dinner.

"Why the long face, Ree?" she asked. "Feeling okay? Dr. Garaff made the medicine stronger for this week. Is it bothering you?"

"Just tired," Henry mumbled.

WEDNESDAY, Hennessy and Will came over for lunch.

"Ready to get out of here?" Will asked. "Bathroom's all done. The last layer of paint went on this morning. The new house looks good."

"I'm sure it's great," Lucy said with a smile.

"Is Adrian going to come back before we leave?" Ree asked.

"I don't think so, honey. He's really busy with work stuff. We're not going far, though. You'll see him after we move. Probably," she hedged.

Hennessy rocked back in his chair, surprise on his face. But he didn't say anything.

His phone started ringing to Bonnie Tyler's "Total Eclipse of the Heart." "Why does she keep fucking doing that?!" Hennessy groaned.

Will laughed. "Because she's the best troll on the fucking planet. Anything we need to talk about?"

"Na," Hennessy said. "Sorry, kid."

Henry was offended by the foul language.

"Yeah, boss. Quit messing with my phone!"

THURSDAY MORNING, Lucy threw all their worldly possessions in the back of the Mazda and drove three miles to the new house. Their beds would be delivered today, but they'd need to get furniture for the rest of the house.

Ree's room had been painted in a *Paw Patrol* theme. Lucy's bedroom had an attached bath with a fancy shower and tub. The kitchen had new counters and appliances. There was a swing set in the freshly sodded backyard.

"Wow, this is super nice, right?!" Lucy said, trying to be excited for Ree.

"Yeah, it's great," he said in a monotone.

"What's with you, kid?" Lucy asked. "This is *way* nicer than the apartment."

Henry shrugged.

AFTER TALKING to Lucy on Monday morning, Adrian packed a bag and left the house.

It's what's best. It's what's best for them. It's what's best. It's what needs to happen, Adrian chanted over and over in his mind.

He managed to drive two blocks before pulling over and puking on the side of the road. When he finally got into his Foundation office, shaking and sweating, he asked Martha to clear his schedule and then he closed his door.

His head was going to cave in. The rage was eating a hole in his brain, and his skull was going to cave in.

Martha knocked on the door. "Adrian, are you sick?"

"Yes," he groaned before blacking out.

In a hotel room later that night, Adrian realized he was missing parts of the day. Not just the blackout, but whole chunks of the day. He had been at the hospital to do a consult for a long-time patient but didn't remember how he got there.

Tuesday morning, he woke up thinking about Ree's doctor's appointment. Thought about Lucy going to that appointment on her own. Thought about his Ree going through chemo. Later, he tried to remember what he did on Tuesday, but it was a black void in his memory.

Wednesday, he went to the hospital. It was a clinical day. The rage had quieted some. He was able to eat without being ill. He could remember Wednesday. There was a text from Will on Wednesday night.

WILLIAM: What happened with Lou? Where are you? Let me help.

Adrian didn't respond.

Thursday, he was supposed to be working at the Foundation. He was supposed to go to the office.

I should be at work, he thought as he watched Lucy throw bags of clothes in the back of her car. Ree was climbing in the backseat. They didn't see him. *It's for the best*, he told himself again.

One of the security cars pulled up alongside him. "Reap's looking for you," the woman said. Adrian couldn't remember her name. He just nodded.

Thursday night, Rage tore the heavy punching bag from the ceiling mount, sending it flying across the room. Once the bag was gone, it punched the concrete basement walls until his hands were crushed. Adrian watched in horror as it happened, felt the pain of it, and couldn't stop it. Once done, Rage disappeared, leaving Adrian a bloody, painful mess on the basement floor.

When he finally got upstairs to refuel, Adrian found the fridge and freezer stuffed full of foil trays of food. Each pan was labeled with the contents and had instructions for how to heat it up.

William found Adrian sitting in the middle of the kitchen floor, sobbing.

"Almost two fucking weeks, I've been trying to find you to have a private fucking conversation. You're busy. You got people here. You're with Lou, pretending like it's fucking rainbows and puppies. Fuck you. I'm your brother. You call me back, asshole. It was important. Now you've fucked it all up.

"The last two fucking days, I've been calling and texting nonstop. You don't fucking answer me. I thought you had this worked out. You were fucking steady on Sunday. What the fuck happened?" Will growled, moving Adrian into a kitchen chair and firing up the oven.

"What happened with Lou?" Will asked again, pissed off. "Leaving a fucking fridge full of ready-made meals does not scream, 'I hate you, and I'm glad we split.' Sitting in the middle of your fucking floor, holding a pan of cold chicken while you fall apart, does not scream, 'I'm making good life decisions.' What the fuck, Adrian?"

"Sorry, I didn't call you back. That was shitty of me," Adrian said eventually.

Will tossed the pan of chicken in the oven, then looked at his brother. "What. Happened?"

"This is not something you're going to understand, man," Adrian muttered.

"OH, FUCK YOU. Wanna play a game? I'll pump you full of terror, and you can pump me full of rage, and we can see who cracks first. I'm betting that I'll win. I have better control than you," Will taunted.

Adrian stared at his older brother, mouth agape, trying to process what he just said. "No fucking way," he whispered.

William sighed. "I can't pump you full of fear right now. You're a fucking mess." Without another word, Will pulled a knife out of the block on the counter and sliced his hand open.

The brothers watched it heal together.

"What happened with Lou?" William asked again.

"Will, how—? Why didn't you tell me? If you knew, why didn't you tell me?" Adrian demanded.

William shrugged. "For as much time as we spend together, we're not great about sharing things as a family. Again, what happened with Lou?"

"Does your thing have a compulsion to it?" Adrian asked. "Like, can you tell someone to do something, and they have to do it?"

Will nodded. "It's the nature of fear and anger, Adrian. They're strong emotions that make people do and think things they normally wouldn't."

Adrian was awestruck. "Holy fuck. How do you know this? Who taught you?"

"OH, FUCK YOU AGAIN. No one taught me anything. It's my working theory. It makes sense to me. Answer my question, asshole," Will demanded.

"A week ago Sunday, I came home from family dinner and was putting Mom's leftovers in the fridge. Lucy and I were talking about fucking Hennessy and that damn file. She apologized. It makes me nuts when she apologizes for shit that's not her fault.

"Out of nowhere, no warning, the rage surfaced and took over. Before I even knew what was happening, it told her to never apologize for something that's not her doing. I freaked out," Adrian explained.

"Why?" Will asked, completely unfazed. "She shouldn't apologize for shit that's not her fault."

"Will, seriously? You seriously don't think that's alarming and wrong?"

"Of course, I do, Adrian. But it's not like that shit has to stay in there forever. Pull it out."

Adrian stared at his brother.

"You don't know how to do that, do you? You're not shy; you're stupid," Will realized.

"How do you take it out?"

William sighed. "The same way you put it in. Pull the rage forward —you know what I mean?"

Adrian nodded.

"Pull it forward, go back in your memory to when you did it. You'll feel the difference. Undo it. It's easier to do when you're with the person. The longer it's in there, the harder it is to undo. The bigger the compulsion—a good word for it, by the way—the more damage you do to the memory. It's easier to undo your own shit," Will said. "She won't even remember that it happened. Something small like that, one fucking sentence that is tied to a bad habit? That'll come right out. But I'd consider leaving it. She should break that habit."

Adrian continued to stare at his brother. "Do you do this often?"

"Nope. Again. I have control. Balance. You, obviously, do not. Before I was balanced, I was a fucking mess. I do, however, give Noah little spikes of fear when he pisses me off. That shit's fun and harmless."

Adrian laughed. And then he really laughed. "Is that why he sees bees everywhere?"

Will started laughing with him. "Fuck yeah," he said as he pulled the tray out of the oven and grabbed two forks. "I love that she did this in fucking banquet trays. She doesn't understand why, but she knows you need a lot of food."

Adrian's laughter tapered off.

"So, compulsion. Fine. But you were together last week. You were fine at Sunday dinner. I thought you had all this shit straight. You put the rage together with Lou's shit, right? After that, none of this shit should have affected her," Will said.

Adrian reverted back to staring at his brother as he ate large bites of chicken and potatoes.

"Oh. Maybe this part's different. Or maybe Lou's not like us. But I really thought she was. She feels like it.

"Was there other stuff? Like the rage but not. Like, zingier lovey-dovey stuff? When you were with her? When you touched her?" Will asked.

Adrian nodded.

"What happened when you put them together? When you pulled the rage forward with that shit running wild?"

Adrian shook his head.

"What does the head shake mean, Adrian?"

"I didn't put them together."

"What do you mean? How did you keep them apart?" Will asked, mouth full of potatoes.

Adrian shook his head again.

It was William's turn to look shocked. "Adrian, do you keep the rage pulled back all the time?"

"Of course," Adrian said. "Holy fuck, yes. Unless I'm working out, yes. You don't?"

"No, absolutely not. That's gotta be fucking agony, man. I take fear from people and cycle it out all fucking day long."

"Cycle it out?" Adrian asked.

William stared at his brother.

"I don't know what you mean," Adrian said. "The only way I've been able to unload it is exercise."

"Wow. Holy fuck, man. You can't keep it back all the time. When you let it co-exist with you, it pretty much takes care of itself. I don't even know how that would work, Adrian. Do you not let yourself get mad? How do you keep it back?"

"I just keep it back. It hurts people. It can't be forward all the time," Adrian argued.

Will looked confused. "What the fuck are you talking about? You don't pull it forward all the time. You just let it be. In the center. Not forward, not backward. Centered. Like having a car in neutral."

"I...don't think I have a neutral."

"I think your shit's out of whack, Adrian."

"How do I fix it, Will?"

"I think you get down on your hands and knees, beg Lou to take your dumb ass back, and then fuck like rabbits until her shit is all blended with your shit," Will said. "I'm still unclear on what happened between Sunday dinner and when I saw her yesterday."

Adrian's cheeks turned a bit pink. "Ah, Sunday night, it came forward at a bad time and wouldn't go back. It could have hurt her."

"You split with Lou because your rage was forward while fucking? Are you kidding me?"

"I won't hurt her, Will. She's had a hard road. I won't add to it. She's better off without me in her shit," Adrian said, voice ringing with sincerity.

Will sighed. "You are dead fucking wrong. She is sad and lonely without you. Henry is depressed and afraid that everyone is going to leave him like you and his mom did. And you're fucking dying without her. You need to have this conversation with her. Explain. Merge the energies. She's like us. You can feel it radiating from her when you pay attention."

"I won't do it, Will. I'd rather die than hurt her," Adrian said, not looking at his brother.

"Adrian, I completely fucking get it. I really do—"

"No, you don't," Adrian snapped. "You don't date. You have no relationships outside our family. That 'ruined for all time' shit makes perfect sense now, by the way. You can't be with someone for the same reason I can't be with someone. Add me to that fucking list. We can grow old playing fucking pinochle and cribbage together."

William laughed at Adrian. Outright, full-on laughed at his little brother. "Oh my God. You have that so fucking wrong and so fucking right at the same time. We are a matched set of fucked up, you and I. Go talk to Lou, Adrian. You're killing yourself. Literally. See you Sunday. Call me if you need me. Eat more."

ADRIAN WAS late for dinner on Sunday.

"Sorry, lost track of time," he said as he entered the dining room.

"We just sat down," Hank said. "Are you okay? You look terrible."

"Oh, yeah. I'm fine. I think I had the flu," he said. "Doing better now."

"Where are Lucy and Ree? No, honey, no kisses if you're sick," Darla said, pulling away from Adrian.

"Uh, they're doing Lucy and Ree things? I don't know. I haven't seen them in a few days," Adrian admitted.

"Why?" Darla asked, her eyes turned to slits.

"They moved into the house on Thursday. I haven't been over there yet. I'll stop by at some point during the week. What's with you, Mom? You don't look so hot," Adrian said to change the subject.

Darla sighed. "Nice attempt to change the subject. What happened?"

Everyone at the table stared at him.

"Nothing. Nothing at all. The house was ready, so they moved into it," Adrian said, trying to look innocent.

I haven't done anything wrong. Why are they fucking staring at me? This is fucking ridiculous.

Will reached to smack Adrian upside the head. Adrian caught his brother's hand before it made contact.

"Stop it," Adrian growled.

"Aww, temper temper, little brother," Will chided. "Henry's been asking about you. Go see him."

"Stop smacking me."

"Stop being an idiot, and then I'll stop smacking you," Will said.

Adrian breathed deep as the rage tried to push forward.

"William, leave me alone." The words vibrated with power.

"No," Will said with an antagonistic grin. He made to slap Adrian again. "You mad, bro?"

"All right, I'm out. Feel better, Mom. I won't spread my germs," Adrian called as he left the house.

Hank looked confused. "What just happened there?"

"He's not in a good place," Will said. "Just making sure he realizes it."

"What happened with Lucy?" Darla asked.

"Adrian's an idiot," Will said. "He needs to get his head out of his ass."

"Hey, Will?"

Will rolled his eyes. He knew what was coming. It was the only thing Sam said to him these days. "Yeah, Sam?"

"What do you love? Why won't you tell me?" Sam asked.

Jake groaned. "Really, man. All fucking week you've been doing this."

"Jacob," Darla scolded.

"Sorry, Mom. But *all* week long with this. Every single fucking time he sees William, *all* day long..."

"He called me at one thirty this morning to ask me, too," Will said.

"I'd stop asking if you'd just tell me. I need to know," Sam said, rubbing his head.

Will sighed. "Here we go, Sam. Stop me when you hear something close to whatever the fuck it is that you're looking for: I love my family, I love my friends, I love a good beer, I love the sun on my face, I love dogs, I love Italian beef sandwiches, I love deep dish pizzas..."

Sam sighed as Will continued to list things that didn't matter.

17

*a*drian wasn't sure what to do after leaving his parents' house.

I need food. I'll go find food, he thought.

An hour later, he was stuffed with pizza and calmer.

Did I even say hello to my family? What happened?

Lost in thought, he wasn't paying attention to where he was going. He looked up and found himself standing on Lucy's doorstep, his car parked in her driveway.

Holy fuck. I lost some time again.

Lucy was pulling open the door.

Oh, no.

She looked good. Really good. The bruising was gone in her face. Blond hair pulled up, blue eyes shining in the dim light, radiant tanned skin everywhere. She was in a tank top and shorts.

"Adrian. Hi," she said, opening the screen door. "You just missed Ree. I can wake him up if you want to say hi."

"Hi," Adrian said, staring at her.

"Do you want to come in?" she asked, confused.

"I do. I really do." He didn't move.

"What is going on? You look terrible."

"I don't know. I mean, I kind of know, but not really. I don't understand it."

"Do you want to talk about it?" she asked, eyebrows raised.

"How are you? How is Ree?"

"Okay on both fronts. He misses you. We both miss you," she said with a shrug. "Worried about you."

He nodded. "Me, too."

"Adrian, come inside. Or go. Either one. But don't stand in the doorway anymore." Lucy grabbed his hand and pulled it toward her.

And just like that, Adrian gave up the fight. Couldn't even really remember why he was fighting to begin with. His arms wrapped around her as his lips met hers, the happy energy surging through him.

"I'm sorry," he muttered to Lucy as he kissed down her long neck to the sensitive skin around her collar bone. He wasn't sure what he was apologizing for, but he was sorry. For being away from her. For coming back to her.

"Okay," she muttered back, arms wrapping around his neck.

Hands wrapped around Lucy's waist, they both groaned as the happy energy cycled when Adrian's finger touched the skin where her tank and shorts met. He was tugging her shirt off before the front door was all the way closed.

HOLY HELL, *this is the most intense make-out session of my life,* Lucy thought as her body tingled with anticipation.

She reached to pull Adrian's shirt off, enjoying the feel of his muscles under her hands. Her bra was gone; she wasn't sure how that happened. Adrian's thumbs were gently circling and pinching at her nipples, making it hard to breathe. He made a very satisfying groaning sound when she nibbled his earlobe.

Lost in exploring the feel of him, Lucy was surprised when her legs bumped against the edge of her bed. Adrian pulled off her shorts as she pulled at his pants. Her body arched up as he sucked a nipple in his mouth and then closed his teeth around it.

When her hand wandered down below his waist, he caught it, pinning both her hands above her head with his left hand. She tugged against his hold when his fingers slipped inside her, rubbing a spot that made her body coil like a spring.

ADRIAN KEPT TRYING to slow down. He kept meaning to draw things out. The rage that was screaming for Lucy wanted no part of it. When her body tightened with anticipation around his fingers, he knew she was ready. Without another thought, he was pushing into her, slowly stretching her.

The energy was going batshit crazy. Adrian was having trouble remembering to breathe. Then it hit him. Lucy's breathing matched the energy. Her body twisted to meet the surges of raw power.

Oh my God. She can feel it.

Her hips pushed up to meet him and hurry things.

"Slow, Lucy. Slow," he muttered against her mouth, letting go of her hands.

"Adrian, not this slow," she muttered back.

Just like that, the rage drove him forward. He was fully inside as she came hard around him. "Oh my God," he groaned as the waves of her orgasm continued to roll.

Adrian tried to wait, tried to wait for the orgasm to pass, for her to catch up. But it was too late. He was moving without conscious thought, slow and steady at first, and then faster. Harder. Lucy moaned his name as she came again, then everything exploded.

HOURS LATER, Lucy woke up, still wrapped with Adrian.

Holy fuck, what happened? she wondered.

Adrian's arms tighten around her in sleep as she tried to scoot away to use the bathroom. "No."

"I'm just going to the bathroom. I'll be right back," she muttered to him.

His arms didn't loosen.

"Adrian, let go. I'll be right back," Lucy said, trying not to laugh.

His arms still didn't loosen.

She pushed against his arms. She couldn't move him.

Lucy didn't want to wake him but didn't have much choice. "Adrian," she said quietly while touching his face. "Let go."

His arms loosened enough for her to wiggle free.

THE RAGE CLAWED at the inside of his brain after Lucy got out of bed. Adrian woke to a wave of vertigo mixed with a stomach roll. He was just sitting up when Lucy walked out of the bathroom.

"I'm sorry, I didn't mean to wake you," she whispered as she searched through a basket of clothes.

The sick, rage feeling quieted at the sound of her voice.

"S'okay," he said, searching through his memory. He thought he might be missing parts of the night. "How are you?"

Lucy snorted a cute little sound as she pulled on pajamas. "I'm just great," she said with a grin. "How are you?"

He smiled a bit at her. "I didn't really intend to pounce on you like that."

"I didn't mind. At all," she said, chuckling.

"You're really okay?"

"Of course. Why wouldn't I be? I'm going to go find the rest of our clothes, so we don't scar Ree for life."

The rage roared back in his brain as soon as she was out of sight.

Food. I need food.

"YOU'RE SERIOUSLY MAKING eggs at two a.m.?" Lucy asked as she walked into the kitchen.

"Hungry," Adrian mumbled. "Sorry, I know it's the middle of the night."

Lucy grabbed a bowl out of the fridge then glasses for water and a pair of plates. "I'm willing to go along with this, mostly because you're doing it shirtless. Thanks for that."

Adrian smiled but it lacked his usual warmth.

"You look so tired, you could be Sam," she said.

"Mmm," he said. "I've been out of sorts."

"I can tell. Ready to talk about it?"

"Can't," he said to the eggs.

Her eyebrows quirked. "It's top secret? That far out of sorts?"

He nodded, but Lucy wondered if he actually heard her.

"Having eggs?" Adrian asked.

Lucy shook her head. "There's watermelon in the bowl. That sounds better to me. Plus, I want to see if you can eat half a dozen eggs at one time."

"I can," he said with a little smile, piling the eggs on the plate. "Thank you. For leaving the food. For opening the door."

Lucy sighed. "Do you need hot sauce for the eggs?"

Adrian cleared his throat. "No, it's fine."

"SO TELL ME AGAIN. Why can't we talk about whatever is going on?" Lucy asked.

Adrian tipped his head back to look at the ceiling and then cracked his neck. "I'm sorry, Lucy. I just can't. It won't make any sense. My brain is not right."

Her brow was furrowed with concern. "You can tell me. I hope you know that. I wouldn't tell anyone else. I hate seeing you like this."

The energies were warring within him. The rage battered his brain, causing a splitting headache at the same time the other energy was trying to tug him toward Lucy. She was talking again, walking toward him. She tried to touch his hand, but Adrian pulled it away.

The hurt was evident on her beautiful face. She was still talking, but he couldn't understand her.

I'm causing that pain. I'm hurting her. Right this very minute, I'm hurting her, he thought. *I shouldn't be here. I need to go. I need to leave. This is not safe. Not good for her.*

"ADRIAN, CAN YOU HEAR ME?" Lucy asked. "Are you going to be sick?"

His pupils were fully dilated; there was no color in his face at all. He pulled his hand away when she tried to touch him. "I'm not going to hurt you, Adrian. I just want to help."

He stared at her with the same blank expression. When she reached up and touched his face, he exhaled hard.

"Sorry," he said. "I'm sorry. What were you saying?"

"I asked if you were going to be sick," she said, hurt now mixed with concern. He was holding her hand to his chest.

"No, better now. One minute," he said, shoveling eggs in his mouth at an alarming rate, still holding her hand.

"Whoa, Adrian, slow down. You're going to make yourself sicker."

"It's fine, almost done," he muttered.

And he was almost done. He'd eaten most of six eggs in less than a minute. "Holy cow, Adrian. Do we need to go to the hospital?"

"No. We should go back to bed, though," he mumbled, pulling her close for a kiss.

"Adrian, wait, what is happen—"

His mouth closed over hers, smothering the words.

ADRIAN WOKE as the rising sun streamed in the windows.

Oh my God. My head. I'm going to be sick again, he thought, jumping out of bed. His legs folded underneath him, unable to support his weight as a wave of vertigo hit.

"Holy hell, what is going on with you?" Lucy asked as she helped him up. "Did you take some kind of drug or something?"

"No, no drugs. I'm so sorry, Lucy. I'm all fucked up."

"Yeah, I got that part. What is going on? You can tell me. I won't freak out, I promise. Okay?"

"Can't," he muttered. "You'll think I'm fucking insane."

"Well, we're already reaching that point. Might as well go for broke, love," she muttered back at him.

"What? What did you just say?"

Lucy's cheeks were turning pink. "I said we're kinda already there, so you might as well share."

Oh God. I can't do this. I can't do this to her. She can't feel this. This can't happen. I'm a fucking monster…

"Lucy, I love you. I love you so much. I can't do this to you. I'm sorry. I—We can't. This can't… I'm sorry," he said, tears running down his face.

Oh God. I can't do this. I don't want to do this. I really am a fucking monster.

Before he could think better of it, before he could chicken out, before he hurt her more, Adrian pulled the rage all the way forward.

"Lucinda," he said, voice making the air vibrate.

Her gaze was glued to his face.

"Lucy," he said as the air crackled with power. The rage rolled through him, disintegrating the happy energy.

Adrian kissed her lips gently, one last time.

"Lucy, you don't love me. You never loved me. You don't want this in your life. You were attracted to me because I helped you, but that's over now. You're happy it's done." Adrian choked on the lump in his throat. "You know that you made the right call ending things. You know Henry is going to be just fine. You don't want to see me again. You want me to stay away. You'll tell Henry that I love him, but that I can't see him anymore. And you know that I love you and have only ever wanted what is best for you."

Lucy blinked at him. "Adrian?"

"Say it, Lucy."

"Adrian, I don't love you. I don't want this in my life. We should make the call now and end things," she looked confused.

"It'll settle in. Rest now, rest until Ree wakes up, okay?"

LATER THAT DAY, Will came by for lunch again.

"Hi, you," Lucy said with a smile, opening the front door. "You don't even text anymore, just show up?"

"Heh, someone's gotta keep an eye on you until Adrian gets his shit together," Will said with a laugh.

"Oh, he was here last night," Lucy said in a distracted voice.

"Was he? He stormed out of family dinner last night. I'm surprised he came here," Will said.

There's nothing. Nothing coming off her. What happened? Will was trying not to freak out.

"Yeah. We talked this morning. I think that's all done now," Lucy said.

"Huh?" Will said, breathing fast.

Lucy shrugged. "I just don't want that in my life? You know? Adrian's great, but I think I was all into him because he pretty much swooped in to save us."

There's nothing. WHAT THE FUCK DID HE DO?

"Yeah, yeah. I know what you mean," Will said, nodding. "Tell me again what happened last night?"

WILL POKED at Lucy's brain for over an hour. Whatever Adrian did, he really did it. There was no sign of it fraying. He couldn't undo it yet. He needed to find the pattern in the words, find at least one thread of the compulsion before he could pull it apart.

WEDNESDAY NIGHT, Sam had the dream where everyone suffocates, but the violet-eyed girl was there with him.

Adaline. She's Adaline. I have a name.

As she took his hand, he could hear her voice.

"This is horrible. All the people. Where are we?" she asked, eyes huge.

"I don't know," Sam said.

"When is this?" she asked.

He shook his head. "I don't know."

"I can't stir the wind here. I can't help them. Have we lost the wind? Your brother. Has he lost Wind?"

"Maybe. He didn't know what Wind was," Sam said.

"No, Sam. No. Wind is not what. Wind is who."

Sam looked confused. "Wind is a person?"

"Well, wind is a thing. A power. But Wind wields it."

"Is Wind like Lady Light?" Sam asked.

"Yes. Yes. The same. Lady Light is light. Heat. She is Fire. Color. Lady Wind —same concept. She is Sky." Adaline nodded like this made sense. And it did, to Sam, at least.

"I don't think I've found her yet. I don't think she is known yet."

Adaline looked around. *"I think we may have lost her already. I'll look for her, too."*

"Why are things changing?" Sam asked.

Adaline shook her head.

Sam's eyes became slits. "What are you hiding? I can feel it. What, Adaline?"

She smiled, reaching up to touch his face. Her happiness at hearing her name from him zinged through Sam's body.

"What are you hiding? What don't you want me to see?"

Her smile faded. *"I'm dying. The power is taking me. Walking doesn't help anymore. There's no way to burn through it fast enough. Even in the house with changing views. I don't think it will help."*

Sam couldn't breathe. "How long?" he gasped out.

Sam's love and fear collided with her resignation, making Adaline's stomach flip.

"Maybe a season. I think I'll see the leaves fall, but not the new snow," she said.

"Can I go with you?"

She looked around again. *"I think you must stay, Sam."*

CV/ hen Will arrived for Sunday dinner, Sam, Ethan, Jake, and Matilda were sitting in the big room, chatting. It was early. Others wouldn't be arriving for a while yet.

"There he is!" Ethan yelled. "Why are we here early?"

"Because I need you here," Will said.

"Will, what do you love?" Sam asked quickly as everyone else groaned.

"Sam, let's do that later." Will brushed him off. "I need you to go spooky."

"Huh?" Sam looked confused.

"I need the other part. Go spooky. Make the room vibrate with your freaky-ass voice. Now."

"I can't do it like that. I don't have control like that." Sam frowned.

"Yes, you do," Will disagreed. "Pull it forward."

"Pull what forward?"

"Whatever your thing is. Pull it all the way forward where it's sitting in your chest."

"I don't know what the thing is, Will. You sound like Luke."

"Luke has a thing?" William asked. "I didn't notice. What's his thing?"

"Peace. He gives peace."

"I fucking hate Luke with my entire mind, body, and soul. I hate Luke more than I hate Ethan," Will said, deadpan.

"Hey! I didn't do anything. Why hate me? I don't have a thing!" Ethan objected.

"Fuck you, yes, you do," Will argued. "And I fucking hate you. We're off topic. Sam, do it."

"It doesn't work like that. I can't do it," Sam said.

"Fuck me. Where are Mom and Dad?" Will asked.

"Mom's in the kitchen. Dad ran to the store," Jake answered. "What's going on?"

"I need Spooky Sam. Fuck." Will looked back and forth between Matty and Ethan. He stood up and pulled a quarter out of his pocket. "Matty, call it in the air. Heads or tails."

"Heads."

"It's tails," Jake said.

"FUCK!" Will yelled. "FUCK! Sam, go spooky. I don't want to do this."

"I can't just do it like that, Will! What's going on?"

Will rubbed his hands on the legs of his pants. "It'll probably go faster with you anyway, Matty. Just. I need Spooky Sam. Okay? You're going to forget why I'm doing this in a sec and be upset. Just. Remember later, okay?"

Matilda started laughing. "William, Sam's the brother that speaks in riddles. Remember?"

Will met her eyes. "Matilda, it's your fault your dad is dead. If you hadn't been born—"

"WILLIAM!" Samuel's voice vibrated through the house, shaking the ground.

"Fuck, that was fast. Can you undo what Rage does?" Will said quickly.

The anger fell off Samuel's face as he caught on to what Will did. "That was clever. More clever than I would expect from you." Samuel —full-powered Spooky Samuel—laughed. Everyone in the room backed away.

As the laughter died down, Darla ran into the room. "Did you feel —? Whoa!" She stopped cold, looking at Samuel. The energy radiating from him was visible.

"You have to tell us, Mother. You need to go where you want to go. Claire is right. It's necessary," Samuel said. "Tell us. Tonight."

"Can you undo what Rage has done?" William asked again, trying to stay on the topic before Spooky Sam disappeared again.

Samuel turned to meet his eyes. "No. Rage is a child of Life, not Time. Time will resolve rage eventually. But not how you want. Not soon enough."

William's face fell. "Fuck. I can't budge it."

"You're pushing from the wrong side, William," Samuel said. "Even if you moved it, it wouldn't help. You understand."

Will sighed as he nodded.

"William, there must be four corners to hold the circle. Four Ladies. Only two are accounted for. One is lost to Rage. Where is the fourth?"

In a heartbeat, Sam was Sam again.

"HOLY FUCK!" Sam yelled. "How?! How did you do that?!"

"Fucking-A. I pay attention, dipshit. Matty, I'm so sorry. I didn't —" Before Will could say another word, Matty punched him in the face.

"Ugh, I deserved that."

"HOW?! TEACH ME HOW!" Sam was still yelling at Will as the family was sitting down at the table.

"THIS IS SO MUCH WORSE THAN THE 'WHAT DO YOU LOVE SHIT!' YOU WERE THERE! YOU KNOW WHAT I DID! PLEASE SHUT THE FUCK UP," Will yelled.

"William."

"Dad."

"Stop it," Hank said, trying not to smile.

"I'm not the one doing it," Will argued.

"I missed this whole thing," Beth complained. "What's Sam wigging out about?"

"William pulled Spooky Sam out on purpose," Jake explained.

"Whoa," Luke looked decidedly uncomfortable. "Was it bad?"

"You shut the fuck up down there, Number Eight. We're going to have words later," Will yelled at Luke.

"What? What? I didn't do anything! I wasn't even here!" Luke yelled back.

"Yeah, Peace. FUCK YOU!" Will yelled.

"Sam, what the fuck?! You weren't supposed to talk about it!" Luke bitched.

"You told me not to talk about mine! You didn't tell me I couldn't talk about yours!" Sam yelled.

Hank put his fingers in his mouth and whistled. "What is going on?! You know better than to do this over dinner."

"Whatever," Will said. "We'll compare notes later. Mom, what do you have to tell us before I beat Luke's ass?"

"Oh, uh…" Darla looked around, lost.

"Spit it out," Will demanded. "It's gonna be bad. We'll cope. Go."

DARLA SWALLOWED hard and looked at Hank. Her gaze moved around the table, looking at each of her children.

Beth was watching her from the other end of the table.

My little girl, I wish you weren't so far away, Darla thought.

Hennessy, her ninth son.

Luke, Matthew. Her eyes filled with tears. The last of her boys.

Noah, watching her with dread.

Sam looked terrible. He literally shook the ground earlier. That was new.

Ethan, her joyful one.

Jake and Matty, together, at least. They'd be fine.

Adrian. Adrian looked horrible. Eyes sunken like Sam, skin grey.

And William. Her first. Her warrior. So alone.

"About three weeks ago, I started treatment for Stage three breast cancer," Darla murmured. "We're treating it aggressively. My odds are good. Everything's going to be okay. Things have been crazy. I was going to tell you last week, but then we weren't all together. There's been a lot going on."

The next few minutes were some of the worst of Darla's life.

Will sat, staring off into space.

Adrian stared at her, not even blinking. She met his eyes. There was anger in that gaze. *My gentle Adrian. I'm sorry, honey.*

Jake sat, pulling Matty close. Sam sat on the other side of her, holding her hand to his chest.

Ethan was weeping. Matthew and Luke looked lost. Beth was curled against Hennessy, sobbing.

Hank sat next to her, holding her hand, tears dripping down his face.

"It's going to be okay," Darla said again. "I promise everything's going to be fine." Darla couldn't get the words out over the painful lump in her throat.

Without a glance, Will took her free hand. Then it wasn't so bad. Sad, but not scared. It was going to be okay.

"What is Claire right about, Mom?" Will said, still staring off into space.

"Claire?!" Luke asked. "What does she have to do with this?"

"Oh, I— At the time, when we were talking, it made sense. But then, I got home and tried explaining it to your father, and I felt like an idiot. So, I blew her off. But I've been thinking about it since then. Look at us, and I'm going to laugh off Claire?"

"What did she say?" Sam asked.

"I had lunch with her a couple weeks ago. She's always been a bit different... But she started talking about energy and life and the ability to harness energy. Anyway, she has a cousin in Texas that she swears can move energy around, within a person and between people. She asked me to go see her cousin with some of you."

"Claire has a Life-Giving cousin?" Luke asked. "Doubtful."

Darla gave Luke a startled look. "Why do you know anything about this?"

Luke sighed. "Because Mom. I give peace. Claire and I stand in the same circle. It's why she wants one of us to go with you. She knows we're...different. Different lights."

"What the hell are you talking about?" Darla yelled. "What people? What did Claire get you involved in?"

Luke sighed again. Without another word, he reached over and touched Bethany, who was still sobbing on Hennessy. She was asleep with a touch.

"Sorry, Hennessy. I meant to calm her. I went a little too far. I'm upset."

"Why won't you do that to me?!" Sam yelled.

"It doesn't work on you! Would everyone please stop yelling at me?" Luke bitched.

"I'll go with you, Mom. We'll go this week," William offered. "We'll check it out. Can't hurt. With all the freaky shit sitting in this room, why not try it?"

"Wait. Before we fly to fucking Texas, can anyone sitting at this fucking table give life or rearrange life energy or anything like that?" Will yelled.

Head shakes all around. The table was quiet for a few minutes.

"Will, what do you love?" Sam asked into the silence.

The table exploded in groans of laughter.

THURSDAY MORNING, Hank, Darla, Will, and Luke flew to Dallas on the Trellis jet.

"Why won't you tell me?" Luke nagged.

"Because, asshole, I'm still fucking pissed at you. Peace. Fuck you!" Will bitched.

"I take it yours is not happy."

"No, Luke. No. Mine is not happy."

"I still don't understand how this happened. We eat dinner

together every week. How has this not come out before now?" Darla complained.

"Frankly, Mom, Sam's weird enough without the rest of us getting involved," Luke answered

Will nodded.

"He really shook the ground?" Luke asked again.

Will nodded again.

Luke grinned. "Matty's bruise is gone."

"It was gone on Monday," Hank murmured.

"It was a full-on shiner on Sunday. No way it was gone on Monday! You wore makeup, didn't you?" Luke grinned again.

"Nope," Will disagreed. "I'd wear that shiner with pride. Carrots packs a good punch, and I earned it."

"How'd you get rid of it so fast?" Luke asked.

Will sighed. "Do you have to focus to give peace? Is it hard work? Is there a maximum amount of peace you can give?"

"I mean, there's a limit to how much energy I can handle. Sam fucked me up good on the night of the fundraiser when Matty freaked out," Luke admitted.

"Let's just assume that I handle more energy than you. There's no cap to mine. The night Matty freaked out, there was a tiny twinge in my gut that was like, 'Oh, something's happening,' and then I burped. Thought it was gas," Will said, starting to laugh.

Luke was quiet. "I puked for four days."

"Yeah, puking peace! I love it," Will said. "This is great. I love this new sharing. We're growing as a family!"

Darla worked hard to keep a straight face.

"Don't worry, Ma, I'll be your fucking battery. Life energy for everyone!" Will yelled, still laughing as he got in the car.

19

Claire's cousin and her family ran a restaurant and bar in a little town outside Dallas. There was nothing around the place but open fields and forests.

"What's this woman's name again?" Will asked as he pulled the car up.

"Ava. Ava and Clyde. Their daughter, Jessica, is around Matthew's age. There are a couple of grandkids, too, but just the mom and daughter do the energy stuff. Ava does something with life. The daughter does something with sight," Darla said.

"No peace." Luke sighed. "Hopefully, they don't fucking hate me, too."

"No one hates you, Luke—" Hank started.

"FUCK YOU, YES I DO," Will yelled over Hank as he pulled the restaurant door open for his parents.

"Well, look at this group. Ma! Claire's people are here," the woman behind the bar yelled.

"You sure it's them? I'm in the middle—" a voice called back.

"They can't possibly be anyone else," the woman interrupted.

"Hey, Peace, who tied up your power?" she asked.

"Huh?" Luke said.

"Who tied up your power? Do you know you're nerfed?" the woman asked.

"I don't know what you mean," Luke replied.

"Oh, for fuck's sake," she said, walking over and taking his hand. "Look. No, not through your eyes, dumbass."

"Ugh," Luke groaned. "Hey, what the fuck?"

"Yeah, see. Your shit's all fucked up. Gotta break that. Bad circle, they're feeding on you." When the woman dropped Luke's hand, he staggered and fell over.

"Oh, suck it up, Peace."

"Jess, did you introduce yourself or, you know, say hi?" a woman said from the back doorway. While she looked to be in her late twenties or early thirties, there was a grace to her movement that hinted at her being older. Still, she looked more like Jess's sister than mother.

"Nah, they know who I am," the woman said.

"Hank, Darla, it's nice to meet you," the woman said, shaking hands. "I'm Ava, this is my daughter, Jess. Welcome. This is your youngest boy, right? Luke? Claire said you had a peace giver. And who's this?"

"This is our oldest, William," Darla said.

"It's nice to meet you, Ava," Will said, extending his hand to shake. Ava looked at it with trepidation.

"William," Ava nodded, still not taking his hand. "I can't see you. I can't see your colors or energy at all. Jess, can you?"

"Nope," she said, elongating the word. "He's a void to me."

"Huh?" Luke said. "I can see him."

"He lets you see him," Jess corrected Luke.

Luke's brow furrowed. "Will, are you doing anything?"

"What would I be doing?" Will asked.

"He wouldn't know how," Luke said. "He's never been in a circle before."

"I'm guessing he's not standing in one today, either." Jess laughed. "I'm not getting in the ring with an unknown that has more juice than Mom. That's terrifying."

"I'm sorry, I don't understand what's happening," Hank

interrupted.

Ava smiled at Hank. "I'm sorry. Let's sit and visit, and I'll explain some of this. And then we can decide how and if we want to move forward. Iced tea? Drink? Have you had lunch? I'm guessing not. It's only ten thirty."

Jess grabbed a pitcher of iced tea and six glasses from behind the bar as everyone sat down at a table.

"Now, what did Claire tell you?" Ava asked.

"Um, she said you can rearrange life energy and that you might help me stay well through cancer treatment," Darla muttered.

Ava nodded. "In our crowd, I'm known as a Life Holder."

Luke whistled. "Holy hell. Why don't I know about you?"

"Because you stand with Claire's circle, from which I am outcast," Ava explained.

Luke's face fell. "Mom, we might not want to do this."

"Says the guy tied by his own circle," Jess snarked.

"Hush, Jess, it's fine." Ava smiled. "Luke, Claire would not have sent you here if I was a hunter, and you know it. I was removed from my circle on my eighteenth birthday. I'm now fifty-three; that's thirty-five years without a circle. Now, you all mostly don't know what that means, but Peace over there does."

Luke turned toward his parents. "When we talk about energy and circles, the strongest of us hold power over an emotion or an element. Elements are typically stronger than emotions, with Life being the strongest.

"There are a lot of us that can't manifest anything but can see the energy. Claire is like that. For those of us that can manifest something, there are a couple levels of power.

"Some of us have a single manifestation. I can give my peace to someone else like I did to Beth, but I have to feel it in myself to give it away. I can't create it. I can't be in turmoil and force you to feel peace. I can't take peace from others.

"Some of us are stronger. They might give energy to a person as well as take energy. They might share something that they don't have within themselves. Give, take, move between people. Like that. The combination of things these people can do varies. But typically, it's only two manifestations. They might give and take. Give and create. Whatever.

"The strongest among us are Holders. They can manifest the raw energy, give, take, rearrange, transform, and sense it in others. These people are...different. They see the world differently. See energy differently. Ava is saying she is a Life Holder, which would make her one of the strongest power wielders on the planet," Luke finished, looking at Ava.

"So, so close!" Jess teased. "There are two more tiers. They just don't talk about them in your crowd because there are so few of them. The next tier up are known as pillars—akin to nobility in our power circles—often called Lords or Ladies, as appropriate."

Luke snorted. "You believe that?"

"Oh yeah." Jess smirked again.

"On Sunday, he mentioned needing four Ladies, four corners," Will murmured to Hank.

That caught Ava's attention. "Who is this?"

"One of our children," Darla answered, following Claire's instructions not to mention Sam. "Okay, I'm playing along. Pillars..."

"Pillars are wielders of elements and base emotions. Things that generate energy and action: fire, wind, earth, water, peace, love, joy, anger, terror, and so on." Ava picked up the lesson. "These folks have an instinctual, core grasp of their elements or emotions. If I had to guess, Peace over there would be a lord if he was untied. And I think this is probably what William is because he can hide from me, and not many can do that. Pillars are typically named by their power, which is why we keep calling Luke by the name 'Peace.' These people typically have no cap to the amount of energy they can use but are limited to a specific *type* of energy."

"They don't exist!" Luke laughed.

Ava chuckled. "Lucas, your energy is so strangled, you can access only a quarter of it. You are still able to give peace to others. On a quarter of your energy. What do you think you are?"

"I don't think it's a quarter," Luke said.

"You can't see it, honey. It's less than a quarter," Ava responded. "We'll poke it in the circle and see what happens."

"What is the last tier?" Hank asked, fascinated.

"There are only two people that stand in the last tier. She is Mother Life, also known as the Mistress. He is Father Time, also known as the Walker. Their titles evolve as they age; Mother and Father tend to be adopted after they've had children."

Luke snorted again.

Ava smiled. "These beings have not been seen in many hundreds of years, but I choose to believe they exist, just as I believe the Lord in Heaven exists, and Jesus walked the Earth."

Darla looked startled. "You're Christian? I would not have expected that."

"Why?" Ava asked, surprised. "I speak of energy sources. That which builds and holds our circles is nothing but energy. Does your use of electricity or your gas stove preclude you from having faith in a higher power? It is the same. Some of us are Wiccans; I am not."

"I'm undecided at this point," Jess said with a grin.

Hank sat back, looking at Luke. "Is there a time holder? Or a time pillar? Like you are a life holder?"

"No. There is only one Time wielder. Saying the Mistress wields life is like saying the Sun is akin to a candle. They both burn but are different orders of magnitude. There is only one Mistress. There is only one Walker.

"She rules emotions and life. He rules the elements, time, and some believe space as well. Our oldest stories hint that they can share energies when in accordance, meaning that she can also touch time, and he can touch life. I don't know. As I said, these are beings of our legends." Ava took a drink of her iced tea.

"Dreams?" Hank asked.

Ava turned her head, curious.

Hank cleared his throat. "Do you have dreams? Of other times? Specific people? Vivid nightmares that repeat or different people you see in every dream?"

Ava looked uneasy. "Pillars are known to be able to Walk in each other's dreams. The Walker and the Mistress certainly could by the very definition of what they are. Who Walks?"

"Holders can do that," Luke said, his face pensive.

"What holders are you hanging out with?" Jess asked.

"Anyway, back to what we were talking about," Ava said. "I have been outcast for thirty-five years. The more powerful we are, the harder it is to stay sane without a circle. The circle gives the strongest among us a way to redistribute our energy to others, so it doesn't build too much. If it builds and we don't redistribute, we go boom. Our minds go first. Then our bodies."

Hank cleared his throat. "Do you taste things in your food? Things about the person who made it or the animal's life?"

"Dad. Stop. That's not something to be discussed. Stop," Luke chided. "No more. Let's talk about it later."

"How have you known this for the last decade and not mentioned it?" Hank snapped. Normally calm and patient with his children, he was clearly angry with Luke. "This didn't strike you as eerily familiar? Like these people might have some answers?"

"Hank, he has cause for concern. If I was interested in raw power, and the person you're describing lacked control, I could do a lot of damage," Ava admitted.

"Yeah, she could tie him to less than a quarter of his power and leave him completely ignorant to what he is," Jess snarked.

"Jess, enough. Stop. Let's get back on track here. We can talk about it later, okay, Hank? I'll answer your questions," Ava promised. "Claire said your children are different, and I believe it.

"Without a circle, things go wrong for the strongest of us, and I am very strong. I was cast out because I refused to participate in what was essentially a genetics breeding program. Powerful parents tend to produce powerful children, and it's generally believed that the stronger each parent is, the stronger the child or children would be.

"I was eighteen and uninterested in making babies with a fifty-six-year-old man. When I refused, repeatedly, they cast me out. I ended up here, with Clyde, who is not empowered in any way.

"I've managed to maintain my energy levels by sharing it with others." Ava shrugged. "I help women get pregnant and give birth, I strengthen cancer patients for treatment, and I help impaired children adjust. I'm happy to help my friends and neighbors by helping myself. This is generally frowned upon in our crowds. I don't really care. They already cast me out. What does it matter what anyone thinks of me?

"Jess lacks my raw power, but her gift is very rare. There are only two others like her on record. Her existence bothers the main circles, as she has only one empowered parent. Lucas, I am curious about what they made of you and your family when they met you."

Luke cleared his throat. "I was in high school. The energy was making me sick. The sight kept breaking through. Claire is a long-time family friend. Her energy was different. She couldn't see mine well, has never seen mine well. She has trouble seeing all of us, actually. My family looks normal to me, like average non-empowered people, except for one."

"That's not unusual, Luke. You see what you expect from those closest," Ava said quietly.

"She explained about energy, at a high level, and taught me how to control the sight better. Then she told me to leave it alone. Stop looking so affronted, Mom. I talked to her about this at Dad's fiftieth birthday party. We talked about it for maybe twenty minutes before she gave me the same warning she gave you. It's energy. Power. Over people and elements. Behavior. Some take advantage.

"I went to school the following Monday, turned on the sight, and looked for kids with lights like Claire. And I found them. She had an absolute shit-fit when I showed up to the first circle." Luke laughed.

"Claire got mad?!" Ava chuckled. "I'm sorry to have missed that!"

"Anyway, we agreed that she'd keep my involvement to herself if I agreed to never bring anyone from the circle home for dinner. She was afraid for one of us. I don't think she realized there was anything more to the rest of us until I ended up manifesting peace."

"So the circle has never seen the rest of your family?" Ava asked.

"I don't think so, no. At Claire's insistence, I've never mentioned any of them. I think the circle believes I'm related to Claire," Luke said.

Ava nodded. "It's entirely possible that you were originally tied because your energy was wonky. It sounds like it broke through unexpectedly and wouldn't focus. This may have started for your own good; it may have allowed them to hold the circle with you in it. I see some of Nora in the deepest part of the tie. She would not tie to drain you. Greggory is less altruistic. Not a hunter, but not opposed to... borrowing from others. I suggest breaking yourself from the circle."

Luke looked a little nauseous.

"Claire sent you here hoping I'd juice up your light, and I will if you want. She told you to bring kids because it seems like your kids have some serious juice of their own. Luke, I don't think I can break that tie. I'm not stronger than Greggory, but we can try. The question remains, though, about William, who has been sitting oh so quiet over there. Drinking his tea."

William smiled a real smile.

"You enjoy it here, yes?" Ava asked. "Feel better?"

"Yes. Much," Will admitted quietly.

"There is a ward here that redistributes energy in natural patterns. I suspect it's taking some of the overflow from you. You've never stood a circle?"

"No."

"Do you know what you are?" Ava asked.

"I do." Will sighed.

"What are you?" Ava asked.

Without another word, Will pulled his energy forward for the world to see.

"Holy fuck!" Luke yelled.

Jessica gasped.

Ava nodded, unsurprised. "Lord Terror, you are welcome here."

"WELL, that doesn't sound dramatic at all. Thanks, Ava." Will laughed. "Why do I have to be Lord Terror, but Luke gets to be Peace?"

"Man, I fucking hate you," he said to Luke.

"*I* didn't make the titles. Lord Fear?" Ava asked.

"Will? William?" he asked backed.

Ava smiled.

"What? What did you do? What have you done to yourself?" Jess asked, tripping over her words.

"Jess," Ava said soothingly, "Fear is black. It's not wrong."

"No, Mom! No! His bindings. What is wrong with his binding? That's the most barbaric, horrible thing I've ever seen. Who would do that to him?" Jess was close to tears.

"I can't see it, Jess. Show me." Ava held out her hand for her daughter.

Ava swallowed hard. "No one did that to him, Jess. Your first guess was right. He did it. It's fine, sweetheart. Leave him be."

Jess bodily turned herself away from William, wiping tears from her eyes.

Ava pressed her lips together. "I'm not sure what to make of this. You have one tightly tied and one pillar. At least one more at home that is empowered enough to Walk. I'm not asking about anyone, Luke. Don't worry. My concern is how you are all sane.

"Power on this scale *needs* a circle. William is clearly still sane but claims to have never stood a circle. I believe him. But this is odd. I don't want to get in a circle with you, where energy is exposed, and then find out there are secrets. I mean you no harm. Please understand I am trying to keep us all safe."

There was an extended pause.

"I have a theory," Lucas muttered. "I've been thinking about this since last Sunday."

"Just a theory?" Ava asked.

"Yeah, I don't even know if it's possible."

Ava leaned back in her chair. "Okay. What's the theory?"

"Uh. I know this sounds stupid. But hear me out. We have dinner together every Sunday. All of us. It's time for us to be together and be a family, share our weeks and our lives. We've done it my whole life," Luke explained.

"Longer than that," Hank interrupted. "William's whole life. Our whole marriage."

"Okay. So we have dinner, and it's fun. Friends, significant others, random people we enjoy, everyone sits around the table for a couple of hours eating Mom's food, and we're together.

"One of my brothers is getting married. His future wife is...very bright. Blindingly bright—"

"Really?" Hank smiled.

"Yes." Luke nodded. "She's elemental light of some sort and at least a Holder. Maybe a lady if you make that differentiation. I'm not sure where I stand on that right now. My brother who Walks insists that he has to be on the same side of the table with her. A couple of weeks ago, he was trying to organize us around the table—"

"You think you have an organic circle with no one holding it?" Ava asked.

"Is that possible?"

"I have no idea. Have you looked?" Ava asked.

Luke shrugged. "I have. I looked that day. I didn't see anything. But, again, all my family looks normal to me. I didn't see or feel the tie on my power until Jess pointed it out. Now that I know it's there, I can feel it."

"I don't know," Ava admitted. "There are naturally occurring places of power in this world. It might be. It'd explain how Will is okay.

"I don't know if I can hold a circle with you, William. I'll try it if you want. If I can hold it, you'll feel better. But we need to go outside for it. If the circle goes boom, I don't want to blow the bar up."

"You think it could blow? Hurt people?" Will asked.

"Not out here. There's no one to hurt. The bar is warded. If the circle goes, it blows outward, not in on us."

"It won't hurt you?" he asked Ava.

She shrugged. "It'd be better if we had more people. A lot more people. I have enough trouble moving energy without adding your exponentially stronger self to the mix."

"Then do it with Luke," Will said. "We'll come back. With more people."

LUKE AND DARLA slept on the plane going back to Chicago.

"He really puked?" Will asked, looking at Luke.

"Everywhere," Hank said. "She said, 'Okay, I'm going to just touch it and see,' and he threw up everything he's ever eaten."

"Fuck. What was the circle like?"

Hank sighed. "Think of the dirtiest, most unpleasant, foulest situation you've ever been in. It was like the best long hot shower ever, after being that funky."

Will laughed. "I'm jealous."

"Fear?" Hank asked.

It was Will's turn to sigh.

"No wonder you hate the peace-giver over there." Hank laughed.

After a few minutes, Hank asked, "Is it why you left? When you enlisted?"

Will nodded. "I knew what I was, what I could do. It was nothing I wanted anywhere near the people I loved."

"What changed?" Hank asked.

"I found balance."

"You think Sam can find balance?"

"Dad. I think Sam's the fucking Walker, and so do you."

"I do," Hank agreed.

"I don't know if there's a balance to that. Maybe the girl is Mother or Mistress whatever? He finds her, and they can be crazy together." Will scratched the top of his head.

Will sighed again.

"Hmm?" Hank asked.

"It's Adrian that needs balance. He's slipping fast."

"Adrian? He's gotta have like life or joy or something, right?"

"Oh, Dad. You have no fucking clue. None at all."

20

"Sunday, Sunday, Sunday, here we are again," Will chanted, walking in late.

"Dinner's half over. Where have you been?" Darla demanded.

"Hi, Mom, it's good to see you, too," Will said as he kissed the top of her head. "I've been pondering the mysteries of life. And love. And Spooky Samuel."

"Don't do it again!" Matty yelled.

"Relax, Carrots. If I ever have to do it again, I'll do it to Ethan. It'll just take longer. And Ethan will probably hate me forever instead of just slugging me."

"Hennessy, my man?" Will called.

"Yeah, Will? You okay?" Hennessy asked.

"I'm good. About to dance. Stay out. Understand?" Will said, meeting Hennessy's eyes. "I mean it. He'll kill you. Literally. Okay, pumpkin?"

"Uh, who we dancing with, man?"

"That's the point. You ain't dancing with anyone. Understand? Beth, he stays with you."

"Yeah, all right, Reap. But what's going on?" Hennessy asked.

"Shit's gonna get real, kids! Time to buckle up!" Will called to the table at large.

"Are you drunk?" Darla asked.

"No. Well, kinda, but not really. I've had a little emotional feast. Mmm, fear. My favorite." Will laughed. "It's gonna be fine, Mom. Probably."

"Hey, little brother! How's Adrian? You don't look great, man. Go bang the blonde again, clear your mind," Will said as he licked his finger and stuck it in Adrian's ear. "Wet Willy!"

Adrian grabbed Will's hand, twisting it. "Fuck off, man."

"Gasp! Mom, Saint Adrian is swearing at the table. You know who I was thinking about earlier. Whitney Fucking Langcaster. Remember that bitch? Oh man, you were so hot for her, then you went and mind fucked her. It took me like two years to sort that shit out."

"What is happening right now?" Matty asked.

"William, what are you—" Darla started.

"So, I don't know, maybe two weeks ago, I was talkin' to Lou, and she starts going on about ending things, never loved you, blah blah blah. And I think to myself, 'Self, this is the perfect fucking opportunity to get hot fucking blonde action.' I mean, what're sloppy seconds among brothers—"

Will stopped talking when Adrian lunged at him. "Just like Spooky fucking Samuel. Pops up as soon as I pick on the girls. Time to dance, man! Outside." Will picked Adrian up and threw him half the length of the dining room.

"Boys!" Hank yelled.

Adrian took a running start to tackle Will to the ground.

"What the—" Jake screamed, pulling Matty behind him.

"You fucking pansy. You're so far gone, you can't even talk right now," Will said, kicking Adrian in the ribs and then dragging him through the house to the back door. "We'll take it out back. Don't want the neighborhood to be disturbed."

Adrian got a hold of Will's leg, knocking him to the ground and twisting until something popped. Will got the other leg under him and launched Adrian off the patio as the rest of the family followed them outside.

"I really don't understand," Matty said. "Is Will after Lucy?"

"No," Hennessy said.

"It sure as fuck sounds like it, man," Jake disagreed.

"No. Promise," Hennessy shook his head.

"What the fuck is happening here, then?" Ethan yelled.

"Right now, Terror is teaching Rage an important lesson in balance," Spooky Samuel murmured, humming to himself. "Mom, don't cry."

"Why are they doing this?!" Darla screamed. "Hank! Get the hose!"

"Luuuccccaaasss?" Samuel sang. "Youngest brother, where are youuuuu?"

"WILLIAM! STOP!" Hank yelled.

"Lucas, come here," Samuel demanded. "It's time. And it's going to hurt."

Luke didn't move. He was visibly shaking.

"Lucas. Come here," Samuel said again. "We have to break it, Luke. One of them will die, and the other will be lost if you don't break it."

"Oh God," Lucas begged, looking sick. "Please, Samuel. There has to be another way. Don't do the fundraiser thing again. Please. Sam, Please."

Samuel chuckled. "No, Lucas. No. This is going to be much worse than that. Much, much worse. But it must be. Come here."

In the yard, Adrian yelled as William dislocated his shoulder. "I mean, here's the thing, man. Rage might let you overcome fear for a short burst, but fear just keeps rolling. The hindbrain kicks in eventually," Will said as he stomped on Adrian's ribs. "Let it take over, Adrian. Let the rage go. You'll die if you keep trying to pull it back. Time to play superpowers. I'll be the villain. Let's do this, Adrian."

"Oh my God," Darla cried, falling over on the patio. "Is Will gone? He's going to kill Adrian. I don't know what to do. Oh my God. Oh my God."

The ground rolled underfoot. "Lucas. We're running out of time. A minute, maybe a little more. Do you want them to die?" Samuel asked.

Without another word, Lucas took Samuel's hand, immediately dropping to the ground, screaming in pain. When Luke's nose started gushing blood, Samuel let go. "Good, good. That's done."

Adrian and Will were literally glowing with power, neon black and red light circling them in the twilight. Back on his feet, Adrian's chest was popping its ribs back into place.

"There you go, little brother! That's it. Now. Pull that energy that is Lou's and merge it with the rage. Seriously, man, weave that shit together. It's more fun to do while fucking, but you know, whatever. You always were a stubborn asshole."

Adrian growled as he dove for Will and dragged him to the ground again. Half of Will's head was bloody, and his jaw was broken before Adrian closed his hands around William's neck.

"Oh my God!" Darla screamed.

Will managed to flip so that he was laying on Adrian's back.

"This is over," Hennessy muttered.

Adrian screamed as Will systematically started breaking bones. "TAKE THE FUCKING RAGE AND THE OTHER SHIT AND PUT THEM TOGETHER, ADRIAN. THEY HAVE TO FUCKING ALIGN."

Will was panting hard. "GOD DAMN, THIS FUCKING HURTS! Do it, Adrian. DO IT. Put them together! I can't fucking hold the terror like this forever. You're gonna die if you don't, man. It hurts her. It hurts her to be like this! She knows it's wrong, but she doesn't know why. ADRIAN, DO IT. NOW. I CAN'T—"

"Lucas," Samuel called. "He's done it."

Nose and ears pouring blood, throwing up, tears dripping from his eyes, still screaming, Luke rolled over and looked at his brothers warring in the yard and let the power roll.

Adrian and Will dropped dead asleep immediately.

Samuel clapped. "Good show! Just leave them there. They're fine. Start cooking."

THREE HOURS LATER, the family was sitting around the dining room table watching William and Adrian eat their way through every bit of food in the house.

"There's like butter and lemon wedges left in the fridge," Jake called. "Someone order pizza."

"I am both fascinated and disgusted by Will eating the mustard as an entrée." Matty laughed.

"Did you really have to rotate my hip out of the socket to start? That shit sucks," Will bitched.

"You kicked in my ribs, man. Deal with it," Adrian retorted.

"Luke, how are you? Still bleeding?" Will called.

"He's out," Matthew said. "Looks like it stopped."

"Peace is fragile. Go figure." Adrian chuckled.

"Can we go back to Whitney Langcaster for a minute?" Jake asked.

Adrian put his head down on the table. "What, Jake? What is confusing to you?"

"The Jedi mind trick part of it. What did you do to her?"

"Ugh. I got pissed off and yelled at her."

"Why did that fuck her over?" Jake asked.

"Man, seriously?" Will asked. "You were there. You saw how she was that day. And every fucking day for like two years. You didn't think that shit was strange?"

"I did," Jake said. "But I didn't at any point think, 'Wow, that shit's strange. Adrian must have accidentally broken her brain.' How did you know?"

Will sighed. "I knew about my fear thing when I was young. Maybe seven or so. I fell out of the tree that Mom told me not to climb, broke my leg. There was a bone sticking out. My nose started bleeding, and then I could just feel it. I was freaking out. It fucking hurt, and I knew I was in deep shit. And then it just popped back in. Still hurt like fuck to walk on, but it was better. I hobbled my ass back in the house. Mom asked what happened to my jeans. I said, 'Nothing,' and she just kinda nodded. Took a while to sort out that mental element of it. Took a while to control it."

"You are in such deep shit, William," Hank muttered as the table laughed.

"Took me a while to figure out what happened with Whitney. She was always fucking irritating. I couldn't decide if she was just a bitch for a while or if something had really happened.

"You really cocked that up, Adrian. Audrey Stevens fucking adored you. She still sends me charming fucking holiday cards with pictures of her family. Jackass."

"I don't have mind-mojo, do I?" Jake asked.

"No, Jake. Your superpower is stupidity," Will said with a completely straight face. "Again, rage and fear can dictate how someone behaves. How they think about life. I'm sure others can do it, but logically, rage and fear are close to the top of the list of emotions that drive a person toward action."

"And what did you do to Lucy?" Jake asked.

Adrian winced.

"I'd actually really like to know that," Will admitted. "I've spent two weeks trying to get traction on that mental hold. That shit is buttoned up tight."

Adrian shook his head.

"I can't pull it out without a hint, Adrian." Will sighed.

"I don't want you to pull it out. I put it there for a reason," Adrian muttered to his hands.

"It was a dumb reason," Ethan stage-whispered across the table.

"Ethan, I love you, but shut the fuck up before I kill you," Will said. "You have no fucking idea. None at all. Particularly before finding balance, trying to control that power is agony. Someone around me would get startled by a bug or think about a nightmare, and it'd feel like my skin was going to fly off my body. I literally ran away from home because I accidentally handed Beth a smidge of fear that gave her nightmares for a month when she was five."

The table was silent for a minute.

Will shook his head. "I can't imagine what dancing with rage is like. Jesus. Driving down the street, a guy in the car next to you is arguing with his wife, and you fucking eat that? I can't fathom it. Working with sick kids. Holy fuck, you're a masochist."

Adrian snorted.

Will sighed. "You gotta fix that shit, man."

"No. I really don't, Will," Adrian said in a dead voice. "She doesn't need rage in her life. I won't do that to them."

"Based on what that woman said on Thursday, you're probably gonna go nuts and then like climb a watchtower with a rifle or something," Will said.

"Meh. Kill me before that, okay?"

A heavy silence settled back over the table.

"My problem is not you walking away. My problem is you not giving her a choice," Will said to Adrian.

Hennessy snorted. "You giant fucking hypocrite."

"Oh, shut it, man. We'll talk about that shit later. Maybe next week," Will muttered.

"Coward," Hennessy taunted, making chicken noises.

"Really, Jessup? Really? Fuck you. How long are you gonna keep sleeping with Beth before you talk to me?"

Beth laughed as everyone stared at her.

"Jesus Christ, man. How long have you known?" Hennessy asked, horrified.

"Day after the fundraiser in April. Guessing the whole time," Will said.

"I can explain, Will—"

"Oh, for fuck's sake. Shut the fuck up. I'm not mad, other than that neither of you fucking said a word. You hurt her, and I'll rip your spleen out through your nose." Will chuckled at Hennessy's expression.

"When is pizza gonna be here?" Adrian asked.

"Twenty minutes or so," Ethan replied.

"That's it? That's all the reaction?" Hennessy asked. "I thought you'd all fucking hate me."

"I kinda want the ringtones to continue. That was genius." Matty laughed with Beth.

"Fucking idiot," Beth said, smacking Hennessy upside the head.

"My favorite was the Backstreet Boys." Ethan laughed.

"Hanson for me." Adrian chuckled.

TUESDAY MORNING, William texted Adrian.

WILLIAM: It's Tuesday. The kid has chemo today. Go talk to her.

ADRIAN: Will, it's done. Leave it alone.

WILLIAM: You're fucking things up again.

ADRIAN: Why would you want this shit in their lives?

WILLIAM: Because this shit is already in her life. It's part of her. It radiates off her. You haven't felt that?

ADRIAN: I have no idea wtf you're talking about.

WILLIAM: Does it hurt to be that fucking stupid?

WEDNESDAY NIGHT, William was pacing back and forth in front of the security terminal exit at Midway airport. Back and forth, back and forth, back and forth. Directly under the sign that told people to meet their arriving guests at the baggage claim.

The TSA people were glaring at him. He glared back. They didn't glare long. The flight landed a few minutes ago, anyway. He'd be out of there soon. Not soon enough, but soon.

Without warning, Will got goosebumps on his arms. He looked around. He couldn't see her yet. This was their game. She'd try to get as close as possible before he spotted her. She made it within five feet once. That was the record. This wasn't a record-setting day. She wasn't really trying.

Pip was walking in front of a group of businessmen in suits that were staring at her ass. The little girl walking in front of her kept turning around to make faces. Pip made faces back at her, making the girl giggle. Twenty-five feet away and in a massive crowd, Will could still hear the girl's giggle. Such was the magic of Pip.

Oh my God. I love her so much, Will thought for the millionth time. Ten millionth time. Every time he saw her. Every time she smiled. Every time he touched her. Every last thought of her. *God, I worship at the altar of Pip, and I know you understand.*

Ten feet away, she could see him. Tipping her head back, they made eye contact under her White Sox hat. Her brilliant smile shone just for him, her love radiating to him. Will forgot to breathe.

And then she was there, in front of him, touching his face with just a finger. The energy that was Pip poured into him with relief that made him want to cry tears of joy.

"Hello, husband," she said in her perfect smoky, mezzo-soprano voice.

"Hi, wife," Will said, holding her to him.

"Missed you," she muttered.

"Missed you more," Will promised.

Taking her bag, Will grabbed her hand and began walking toward the elevator. "Did you check a bag?"

"I did, but maybe we can pick it up later? After people clear out. Did you eat? I didn't," she said with a smile.

He snorted. "Let's go get food, then. We'll come back for your bag. Is it checked in your name?"

"No, it's fine."

Will nodded as they walked toward the car. "What would the lady like to eat?"

She laughed. "Something extremely unhealthy and very fattening, as per usual."

PIP WATCHED him across the table. "Are you okay?"

Will nodded. "Yeah, I was pretty much healed up by morning."

"That's not what I mean, and you know it."

His face flashed with grief. "It was the worst thing I've ever done, and that's saying something. I wanted to die as his bones broke. I will have nightmares about that for the rest of my life."

"It had to happen, Will. It sounds like he was ripping his mind apart," Pip said, sympathy in her eyes. "What is it that Lucy can do?"

"I have no idea," he said. "It's not like you. You told me how it was going to be, and that was it. She doesn't seem to have that kind of thing."

Pip snorted. "Clearly, I don't have that kind of thing, either, or I wouldn't be living half a country away."

Will rolled his eyes as he smiled. "I'm a stubborn asshole. I've never claimed otherwise."

"And what is it that you think I'm going to do to help with this?" she asked. "Don't get me wrong. I'm fucking delighted to be here and nervous as all get-out to meet your family, but I think there's a significant chance I'm going to do nothing."

Will exhaled, blowing the air out his mouth. "I don't know. It's easier to remember the good stuff when you're around. It's easier to count blessings. I'm hoping your mojo will at least smack him upside the head. If he can tell me the words, I might be able to help it crumble."

"You think it'll crumble?"

"Yep. I think it'd crumble faster than anything I could do. If I did such things. Which I don't." He grinned at her.

"Uh-huh." She squinted her eyes at him.

"Anyway, I think you might be able to help Sam. Even if you can't help Adrian, I'm reasonably confident Sam will curl up at your fucking feet and take a good nap. Maybe eat a meal."

"He still hasn't broken through this phase?"

"When I saw him yesterday, he looked like a cadaver. I don't think he's slept more than ten minutes at a time in the last two weeks. Keeps saying he can't find the girl, that everyone suffocates and he can't find her. He won't eat. Says shit like, 'It tastes mad.' Or, 'This is way too angsty,'" Will said as she snorted.

"I really can't wait to meet him. Honestly, some of the shit he says." Pip smiled a sad smile, knowing it bothered William that he couldn't help his brothers. "Matty is done being mad at you?"

"Yeah, she was done after punching me."

"And you booted Jessup and Beth out of the closet. Poor form, William." She mocked frowned. "He hasn't booted you out of the closet for SEVEN years. They got like three months."

"He made chicken sounds at me. Fuck him," Will said with a grin. "Beth kicked them out of the closet with the ringtones. If you were a better troll, we wouldn't be here now."

"Ugh!" She threw a dirty napkin at his head. "Do they know? Do any of them know about me?"

"I don't know. It's impossible to know what Sam knows. Most of the time, Sam doesn't even know what he knows. I don't think Hennessy has told Beth. She doesn't have much of a filter. This gossip would be way too good for her to sit on," Will said, looking at his hands.

"Your parents?" Pip asked, looking sad.

"No, I don't think so," Will said quietly.

"What are we going to do if they don't like me, Will?"

"Pip, there is seriously a *zero* percent chance of that. *Zero.* They're gonna be *super* pissed at me, but they're gonna fucking love you. Still eating?"

"There's no pizza left. I had a slice and a half of deep dish. You had eight and a half slices. What would I eat if I was still eating? Sugar packets?"

21

"There! We're home," Pip said, walking through the door of Will's house. "Can I have my ring now?"

"Impatient?"

"Yes. For many things," she said, tossing the baseball hat on the side table.

Will smiled as he undid his dog tags, taking Pip's wedding ring off the chain. "You can't have yours until I have mine. Woo, it's an anklet today." He laughed as she unwound the chain from around her ankle.

"Husband," Pip said, smiling as she kissed him and slipped his ring on.

"And wife," Will muttered against her mouth, completing their little ritual.

She pulled her mouth away. "Will, I'm not going back. I mean, I'll finish the project. But I'm not staying there. I'm not doing this anymore."

Will sighed. "Pip—"

"No. This started because you thought I'd regret missing the opportunity. Regret us. I have no such regrets. I hate this. I hate being there. I hate not being with you. Unless you regret us and want out, I'm staying."

"Pip," he muttered, resting his forehead against hers.

"Do you regret us, William?" she asked. "Regret me?"

He sighed. "No. I love you. I will always love you. I will fucking murder the world for you, laying the bodies at the altar of Pip without remorse. The part that I regret is that you love me. I want better for you. I will rot in hell forever, and I would not choose for that to be bound to you."

"William. That's probably *exactly* how Adrian feels, and you have enough sense to know that's wrong. Why is this different?"

"It just is, Pip. Adrian hasn't killed people. Lucy has had a tough road. They just go together. I'm a fucking black void. That witchy woman said my bindings were disgusting, and I know that's accurate. You are the polar opposite of that, and I feel like I'm getting my shitty soul in your angel brilliance every fucking time I touch you."

"Will, you're taking that witch shit too seriously. If it really bothers you, let's go see them. Seriously. Let's go there and talk to that woman. Without your parents there. Let's go see what she says. I'm not afraid of whatever the fuck your 'black void' soul muck is." Pip's face was severe, but Will was grinning.

"Soul muck?"

"You started it," she said, smiling.

"I love you,"

"I know. I'm pretty great." She grinned.

"You are," he said, running his fingers through her honey blond hair as his lips met hers.

In less than a minute, Pip was pulling his t-shirt off as Will was pulling her toward the bedroom.

Mouth to mouth, bodies joined as Will moved slowly, she sighed. "Missed you, Will."

Will gasped as her hips shifted. "Love you, Emma. Always."

SUNDAY MORNING, William texted his family.

WILLIAM: Bringing someone to dinner.
JAKE: Seriously?
DARLA: Hallelujah. I love whoever this person is, and you should marry them. Now. Grandkids. I could be dying.
ADRIAN: Really, Mom?
DARLA: He's thirty five years old. It's time.

Pip couldn't stop laughing over Sunday breakfast.
"See, they love you!" Will exclaimed.
"Are they gonna be pissed to have missed the wedding?"
"They have Jake for that."

SAM RUBBED HIS EYES. He kept losing track. The echoes of the past and future were too close right now.

Sleep. Go to sleep, self. Just nod off. Family is here. Drink in their love and go to sleep. Just a catnap. Just to quiet the echoes. A little. Just a little.

As his eyes drifted closed, he was falling backward through time. Hank and Darla as children.

No. Sleep. Go find Adaline. Not Darla. Adaline.

Sam tumbled out of history, back to now. At least, it seemed like now.

"When is Matty going to be here?" he asked. Matty's light made it easier to keep track.

No one answered him.

He looked around. "Oh, I'm in the apartment."

"What, Sam? What did you say?" Matty asked.

Sam blinked again. He was in the big room. "Oh. Sorry. I didn't think you were here."

"Sam, you rode with us here. You need to eat. Would you try eating? I'll make you anything you want," Matty offered. "Mashed potatoes? You ate them the other day. Remember?"

The mashed potatoes tasted like a campfire mixed with worry. He ate them so she wouldn't worry.

"What's for dinner, Mom? I'll eat dinner."

Dinner will taste like fear and death and make me sick, but I'll eat it. I'm so hungry. I'm so tired. I don't want to see anymore. Please, God. I want to sleep.

Sam closed his eyes. Falling forward, Matty was pregnant. Darla was dead.

No, not right. This one's not right. Mom doesn't die in the right one. Where is the right one?

Beth touched his hand. "Want to go sleep upstairs, Sam? I'll walk with you. Stay with you. Okay? Please don't die. I don't want you to die. You look dead, Sam. Please don't die."

"I'm not dying. I have to stay," Sam said.

There was a startled gasp.

Oh, that must have been a thought, not words.

"Oh my God," Beth muttered as she choked back tears. "Luke, can you?"

"It doesn't work on him. Even now," Luke said, concern and frustration evident.

"It's okay, Beth. I'll be fine. Just tired. I'll sleep soon. It'll be fine. You'll see," Sam murmured, words slurring. "What's for dinner?"

"According to you, fear and death are for dinner," Ethan said. "You need to eat and sleep, Sam."

"Pot roast, Sam. I made you pot roast. You'll eat it for me, right?" Darla asked, eyes full of tears.

Sam had never been the image of health and well-being. But now, he looked like death. Eyes glassy and unfocused, cheeks caved in. Neck hollow. Bones visible. Skin waxy. Lips cracked. He had lost at least forty pounds in the last month, and he didn't have it to lose.

Spooky Samuel spent more time in the foreground over the last two weeks. Their soft-spoken, kind-hearted, generous Sam was gone. Spooky Samuel told Hank on Thursday that Sam would die soon without the girl. And they couldn't find the girl. They'd been looking for her for almost twenty years.

Sleep. Eyes are closed. Go to sleep.

No, falling through time again. Baby Beth. Beaten Hennessy, back when he was Jessup—

Sam's brain snapped back to the big room without warning. It smelled like cookies and hot cocoa. Pine trees at Christmas. Fresh oranges and ripe watermelon. Flowers in bloom.

"Cookies? Are there cookies?" he asked.

"I'll make you cookies, Sam. Whatever you want," Darla offered.

It tasted like Jake's kindness and Ethan's laughter and Matty's smile. Hank's pride in his family and Darla's hugs.

It felt like summer thunderstorms and rolling in the grass on a hot day, swinging on a playset as the air whipped at his face, hot apple cider when the apples were happy.

"Love. Love. This is love. Where? Where is it? WILLIAM! WHAT IS IT THAT YOU LOVE?"

"Sweetheart, he's not here," Darla said as tears dripped down her face.

"Where? Where is—?"

Sam stopped talking as the front door opened. "Oh God. Better. So much better," he groaned as the echoes resolved and his mind cleared. For the first time since the suffocating dream with Adaline more than two weeks ago, he was himself again. He was sucking in air like he was rescued from drowning.

William. William brought Love. William loves Love.

From the entryway, a woman's voice said, "Hi, Roscoe! Who's a good boy? No, you sit and be a good boy, yes, just like that. So handsome—"

"PIP!" Hennessy bellowed as he jumped up and ran from the room. "There's this thing I gotta do! PIP!"

Five seconds later, there was a squeal of delight as Hennessy yelled, "SQUEEZE! YOUR! GUTS! OH MY GOD, PIP! OH MY GOD!"

"What the hell?" Jake asked, starting to get up.

As Darla started walking toward the big room door, Will turned into the room. "Hi, Mom. Hi, everyone. Mom, sit, please. This is a 'sit down' kinda thing."

"PIPPY! I CAN'T BELIEVE YOU'RE FUCKING HERE! HE SAID LAST WEEK BUT I—"

"JESSUP! Calm down, man. She can't breathe. Don't make me hurt you," Will scolded.

"Sorry, Pip, sorry!"

Will turned back to the big room. "Okay, there's no good way to do this, so I'm just going to do it. My wife is here for dinner. She's standing on the other side of this wall trying to get Hennessy to stop crying like a little girl."

The room was utterly silent and still.

"Uh...your wife?" Jake asked.

"Yeah. Yes. My wife," Will confirmed.

"As in marriage?" Ethan asked.

"Indeed."

"Ah, when...? When did this happen?" Hank asked.

"Not quite seven years ago," Will admitted.

"YEARS?!" Darla bellowed.

"Yeah, Mom. It's a long story, and I'll tell it, but can I introduce her first? She's nervous."

"Oh, PIP! No nervous. No! It's gonna be fine!" Hennessy was still yelling everything.

"JESSUP! Let her go. Get over here in the room. You've lost your shit, man," Will yelled at him.

Hennessy was vibrating with joy, tears on his cheeks as he leaped around William. "Where is my fucking phone?! Not yet. Wait! Wait! I gotta get a picture of the faces! Wait!"

Will was grinning. "Sorry, Pip. I intended this to be more dignified. Roscoe, go! Leave her be!"

The dog growled as Will tried to shoo him away.

"He's fine. He'll sit and be a good boy. Yes, just like that," the voice said.

"Okay, I'm good!" Hennessy yelled.

Will rolled his eyes. "Family, this is my wife, Emma Gracen."

Every face in the room dropped into a look of shock as Will put this arm around the most beautiful woman in the world.

The only sounds were the dog's tail thumping, Sam gasping for breath, and the shutter sound of Hennessy taking a lot of pictures on his phone.

"H-HI," Emma said with a little wave. "Hennessy, please stop. Please?"

The entire room was still.

Emma looked up at Will with concern.

"Stop shaking. I can't take nervous from you. Can you do fear? I can help with that." Will grinned. "It's fine. They're processing. Just wait."

She turned back to the room. "I-it's. I'm. I'm thrilled to meet you. All of you." She swallowed hard.

No one moved.

Sam started trying to get up, but Beth was leaning back on him.

Beth, move. Move, Beth. Please move. I can't move you right now, he thought as he tried to wiggle sideways away from her.

"DAD! Come here and say dad things!" Will yelled.

Hank shook his head as he started moving to the doorway. "Emma, it's so nice to meet you, too! I can't wait to hear this story. I'm sorry, we were entirely—"

Before Hank finished his greeting, Sam had reached them. Wrapping his arms around her, he pulled her off balance and to the floor. Holding Emma as close as he could, his body folded around her as he sobbed.

"You're here. You're here. He wouldn't tell me. I kept asking. I knew you were somewhere, but you weren't here and I couldn't find you and I couldn't see you and it was horrible. I'm so hungry, all the time, so hungry and I can't eat because it makes me sick and I'm losing track. I can't tell when it is or where it is. I can't find Adaline." Sam gasped for air. "She's dying, and I can't find her. Would you please take me to her? I need to go to her. I think I might be dying but maybe not now that you're here and I can't control—" Sam babbled incoherently

"Shh, shhh. Sam, shhh, it's okay. I'm here, I'll help, but I don't know how. If you tell me how, I'll help," Emma promised over his sobbing as she looked up at Will.

Will shrugged. "I thought he'd curl up and take a nap while you sang a lullaby. This is a new one for me. I don't think I've ever seen him cry."

"I'm so hungry. Can we eat? Please, can we eat?" Sam begged.

"It's an hour before dinner. It's still cooking," Darla muttered. "I'll go find something. Okay, Sam? I'll find something else."

TEN MINUTES LATER, Sam had scarfed down three sandwiches and a giant glass of water, still sitting in the middle of the doorway to the great room, wrapped up with Emma.

"Will! Don't tell the story yet. Not yet. I don't know how this happened, and I want to know, okay?" Sam called.

"Okay, Sam. Okay. How about you go back to sitting on the couch? It'll be more comfortable, man. Come on. Emma's coming with you. Right, Pip?" Will cajoled.

"Of course I'll come with. We'll go together, okay?" she asked.

Sam didn't respond. His breathing had evened out.

"I think he's asleep," she said to Will.

The dog growled from Emma's side as Will tried to shift Sam. "Roscoe, stop that. Go on! Go lay in your spot," Will said, gesturing to a spot between the sofas. The dog didn't move, still baring teeth at Will.

Emma scratched the dog's ears. "There now. Go to bed, Roscoe. Go to your spot. I'm okay."

The dog got up and started to walk away, glaring at William the whole time.

"That's hysterical," Jake said. "What the fuck? I've never seen him growl before."

"Oh. Um. Dogs like me. Most animals like me, but dogs especially," Emma muttered, a blush heating her cheeks.

"Hennessy, help me unwrap Sam so she can get up. I don't want to hurt him, and this is awkward as fuck. He won't let go of her," Will said. "Ma, scoot out of the chair. We'll put him there for now."

"Take him up to bed. He needs to sleep!" Darla instructed.

"If we can, we should wake him for dinner when it's out and on the table. I think he'll go back to sleep after dinner. He needs food, honey. Before the sandwiches, I don't think he's eaten in days," Hank said.

Sam didn't move as Will picked up his torso and Hennessy picked up his legs. He didn't even stir when they dropped him in the reclining chair.

By the time Will turned back around, Hank had helped Emma to her feet.

"Just so we're clear," Will began. "This didn't go how I thought it would, Pip. I expected Hennessy to do his 'squeezing guts' thing and then laugh. I thought I'd introduce you, they'd be startled for a second, then be super pissed at me. I forgot about the dog thing. I didn't see the Sam thing coming at all. You're okay?"

She smiled a nervous little smile. "I'm fine."

"Okay, let's try this again. You met Hank. This is my Mom, Darla—"

Darla's arms closed around Emma in a giant hug. "Oh! This is wonderful. Absolutely wonderful. I told Hank. I told him."

"No, Darla. No, you did not tell me he was married to *literally* the most beautiful woman in the world," Hank said, laughing as Emma turned bright red.

"I did tell you! I told you he was stuck on someone from being in the service. I told you! The rest of it is just minor details," she yelled at Hank.

"Honey, this is a hell of a 'minor detail,'" Hank said, still laughing.

Arms still wrapped around Emma, Darla gasped. "Jake! You need to go to the store! Right now. Go to the store."

"For what?" Jake asked, surprised.

"I don't have any salad or lemon wedges or anything like—"

"Oh, Mom. No," Will said, laughing. "No. She will eat her body weight in whatever it is that you're making. When she's working, people take food away from her and give her like cucumber slices and shit. She scarfs food when she's not around work people."

Emma nodded. "It's true. I'm not picky. Plus, it smells like maybe some kind of beef roast?"

Darla nodded back. "Pot roast. Sam's favorite, I thought he might eat it."

"Hurrah!" Emma did a little cheer in place as Darla continued to hug her.

"Okay, Mom. Let go," Will coached.

"Oh! I'm sorry, sweetheart. I'm sorry," Darla said, kissing her cheek.

Matty was bouncing in line behind Darla.

"Hi, Matty! It's so nice to meet you!" Emma exclaimed as Matty threw her arms out in a vigorous hug.

"I CAN'T BELIEVE THIS! OH MY GOD!" Matty squealed. "I'm so pissed at you for not telling me, Will! I wouldn't have told anyone. Okay, that's not true, I would have told everyone. But you still should have told me!"

"Oh, calm your shit, Carrots. This was coming out before the wedding no matter what." Will chuckled.

Matty pulled away from the hug but was still bouncing in excitement.

"Ethan, right? You're Ethan?" Emma asked with a smile.

"OH MY GOD, EMMA GRACEN KNOWS MY NAME!" Ethan squealed as he hugged her. "I can't believe this! I can't believe this!"

Will was still chuckling. "Man, you gotta calm your shit, too. I don't know how to break this to you, but you're related to her. She's your sister-in-law. She's been your sister-in-law for longer than she's been famous. She's rather embarrassed and nervous right now. Quit fanboying it."

Ethan let go of Emma and joined Matty in bouncing and clapping.

"Hi, Beth, it's nice to meet you," Emma said, still red in the face.

Beth looked around. "See this, you ninnies," giving Ethan and

Matty side-eye, "I'm gonna play it cool when I hug the famous actress and singer. Because whatever, she's here for dinner."

When Beth pulled out of the hug, she joined Ethan and Matty in their bouncing. "Just don't look at us right now. We need to get acclimated!" Beth giggled.

"Hi, Jake." Emma laughed as Jake hugged her, picking her up and swinging her legs a bit.

"Hi, Emma," Jake said, grinning. "It's very nice to meet you."

"We're missing Adrian, Matthew, Luke, and Noah. I'm quietly hoping Noah doesn't bring a date, cause that shit will be awkward," Will explained. "More awkward than weeping Sam, and that was fucking uncomfortably awkward. You okay?"

Emma smiled a small smile at him and nodded as she took his hand.

"I know he wanted us to wait, but the suspense is killing me," Hank said. "How? How did this happen? Maybe just the short—"

The front door opened. Matthew and Luke were walking in the door.

"No, I don't think—" Luke paused in mid-sentence as the energy of the house hit him. "What's going on, all?"

He and Matthew were walking around the corner into the room, Luke looking suspicious.

"Wow, you are the spitting image of Emma Gracen!" Matthew exclaimed. "No wonder Will finally has a date."

Will sighed. "Matthew, Luke, this is my wife, Emma."

"No fucking way," Matthew exclaimed.

Luke glared as his closest brother and shook his head. "Hi, Emma, it's nice to meet you," he said while giving her a small hug.

"Oh!" she exclaimed. "Oh yes. You're the peace one. Yes. That's better. Thank you."

Luke smiled at her and then whacked Matthew in the chest. "Stop staring."

"H-Hello!" Matthew stammered. "Um, nice to meet you?"

Emma's lips turned up. "It's nice to meet you, too."

"Okay. That's all I got for now. I'm going to go freak out over there with the others," Matthew said, walking toward Matty, Ethan, and Beth.

"Let's go back to that wife part—" Luke was cut off as the front door opened again.

"Hey, where's the dog?!" Noah called, walking into the room. After a glance at Emma, he turned to Will. "Wow, you don't fuck around when you bring a date to dinner. Hi, Emma, it's nice to meet you. Wanna get—?"

Without a thought, Will grabbed Noah by the throat and dangled him in the air with one hand. "Noah. You get one warning, and this is it. Listen. You will not disrespect my wife. You will not touch her inappropriately. You will not make rude comments. You will behave as if she is Beth because she is your sister-in-law." Will dropped him, gagging for air, to the floor. "Do you understand?"

"Holy shit, man! I was just kidding!" Noah yelled.

"Noah, I can't stress this enough. DO NOT test the boundaries on this. DO NOT try to push my buttons. The impulse to protect at any cost is *very* high. I don't know that I would think before I killed you. I'm not kidding. At all. Do you understand?" Will said in a quiet voice.

"Noah, really," Hennessy said, voice uncharacteristically serious. "This is not something to play with. You'll understand more after we tell the story, but don't test. Don't aggravate just to aggravate. He's faster than me. I'm not sure I'd catch him before you're dead. I'm not talking about a beat down. I'm talking about death. Literally dead."

"Will," Pip said, touching his hand. "I'm okay. No one here is going to hurt me. You know that."

"Hey," she said, turning his face toward her. "Everything's fine."

"I know," Will said, giving her a little kiss. "He needs to understand, though. He's an instigator. This is not something he should start shit with."

Noah was backing away as Emma gave him a sad smile.

With a sigh, she asked, "So, it's just Adrian we're missing?"

"Yeah," Jake said, still staring at Will. "I actually just texted him to see where he's at. He thought you were bringing Lucy. I told him you brought your wife; I hope that's okay?"

"Perfect." Will smiled. "The curiosity will kill him."

"So you're married? Actually married?" Luke asked. "Is that what you were doing over your long weekend?"

Will laughed. "No, Luke, no. Pip and I have been married for almost seven years. I picked her up at the airport on Wednesday night. We've just been spending time together."

Before anyone could say another word, the front door opened. "Fuck, Jake. Stop texting me. I'm here. What?" Adrian called from the entryway. "Where's the dog?"

"Roscoe, go see!" Pip whispered.

The dog took off scrambling for the door.

"That is fucking weird." Jake laughed.

Emma turned pink again.

"It works like that on me, too." Will laughed with the rest of the room.

ADRIAN HAD no desire to attend Sunday dinner. He didn't want to see Lucy. Leaving her was by far the hardest thing he'd ever done. For a guy that had to tell parents that their child was dying, that's saying something.

But he knew Will would continue to push if he didn't show. So there he was. Showing up to listen to Lucy ramble about how glad she was that they weren't together. It was going to be a long, terrible dinner.

And Ree. Ree was here, too. There was nowhere else he could be. Ree started chemo last week. Adrian checked the chart. His blood work looked okay. Not great. Not even promising. But okay, so they were trying. But Henry was probably going to die. Adrian was too late. Ree was going to die a slow, terrible death by cancer because Adrian missed the window of opportunity.

Darla might not die. It hadn't spread. They'd do surgery; she'd do chemo. She might be okay. Odds were that she'd still be around for a couple more years.

Jake was blowing up his phone with texts as he drove. Something about Will. Adrian knew Will was bringing Lucy. There was nothing else to prepare for. It didn't matter. Today was going to suck; tomorrow was going to suck. And the day after that. And the one after that, too.

Adrian's phone vibrated again as he was walking in the front door. "Fuck, Jake. Stop texting me. I'm here. What?"

Damn. Even the dog wasn't interested in seeing him. *That's cold, Roscoe.* "Where's the dog?"

A round of laughter broke out from the big room as the dog turned the corner into the hallway. An ear scratch later, Adrian was looking at his family, standing in the middle of the big room, laughing.

The dog pranced back to the side of a beautiful woman standing with William. Maybe five-six or so, honey blond hair, glowing skin, a brilliant smile, in a little pink sundress.

And then Adrian was falling backward through time. Holding Beth as a baby. Harley, the first dog that was truly his. Darla hugging him when he was upset. Hank, smiling with pride when he graduated from medical school. Jake, holding Matty's hand in the hospital. Ethan, teasing. Noah, joking. Luke laughing. Matthew, grinning with a group of second graders at the zoo, posing for the field trip picture. Hennessy, holding Beth when Darla talked about her cancer.

Lucy and Ree. Meeting him as he came into the house. Eating dinner. Cutting apples for a snack. Putting Lucy in her bed. Lucy, slapping his hand, looking at him with her big blue eyes. Henry sitting on the bench. Henry, sleeping on the couch with the tablet in his lap. Lucy folded into the guest chair in that stupid, small exam room. Lucy, smiling, talking about chicken. Lucy, glowing with beauty, even in the darkness. Lucy...

"Adrian! Come on, man!" Will slapped him again.

"I'm okay," Adrian gasped. "What happened?" he asked as he started to sit up from the floor.

"Uh. I'm guessing you got Pip'd and then fainted like the giant pansy you are," Will said with a laugh.

"I feel...weird."

"Yeah, give it a minute. Then you can meet my wife."

Still woozy, Adrian lifted his eyebrows. "Your wife?"

"Yeah, dumbass. Didn't you wonder how I knew about the two streams to weave together?"

"Yeah, but...I don't know. I didn't think you were married. How long you been married? Maybe secret weddings are the way to go. How the fuck do you pick a best man, you know?" Adrian rambled.

"You know what I haven't had in a long time? Mint Chocolate Chip ice cream. I should get some fucking ice cream," he continued to mumble. "In a waffle cone. Adults don't eat ice cream in waffle cones, and I feel like that's fucking bullshit. Ice cream cones are great."

"This is even better than Sam." Jake laughed.

Luke looked at Sam, sleeping in the chair. "What'd he do? He's zonked out."

"He fucking dragged her to the ground, wrapped himself around her, and cried like a baby until Mom made him sandwiches," Jake explained. "He scarfed them and passed out. Will and Hennessy unwound him and put him in the chair."

"Midas cried?" Noah asked incredulously.

"Fucking bawled," Jake said, nodding.

"Can you stand up?" Will asked Adrian.

Adrian shrugged. "I dunno. What's for dinner? I'm hungry."

Everyone was laughing again. The laughter was sweet; it made Adrian happy. His house was so quiet and lonely now.

Maybe he'd get a dog.

"Pot roast, honey," Darla said, laughing.

"Oh. I like that. Are there potatoes? That's Sam's favorite." Adrian still sounded drunk.

The blond woman was kneeling down in front of Adrian.

"Your eyes are like a starburst. Blue and green starbursts. So pretty," he rambled.

"Adrian, can you stand up? I'd like it if you'd stand up. Will you try?" she asked in a beautiful voice.

"Sure. I'll try it." Adrian started to push himself to his feet as Will steadied him. "I should probably sit down before I fall. My blood pressure is low. Luke, turn off the mojo."

"That ain't my mojo, man," Luke called.

"Yeah, this is going to work great," Will said as he ushered a wobbly Adrian over to the couch. "Do you feel the anger at all right now, man?"

"Hmm?" Adrian asked. "Oh. No. I'm not mad. Should I be mad? Hey, is she your wife, Will? That's a good choice right there. So pretty."

Will was grinning. "Yeah, man. That's my wife. Emma. Or Pip."

"How come he doesn't get the death threat?" Noah bitched.

"He can't even stand on his own right now, Noah. Shut the fuck up," Jake said.

"Did you get the death threat?" Noah asked Jake.

"Nope, because I'm not an asshole. Shut up."

EMMA WASN'T sure what to do. She wanted to help but wasn't sure how. She didn't know how to do whatever it was that needed to be done.

The dog was growling as Hennessy walked toward her.

"Roscoe, go lay down. Be a good boy," Emma said.

The dog went back to his spot.

"You know, the next time that dog pretends like he doesn't know what I'm saying, I'm going to remember this and not give him any more treats for a week," Hank bitched.

"Pip, go ask him about Lou. Let's just see how it goes. I think Reap mighta got this one right," Hennessy said.

Everyone but Will and Adrian were staring at her. "O-okay."

Emma knelt down in front of Adrian, taking hold of his hand. "Hi, Adrian, it's nice to meet you. I kinda want to say thanks for making him bring me here, but I wish you weren't hurting so much."

"Why didn't he bring you before? I'd bring you everywhere. What the fuck, man? What the fuck you been doing?" Adrian slurred at Will.

"Yeah, this is going to work just fine. Go ahead, Pip," Will said, backing away.

"Uh, I'm not sure what to do," she admitted.

"Just, you know, do Pip things. It'll be fine. Talk to him about it," Will suggested.

"Uh, okay." She paused for a minute to think.

"Adrian, where's Lucy?"

"Oh. At her house. She's safe there. Safe. Away from me," he muttered.

"Does she want to be away from you?" she asked.

"Yep. I told her so. I told her."

"What? What did you tell her?"

"I told her she never loved me, that she was glad things ended, that she only liked me because I helped. So, she's glad."

Will sighed. "What were the words, Adrian? The exact words."

"I told her Henry would be okay, but I looked at the chart. He's probably going to die. I was too late to help. My Ree's gonna die."

"Wha—" Ethan started, looking like he couldn't breathe.

Will cut him off with a glare.

"Adrian," Pip said. "Do you love Lucy?"

"Oh. Yes. Yes." He sighed out the word.

"Why did you make her not love you then?" she asked.

"Huh? I thought you knew. Didn't he tell you? You should know. I'm a monster," Adrian mumbled.

Pip's brow furrowed. She didn't like that at all. "Why do you think that?"

"Are you upset with me? I don't want you to be upset with me. I'm sorry, Pip." Adrian blinked hard to avoid tears.

"I'm upset that you think you're a monster. I don't think you're a monster. Just like Will is not a monster. He's just ridiculous. And stubborn."

"I'm kind of a monster, babe," Will muttered.

Pip turned an annoyed expression on him. "Really? Right now? We're doing this right now?"

The room exploded in laughter. "Yeah, they're really married." Hank laughed.

Turning back to Adrian, Pip said, "You're not a monster, Adrian."

"I have this rage thing. It eats at me," Adrian started.

"Uh-huh. I know. Do you let the rage hurt people? Does it try to hurt Lucy? Or Henry?" she asked.

That gave him pause. "No, not really. It doesn't seem to want to hurt her. It's just always there. It might hurt her. I can't do that."

"Adrian, everyone gets mad. Everyone gets angry. The anger itself isn't bad. It's okay. Would you ever purposely hurt Lucy?" Pip asked.

"No. But I might do it accidentally. I don't want to get my rage mixed up with her," Adrian mumbled.

Emma's eyes were slits as she glared at William.

"I still maintain it is not the same thing," Will said defensively.

"WILLIAM, IT IS THE EXACT SAME THING," Emma yelled.

"Oh, she's mad. No, Pip, don't be mad. I'm sorry," Adrian said.

"I'm not mad at you, Adrian. I'm mad at Will."

Adrian looked perplexed. "Why?"

Emma sighed. "Because, Adrian. He's like you. Will keeps me away. He thinks he's going to hurt me. He thinks he has soul muck."

"Yeah," Adrian said. "Soul muck. That's a good way to put it."

"Adrian, William's soul muck doesn't hurt me. You know what hurts? Being away. Being away is not what I want. I know about the soul muck. He told me. Explained it. Years and years ago. It's okay. He's still mine. But he won't let me be his; that hurts."

Adrian looked up at Will. "You're hurting her feelings, man. You shouldn't do that."

Emma touched Adrian's face, bringing his attention back to her. "See? You understand that he shouldn't do that to me. Why are you doing it to Lucy?"

"Oh. Yeah. I should probably explain the soul muck to her. But I already made her forget. Too late." Adrian sighed.

"What if Will makes her remember? Will you talk to her then?"

22

"*D*inner is done," Darla announced. "Adrian, can you stand up yet?"

"Yeah, Mom. Yeah. I think I'm a little better. Less loopy. Starving."

"What should we do with Sam?" Matthew asked. "He needs to eat, but he's out."

"SAM!" Jake yelled, shaking Sam's shoulder. "He's toast. He didn't even blink when they picked him up."

Emma reached down and touched his hand. "Sam, come on. Time to eat."

Sam's eyes flickered open. "How long was I out?"

"Fucking weird," Jake muttered. "Please don't turn the mojo on me."

"I'm not doing anything, I swear." Emma looked embarrassed again. "Only about an hour, Sam. Dinner's done, though."

"I'm so hungry," Sam said, eyes still glassy.

"It's okay. Come on. We'll eat," Emma said softly as he grabbed for her hand.

"Come on, man. You gotta walk. Let go of her, just for a sec," Will was saying as he tried to get Sam up on his feet.

Adrian wobbled as he stood up from the couch but stayed upright. "I honestly don't think I've been this chill since before puberty."

As the room broke out in laughter, he grinned. "I know that's ridiculous, but still true. What did you do?" he asked Emma.

"I don't know. I don't think anything. Honestly. I don't know," she said, still embarrassed.

"I'll go sit on the other side of the table," Adrian said. "Sit between Sam and Will," he told Emma as the family warily played musical chairs. There was no reaction from Sam.

"Pip, I'm curious. Are you able to call Spooky Sam?" Will asked.

"Other-Sam," Luke said. "He calls it Other-Sam."

"She doesn't need to call to me," Samuel said, voice vibrating with power. Everyone in the room shifted a bit.

"I'm here. All parts of me," Sam said, in his normal voice. "As I'm meant to be."

"Other-Sam is forward?" Luke asked. "Can I look?"

"There is no Other-Sam right now, Lucas. Just Sam. One. Look if you want. I don't know what you'll see."

"I don't see anything," Luke said. "It's a big void space. Not even life signs. In all seriousness, is his heart beating?"

Emma touched his wrist and nodded. "What are you looking at? What do I look like?"

"Very purple," Luke said. "All shades of purple. Almost no other colors at all. I guess I'm looking at auras or life energies or something like that. I don't know. I don't know what's right and what's crap at this point, honestly. We need to go talk to Ava again. Clearly, my information is suspect."

"We will go. We will all go. Together. But we need Wind. There must be four, Adrian. You must undo it," Samuel said, voice echoing in the room. "We are running out of time."

"I don't know how to undo it," Adrian said, looking at his plate.

"Lady Love will help," Samuel said, smiling fondly at Emma. "It is nice. Between Light and Love, I can rest. Much easier to be one. I kept asking him for what he loved. He did not name you."

William sighed. "You told me repeatedly that it was a *what*, not a *who*."

Sam's brow furrowed. "Love is what. It is a power. It is also a who. Adaline and I talk in this circle, too. It'll be easier now that I'm one."

"One what?" Emma asked.

"One Sam. When I am many, I lose track. There is no anchor. Light can't always anchor on her own. Hope does not belong with me. But with you, I am here. All of me."

Emma looked at Matty.

"I dunno," Matty said. "He's called me Light before, but I don't know what it means."

"Okay, moving on. Storytime!" Hank yelled. "The suspense is killing me, William. How in the great wide world did this happen?"

"Uh, I'm not sure it's a dinner time story," Will said.

"Too bad," Darla said over Hennessy's laughter.

Will scratched the top of his head. "Pass the mashed potatoes. I want some before Mom beats me with the serving spoon. I can't believe we're eating pot roast in July."

"Stop stalling." Hank laughed.

"All right. I will preface this story by saying I am a dirty, disgusting pedophile of an old man," Will started.

Pip snorted. "It was weird when I was fifteen. No one gives a shit now. Get over it."

The table erupted in laughter.

"This is actually easier after last week. Thanks for being an idiot, Adrian!" Will laughed as Adrian nodded in acceptance.

"So, I enlisted to get the fuck out of here—"

"William," Darla said.

"Ma, I'm going to need a pass this week. There's no way I'm going to filter. If you want the story, you're getting the language," he said as the table laughed again.

"So, I enlisted, knowing that I had a weird fear thing. Thought I'd put it to good use and fully intended to die in service to my country. I enlisted with the intent to go for the SEALs, got accepted, made it through the training.

"First op out, everything goes fubar. Jackass over there is missing, out of position, insurgents amassing, and we're heading out, knowing we'd be going back for a body, not a brother. I wasn't wild about that.

"When we were set to rendezvous, I felt his fear fucking screaming at me. Went for him. Got him. Killed six people getting him out and lugging his giant fucking ass down that mountain. You've heard that story.

"I didn't have regrets about going for him. Really didn't. But I took six lives that day without a thought. Two women. Maybe they had families. Maybe one of them had eight fucking siblings and great parents waiting to hear from him at home. Maybe it's not their fault that the dead asshole got into the shit he was in. Now that asshole was dead, and that family was fucked because I went and got Hennessy.

"Taking lives is hard. I had trouble justifying it to myself. The pain I was inflicting. I was fighting for a lot of things I love, but fuck. I'm sure the other guys felt that way too, mostly.

"Anyway, about a year after that first mission, we had a lousy op. It was successful but bad. The bad that sticks in your brain forever. Got back stateside, all Hennessy and I wanted to do was fucking drink ourselves stupid, forget all about it. Maybe block that shit. I don't know.

"Bars near the base were gross. Assholes and bar-stars, looking for guys like us. We went further out. Found this little joint, off the beaten path. It was homey. The couple running it reminded me of Mom and Dad. The food was good. Pool tables were level. Darts. No one bothered us. Just kind of a nice place. Ordered a bottle of whiskey, first of many pitchers of beer, sat down to get our drink on and bullshit.

"So I was sitting there, minding my own business, drinking my fucking liquor with my buddy, talking about something stupid. I don't even remember what. Side door to the bar opens up, and a girl walks in. And I'm not being a pig. She was fifteen. A girl in a school uniform with fucking knee-high socks."

"Pippy Longstocking!" Hennessy yelled in a cheers gesture as everyone laughed.

Will grinned at Pip. "Anyway, I had never seen anything so beautiful. I loved her immediately. With everything I was, every bit of life I had in me, I was hers to do with as she chose. I couldn't stop staring at her, and I knew I was a fucking creepy pervert. It was similar to Adrian's reaction to her. Not as bad, but similar."

"Oh my God, you are so full of shit. It was a THOUSAND TIMES worse than Adrian. At least!" Hennessy yelled. "She comes over to pick up the damn empty beer pitcher. He full-on babbles nonstop about how much he loves her and how beautiful she is and how he's a horrible person, but she's fucking amazing. I mean, any fucking random thought in his brain came pouring out his mouth."

Bright red, Pip was laughing. "My favorite part was, 'I love hushpuppies. I haven't had a good deep-fried hushpuppy in years. We should find some hushpuppies.' He was drunk. It's funny that Will and Adrian both went to food rambling, though. Food must be dear to them."

Once the table laughter settled back down, Will continued. "So, the next morning, I woke up thinking, 'I made a damn fool of myself, I will never go back there again!' Hennessy ribbed me about loving little girls in knee-high socks. He started calling her Pip because we didn't know her name at that point.

"Next op, we go out, and when it came down to it, I had no trouble taking a life. I gave zero fucks. The bad guys couldn't get away to ride another day, they might find their way to Pip, and then she'd be hurt because I was too much of a fucking idiot to do my job. So, money-shots, as needed.

"I have no idea how many people I took out, no idea how many bodies I laid at the altar of Pip, but I didn't regret it. I did my job because if I didn't, they might hurt her. More than a hundred lives. Probably more than five hundred lives. Not a thousand."

Hennessy made a so-so gesture. "There was a point in time before we met her, where he'd try to not kill. Disarm. Disable. Take captive. Even if it was a risk to us in the situation."

After a pause, Hennessy continued in a flat voice. "After we met her, those times were over. He was never bloodthirsty. Never war crimes material. But the hesitation was gone. If it needed to happen, it happened. The Grim Reaper showed no fucking mercy. It was hard to watch.

"Maybe a thousand. I don't know. We'd need to think about the missions over those two years. They started putting us on ops that would likely have a high body count," Hennessy finished.

"You get the idea," Will said. "A couple of months go by, going back to that bar with the girl didn't seem like a bad idea. Hennessy yucked it up, had a great time with it. Went back, there she was, bussing the tables on a Saturday evening. We walked in as she was clearing a table. She bent forward to grab something. A guy at the table behind her tried to put his hand up her shorts. Of course, I saw it because, again, I'm a creepy fucking pedophile. I broke his hand. Dislocated his shoulder. Didn't even think about it."

"To this day, I remain impressed that you did not kill him," Hennessy interrupted.

"Bah. That'd upset her. I couldn't upset her." Will took a bite of roast.

"Her dad walks over, buys me a beer, says thanks. He didn't see it, was on the other side of the bar. The sheriff shows up, and Pip explains what happened. Sheriff buys me a beer."

Pip rolled her eyes. "He's my dad's best friend. Effectively my uncle. There was no way you were going to jail."

"She remembered me as the drunken fool, teased me a bit. Started talking. Shot some darts. Played some pool—"

"Yeeee!" Matty squealed, clapping her hands.

"Pfft." Emma grinned. "I excel at all bar sports. We'll throw down later. But not your pool table. No telling what's on that thing."

The table exploded in laughter, and Matty turned bright red as Will laughed. "You should all know I tell her fucking everything. We talk twice a day."

"Yeah, okay, tell your story, you fucking creepy old man," Matty, cheeks red, yelled over the laughter. "I love you, Emma. Please don't think I'm gross."

"Wait, pass the roast," Sam muttered, well into his third helping.

Will was laughing. "It went on like that for a while. More than a year. We were friends. Just friends. I couldn't deal with the age difference. Plus, soul muck." Will shared a nod of understanding with Adrian.

"She'd be upset when I went wheels up. Upset if I wasn't back when I thought I'd be. Worry about me when I was gone. She pretty quickly became the last person I talked to on the way out and the first person I called on the way back.

"As she got older, the bar folk got more handsy. By the time she hit seventeen, there were a few incidents. Still not sorry. Skipping over that, though. Pip still bussed tables and cooked in the kitchen. She and her sister rotated chores. One Friday evening—it wasn't even late yet, maybe dinner time—it was her turn to take the garbage out. We were shooting pool at the other end of the bar.

"So, we pause the game, and she collects the shit, goes out the back door to toss it in the dumpster. And then I felt a stab of her fear. Real terror. I was out the back door and had literally laid two dead bodies at her feet before I even knew what was happening.

"Ultimately, I was lucky those fuckers were tied to other crimes. I didn't stop to assess what was going on. I just spun their heads like tops, dropped 'em. Scooped her up to get her out of there. If they'd been asking her for directions after she saw a rat or something, I'd be in jail forever."

Hennessy cleared his throat. "Noah, he's not kidding about this. There was no pause. I was there. When he dropped the pool cue and started hauling ass, I followed him. I wasn't more than five steps behind him. They were dead before I got out the door."

"Geez, I get it. I'm not that dumb." Noah groaned. "Don't scare Pip. Fine. I don't scare the ladies anyway. We've already established this; I'm the flirt. It's fine. I'll behave."

Will glared at him. "Anyway, they had injected something into her, she kept fading in and out. They were trying to put her in the trunk of a car. She was fighting as best she could, but she wouldn't have made it much longer. My freaky-ass soul muck saved my Pip.

"Things got worse after that for a while. Like where Adrian was. Worse than that. I didn't know what the problem was. The energy that came from Pip did *not* belong with my soul muck. She was scared to be away from me, and I was scared for her to be near me. It was not good."

"That's Will's shorthand for 'I was looking for a way to die,'" Hennessy added.

Will shrugged. "In the end, I came home from an op and found her sitting in my apartment, waiting for me. That was it. I was done fighting it. I explained the fear as best I could, told her to stay away. She said no. I belonged with her; she wasn't accepting anything else.

"Two days later, I got up the stones to ask her parents to sign the forms for us to get married. I was hers. I'd be hers forever. She couldn't stay on base with me as an unmarried minor. We were married before the week was out.

"You guys didn't come to see us. I certainly wasn't calling Hank and telling him I married a seventeen-year-old girl. I just figured we would talk about it when I was home. My tour with the SEALs was almost up. I wasn't re-upping. Sam was starting to rake it in at that point. Figured I finish out the contract, move home, and do some groveling for forgiveness."

Emma sighed. "I was in drama in school. Early in my senior year, the drama teacher took videos of all us kids and submitted us to a contest. I didn't win the contest."

"About six months after we were married, a Hollywood producer came looking for me, wanted to make me an actress. Saw the video, wanted me to audition. I was...let's say skeptical. Told the guy to piss off. Will was livid. Felt I was passing on a 'life experience.' He wanted me to audition. I did. Got the part. He came back to Chicago; I did the movie. Another role came up. And another after that. And so on. Here we are," Emma said, somehow sad.

"I thought being away from me, she'd change her mind. She'd get the experience, taste the fame, go for it. Be with some actor type that wasn't fucked up. I wanted her to be able to make a clean break with no bad press. So I didn't mention her. I told her that it'd be bad for Sam's business if she mentioned me. We kept our secret. I've been flying to her every other weekend for years. I just made sure to be back for Sunday dinner. Didn't go anywhere public."

"Last week happened. Hennessy called bullshit. Dumbass refused to go see Lucy on Tuesday. Pip was in Chicago before dinner on Wednesday. Thought maybe she'd have better luck talking to him. Maybe she could help Sam. There's some kind of magic about her. I didn't know if it'd work on them. Turns out, it does."

"The end was in sight anyway. She would have come to sing for Matty and Jake."

The table was silent and still for a full minute.

Darla cleared her throat. "Now what?"

"It remains undecided—" Will started.

"I'm not going back," Emma said in a tone of finality. "I'll go back for whatever reshoots they need, but I'm not doing this anymore. I've had the life experience. Totally over it. I didn't want it in the first place. Never wanted it. Still don't want it now that it's done. Seven fucking years wasted. It's done. If you want me to leave, convince me you don't love me, then file for a divorce."

"Pip—"

"No," she said.

The table was silent again.

Hank snorted. "If you try to make her leave, your mother is going to have a shit fit of epic proportions. You know that, right?"

"Well, this isn't really about Mom, so—" Will started as his siblings looked decidedly uncomfortable.

Darla smiled as she cut Will off. "Emma, sweetheart, it remains unclear to me if William knows that he's going to be a dad. Is that cat out of the bag?"

Emma's mouth dropped open in shock as the table held its breath. "Umm...how? How would you know that?"

"Huh?" Will said, unsure what expression to put on his face.

"Uh. I mean. Maybe. I haven't done the test. I'm not even a full week late," Emma said, blushing deep red. "I was going to give it a couple more days..."

"You are. You absolutely are. I can tell," Darla said, nodding. "There, now you don't have to argue about leaving. I'm going to be a grandma."

"We're going to have a baby?" Will asked, tearing up. "Really?"

"I—I don't know," Emma said, still stunned.

"I'll bet ya ten bucks. Who wants in?" Darla called. "Jake, go to the store."

"What? Why me?" Jake looked appalled.

"Because I said so. Adrian's all funky. Emma can't do it. If someone snaps a picture, it'll be everywhere. Go to the store. Matty, go with him," Darla directed. "He doesn't know what the hell he's doing. It'll be practice. Make him buy tampons and anti-fungal cream, too. It'll be fun. Go. Right now. I'm not kidding."

THIRTY MINUTES LATER, Will was staring into space. "I'm going to be a dad. My wife is having a baby. I'm going to be a dad."

He remained unaware that his entire family was laughing at him as they placed wagers on everything from gender and birthday to weird powers.

"That had to be a lucky guess, Mom. There's no way to visually tell this early. None at all. Emma, were you like touching your belly or something earlier?" Adrian asked.

"No, I hadn't really been thinking about it. My cycle isn't that steady. I just thought it was late. How did you know?" Emma asked Darla.

"I just do, sweetheart. I've had a lot of babies. Still hungry? Want some ice cream?"

"Uh, no, thank you. I'm full," Emma said, still stunned.

"There's ice cream?" Adrian asked, hopeful.

"Mint chocolate chip, just for you, buddy. Matty thought of it." Jake laughed. "No waffle cones at the corner store, though. Sorry."

"Hey, I want in on that," Sam muttered. "Make me a bowl before you eat the remainder, okay?"

"You're gonna be sick if you keep scarfing like this after not eating for so long," Adrian said. "Take a breather. I won't eat it all."

"I'm okay," Sam said. "Ice cream sounds good."

"So, what changed with the food?" Ethan asked. "You haven't really eaten Mom's cooking in weeks. Last week you were eating the inside of a piece of white bread because the crust 'tasted like metal and hate' and you wouldn't eat peanut butter and jelly because 'the jam was too angry.' What changed?"

"I'm sitting next to someone that radiates love. Everything tastes like love," Sam said with a shrug.

"What does love taste like?" Emma asked.

"What does blue look like?" Sam asked back.

"Oh, yay! He does that to someone other than me," Matty said with a little cheer.

"It's like a rite of passage, Emma. Weird Sam questions are our version of hazing." Jake laughed.

"Now, if he tells you to use your colors, we can really bond." Matty laughed.

"Nope, that's just you. You have all the colors. Emma is sparkly purple. All different colors of purple," Sam said. "Emma needs to learn how to hide her purple."

"Why? I thought that made it easier for you...right? The purple is the love thing?" Emma asked.

"It does, and it's fine around us. But people feed off your energy with it all out like that. Makes you tired and weaker," Sam said, stuffing another piece of bread in his mouth. "Someone tried to tie you like they did to Luke, but it didn't work."

"What?" Will snapped back into focus. "Tie her? What does that mean? I'm really unclear on what the Luke thing was."

"I don't really know how it's done. Or maybe I do somewhere. I'd have to think about it. But people that know what they're doing can siphon energy off others that don't know how to protect themselves. In Luke's case, someone tied up his energy so he could only use a little bit of it while the other person fed off the rest of him. That's harder to manage, has to be done by someone you trust, that you'd allow into your energy," Sam explained. "It's over now, though."

"Yeah, thanks, Sam. We couldn't have done that in some other way at some other time?" Luke bitched. "You couldn't have mentioned it before last week? Kinda would have liked to have known that."

"I didn't know what the hell it was until that woman told you," Sam said. "And you refused to talk to me about this shit, so that's on you, man."

"Go back to someone trying to tie Pip," William said.

"Someone tried to tie her. Repeatedly. There are marks in the colors where it failed. Like scars, but not," Sam said. "Luke doesn't have the scars, so I'm not sure if those are from it failing or if it means something else."

"Will it heal?" Will asked, concerned.

"How would I know?" Sam asked back.

"I don't know, Sam. How the fuck do you know anything? Think about it and get back to me," Will deadpanned.

"We need to go talk to that woman. I want to meet her," Sam said. "Maybe she knows how to find the girl. It was a restaurant? Not a bar?"

"It was both," Will said. "There was a bar, but there were at least thirty tables in the restaurant. You would describe it as a restaurant. You wouldn't call it a bar."

"Yeah, the bar only had a handful of bar-height tables," Sam muttered. "Emma, have you ever met or talked to a girl with violet eyes? Lucy knew of her. Maybe she's familiar to you?"

Emma shook her head. "I'm sorry, Sam. I look everywhere I go. No Wile E. Coyote and no fires without fuel."

Sam looked at Will. "Really? Full details?"

"My wife is the secret, not someone I keep secrets from, Sam," Will said with a straight face.

"Woo, do I get to know now? He never would tell me." Hennessy gave Will the finger.

"I told you like a year and a half ago," Beth said.

"I know, but they don't know that," Hennessy muttered.

"Who told you?" Sam asked.

"Mom," Beth said.

"What?" Darla said defensively. "It was wrong that everyone knew but her."

"Who told Matthew?" Sam asked.

"Luke," Matthew said. "Years ago. Haven't seen her, man."

"I like this new paradigm of sharing," Sam said. "Adrian, what the fuck are we gonna do about Lucy?"

Adrian shook his head. "We can't just leave her be? Let her be happy? You're sure?"

"Stop it, Adrian." Samuel's words vibrated with power. "You do not believe me?"

"No," Adrian said. "I just...soul muck. I don't want to hurt her."

"The soul muck thing is ridiculous. You know that, right?" Emma asked.

"Pip, it's absolutely a thing. The Ava woman even saw it, said I did it to myself. Her daughter couldn't even fucking look at me. My soul is mucky. You're having a baby with Soul Muck William."

Luke rolled his eyes. "She wasn't talking about your energy. She was talking about your binding to Emma."

"What binding?" Will asked.

"There's a binding that happens between people that share love. All kinds of love. Family love. We all share that binding. If someone that could see it was looking, this table would be a giant spider web of family binding. The romantic love binding, when it's there, is solid. It's hard to build and hard to damage."

Will's eyebrows went up. "And you're saying my binding to her is damaged? Or it's got some freaky muck hanging out in it?"

Luke shook his head. "No, it's been cut and reforged a lot. I couldn't see it until Sam roasted my brain last week. It's a brilliant gold strand that's perfectly smooth and even from Emma, and it's frayed and knotted and kinked from you. My guess is that you cut her free every other weekend for the last seven years or so, and she just keeps coming along and fixing it."

Emma gave him a smug look.

Will laughed. "You're a pain in the ass, woman."

Matthew sighed. "He's smiled and laughed more today than he has over the last seven years combined."

"That's true as fuck. I thought that before we sat down to eat," Noah said. "He doesn't even look like the same person. Did you really think we'd lose our shit over you being happy? I don't understand why you did this."

"I didn't think you'd lose your shit. Especially after you all took turns freaking out about the fact that I wouldn't date anyone. It just got away from where I thought we'd end up. Honestly, I thought Pip would get over her schoolgirl crush and want to move on. I was trying to make that easy for her to do."

"I know you thought that, and I know you meant well, but I want to stab something in your eye every single time you say that. Just so you know," Emma growled. "You can stop saying it now."

"I'm not trying to suggest I was right, Pip," Will said defensively. "When this started, you were going off to become a fucking movie star. You're literally the most beautiful woman in the world."

Emma slapped him upside the head. "We've talked about that, stop it."

"Emma, I'm not trying to be a dick here. Seriously. You were going off to become an actress. It still remains unclear to me—and probably to everyone else here—why you have not kicked my ass to the curb. I'm not complaining. I just didn't want to be a hindrance to your happiness."

She shook her head at him, visibly angry. "You are such a condescending fucking moron sometimes. I'm not arguing with you in front of your family. Just shut up."

"What is it that we need to do with Lucy?" Emma asked Sam.

Samuel touched her hand. "Be calm. He does not see his worth."

Emma lifted her eyebrows, unaffected by the boomy, quiet voice. "Lucy?"

"You can't help her until he releases it," Samuel said. "And he does not yet believe that he must release it. It was a huge compulsion that went directly against what she wanted. There will be memory gaps."

Adrian sighed. "By my count, there are three Ladies. Emma, Matty, Lucy. We're still one short. Go find the fourth, and then we'll talk."

Samuel's eyes flashed with anger. "There are four. She is the last. Stop this. Now."

"You know what I don't understand, from either of you?" Emma asked, looking between Adrian and William. "Who are you to decide what Lucy or I want in our lives? Why do you get to make that decision for us? Are you really too big of a coward to let her make her own choice? Why do you automatically assume you know better?"

"Emma, you really have no idea—" Adrian started.

"Holy fuck, you're as bad as him. Adrian, I understand anger *pretty* well by now. My husband's been hiding the fact that I have existed for seven years, like I'm some horrible fucking shameful embarrassment. Surely you can feel that rage," Emma ranted.

"Oh yeah, it's rage, babe. Pain, too. Deal with it," Emma yelled as William flinched.

"Why in the world would you think your rage is any different than mine? Do you seriously believe you're angrier than I am at this moment?" she asked.

"For fuck's sake. Both of you. William, you fought a war. You saved my life. You're the only man I've ever loved. The first person I talk to every morning and the last person I talk to every night. We're going to have a baby. When are you going to finally understand that I DON'T WANT OUT! I don't regret the choices I made. I made those choices with my eyes wide open.

"Adrian, you've spent your adult life taking care of fatally ill children the world fucking discarded. You run an organization that saves millions of lives. If you seriously think you're not good enough for her, I have to wonder who you *do* think is good enough for her. I'm not sure that guy exists."

The table was quiet for a minute as Sam squeezed Emma's hand.

"Want to punch me?" Will asked, not looking at her.

"It's not as much fun when you expect it," Emma said, biting back a smile. "Shut up. I'm still mad at you."

"What kind of kinky foreplay shit are you two into?" Noah asked as Jake burst out laughing. "Can I get in on that?"

At William's glare, Noah talked fast. "I'm all the way on the other side of the table, man, not touching her. Just teasing. Just a little bit. Breaking up the tension."

"Roscoe," Emma whispered. "Go lick his toes."

"That's disgusting!" Matty yelled as the dog moved toward Noah.

"I know!" Emma laughed. "Poor Roscoe. I was just kidding, baby. Come here, who's a good boy?" she asked, scratching his ears. "He doesn't get my humor yet."

"More kinky shit!" Noah yelled.

Emma lifted an eyebrow at Adrian. "What's it going to be, you big fat jerk?"

"Do you always get your way?" Adrian asked.

"YES," Will and Hennessy yelled together.

"Always. Even when you think she's not going to pull it off, she just waits it out." Hennessy laughed.

"You're going to keep yelling at me, aren't you?" Adrian asked.

"I thought I might try crying next," Emma admitted. "Mix it up a bit."

Adrian sighed again. "I don't have any idea what to say to her. How does one explain this?"

"Pro tip: 'I'm sorry' is a *great* place to start," Hank coached. "Because it sounds like you should absolutely be sorry. You told her you didn't love her?"

"No. I told her that she didn't love me and made it stick."

"Ugh," Hank said. "That's so much worse."

"Okay," Sam said. "Let's go."

"Right now?" Adrian asked, sounding panicked. "Let's go talk to her in the morning. It's almost ten. We don't want to wake up Ree."

"No," Sam disagreed. "We go now. Tomorrow, we'll go talk to the witch. I meant what I said. We're out of time."

23

*L*ucy heard a car pull into the driveway after ten thirty. Ree was long past asleep. She found herself wishing she had a dog.

"Hey, Lou, it's us. Open up," Will's voice called.

"Will, what the fuck?" Lucy said, throwing the door open. William, Sam, a beautiful woman with honey-colored hair, and...

Adrian. I forgot about him, Lucy thought. *How could I have forgotten?*

"Hey, let us in, Lou. Hurry it up," Will said with a grin.

Lucy opened up the screen door and stepped out of the way of the crowd. "Ree is sleeping upstairs."

"Okay," Will said. "Lou, this is my wife, Emma."

"I didn't know you were married. Is that new?" Lucy asked, curious.

Will snorted. "No. Don't get me in trouble. I'm still in the doghouse. We'll talk about it later."

Emma glared at him. "I'm going to punch you later."

"I'm aware," he said.

She glared again. "I'm going to wait until you've forgotten."

"Figured," he said. "I love you."

"That helps." She showed a small smile.

"Do I know you?" Lucy asked. "You look really familiar."

Emma sighed. "Yeah."

When everyone turned to stare at Adrian, Lucy looked startled. "Adrian, I'm so sorry. I…I don't know. I'm sorry. I forgot… Anyway, sorry. Hi," she said, giving him a hug.

"Hi," he almost whispered. "How are you? How's Ree?"

"He's upstairs. I can go wake him. He'll be sorry to have missed you…" Lucy looked confused. "Again? Were you here before?

"I'm so sorry, all. I don't feel well. I'll be right back." Lucy turned around and ran from the room, barely making it to the bathroom before being sick.

"WHAT'S HAPPENING?" Adrian asked.

Will glared at him. "It's crumbling. This happened to Whitney, too. It's not pretty to watch."

Adrian stared at the floor, not reacting to Will's taunt.

A few minutes later, Lucy walked back into the room. "I'm back. I don't know what happened…"

Lucy's words trailed off as she glanced at Adrian.

"I feel so strange," she said as she abruptly sat on the floor.

"Lucy, I—"

"Ahhh!" she yelled, holding her head as her nose started bleeding like it was broken again. "Holy hell, I'm so… I don't…"

A breeze flitted through the room, though the windows were closed with the air conditioning on. A gust followed the breeze as if there was a wind tunnel through the house.

"Wind," Sam said with a smile.

"What…? What did you do to me?" Lucy asked Adrian, blood still dripping down her face as she held her head. The betrayal was evident in her voice.

"Oh, this is going much faster than middle school," Will muttered. "Good."

"What? What did you do to me?" Lucy asked again. "I remember… You were here that night. What did you do?"

275

"Lucy, I didn't—I don't want to hurt you. I just wanted what was best for you—" he started.

"What did you do to me, Adrian?"

His head tilted, still staring at the floor. "Uh. Holy fuck. I can't. I... Will? How do I...?"

"Just start talking, man. At some point, it'll click," Will said, swallowing hard, knowing what this pain felt like.

"Right now, you are angrier with me than you have been with anyone, ever, in your life. I, uh, can feel your rage. Feel your thoughts. You're thinking about your dad trying to sell you. And being stabbed. You think this is worse, because you know I did something horrible. The betrayal from someone you trusted is worse."

Adrian scrubbed his hands over his face. "I can't do this. I can't, Sam. I can't."

"It's already done, Adrian," Sam said quietly. "Just time now."

LUCY STARED AT HIM. *What the fuck? What the fuck just happened? What the fuck just happened? What is happening here? I don't understand. I don't understand.*

The air stirred around her, blowing her hair, making her tank top flutter.

Where did the breeze come from? she wondered.

"You," a tiny little voice whispered to her. "I came from you."

Lucy looked around. "I think I'm losing my fucking mind. Did anyone else hear that?"

Headshakes all around.

"What did you hear?" Sam asked.

"Fuck if I'd tell you," Lucy said before she could reconsider.

Sam's lips turned up in a little smile.

"What the fuck do you people want?" Lucy asked. Hurt, angry, and betrayed, she wasn't sure what exactly Adrian did to her, but there was something wrong with her memory.

He was eating eggs in the kitchen at some point, and then she didn't remember anything until Will showed up for lunch. The following day? The day after that? She wasn't sure.

"Emma, will you help?" Adrian sounded like he was crying.

Fuck you, Adrian.

Emma sighed. "I'm not sure what to do or say, so I'm just going to talk. Stop me if you have questions, okay?"

Then the fine-boned, beautiful blonde wove a tale about how she and William met and fell in love, his shame at loving her, his certainty that she'd be better off without him, and then an explanation about fear that Lucy didn't understand.

Lucy looked at Will. "I don't understand."

"Yeah," he said. He pulled a large pocket knife out of his jeans and sliced his hand open.

"What the fu—?" Lucy stopped talking when he wiped the blood on his shirt and showed her a perfectly healed palm.

Lucy's eyes snapped to Adrian. He wasn't looking at her, but he exhaled hard when her eyes landed on him. He took Will's pocketknife and stabbed the blade through his hand, out the other side.

Holding the hand up to her, he ripped the knife out. The wound gushed blood for a minute, dripping blood on the floor. Then it was closing.

"Fear? You feed off fear?" she asked.

"No, Lou. Wrong direction. And he's not fear. Mine is fear. It feeds off me. Talks to me," Will said.

"What then? What?" she asked. "WOULD YOU FUCKING LOOK AT ME? Your feet can't be that interesting. You've been staring at them since the day I met you!"

Adrian sighed as he picked up his head. "Anger, Lucy. Rage. I've been staring at my fucking feet for twenty years. It's harder to fuck up someone's brain if I'm not looking them in the goddamn eyes. So I don't look at anyone. I'm careful with my words, too careful. I stutter and stumble through sentences and sound like a moron."

"I don't understand," Lucy said. "What is it you do to people? What did you do to me?"

Adrian nodded. "Anger and rage make people act in certain ways.

It's like a mental compulsion, I think. Words spoken in anger, directed as a command, focused on someone—particularly with eye contact. People do as I say."

"And you've done it to me? Around me?"

He nodded again. "The day we met, I told Erika to go away from your apartment—"

Will started laughing. "I didn't catch that. That bitch wouldn't leave the stairway door when we were there. I should have caught that."

"And what? Will? You've been following around after him, cleaning up?" Lucy asked.

"Nah. My shit surfaced earlier than his. By the time his shit hit, I had control of mine. He accidentally hurt a girl in middle school when his anger busted through. It took a while, but I got that worked out. Otherwise, there's been nothing to clean up.

"He's nothing if not methodical and careful. Terrified of hurting people. Acted shy to keep things safe. Dated only stupid women—less chance of damage. Beat the fuck out of his body daily so he'd be too exhausted to be dangerous."

"So what happened to me? What changed? What did you do to me?" Lucy asked.

"The night you got hit, I quietly told you to rest. A tiny nudge. You slept for a day and a half.

"When you talked about used cars that morning when you made eggs? I told you to come to the table and look at my phone. It was unintentional. I should have left then. Disappeared into work until the house was done. Left you in peace. I knew that. I hadn't lost control like that in a very long time."

Adrian paused, looking for the words to explain. "Other than my immediate family, who seem to be unaffected by my weird shit, I have been alone. I don't want to hurt anyone. I want to do the right thing. But the thought of leaving you and Henry that day made me ill.

"So I was selfish. I convinced myself that I just needed to be careful. More careful than I already was. It'd be fine. I could be safe, keep you safe, and be safe.

"That night, the energy went haywire. You were crying, we were laughing, and then it all changed. There was more energy, and it was different. I went downstairs and worked out too long. Six or seven hours. My muscles gave out, bashed my head into the concrete wall, split it open, bled some. I went upstairs to the kitchen, ate all the chicken and potatoes leftover. You came out of your room, alarmed. Wanted to go to the hospital. I told you it was a dream, made you sleep.

"The Sunday that I went to dinner without you, I came home talking about Hennessy's fucking file. You apologized. The rage surfaced of its own accord and told you not to apologize for things that were not your fault.

"A couple weeks ago, I came here all fucked up. The energy was out of control—the happy stuff and the anger. I was sitting in your driveway, unsure how I got here. You kept asking what was wrong. I kept fading in and out. I couldn't get a handle on it—"

"He was dying. The energy was killing him until William helped align his energy with your energy last week," Samuel said, quiet voice resonating.

"Anyway, you called me 'love,' and I panicked. Pulled the power forward. All the way forward. Embraced it. I told you that you didn't love me, you were glad to end things, we were only together because you felt obligated after the Foundation helped Ree.

"And I didn't come back. I stayed away because you don't need the fucking embodiment of rage in your life. Because you deserve better."

The room was silent for a few minutes. "The following Sunday, Darla told us she had cancer, and I went around the fucking bend. I knew I wasn't safe. I stopped going to work. I wrestled with the power, spent too much time working out.

"By the time Sunday dinner rolled around again, I knew my clock was ticking down. My brain was all fucked up. I went to dinner to be with my family again, knowing it'd likely be the last time I saw them."

"Spoiler alert!" Will laughed. "It wasn't. I beat the ever-living fuck out of him until he figured out what to do with the energy, and then we ate all the food in Darla's kitchen plus a dozen pizzas."

"Will spent most of the week bitching at me to come to see you. I refused. Emma showed up to dinner tonight, yelled at me. Told me I had no right to make decisions for you. So, now we're here, and you know." Adrian fell silent.

"Lucy," Sam began. "I need you and Ree to go to Dallas with us tomorrow. I don't need you to be with him or talk to him. I don't need you to like what happened. I do need you to go with us."

Lucy looked at him without expression. "Your mojo doesn't seem to work as well, Sam. I'm not the least bit inclined to do what you want me to do."

Sam smiled. A real smile. It made the hairs on her arms stand up. "No, Lucy. I'm something else entirely. Not like them. I need you to go with us tomorrow in the same way I needed Ree to not go back to the apartment and in the same way I know he'll die if he doesn't go with us tomorrow. You must come with us."

"If I agree to go with you tomorrow, will you all go away now?" she asked.

"We will," Sam agreed.

"Ree has treatment on Tuesday," she said.

Sam nodded.

"Fine. Get out."

LUCY SAT on the couch she didn't buy, in the house that wasn't hers, staring at the wall with the paint she didn't choose. She thought about the little boy upstairs that was fighting for his life, getting help from people that really didn't have to help. The little boy that wasn't hers, but she'd happily give her life to protect.

And Lucy thought about Adrian, the holes in her memory, and oddly, the amount of time he spent *not* looking at her. She thought about yelling at him in the billing office. Freaking out when she got home from work that night and found him on her couch. Making shit uncomfortable over lunch that first day.

Now that he'd told her when he had messed with her thoughts, she could sense the difference in the memories. They were blander. Lacking in feeling. Thinking back over the last few weeks, she couldn't come up with an instance that he didn't list.

I wish I could remember that night he was here. He was acting strange. Didn't want to come inside the house. Lucy tried to remember, but the memories just were not there.

Somewhere in the middle of her deep thinking, Lucy fell asleep without realizing it.

ADRIAN STARED off into space in the back of the Suburban. He didn't want to do this anymore. Didn't want to live like this anymore. This was no way to go through life.

"Adrian. I know *exactly* what you're thinking. Stop it," Will said, looking in the rearview mirror as he drove back to Hank and Darla's.

"What? Adrian, what?" Emma asked from beside him. She tried to take his hand; he jerked it away.

"I'm fine," he muttered.

"It'll get better, man. Give her a little time to process. We dropped a ton of heavy shit on her tonight without warning," Will said.

"I'm not going with you guys tomorrow. You need her. Not me. We don't need to make this unnecessarily hard on them. I will stay here."

"I know you think that's true. And I won't make you go. But you'll go with us tomorrow. Things will change. Rest, Adrian. Your road has been long. It's time to rest now," Samuel said, words heavy with power.

Without warning, Adrian nodded off to sleep.

"I thought you said you couldn't do that," Emma objected.

"I didn't say I couldn't do it. I said I was something else, and that's true," Sam said.

LUCY WAS WALKING through a forest when she found Adrian walking in the same direction.

"Where are we?" she asked.

Adrian started. "Holy fuck, you scared me. How are you here?"

"I don't know. Where are we?" she asked again.

"I think we're walking toward the girl with violet eyes," Adrian said.

They walked together for a couple of breaths.

"Why did you do the things that you did?" she asked.

"I tried to explain earlier, but—" he started.

"No, that's not what I mean. Why did you do those things and not others? You could have just told me to shut up in the billing office. You could have told me to be calm in the apartment that night. You could have shut down my questioning in the cafeteria. Why did you do the things you did but not the others?"

Adrian sighed. "The night your nose got broken, you were fighting off sleep, trying to take care of Ree and ensure everything was handled. You needed to stop worrying and rest. So I nudged. Will knew I did it, too. I didn't realize it at the time, but in retrospect, he knew it. The pain pill would have knocked you out soon enough. You were just stressing yourself out needlessly. I wanted to save you the grief.

"The thing with the bank balance and the phone was an accident. I was angry and upset that you were apologizing for kissing me. I wasn't sorry about kissing you," he admitted.

"Late that night, I had to either explain the weird energy shit or make you forget it. You were wigging out. There was no good excuse to use. You had enough on your plate.

"I don't use it for convenience. I don't want to hurt anyone. The billing office, your apartment, the cafeteria—you were a stranger, then an acquaintance, doing your best to take care of a sick kid. I don't just force my will on random people's lives. Other than shit like the Erika thing, where she needed to go away, or I'd lose my temper, I try not to do it," Adrian finished.

"Not on random people's lives, just the people that love you?" Lucy asked.

They walked a couple more paces in silence. Adrian scrubbed his hands down his face.

"Can you undo it? Bring the memories back?" she asked. "I don't remember that night well. It's like trying to remember kindergarten. Distant."

"I have no idea," Adrian said quietly. "The woman in Dallas might be able to help you remember. It seems like it would be pointless to remember now, though. Why try?"

"You don't want me to remember it?" she asked.

Adrian sighed. "I want you to be happy and well. Memories of me hurting you are not going to make either of those things happen."

With the next step, they were standing in the clearing with the violet-eyed girl.

She was waiting for them.

"Hello, Adaline," Adrian greeted her.

Her eyes filled with tears as she met Adrian's gaze and nodded in greeting. Touching one fingertip to his hand, Adaline shared her raw love and understanding with him. Adrian couldn't breathe for a second.

Tears dripping down her face, she turned to Lucy with a small smile.

"Hello," Lucy said. "Why are we here? Where are we?"

Adaline walked over to take Lucy's hand. *To understand. I will help.* Without another thought, Adaline touched Lucy's forehead.

"You will see me tomorrow. You will come with him," Adaline said to Lucy and Adrian, together.

LUCY WOKE UP WITH A START.

Ugh. Going to be sick again, she thought, running for the bathroom. After the dry heaving stopped, she tried to sit back and relax her body, thinking back over the dream. The conversation with Adrian. With the girl.

Her mind jumped back to that night with Adrian. Her memories were different. She saw herself open the front door of the house; she felt the rush of love and admiration at the sight of her. Felt the internal struggle of staying outside, not entering the house.

Holy fuck. I don't have my memories of that night. I have Adrian's memories.

The clawing agony in his head when she went to the bathroom. When she walked out of the room to find their clothes. Hunger. He'd been starving, stomach tied in painful knots when he went down to the kitchen and made eggs.

The energy eating at his brain, the realization that he was causing her pain, that he needed to leave. The feeling of relief when she touched him. The resonance of the word "love" coming out of her mouth. His overwhelming terror at the idea of hurting her.

"Lucy, I love you. I love you so much. I can't do this to you. I'm sorry. I—We can't. This can't...I'm sorry," she heard him say in the memory.

She saw the confused expression on her own face. Could feel his agony at the words.

For a second, he thought about not doing it, thought about explaining it all, and keeping Lucy and Ree with him. She felt his loneliness, sensed his self-hatred.

Oh, God. I can't do this. I don't want to do this. I really am a fucking monster, he had thought. Then the overwhelming desire to keep them safe took over as the rage came forward.

"Lucinda," Adrian's voice said, making the air vibrate, even in the memory.

ADRIAN STARTED awake in the car. "SAM!"

Will jumped. "What the fuck, man!"

"I'm sorry. I'm sorry. Sam! I saw her. I saw her. She's there. She's in Dallas," Adrian gasped.

There was no response.

"SAM!" Adrian yelled.

"What the fuck?!" Will yelled as he swerved out of traffic. "Where is he?!"

The front passenger seat was empty.

"I DON'T KNOW!" William yelled back at Darla. "HE WAS THERE AND THEN GONE."

"Well, he's figured out how to apparate, obviously," Noah said with a laugh.

"This isn't funny, Noah!" Darla yelled at him.

"Mom, there's absolutely nothing we can do. Nothing at all. Yelling at us is not going to make him show up. Luke, do that thing. Make her all calm and shit!" Noah yelled.

"Lucas," Darla growled.

"Wouldn't dream of it, Mom." Luke backed away.

"I don't know what to do!" Darla yelled. "How would we even make a police report?"

"Mom, let's just—" Will stopped talking as the front door slammed, and the house vibrated with raw power.

When Samuel walked into the big room, his eyes were glowing, his footsteps were echoing. Rage radiated off him, a haze of red visible to the naked eye. "They are keeping her from me. They intentionally hide her. FROM ME."

Lightbulbs in the ceiling overhead exploded with his words.

"We leave in an hour," Sam said.

"Get the plane ready and loaded. Call Lucy," he directed at Will as he walked out of the house.

Thirty-five minutes later, the Trellis family was getting loaded into cars to head to the airport. By the time they arrived, Sam was no longer glowing, but he was not yet talking. Once on the plane, he walked to the back, sitting away from everyone else.

"If he freaks out, are we going to crash?" Noah whispered to Jake.

Jake raised his eyebrows. "You wanna get off the plane before takeoff and see what he does? Not sure I'd fuck with him right now, man."

"Leave him alone," Emma said. "Just turn around and sit down."

"Lookit here, PIP, you've known me for, like, less than twelve hours. You can't boss me around yet," Noah bitched.

Emma painted an adoring look on her face with a sweet smile. "Noah, please sit and buckle in?"

Noah's ass was in his seat and buckled before she finished the last word.

There was a pause in the familial muttering.

"She is *way* more terrifying than Matty," Noah said to Jake.

"Yeah. Another one that I wouldn't fuck with."

"Lou's here," Will called. "I'm going to go get her from the terminal."

HENRY WAS WAVING like a mad man when he saw Will running toward them.

"Hi, Ree," Will said quickly. "Lucy, I'm so sorry for the middle of the night call. Change in plans. Sam is off the charts freaky right now. We just need—"

"It's fine, Will. Let's go," she said quietly.

"Henry, you're riding, man," Will said, scooping him up as they started walking fast.

"Is Adrian on the plane?" Lucy asked, staring straight ahead.

"Yeah, Lou. Just...sit with Emma and me. Or Jake and Matty. Okay? You don't have to look at him or talk to him or anything," William said apologetically.

She didn't respond.

"THERE THEY ARE. COMING OUT NOW," Emma called.

Lucy ran up the steps to the plane and through the door. She muttered a general, "Hi," as she searched for Adrian. Ree ran between people getting hugs and kisses.

Adrian was toward the back of the plane, sitting by himself in what should have been an area for conversation. Six seats faced each other in a semicircle, with a table in the middle. He was decidedly not looking at her, head resting on the plane window. Lucy headed straight for him, sitting down next to him and buckling up. Ree followed her, charging Adrian with a vigorous hug.

"Adrian! I missed you so much. I read a new book, and Dr. Garaff is making me better, and Aunt Lucy and I went shopping..." Ree rambled, arms wrapped around Adrian's neck, head buried in Adrian's chest.

Adrian bent to kiss the top of Ree's head, ruffled his hair, and then pulled Ree into the seat on the other side of him, helping him get buckled in for takeoff without a word. Henry was clinging to Adrian's arm like he was afraid Adrian would disappear again. He continued talking nonstop about his new room and a backpack he got with dogs on it.

Lucy and Adrian were quiet through takeoff. They hadn't said a single word to each other or to Henry.

"Ree!" Ethan called once the plane leveled off. "Come play Go Fish with us!"

When Lucy nodded her approval, Ree unbuckled his belt and ran for Ethan. "Uncle Ethan, did you see my bag?!"

LUCY WASN'T sure what to say or where to start. Adrian hadn't even looked at her. She sighed, somehow feeling lost again. The words weren't right yet, so she took his hand instead. He flinched at her touch but didn't pull away.

When he finally turned and met her gaze, Lucy said, "She didn't give me my memories back, Adrian—"

"I'm sorry, Lucy," he interrupted before she could finish. "I didn't want to hurt you."

"I know. She didn't give me my memories back. She gave me yours," Lucy finished quietly.

The look of shock on Adrian's face would have been comedic under other circumstances. "My memories?"

"Yes."

"Of that night?"

She nodded.

"What portion of that night?" Adrian asked, embarrassed.

"The portion that involved me," Lucy answered.

"All of the portions of that night?" Adrian's cheeks were turning pink.

She laughed a little bit.

Adrian went back to staring straight ahead.

"It's painful? It hurts your head? All the time?" she asked. "When I stepped away that night, you were in terrible pain."

"Uh, it was. That night. That was the start of things going very badly. Well, really, Monday that week, when I started avoiding you. By that Sunday, it hurt, clawing at my brain. The following week was agony. The week after that, I think I was demented. On my way to insane. Fairly certain I was going to die," Adrian admitted.

"It got *worse* after that night?" she clarified.

"Yeah."

"What changed?" she asked.

"William kicked in my ribs and broke a lot of bones until I figured out how to align the energy correctly," Adrian said with a small smile.

"And now you're okay?" she asked, wondering if she should just leave him alone.

Adrian shook his head. "Not really."

"It's still painful?"

"Not in the same way. No. It won't stay like this forever, but I have more time now."

In the quiet that followed, Adrian had an internal war with himself. She was right there. Sitting with him. Holding his hand.

There was no more anger coming off her. This was the best he felt about life for a month.

He wanted to tell her that, tell her how much he loved her, missed her and Ree, how lonely life was now without them. But nothing had changed. He was still a monster; soul muck was still a thing. He couldn't ask her to stay with him and the fucking rage. He couldn't put that decision on her shoulders.

"Adrian?" Lucy asked quietly.

"Hmm?"

"Do you really think you're a monster?"

"Yup," he said without hesitation.

"Why?"

"You're really going to ask that after what I did?"

"No, I'm asking that after what you didn't do," she said. "But fine. Let's talk about it from the negative.

"You made me sleep well, made me look at your net worth, made me forget something you couldn't explain, broke a bad habit, and tried to make me avoid what you thought would be a painful and horrible situation.

"I know how much that hurt you. How hard that was to do. Maybe I'd be angrier if I didn't know that, but I do. You honestly thought you were protecting me. I'm not happy about it. I still feel weirdly violated, like my mind isn't entirely mine anymore. But I understand it better now.

"While we're talking about this, you also helped my kid, sat with him all night when my babysitter flaked out, didn't take advantage of the fact that I literally zonked out in your arms, found a great doctor to help us, let us live with you while I was severely beaten, gave Ree a bunch of books, made dinner, and just tried to be a good person, all around. I'll leave the Foundation help out of it and not talk about the absurd amount of money in that trust fund.

"You did not, at any point, use the freaky mind mojo to take advantage of me. And I've been taken advantage of enough to appreciate that detail. I took you to bed of my own accord and still don't regret it, even after everything."

After a pause, she continued. "I feel like the overall weight and measure of dealing with a monster would be different. Are you murdering people in your basement or something? Drowning puppies in your spare time? Because, otherwise, I do not see 'monster' in you. I see 'terrible judgment call' and 'stupid white knight syndrome' in you."

Adrian snorted. "Lucy—"

"On that day you first brought us to your house, I didn't realize Beth was your sister. I kinda hated her for a little while," Lucy admitted.

His lips quirked up a little bit. "But—"

"That night Ree had the nightmare, I just about died trying not to stare at your shirtless body. Being that fucking toned and hiding it in doctor clothes just shouldn't be allowed," she continued.

There was a long pause. Adrian's face was utterly blank until a small smile broke through.

"That is not a stone that should be thrown, oh she of the tank top and short shorts pajamas. Holy hell. And then you went and kissed me after I had this entire internal dialogue about how *not* into me you were and that I needed to get my shit together. I'm a doctor; I've seen plenty of naked women. It should not have been that distracting. I was appalled with myself." He laughed.

"I started crushing on you when I woke up that Sunday morning to find the door locked. How'd you get the keys to fit in the crack under the door? There wasn't much room."

"Magic," he said.

"Really?"

"No. I wet the carpet where it met the door jam. It was a tight squeeze, but it worked." He laughed again.

"I spent at least ten minutes trying to think of ways to get both you and Ree out of the apartment and into my car at the same time without looking like a creepy fucking asshole. I kept trying to wake you up so I could talk you into getting the fuck out of there. I thought about sleeping on the couch and then trying to get you to leave with me in the morning. In the end, I realized it was your life and your place, so I left."

They were quiet for a while again.

"I love you. I don't want to be without you, Adrian," Lucy said eventually.

He took a deep breath, tipping his head back to look at the ceiling of the plane. "I love you. I want you to be happy," he whispered.

"Then you should probably stop trying to make me dump you," Lucy said. "I dislike that tendency. It makes me unhappy."

When Lucy touched his cheek, he turned his face to meet her lips.

"EEEEWWWW! They're making kissy-face back there," Ethan yelled. "Holy shit, man, I thought we were going to be on the ground before you got that worked out. Then it was going to be weird and awkward, and I just knew I was going to get stuck in the car with the two of you."

"Hey, some things take time," Jake said. "They've known each other, like, six weeks. Cut him some slack."

"No one asked you, three-minute-man. You rush the wrong things." Matthew grinned as laughter erupted from the family.

"ADRIAN, YOU WILL NOT TELL THAT STORY!" Matty yelled.

"Already did!" Adrian yelled back.

"Hey, is Will married to Emma Gracen? That's her, right?" Lucy whispered.

24

"*D*rive, Lucas."

"Sam, there has to be some kind of misunderstanding. These people wouldn't—"

"Lucas, do you want me to drive?" Sam asked, voice quiet and calm.

"No, Sam. I just want you to chill a little bit. We don't need to go in loaded for bears," Luke said reasonably. "These people were fairly—"

"Lucas, start the car and drive, or I'll tear the city of Dallas out of this reality and put it in the year 1365. It's time to go."

"I'm driving, we're going. Just calm down, okay?"

"Sam," Matty said from the backseat.

"Matilda, nice people don't hold a woman captive for twenty years, forcing her to power wards to hide her presence from the world."

"How is that possible? How do you know that?" Jake asked. "Can you see it?"

"No, I can't see anything at all. I couldn't see the bar or the forest. It was a complete void space. For twenty miles around the bar, it was just gone. Not a living creature around. It was completely hidden from me, and I couldn't fucking see it was gone until I hit the damn ward."

"Hidden from you specifically?" Jake asked.

"From psychic energy," Sam clarified.

Jake sighed. "What happened earlier? In the car?"

"Adrian saw her in the dream. She told him she'd see him tomorrow, which is today. I heard the words clearly as she said them. I can feel Adaline very clearly with Emma around. I followed the voice, the link to Adrian's mind back to her when she spoke to him. I couldn't tether down. There was nothing but void. Nothing alive to anchor myself to. It took me a while to figure out how to get back."

"Back where? Your body was physically gone! You've never done that before," Jake said, getting annoyed.

"I thought I might need it, so I brought it with me. Lucas, how long?"

"It took us forty minutes that morning. We're going faster now, and there's no traffic. Maybe twenty more minutes."

"You're certain she's being held captive?" Matty asked.

"No, Matilda. I'm not certain they're holding her captive. I just know she wouldn't hide from me. She wouldn't do that. If I was close, she'd pull me to her. I know she would."

They were quiet for ten solid minutes, following the car with Hank, Darla, Will, and Emma.

"Lucas, stop. Pull over," Sam said suddenly. "There's a ward ahead. Do you feel it?"

"No," Luke said. "What is it?"

"I don't know. Jake, tell them to keep going. We'll be the last to arrive," Sam said, getting out of the car on the side of the road.

"It was a protection ward," Sam said, getting back in the car a minute later. "I tore it down. They know we're coming."

Lucas winced.

"DID YOU FIND HER?" Ava asked, panic clear in her voice.

Jess was shaking her head. "No, she's not answering me, and I can't see her."

Ava was wringing her hands. "They'll kill her if they find her. I'm going to go look."

"Mom, I don't have the chops to make them stay away. You can't leave. If the ward trips again, I can't put it up by myself. You know that," Jess said. "We're just going to have to trust she'll stay away."

"They tore down the outer ward. They're coming for her. They know she's here. It has to be," Ava said, eyes huge with terror. "I don't understand how they know. I don't understand. But they threw a giant punch right in the middle of the ward tonight. Slammed into it like a battering ram."

Clyde sighed. "We knew this was possible. So did she. We need to trust that she can handle it herself."

Tears leaked down Ava's face. "Our baby girl, Clyde. They can't have her. Over my dead body. They will take her over my dead body."

Ava groaned. "Go. Both of you. Like we planned. Get out. They're not looking for you; you'll be leverage for them if you're here."

"Mom?" Jess asked.

"Go. They're coming. And they're stronger than me. A lot stronger than me. The wards won't hold. Go," Ava said, pulling power into the wards on the property as fast as she could.

The sound of tires in the gravel lot could be heard about a minute after Clyde and Jess headed out the back door.

THE OUTSIDE LIGHTS flipped on as William got out of the car he was driving. "I guess we'll go inside?"

Hank held the restaurant door open, gesturing for indestructible William to walk in before Darla and Emma.

"William? Darla? What are you doing here?" Ava was clearly startled and expecting someone else.

"Ava, my son, my middle son, has dreamt—" Hank began.

"YOU HAVE TO GO NOW. WILLIAM, YOU HAVE TO GO. THERE IS DANGER COMING. THEY WILL TRAP YOU. THE

WARDS ARE DROPPING LIKE DOMINOS. GO. NOW, GET IN THE CAR AND—"

Emma was now visible behind Hank and Darla. Ava was still staring at her as Noah, Matthew, Beth, and Hennessy walked in. When Adrian, Lucy, Ethan, and Ree followed, Ava stepped back, mouth agape in shock and fear.

"What is happening? Who are you people? I tried to help you. Why would you—" Ava groaned in pain as the door opened again. Matilda walked in, followed by Luke, Jake, and Samuel.

The air vibrated with each of Samuel's steps. "Where is she?" he asked, quietly, patiently.

"Oh my God," Ava gasped, staring at Samuel.

"Where is Adaline?" Samuel asked again. "Why are you keeping her from me?"

"Walker," Ava breathed.

"Where is she?" Samuel asked for the third time. "If you've harmed her, you'll spend a thousand years begging for forgiveness."

Power was flowing into Samuel in giant waves, pulled from all directions, visible to the naked eye. He glowed like a lighthouse in the night.

"No, Walker. Never. I would never hurt her. She is my daughter. I would not harm her. I would not keep her from you."

"You do keep her from me. Your ward hides her. Twenty years, I've been searching for her. You've been hiding her," Samuel said, words echoing.

"No. No, Walker. Not from you—"

"Where is she? I will not ask again," Samuel said in the same quiet, heavy voice.

"Sam," something akin to a voice breathed from the back door.

Like an apparition formed from Samuel's haze of power, a young woman appeared. She had raven black hair that hung to her lower back and pale violet eyes that glowed in her milk-white complexion.

Everything paused for two heartbeats. Then the girl ran. Out the back door and into the forest. Sam charged after her, gone in the blink of an eye.

"ADALINE, STOP!" Sam screamed. "I won't hurt you! Stop! Please!"

The girl still ran, her white dress barely visible in the black night. Sam followed.

"Adaline! Please! Why are you running from me?!?" he continued to yell as the girl ran. "Addy! Please!"

The spot of white that was her dress was gone. "I don't understand!" he yelled, continuing to walk in the direction he thought she went, knowing that it was useless in the dark, glowing with energy as he was. She could easily see him coming and hide.

Ten yards later, he emerged in a clearing. A perfect circle of a clearing. It was the clearing of his dream.

"The circle. We need the circle," Adaline said in Sam's head.

Thank you for reading!

The Trellis family's adventure continues in The Center - Building the Circle, Book 3, available now.

For alerts on new releases and other book news, join my email list at https://maggielilybooks.com/sign-up.

Finally, your Amazon review of this novel would be much appreciated. Reviews are critical to the success of brand new authors (like me!)

ALSO BY MAGGIE M LILY

BUILDING THE CIRCLE SERIES

Building the Circle - Volume 1

The Call

The Power

The Center

Building the Circle - Volume 2

The Corners

The Pillars

The Close

Becoming Hank - A Trellis Family Novella

PEACEKEEPER'S HARMONY SERIES

Ransom

Reaping

Rise

Made in the USA
Coppell, TX
16 April 2022

76684170R00167